A TAIL OF T\

Clive Van

This novel is sort of entirely a work of fiction however any resemblance to persons living or dead is purely coincidental. The moral right of the author has been asserted

All rights are reserved. No part of this publication can be reproduced without the author's explicit consent

ISDN 979-8-6643-8042-2

Amazon Publishing

Paperback original December 2020

Copy also available as an Amazon e-Book

Book Layout by: White Magic Studios
                    1 Brunel Way, Slough, SL1 1FQ, GB

ACKNOWLEDGMENTS

None of the names in this book have been changed as there is no innocence that needs protecting!

Here goes: I would particularly like to recognise my amazing mum and dad Clive Snr and Gloria Van Cooten, my wayward sister Kay, my charming, stunning and witty wife Linda and Jack, my superson. Also all the wacky and interesting people of London's East End, my teachers and schoolmates at Harry Gosling Primary and Westminster City Grammar School. The Boom-A-Lackas of the Oxford & St George's club, not forgetting the English teachers who taught me to schpell. - Let's not disregard the wonder that is New York City and of course London itself, the greatest metropolis on the planet. London is currently forlorn and distressed during this sad Lockdown but ready to blossom again into the world's first true 21st century renaissance capital!

Clive Van Cooten – December 2020

Three things to watch out for:

The 'Tail of Two Cities' stage musical. Words and music by this author

The second novel of this unconnected series 'A Tale of 3 Cities' out now, written by this author

'A Tale of 3 Cities' stage musical currently in production, words and music by Gary Ogin and this author

CONTACT CLIVE VAN COOTEN DIRECTLY ON
trafford365@gmail.com

See also
www.clivevancooten.com

INDEX

1. London 1969 – A man on the moon
   (Song from the stage musical: 'Bang!' sung by whole cast) 7

2. A tall tale from the tall trees 19

3. The Bag O'Nails 30

4. Boxing Clever 41

5. Get Back 52

6. A change is gonna come
   ('Best of Friends' sung by Janey) 63

7. The Good, the Bad and the Vermin 76

8. Just gimme some kinda sign, yeah
   ('Ingleton' sung by Oliver) 92

9. The Cowboy and the Angel
   ('Bubbles' sung by party-goers) 109

10. 'A bleedin' great decision' 120

11. Where do you go to my lovely? 132

12. Monopoly, Daffodils and Chelsea
    ('Not to be Trusted' sung by Jeff) 141

13. 'Dastardly Deed Day' 150

14. Lulu in a stew 159

15. True love's a many splendid thing 172

16. Peace in our times 181

17. 31st August 1969 192

18. 'I need to speak to Mrs Spencer!' 203

19	Hey look, its Mary O'Brien!...	212
20	NYLON *('Digital World sung by cast) ....*	224
21	Noah, Jeremiah and the Jews	242
22	'We want to be alone'..	254
23	Books Smooks! *('When I'm 65 sung by Izzy)...*	265
24	Person of the Opposite Gender *('Flat Shoes' sung by cast) ....*	273
25	The Good, the Bad and the Shaven-Headed Dyke Witches *('His Heartbreaking Smile' sung by Belindy) ....*	288
26	The Naked Truth *('Pie in the Sky' sung by Louise & 'Recollections' ....*	300
27	Visitors	325
28	And in the end…	337

Chapter 1

London 1969 - A Man on the Moon

'Stature, ruthless strength and determination has been deemed to you Oliver this day', declared Caesar.

'You shall impress upon the feeble usurper your unshakeable will. You will succeed in any battle. You will lay waste to all before you. You will slaughter with no mercy those upstart resisters and do so with poise and grandeur.'

Oliver started most school days with a degree of pretence and self-examination that recently had become more extreme and imaginative. His chosen personae this morning was that of Julius Caesar which gave the 29-year-old academic plenty of creative latitude. He had read in one of the Sundays that remonstrating to one's bathroom mirror would ultimately assist the reflected in grasping the soul within, hence everything thereafter will be 'JC or just cool' and wherever he should venture thereafter his 'true majesty' will be groovily appreciated. That this was likely the 127th prognostication of Zane Markovitch, a 22-year-old 'Professor' from

A TAIL OF TWO CITIES

the Please-Yourself-University, California simply passed Oliver by as did much of reality in recent months.

Oliver picked out his purple chemise, which he thought quite fitting for his new-found temporary regal status and, to contrast he plumped for his off-white suit. Oliver had a calling; he knew as much, but remained vague about what precisely this was to be. With his friends he would rail against jazz and ballet as simply fatuous concepts and made it clear where he would shove Harold Wilson's pipe if he agreed to allow the UK into 'Nixon's war against the Vietcong'.

Once Oliver had finished grooming himself he felt quite the dandy, relaxed very much the man in-form and headed for the Tube, chest protruding, as any Imperial Leader would. One last thing he thought - Just before he closed the door he ran back to the mirror and shouted 'SPQR!' Although usually grounded and self-aware, putting himself on a heroes' plinth was never Oliver's want, but this disposable Roman facade certainly emboldened him.

The journey to work on the District Line was paradoxically a most relaxing interval for Oliver. Today was particularly quiet with little of the rush-hour mayhem or commuter torment to off-balance him. This rendered him head space to plan. He recognised that the week ahead was sure to be one where he would have to confront, step back, seduce and reap the rich pickings he had sown for the previous three years. Tube time was also used as a distraction for the real journey ahead and gave him the opportunity to indulge in his favourite pastime, that of the BLG: The Beatles' Lyric Game.... You randomly pick a number from 1 to 26 where A is one. Then just as randomly decide on a Beatles song title that starts with that letter. From this you pick any relevant line from that song that matched the mood he had chosen to engender. In turn, the lyric could then be brought to mind throughout the day and used as an inspirational motif. It was simple, private, not rule based and best of all was Oliver's own little invention that truly echoed him. If, however the sentiment complimented the day's chosen persona then all the better.

As the train pulled into Whitechapel station his chosen number formed as 19. His song hence was John Lennon's, 'Strawberry Fields Forever.' His chosen lyric 'It's getting hard to be someone but it all works out. It doesn't matter much to me.' As he neared the escalators he convinced himself that this was the profound rhetoric Caesar would have used at the Senate when told that the Britons and Gauls were giving him grief again. In furtherance, he concluded that both Lennon and Caesar were both tremendously successful yet recklessly fell in love with a foreign woman against the advice of their colleagues.

That Caesar was then brutally murdered by apparent admirers was a difference that Oliver consciously put to one side. He was happy to mix the tragic lives of two ancient Romans if it meant the Lennon comparison prevailed.

A TAIL OF TWO CITIES

Tower Hamlets was a large Secondary Modern Comprehensive school in the heart of the capital's predominantly Jewish East End. Most 1960s monoliths dedicated to education lending everything to convenience, not aesthetics. Tower Hamlets was no different in that it was built so flimsily and with such inordinate haste as ordered by the London County Council that even minor inclemency unsteadied the building's fabric. It was the near hurricane force storm of November 1965 that rendered it practically classroom from classroom. The rebuilt school was a marvel of its time; indeed, its majestic foyer area was even likened to that of the Taj Mahal! At the school's 'rededication' the teachers clapped incredulously at such a comparison but to many of the pupils the Taj Mahal was an odorous Indian restaurant off the Commercial Road that sported sticky carpet as floorcovering with matching slowly peeling dank wallpaper.

What made Tower Hamlets the East End school par excellence back in 1969 was its 1177 girls. These were some of the most studious, aggressive, witty, slovenly and charming youngsters in all London. It could even count Lesley Hornby (better known as Twiggy) as an old girl. Its principle claim to fame in recent years was Michael Caine's attendance at a Prize Giving ceremony. Local luminary, Steven Berkoff was guest of honour the following year but left early because it was 'too bleeding hot.' Most of the older girls however recall with glee that the school was the only one in England to have been forcibly closed by insects. This was a reference to the summer 1967 cockroach invasion. Consequently, Head Master Mr Press had been renamed Mr Cockroach, an epithet at which most of the staff secretly chuckled and seldom corrected the pupils that referred to him so.

Oliver was a tall, lean and well proportioned, handsome but slightly less than trendy teacher. He was an only child to a Caribbean father and a Scottish mother hence his loose curled light brown hair and lightly freckled nose. His father, a docker and his boyhood champion died in June 1963, the day John Profumo resigned, whilst his mother drank too much but remained an ever-optimistic extrovert who nurtured him well.

His core strength and self-assurance anchored him, but it was at Tower Hamlets school that Oliver felt most at home. He believed that he could make things happen there for the girls and positively enrich their futures. With so much fervour he was far from being burnt-out as many of his contemporaries. Rare moments of self-doubt and naval-gazing were firmly cast aside: He rejected a free 30-minute session with the staff Counsellor last term as he was certainly heading for the top and would get there without recourse to any malice but with a mile-wide smile across his face. -

The 8.30 Monday morning staff meeting was Mr Press's new pioneering idea, 'ideal for planning and promoting' as well as prattling on about TH's place in society, its readiness to embrace children 'from all the Colonies' as well as its preordained right to pummel any other school's hockey or netball teams, should they dare take up the challenge! Oliver respected Mr Press but lately their fine working relationship had been cooling.

There was an unusually buoyant mood amongst the teaching staff this particular Monday morning. Oliver put this down to the excitement and relief that all felt as this was the last full week of the 1968/69 school year. The 8-week summer holiday was just days away wherein the staff could finally rid themselves of the 'Banshees'

A TAIL OF TWO CITIES

and each. As Mr Press detected that the babble had descended to a respectful hum, he took to his feet:

'I speak at this truly momentous time in human history. As of yesterday school will never ever be the same again. The weekend's events have changed all that. We can now only look to the future; the former things have passed away.'

Was Mr Press about to announce his long-awaited retirement? He went on: 'I am of course referring to Mr Armstrong and that other American chappie taking Man's first shaky steps on our moon. This you will appreciate is just the start for Mankind and indeed for Tower Hamlets. Edith, my wife of course and I took the grandchildren to our caravan in Wales and watched the events on TV there. Many of you younger teachers will be taking lessons actually on the moon by the year 2000 and that's only 31 years away. So we need to prepare now!'

At this point, when the incredulity and disappointment had subsided, Jeff Slater interjected. 'Funny you should mention that Mr Press but a few weeks ago I went to a rave up with a couple of cats on the moon but I left early because there was no atmosphere .... I've been taking my birds to places beyond the planets almost every night!'

'I'd have thought that cats and birds don't quite get along Mr Slater' came the droll reply.

'Did Mr Armstrong take his trombone with him to the moon?' countered the teacher obliquely.

'The moon is certainly a Wonderful World Mr Slater,' a comedic reply not expected hence completely missed by the staff.

As ever the masses there responded with barely hidden chuckles and a few guffaws.

Jeff Slater was the teacher with it all. He had a wit, sharpness of thought and joie de vivre admired by most. He was also the possessor of some alternative and even outrageous opinions, and in attempting to reflect the local Jewish community he once suggested that all lessons should be conducted in Yiddish or Hebrew, as he believed that 'if you can't beat 'em then join 'em.' Jeff was also of striking appearance standing at 6'1" and manfully built. The son of an Irish mother and wealthy home-counties father, Jeff was well-heeled with the sureness that money and connections often bring. His father had done well for himself in recent years and directed and produced several of the top West End stage shows. Jeff's golden complexion radiated supreme health and poise. On top of this he was Tower Hamlets' only sports teacher and accordingly dressed differently, always choosing top of the range sportswear. Jeff Slater stood out. He knew it; his colleagues knew it and all the fawning pupils too. If this wasn't enough, this Classroom Casanova lived in a Chelsea Mews and accordingly drove an E-Type Jag, both courtesy of his successful father Arnie.

Following a shaky start in their professional relationship Oliver was regarded as Jeff's best mate and this reciprocated. They were schooled together even sharing the same birthdate. In fact, their mother's met in the delivery suite at London Hospital's East End Maternity in Stepney. So as friends Oliver and Jeff went back as far as it was possible. They complimented one another well and shared a mostly similar approach to life as well as a keen interest in football, politics, music and snooker. In a blokish way they also laughed at the same things at the same time and enjoyed competing with one another. Their longstanding friendship was solid much of the time, but times were changing.

Healthy Schools
TOWER HAMLETS

Mr Press meanwhile was an out of touch, seemingly innocent, portly Head but imbued with an unlikely steely cynicism. His only real input to the well running of the school was his Monday morning rallying call but he yearned to leave his mark somehow. As a consummate middle-class Englishman with a pre-war approach to everything Mr Press was inevitably going to find 1960s swinging London unsympathetic and often hostile. He was simply biding his time waiting for Edith, his 'wife of course' to order him to retire. It was clear that all he desired was to see out his days in rural Tring where he could continue his study of calligraphy and dream of becoming the first retired Englishman on the moon. His only way of parrying Jeff's crudity was to side step or even ignore such flippancy although sometimes it was felt that he comprehended all.

'As the headmaster this school's reputation and standing during these liberal times is of tremendous import. I am however more continually concerned about the small minority of our girls who, some as young as 16 spend much of their leisure hours at weekend involving themselves with boys and narcotics. Some even smoke pot and are seemingly unconcerned with their studies. It's being sold outside the school gates and even being brought inside school. For those who don't know, pot is a killer drug that can kill many unfortunates stone dead the first time inhaled. I've got a Sunday Times editorial for those teachers here that want to know more about these killer drugs. Of course the Police at Leman Street are aware of this stain so I would ask that all staff this week watch for any girl who seems to be hallucinating,'

'Drugs? I blame Mick Jagger and that other one in the Rolling Stones,' said Jeff sarcastically.

'Cliff Richard?' ventured the Head.

'Yeah Cliff Richard, that's the chap. In fact, I fully uphold the BBC's view that 'Let's spend the night together' should be banned along with Jane Birkin and that foreign gentleman!' said Jeff, complete with straight face and much to the amusement of the others.

'It's good to know I have an ally in you Mr Slater,' said the apparently gullible Head to more stifled sniggering. Mr Press was well-aware of both Cliff and Keith but presenting as simple served a purpose.

He then bid his staff a good and productive last week and holiday and sent them on their way. As he had rarely seen his teachers in such jovial mood his ego led him to believe that, yet again, he had really pulled it off!

Oliver's mood that day was a mixture of anticipation and apprehension. There was alot going on in his mind and a few major issues to be addressed with two months at most to resolve them. His approach and resilience however he hoped would see him pass through the troubled waters of the tottering education system and come out dry as a bone. This resilience was the key to teaching the Greek, Latin and Roman Classics at the toughest of East End institutions with an enthusiasm that Oliver never struggled to uphold. Alas many of his students thought otherwise, one even complaining that Oliver delivered his classes with so much passion she could barely sleep. Even his best Latin wise-crack "A Roman Centurion walks into a pub and ask for a Martinus. The landlord says 'Don't you mean a Martini?' The Centurion replies 'If I'd wanted a double, I'd have asked for one'" always fell on deaf ears. His well-known thick skin had him put to one side such incongruity prompting his private moto for the school as *Maxima debater puree reverential* (The greatest respect to the children), although he was planning to update this sometime soon. He loved his vocation and would have gladly gone another 10 or 15 years therein with no regrets and no easing of pace. Oliver was certain that it was this sort of devotion to duty that would result in him collecting an OBE as was recently bestowed upon the lolly pop lady that had patrolled the crossing opposite the school for decades.

Perhaps the aspect of Oliver's working day that really put a spring in his step was fellow teacher Miss Elsmore. Louise Elsmore was the stunning doyen of the staff group and incredibly aware of being the unchallenged diva teacher. Standing at 5'9" and of near perfect proportion everything she wore sat well onto her fulsome mermaid-like curves without being skin-tight. It was as if the fabric was just content to lay upon her without having to caress too closely. Her hair was long, substantial and coal black. With shimmering magnetic green eyes, Jean Shrimpton's sultriness and Diana Ross's allure she was as close to the complete woman as could be. Everything sensual that could be oozed, Louise oozed. Her tendency however to utter working class profanities belied her Brighton Finishing School upbringing. In point of fact it was difficult to attribute her to any particular class. What was certain however was she had plenty of it! Her regular recourse to industrial language along with her perplexing disposition were seen as minor flaws or possibly assets to her character. Being so pleasing to the eye greatly augmented her life chances and exploit it she did.

Oliver meanwhile felt extraordinarily protective toward Louise so what irritated him as much as anything oftentime was overhearing his male colleagues staff room banter lewdly wagering amongst themselves as to the colour of her panties, the measurements of her breasts and other such mysteries. These questions however were assuredly and definitively answered by Oliver.... 'Miss Elsmore wears only black underwear in the winter months and rarely any undergarments at all between June and September. Her breasts are 36 inches, that's combined and not each and they fit wholesomely into a D cup!'

Of course whenever he answered with such surety his colleagues knew that Oliver was simply being Oliver, the tad obscure Classics Master. He too felt safe in that knowledge however he knew, Oliver actually knew the truth about her! You see, he and Louise had been passionate, hotly passionate lovers for nigh on three years.

A completely unlikely pairing. Indeed, no one, not a soul knew of this undisclosed and most romantic of trysts and Oliver and Louise determined to maintain this.

To his colleagues and pupils Oliver Cherry was a head-in-the-clouds, stick-in-the-mud but Lulu so loved her man and he truly loved her back.

ఌఌఌ

Chapter 2

A tall tale from the tall trees

The summer of 1969 was as glorious as was it immense. London had a brash and confident air about it. Though not one of the hottest on record the real heat on the shimmering streets was generated by the multitudes of exuberant, talented, eccentric and curious people it attracted from the world over. Designers, models, musicians, photographers, poets, philosophers of the new religions and thousands, even tens of thousands of hopefuls. Two summers prior the capital abounded with gifted idealists. Now many of those concepts had been realised and new fresh horizons were there to be pursued and gained.

The West End fizzed too: Carnaby Street burgeoned with new designs, Shaftsbury Avenue, the Palladium and her environs offered more theatrical treats than all Broadway and still curiously the city's naivety remained untouched. The Beatles had just recorded their finest album to date, Abbey Road in St John's Wood and it seemed from almost every open window kids sang 'Maxwell's Silver Hammer' and 'Octopus's Garden' and lovers, 'Something' as they came together. It was cool to be chic and chic to be cool we were told. Mayfair and Belgravia sat sedately whilst Leicester Square hummed and bustled as Trafalgar Square gushed majestically and Piccadilly Circus stood at the true unchallenged crossroads of the known universe. A little further afield Portobello, Notting Hill, Camden Town and Islington stirred and fermented with a deluge of ambitious communities anxious to carve a place for themselves in this great swarming metropolis of nearly 10 million souls. London stood grand, unhindered, purposeful and beautifully aloof. In essence, London was it!

The East End as well continued to hurtle along remorselessly. Whilst rack upon rack of glamorous and trend-setting garments clattered and shunted across Commercial Street into Spitalfields and seedy goings-on continued particularly when the working girls hit the streets at dusk to ply their trade and earn some good-will! Not far from this hive of business, Tower Hamlets Girls School stood alone in 4 and a half acres of prime real estate. Surrounded by tall trees and surprisingly well manicured hedgerows and flowerbeds, the school was a true calming haven as well as a great symbol of pride for its caretaker, Ruff Carnegie a less than gentle Scotsman. To Ruff the school was his baby bequeathed to him indefinitely by an Education Authority who in him, he would often say, found the 'best man for the job!' He took no prisoners and woe betide anyone who'd even consider messing with his baby. -

It was the last week of term when Ruff spied a lot of unnatural movement in one of the tall beech trees that bordered the hockey field. The movement was unusual enough to warrant further investigation. As he approached, the tree reverted to its usual repose but the caretaker remained curiously unsatisfied. The silence and stillness continued then, with no notice Ruff was struck square on the head by …. an object, which fell away into the undergrowth.

'Who's up there ye? Out with ye, ye weak piece of piss,' he yelled. There was no reply.

'I'll give ye 10 seconds then I'm gonna climb up there meself and bring me dog too. If he gets his teeth into ye throat he won't be able to let go until ye is dead and dead ye will be,' he continued. The gruesome threat again went unheeded but Ruff all the more, sensed that the branches undoubtedly held a secret.

At this very moment, Miss Elsmore was taking her first drama and dance class of the week when she spied Ruff outside gathering stones and discarded tin cans into a large plastic bucket. He then marched hurriedly across the field toward the troublesome tall tree wherein he vigorously pelted the branches with all the strength he could call upon whilst furiously flailging around, cursing and screeching. He was not a man to be denied.

'Ye had ye chance to save yeself. I canne help what's gonne happen to ye now ye blithering buffoon ye!'

Louise then gave the evolving scene her full attention and when Ruff's ire reached a critical level the whole class joined her at the window watching as Ruff reached apoplexy.

'Girls, get back to your seats there's nothing of interest here' she said as she left the classroom to see for herself. She then scurried out of the school and across the playing field followed by her entire class.

'Ruff, Ruff slow down. You'll do yourself an injury' said the breathless teacher who was by then surrounded by 30 or more equally breathless 5th formers.

'There's someone up that tree. I've seen him move an' he's attacked me with something or other. I might even be bleeding from the wound' said Ruff.

'Who's up there and what wound? Wound! Do you mean a proper wound?! A gunshot wound? Has he got a gun?' yelped the teacher.

'Ye canne be too sure. I think he might even have an eye for your girls Miss Elsmore.'

For several heart-thumping seconds Louise had to decide whether to take cover to save herself and her charges or support the Scotsman. She did neither because it was here that Linda Greenhalgh the unrivalled leader of the older girls came to the fore.

'Right girls' said Linda 'get anything you can lay your bleeding hands on and chuck it up there. We'll soon show him who's who at Hamlets!'

It was at this point that one of Linda's more imaginative peers shouted that she could see at least three men up there possibly toting 'tommy-guns'! Then, to a-girl the class instantly and fearlessly took to arms relishing the opportunity to be part of future school folklore. This scenario could even warrant a front page headline in the East End Advertiser:

-Teenage Girls Capture 3 Communist Gunmen -

'We're running out of ammo so shall we set fire to the tree now Miss?' asked Linda.

'No, no, no of course not Linda. A fire, are you mad girl?! Get back inside. Get away from the tree all of you. I'll write a letter to all of your parents you know.'

screamed the teacher.

'Aye, I think ye girls know what they're doing Miss Elsmore. Leave it to 'em Miss. A limited blaze may be the only way!' said Ruff sincerely.

'Thanks for your bloody solid support Mr Carnegie,' said Louise sarcastically.

It was then that a shrill voice emanating from the upper reaches of the tall tree could be heard over all the commotion.

'If you want me to come down you're all gonna have to get lost so I can scarper,' the voice said.

It soon became clear that the alleged machine gun maniac was simply one mere boy and too little a challenge for the girls who perceived their moment in the sun had passed. They filed back into the school disappointed and dejected. Their time was not yet.

'Well I think I best be getting back meself Miss Elsmore. Better one of the teaching staff sorts this out I think,' said Ruff without a jot of consideration to the tumult he was responsible for creating.

'Yes, go and have a strong cup of tea Mr Carnegie and you'll need to get a plaster on that gunshot wound too, won't you!' said Louise, now relieved that nothing serious had unfolded.

Louise took a moment or two to recapture some of her usual composure and peered into the tall tree's thick, lush foliage.

'It's all quiet down here now. I'm on my own,' said the teacher tentatively.

There was no response.

'Ahoy there young man is there anyone up there who's in charge? You can talk to me ……. I'm on your side.' said Louise in an effort to relax the boy.

A TAIL OF TWO CITIES

'I'm coming down now but that's all I'm gonna do. Don't wanna talk to no teacher,' said the youngster firmly.

Louise could see some stirring of the boughs. It was a boy, no more than 10 years of age and clearly dressed in the uniform of Harry Gosling a nearby primary school. As the child descended further his most striking feature was his bundle of tight red hair. It was clear that as he finally touched ground he was content that his ordeal was over even though another was about to start.

'Where's me shoe?' he enquired nervously.

'Do you always climb trees with just one shoe?' said Louise jokingly, designed to put the lad at ease.

'No I threw it at that madman. He…that man he he… was gonna set his big dog on me,' said the boy. 'I ain't gonna take that from him. He don't even talk proper.'

At that the boy waded through the long grass in an effort to find the missing footwear. Louise was finding it difficult to refrain from asking more about the waif but knew she had to win some degree of trust at least, prior.

'What does the shoe look like?' asked Louise in a failed attempt to get the boy to respond with the obvious gag.

The boy remained uninterested.

'Well my name's Miss Elsmore I'm a drama teacher here. What shall I call you?'

'I know what a teacher is but I don't know dramarr?' he replied.

'Drama is a bit like acting,'

'Acting, acting like on the telly, like James Bond, The Saint and like The Avengers?'

'That's right,'

'Are all teachers at that school …. sort of … a bit like you?' he asked.

'Like me?'

'I mean are all the teachers at Tower Hamlets … lady teachers?' he clarified.

Louise chuckled at this odd line of questioning and told him that there were lots of men who taught too. They continued to look for the absent shoe.

'You could be a teacher too one day,' she said.

'Can I be one at this school soon Miss?' said the boy excitedly.

'Give it a bit more time, let's at least find your shoe first. Well look I've told you my name and my job but I don't know anything about you yet. You must only be about 8?' Louise speculated.

'On September the 23rd I'll be 8 and my name's Terry, Miss.' 'Have you only got one name?' replied Louise, now confident enough to get a little pushy.

'Shit' said Terry 'Shit Miss, I found me shoe and it's got shit on it. Dog shit all over it even on the laces. It's that madman's fault it is. I can't wear that. I'm not gonna put that on. Shit! Shit! Shit! ….'

At this the boy kicked the offending shoe with his good foot further into the long grass and ran off toward the Commercial Road. Louise knew there was no point chasing after him or even calling him back. She knew from experience that many of her girls at some point arrive in the morning with two shoes only to somehow or other lose one by the final bell. They just take the other one off or simply hop home. All survive, and young Terry would be no different.

Louise was inquisitive enough to take matters a little further and there, inside the offensive dark blue plimsoll was sure enough written his name, 'TERRY' in black magic marker. There was a surname too but, alas obscured by excrement. Louise had seen a lot and been involved in many a situation during her years at Hamlets but this whole saga proved without doubt to be up there with the most bizarre. She seemed to develop an almost immediate empathy for the boy in the tall tree and her curiosity led her to want to know more.

The following day Louise approached a rather sheepish Ruff and asked how exactly the boy came to be in the tree?

Vehemently he replied: 'The boy's a born nuisance. He won't heed anything I say. Sometimes he's up there for hours but yesterday was the closest I've come to getting me hands round his scraggy neck. He does ne care for me flowerbeds. He does ne care for me borders. He does ne care that I've been workin seven days a week. He does ne care that Cockroach expects the whole place looking …'

'Our Headmaster is called Mr Press can I remind you Mr Carnegie, Mr Press!' retorted Louise.

'You're right Miss Elsmore. I was ne thinkin.' conceded Ruff.

'The boy.... er did you say that he's been hanging around a while?' asked Louise.

'Aye Miss since the beginning of term. Every other day I can see this wee ginger heed through the branches. I think he might even fall asleep up there. Surprised he does ne build a tree house. Don't go to school much I think.'

'What do you know about him, does he live nearby, do you know anything, anything more?'

'Well Miss, the lad does ne care about me flowerbeds and I disney care too much for the lad. He's heading for a good hiding, he's gonna feel me boot before long. I just need to see the back of him once and for all.' said Ruff and scuttled off murmuring further malcontents.

Ruff's minor disclosure made it all the more difficult for Louise to combat her curiosity. Finally giving in, she did something only the day before she promised herself she'd never and telephoned the Head at Terry's school, Harry Gosling Primary. With remarkable ease Louise found the Head Mistress Miss Parry very forthcoming and with boy's first name, description and even date of birth '23 September 1961' he was easily pinpointed.

'That can only be Terry Saunders,' said the helpful Head. 'Terry's a boy that everyone will hear of before long and not for the right reasons. We don't see much of him lately. His mother sends him to school each morning, they only live in Dellow Buildings, but he hardly ever arrives. He seems to think he should only drop in when he's got

A TAIL OF TWO CITIES

nothing better to do. His mother seems to be finding it all too much for her. Many of the other mothers call her Jezebel, I prefer Peggy as in Peggy Mount. Got her head in the clouds that woman and won't accept that she is responsible for getting him here and ensuring he stays. No one else! Terry's dad doesn't seem to be much involved but his grandmother in Islington has his best interests at heart and helps out when she can. Terry, I'm afraid is sadly going nowhere fast ......'

DELLOW BUILDINGS

It was all beginning to turn into a rant reminiscent of Ruff's outburst the previous day. Louise wanted to know more of this 'Jezebel' but felt further prying was going beyond normal professionalism.

'It seems that Terry dropped a plimsoll out of his school bag the other day and it ended up on our hockey field. One or two of my class live in Dellow Buildings I can get the plimsolls back to his mother through them,' said Louise expectantly.

'Ha that explains it. That explains why the boy's wearing odd shoes. Well yes I'm sure that will be a great help. 27 Dellow Buildings off Cable Street, E1. Perhaps if Terry happens to pop into school tomorrow he'll be clad appropriately,' said Miss Parry sarcastically.

'Perhaps,' said Louise. 'Perhaps!' and thanked her for assisting.

෴

Chapter 3

The Bag O'Nails

Oliver and Louise lived nearby one another. In the same block of flats even. She on the 3rd floor, he the 9th of Gouldman House part of the newly built Cleveland Estate off the Cambridge Heath Road. Proximity meant they could keep an eye on each other, not that their respective fidelity was in any doubt but they were just genuinely interested in each other's lives, the result of being deeply in love. That way too made it easy to meet up each day away from nosy colleagues, noisy girls and the world at large. Their connection was as light-hearted and pithy as it was ardent and sincere. Spending the evening together was the ultimate daily highlight for these intense lovebirds. 'The swans' as they referred to one another vowed that they would become impervious to all the machinations and pressures of life and work and that they would remain as one indefinitely and renew that 'vow' often.

GOULDMAN HOUSE

Traditionally, or for the last 12 months or so Wednesday evenings Oliver went out to find his own entertainment without her. In fact, it was even encouraged by Louise, the only rule being that she must know which night-club, dance hall or music venue he planned to go.

'My sweet, sweet lady friend. My gorgeous piece of fruitcake. I love you more than a bumble loves a bee. I adore you more than Helen loved Troy....Tempest. I think of you even more than Cockroach does Edith, his wife of course!' confessed Oliver to Louise wistfully.

'Salute my scrummy Classics Master. I love you more than grass loves green. You mean more to me than Sonny does Cher. In your arms I am tripe! Pray tell this fair maiden my twinkle toed lover where doth thou frequent this eve?' she responded, in similar manner.

'When the cock doth crow ten I frolic at the Bag full of Nails. Yes indeed, The Bag O'Nails night venue in the Square that is of Leicester in the heart of our fallen city. Henceforth I must away to iron my slacks and bri-nylon shirt anon. Now place your sweet lips upon mine. I must hasten away Lulu!'

Oliver and Louise held each other close and passionately kissed. Then he left and went up to his flat on the 9th and prepared to head up West. Oliver was a man with a surprisingly substantial wardrobe. Classical languages, The Beatles and clothes were his three main passions in addition, his love for Louise of course. Getting ready to go out therefore usually took Oliver at least an hour. -

Wednesday night at the Bag O'Nails was generally quiet. Mostly a regular crowd, in the main there for the music: Tamla Motown, Aretha, The Monkees and of course The Beatles, The Stones, The Kinks and The Who. However, the vinyl spun this particular night were mostly The Doors, Byrds and Credence. For Oliver this made a refreshing change. Something else was different too. At the bar sitting on his usual stool sat a girl that had Oliver salivating the moment he spied her. With no compunction and without a moment's recourse to Louise the woman he had kissed and departed from only a couple of hours prior, Oliver prepared himself for an introduction. As he strode the dance-floor, his eyes fixed lasciviously on his quarry confident it would be a successful kill. All it took to score was charm, radiant appeal and a sense of fun. After all it was Wednesday night!

'Oops, I seem to have lost my phone number. Can I have yours?' joked Oliver to no avail. He continued.

'You do know that I've been coming to The Bag for almost a year each Wednesday and I've made the stool you're sitting on my own.' said Oliver.

This second gambit was slightly more direct than usual, with even a slight degree of menace. The woman however was made of sterner stuff and after she had taken another couple of sips from her glass of Champagne said coldly:

'I too come frequently and I've never seen *you* around. Usually when men approach me they ask me if I 'come here often' but you…no.' said the woman.

She spoke assuredly and in a polished rich South Kensington-type accent. Oliver's reaction was mixed but he was mostly more than a little taken aback. He did not expect such a forthright response from a stranger on his own patch but he was pleased she noted that he was a little more original than the competition. He struggled to come up with a suitable response be it witty, cool or apologetic. The woman sensing his unease was in no mood to help the helpless, preferring instead to transfix him with a withering glare. He recalled privately that Louise never gave him this grief when he made his first advances a couple of years prior.

As the sweat channelled down his spine Oliver was about to turn tail and willingly give up his stool, however from nowhere he summoned more mettle.

'I'm having a drink. I suppose yours is a Cherry B?'

'Do you honestly think I drink Cherry B or Babycham or Snowball? Do you?' she hissed.

'Well I do, so I thought that perhaps you err ….. ' he mumbled.

'Well you know what thought did?' she replied, more irritated than before. It was clear that his quarry was impenetrable, having no need for the company of this East End charmer or a drink. He'd given it his best shot but it was now time for a dignified departure.

'I'll be sitting in that alcove over there if you sort of … sort of need me for anything or whatever,' said Oliver chastened.

At that he spun on his heels and hotfooted it, however almost simultaneously the woman jumped up from her stool and followed the bewildered man stride for stride to the alcove.

'I knew you'd see things my way,' said Oliver with renewed but excessive confidence.

'Don't get too cocky Casanova but do go along and get me a glass of dry white,' she said much more disarmingly.

Oliver returned with the refreshments sensing the Ice Maiden had at least partly been won over but did not know quite why.

'I'm Oliver and I don't have to ask you now if you come here often, do I?' To which the woman smiled and then chortled. Amazingly for at least ten minutes the conversation ebbed and flowed without faltering, then she asked:

'What do you do Oliver?'

'I'm a teacher. A teacher of Greek and Roman Classics, you know, Latin and all that stuff.'

'Well how about that!' she replied

'Yes lots of people are surprised when I tell them I teach. Most think I'm an international playboy,' said Oliver reverting to bravado.

'No, I don't mean that. I'm a teacher too,' replied Oliver's 'date'.

'A teacher! You don't strike me as that sort of person. I mean teaching's a noble profession and that, in fact probably the most noble but how come you talk like some kind of …. err princess?'

'It's not my true vocation though. You see when I was a child growing up I yearned, simply yearned to be an actress. Then when I was in my teens I yearned, simply yearned to be an actress,' said the woman theatrically.

'And now that you're a teacher,' said Oliver satirically. 'Do you still yearn, simply yearn to be...'

'...to tread the boards. Yes, yes and yes again. Oh more so than ever, ever, ever,' she interrupted flailing her arms skyward and attracting attention. Oliver soon formed the creeping suspicion that he had come across yet another of London's myriad of eccentric nutters.

'Tell me ... err ... at what school do you teach?' asked Oliver.

'Tower Hamlets' she replied.

'Tower Hamlets.....Tower Hamlets Girls in the East End!!!' blurted Oliver.

'The very same,' came the reply.

'Ah ece destra educatum institu, ece in institu omega educatum et. Amo fecil Lulu est!' said Oliver.

'In English please?' she replied.

'It means that of all the teachers at all the schools, she had to teach in my one. I simply adore you Lulu!' he said, passionately gazing into her eyes.

'And Lulu simply adores her Ollie too and will always, always alwaaays.'

With that they flung themselves together, nuzzled each other intimately and kissed then kissed again. Throughout the proceeding minutes Oliver and the reverted Louise spoke only of their mutual adoration. Then under the cover of the darkened alcove Oliver took the cheeky opportunity to place his hand on her knee before proceeded to slide it upward.

'Ay you, what have I told ya ... tits first!' she joked.

> THE
> BAG O'NAILS
> CLUB
> Paul McCartney
> met
> Linda Eastman
> here on the
> 15th May 1967

Of course Wednesday evening was Oliver's time 'on his own', however such a separation was much to the often untrusting Louise's chagrin. As a pseudo-compromise

Oliver and Louise developed this complex charade to go out independently whereby either a diffident, bashful, engaging or gallant Oliver would undertake to chat up, then pick up his erstwhile lover who herself took on varying dispositions in response. Invariably he would eventually succeed and never left 'The Bag' without Louise on his arm. To the regular patrons at this sultry night-spot this apparent futile palaver was appreciated and ignored, 'each to their own' they would proffer. Potential suitors however, unaware of this wacky rendezvous began to seriously question themselves on witnessing the likes of clumsy Oliver succeeding where they themselves had been rebuffed so unceremoniously just minutes before. In many ways Wednesday night at The Bag O'Nails was the week's highlight and was used not only as a little light-hearted relief but as a venue where the couple could discuss their respective and joint concerns. This particular night was no exception.

'I gotta get something off my chest Oliver,' said the real Louise.

'Don't worry sweetie, I'll slip your bra off as soon as we get back to your flat,' he replied, still in frivolous mood.

'No come on let's get serious now. This is important,' said Louise pleadingly.

Oliver stiffened and sat a little more upright, altered his expression and with brow furrowed said.

'OK baby shoot, but I've got something for you too.'

When they finally agreed who would go first Louise related in great detail the incident with Ruff, the boy in the tall tree, having her class effectively taken over by Linda Greenhalgh and the attempts made to track the boy down.

'Hang on, I don't believe you sometimes Louise!' said an astonished Oliver. 'You actually phone another school because you found a shitty shoe, that was flung by a wayward kid from a tree at the head of a homicidal Glaswegian tyrant?'

'Well yes if you have to put it that way, but there's much more to it. Terry has been spending a lot of time up that tree and we need to find out why,' she replied apprehensively.

'*We* don't need to do anything. *We* need to be professional. Haven't we got enough problems with the girls at Hamlets? There's pills and pot coming into the school, the exam results are down and Lynn Snow is pregnant…. again. I could go on! The East End's full of Oliver Twists,' complained Oliver becoming increasingly exasperated.

'Occasionally, only very occasionally, you can talk a lot of sense Ollie …..' said Louise in an uncertain tone. '…and this is one of those occasions when …. I … I … have to agree with you. And by the way you forgot to mention that LBJ is bombing the hell out the Vietcong. Ah … Oh well you're right Ollie I know I do sometimes get too involved. Anyway never mind all that, what you got for me?'

Oliver was pleased that he had seamlessly shifted her attention away from the 'Terry thing' and onto what he thought a more pressing dilemma.

'You know that all the applications for the Head of Year post have got to be completed by the end of the week? I've given it some thought and …... well I reckon I'm just the man for the job. It takes a certain type and I've sat myself down and had a long chat with my Naked and decided to give it a go. Well perhaps give it a go. What do you think Lou?' said Oliver hopefully.

'Naked, that's one smart dog you've got there!' came the smiling reply. 'Get me a drink and let me think about it,' said Louise.

At that Oliver scuttled around the alcove's table and through the trendy throng swiftly moved to the bar. He returned a minute or two later with two small glasses and having shooed away a suave would-be suitor who was making a play for Louise he resumed the conversation with anticipation written large across his twitching face.

'I thought we'd try the malt whisky. It's different here tonight don't you think Louise? They're playing The Doors alot, they don't usually play The Doors so much or Credence or …' bumbled Oliver apprehensively.

Louise looked sternly and said. 'Do you have any idea who the other candidates for the post are?' Oliver replied that he didn't and that he had never really given it much thought.

'There's that Stewart Segal, Liz 'what-day-is-it-today-girls' Tucker, Tim Petyt, the oh so lovely bottled-blonde Ann Hall, Christine Newton, Sarah 'Stupid' Stringer, Angela 'mine's a double' Hughes and the muscle man that is Andrew Tansey. And do you know what they have all got in common, Oliver?'

'They're all going for the same job Lou!?'

Oliver was prone to state the obvious when he was nervous or just plain stuck.

'No I don't mean that … They're all a bunch of has-been losers or wanna-be chancers. None of them can match you in anything … anything! Your time has come Oliver go for it … go for it now!' protested Louise more fervent than Oliver had ever seen her, outside the bedroom at least.

She spent the next few minutes tearing strips off her man's rivals individually emphasising their lack of charisma and experience or unsuitable temperament. Oliver was completely taken by Louise's vehement encouragement. How could he have even doubted she would be any other way? After all they were a young couple madly in love and were planning a future together. Consequently, if Oliver succeeds in any endeavour wouldn't Louise do too? In fact, Oliver was so wrapped up in the pep talk he had just received he did not think to question how Louise had such a complete list of all the other applicants. This was confidential insider information, wasn't it?

'I'll get my application in as soon as I can,' said the prospective Head of Year candidate gleefully.

'Yes, and you better be quick about it as well. Oh and Oliver remember the next time you have a life-changing decision to make perhaps you might deem it more appropriate to discuss it with me before Naked!'

Then Louise reached into her handbag and from it handed Oliver a small, fluffy rabbit's tail key ring.

'What's that for?' he asked.

'Well its not a superstitious thing or lucky charm. I know you're not into that sort of thing. It's just something to remind you of me during our adventures together. Anyway, it could help us get what we want, what we deserve!' said Louise.

'So there's a mutilated rabbit hopping around somewhere. I don't think little bunny wanted or deserved that, do you?

At that they cuddled and giggled affectionately. They left the Bag O'Nails renewing their 'vows', arm in arm, lifted by the progress they had made that evening and all the more looking forward to their future with one another. He came to know that when she spoke with messianic-like dynamism and faith she was determined to see results, and soon.

ಊಊಊ

Chapter 4

Boxing Clever

'Good morning girls, before I get you all panting its quiz time. Ah, but before I come to that here's a few important notices: Well this is your last PE lesson with me before the end of term. However, I have to remind you that the last few months will go down in the history of Tower Hamlets as without doubt our most successful on the sports field ever, yes ever! Our under 12's girls wiped the floor with all opposition in both netball and hockey. Our under 14's took the all-London swimming shield for the fourth year on the trot. It is our under 17s however that will be long remembered throughout the East End for winning the South East England inter-school's Rounders championship and as a consequence of their efforts won TH a new fully-equipped mini-bus! Will there ever be a year like 1969? I think not!'

So began Jeff Slater's up beat July rallying address to his top girls' class. His approach was Churchillian with a touch of Eric and Ernie some colleagues thought. He knew that just about all of these girls excelled in their chosen sport, some even representing their borough.

All were aware that Jeff's coaching skills and method of engendering enthusiastic devotion to any sporting cause brought the school more prestige and adulation than any academic achievement. Teaching staff knew they were never going to produce a Mrs Bamber Gascoigne. Further, Mr Press was unashamedly prepared to bask in the glory of Hamlets' sporting success and positively milked it to extreme, so much so that he kept a fresh wardrobe of clothes in his office should yet another media photo opportunity arise. The head always made it a priority to eavesdrop on Jeff's major pronouncements to the girls as experience showed that Jeff always had an idea or two up his sleeve again designed to put the school even more firmly on the London map. Jeff continued:

'Girls we have one final challenge, a challenge which I am sure you will be only too pleased to take up. You'll know that not everything went our way this year. Our nearby biggest rivals are still Robert Montefiore Girls School.'

At this howls of derisive and scornful jeers echoed and bounced around the assembly hall.

Robert Montefiore was a Secondary Modern Comprehensive school in nearby Bethnal Green. Probably because it had boys as well as girls its reputation for unremitting toughness was fabled. On top of this its sports facilities were envied throughout east London however their head of sport, Glenn Greaves said of his charges that if procrastination was an Olympic sport they'd compete in it later. Jeff was aware of their lethargy and this encouraged him in bringing out the best from his 'warriors'. Jeff and Glenn were friendly enemies aiming to outdo each other at every opportunity not for their own ambitious personal prestige of course, but for the enhancement of their students!

Jeff went on: 'Before the end of term I have discussed a way with Glenn Greaves a method of deciding once and for all which of our schools will be the 1968/69 top dog.'

Language like 'top dog' was sure to raise the competitive hackles of the girls and Jeff was certainly aware of this.

'In two days from now Hamlets and Monty will meet for a showdown. A final showdown. There will be a massive difference though this time girls.'

This pronouncement was met with a little uneasiness before an enquiring silence ensued.

'We will be challenging the Monty girls at boys' sports! No hockey or netball but ..... boxing and wrestling.'

There was numbness in the air but after a moment's speedy contemplation the mood changed decisively pro.

'There's no way we can let that lot of nancies get one over on us. They're just a loada girls!' yelled Karon Cashman ironically, who along with fellow students, Maureen Camilleri, Sandra Drier and of course Julie Blair held much more sway on any such decision than ever did Jeff.

'Are we all up for it girls, us against Monty?' bellowed Jeff. Without any hesitation the girls took to their feet cheering, tugging each other in a very manly way whilst baying to bring the clash forward.

'Just one final point girls. Let me go back to our quiz. Now girls, what happened on 30th of July 1966? If you know, don't shout out put your hand up.'

A TAIL OF TWO CITIES

Big Susan Wolfe, noted as one of the school's many dolts, ignoring the direction shouted:

'I think it was the day that my brother Tony broke his wrist when he was playing out on his roller skates. My mum took him to Casualty at The London and had to take us all cos me dad was at the pub so we missed England winning the World Cup on the telly.'

Jeff, in an effort not to dismiss Susan's attempt outright and to get her back on track replied. 'So what big event happened on that date back in 1966 Susan, you were very close?

'I've just told you Sir, Tony broke his wrist!' she repeated failing to grasp her teacher's direction.

'Sir, England won the World Cup beating West Germany 4-2 in extra time. Scorers, Peters and a Hurst hat-trick.' said Julie Blair the cocky and confident 11+ passer.

Jeff skilfully assured both girls that they were correct and went on to make his specific point:

'Next year our boys will be going off to Mexico to defend *our* World Cup. We are the inventors of football so the cup now here should never be allowed to leave our shores. Alf Ramsey will soon be gathering together an unbeatable squad. Bobby Moore, Bobby Charlton, Banksy and Greavsie …'

Susan Wolfe now filled with confidence chose this moment to interrupt.

'…. and Georgie Best, Sir!'

Determined not to get into a discussion on nationality and have his flow disturbed Jeff continued:

'They will be travelling half way across the world with but one objective. To come back successful having achieved the ultimate yet again. This, girls is what you too must aim for when we box and wrestle those losers from Monty. How dare they come to us hoping to compete with the best! Can the invincible ever be beaten? Can they? Can we ever come second to that lot, when they don't even know how to put on a pair of boxing gloves?!'

'They'd probably want to stuff 'em down their bras like they do their socks,' joked Elizabeth Tucker from the back of the hall, to much coarse laughter. 'Lizzy T' as she insisted was the staff's hot favourite as the next girl to fall pregnant.

Jeff's rabble-rousing continued for a further ten minutes but by then the girls had got themselves into such a frenzy it attracted the attention of many of the other teachers who gathered around the edges of the hall to see what had caused such a hullabaloo.

Jeff, with recourse to his favourite film 'Spartacus' and aware of his new audience summed up in similar fashion.

'In the next few days you girls are going to become the finest scrappers London has ever seen. But not without cost ….. no not without cost. It will mean sacrifice though girls. Great sacrifice! The task ahead may be too daunting for some that stand before me today. The Monty girls won't hit the canvas easily. Only the strongest will survive in the dog-eat-dog world of the ring. So rest tonight my young ones. Rest well and gather your strength. Training starts first period tomorrow!'

At that Jeff, when he could take the class no higher, dismissed the noisy, ecstatic and enthused throng knowing that his use of some well weathered rabble-rousing clichés clearly won them over. Now for the tricky bit, persuading his colleagues to let the girls scrap! -

Later that morning Mr Press called Jeff to his office to discuss how best the school could handle the remaining few days of the school year. Many of the girls in the 6th form leave school at this time to either go onto further education or seek a job. Hamlets' girls usually fell into the latter group. Either way this period of the school year was generally unsettling for most and away from the normal rigid routine.

'A couple of things to run by you Mr Slater,' said The Head, 'next week the school will be holding its usual end of term party. In the main, arrangements for that event have been finalised by myself and Louise.'

Jeff inwardly balked at Mr Press's rare and overt familiarity.

'What we now need is a special event something just a little away from the norm. The idea I have come up with I've discussed with Edith, my wife of course. How about some sort of sporting challenge..... perhaps against the old enemy Robert Montefiore High School!'

Jeff was well-aware of Mr Press's massive ego and was therefore only too happy to play the eves dropper's game and share the spotlight if it meant that he could be allowed to construct a boxing ring within which teenage girls could pummel. Such a thing had never been considered never mind enacted. Jeff appreciated that controversy and even disapproval would inevitably come from outside the school but if it had The Head's blessing Jeff figured, indeed if it were The Head's original concept then how could it possibly fail?!

'Funny you should say that Mr Press but only this morning an idea, probably similar to but not as exciting as yours of course came to mind. I was thinking that if we were to...'

Mr Press, as he so often did, interrupted.

'No Mr Slater don't just give me any old tosh of an idea. I want you to go away and sleep on it and report back to me first thing tomorrow with some fresh thinking. That'll be all for now, thank you.'

Jeff left the office hurriedly, knowing that the deal was as good as done and that if the inter school's boxing and wrestling match was a success Mr Press would allow some of the reflective glory to come his way. This could possibly result in Jeff's long hoped for transfer to an all boys school that played football and cricket, Jeff's true sporting passions.

Word of the 'fight' had got around the staff room by lunch time to universal scepticism and no little derision each believing that getting girls to batter one another folly in the extreme and that the

London Education County Council would anyway dismiss the idea out of hand. So too did Oliver. Louise, ever the opportunist was a little more farsighted and canny believing that it might just work and that the school and her Ollie could somehow benefit if involved in the contest from the outset. With this in mind Louise sought to elicit Mr Press's reaction. She was always aware that he had a soft spot for her and indeed for any pair of fluttering pretty green eyes would soon have him swooning which unquestionably left him more pliable. Louise's ambition for herself and particularly her one true love Oliver was in no way limited. Her attitude was that if toadying was the name of the game, a toad she was content to become.

Mr Press always considered that he was free to speak discreetly to Louise and she regularly reassured him that to be the case, of course with her fingers crossed firmly behind her back.

'Tomorrow Louise, I am confident that Mr Slater is going to approach me with the idea of a boxing bout or some such thing with the girls from Monty. Of course I will be shocked and eventually he will win me round conceding that it was in the main my idea as it was I who granted him the freedom to come up with something quite unusual before the end of term party. I'll then have a duty to make it a most successful and enjoyable event. I'm sure it'll be something the local and national media will revel in, don't you think Louise?' he said smugly.

Louise saw no benefit whatsoever informing him that Jeff's proposal was already the talk of the teachers' staff room.

'I don't know how you manage it you, wily old fox you,' said Louise careful to praise and not patronise.

'When you eventually retire I don't think anyone will be able to fill your shoes Arthur. You're the beating heart of this school, you are Arthur, you really are!'

They both then chuckled but for differing reasons.

Louise continued 'By the way, have there been any err … late entries for the Head of Year job?'

'Oh yes, most intriguing. Young Mr Cherry submitted only this morning. He truly is a splendid chap. I'm very fond of him you know. The interviews are as soon as we return from our summer vacation in September. Between you and I, Mr Cherry's certainly got the position even before the interviews. The others seem so staid. Cherry's got class. We need much more of that here at Hamlets, Louise. Class!'

She could barely contain her excitement. Everything was falling into place beautifully. She bade Mr Press a warm farewell, flung him a few more disingenuous compliments and left the office saying she would return tomorrow to see what other eye-popping strategies he would have devised overnight! -

Later that evening Oliver and Louise enjoyed each other's company with a bottle of Claret in his flat on the 9th floor. Naked always mooched around uneasily when Louise visited. The dog was never certain of her and she didn't care too much for the dog either. Inexplicably Naked could read her in a way Oliver was never able to. Once the lovers had had their fill Louise casually brought up the topic of The Head of Year post. Shrewdly she informed Oliver that she had discussed it with Mr Press and he had indicated that Sarah Stringer was the front runner and indeed almost certain to be successful!

'Well that does it Lou. It was pointless anyway applying. I don't know why I bothered. I know Sarah well she'll do a great job. I know she will. Good luck to her. Let's raise our glass to Sarah 'Stupid' Stringer. God bless her and all that are taught by her,' hissed a drunken and disappointed Oliver.

This twist on truth, as it turned out was Louise's way of testing Oliver's mettle and commitment to the cause. It may have backfired however as Oliver now spoke of withdrawing his application altogether.

'Come on Ollie,' she wooed, purposefully nuzzling his ear. 'Why is Sarah known throughout the East End as 'Stupid'? Think about it Ollie Wollie, if you don't go for it what does that make you? A quitter never wins and a winner never quits. I never thought you'd be beaten by a woman even before the start.'

'So why do you think I've got a chance when the job's as good as Sarah's. What qualities have I got? Yeah tell give me …. er 17 things about me that'll convince the panel I'm the man for the job? Go on!'

For love-struck and ambitious Louise this was a cakewalk.

'Well Oliver you're decisive, talented, hard working, ambitious, extremely knowledgeable, creative, understanding, honourable, optimistic, ingenious, resilient, talented, you can speak fluent Latin, God knows why, your versatile, adroit, experienced, charismatic, you're great in bed and you never ever run away from a challenge!'

Inevitably and with little effort Louise had got her man back on track. When had she ever failed? As the sunset over the East End they renewed their vow of love and devotion, held each other and kissed sensually giving way eventually to intimacy.

'Oh by the way Lou, that was 18, you said talented twice and you omitted any reference to my rugged manliness!'

Naked mooched once more.

ঌঌঌ

Chapter 5

Get Back – To where you once belonged

8am and bang on cue the following day Jeff approached the Head teacher's office. Not yet changed into his tracksuit, Jeff first straightened, arched his back, cleared his throat a little and knocked resolutely on the door. The Head wasted no time:

'Enter Mr Slater, take a seat and tell me what you've come up with. I trust it will be entirely to my liking. Ah but before your proposal however I've one of my own. I've been thinking that we should perhaps liven things up for the girls' sports day. Last night I was discussing with Edith, my wife of course, introducing traditional boys' pursuits, say boxing even wrestling and then testing our prowess in those areas against those from our rivals at Montefiore school!'

Mr Press went on to explain that his plan to pitch girl against girl though anathema to some could prove a turning point for girls' sport throughout the entire nation. Consequently, Tower Hamlets and its forward looking and enlightened leadership would be remembered as pioneers lauded by the entire British education establishment. Even the new and burgeoning Women's Liberation Movement would see the idea as refreshingly equitable!

'Ah, what can I say!' Jeff sighed then unassumingly further gave way.

'I feel that between us here Mr Slater we could be onto something that may make a lasting impression on the playing fields of England. I will inform the media whilst you get to work training our most powerful girls in the art of unarmed combat!'

It was at this point that Mr Press unexpectedly redirected his monologue.

'Before you go about your business Mr Slater I have long been aware of your eventual wish to coach in an all boys' school.'

This unnerved Jeff a little as for the last two years he had regularly broached this only to be rebuffed as often. Then in a sinister tone Mr Press continued:

'You'll know that a Head of Year post has become available. I trust that without hesitation you'll put yourself forward for this prestigious position. Should our match against Monty prove to be successful, very successful then your application for the post will no doubt be equally successful. It will then only be a matter of time before your transfer application papers to any London school of your choice will fall onto the appropriate desk. Put simply, sporting success equals promotion and promotion equals passport. Our sporting challenge against our rivals Monty has, as an imperative to succeed. I'm sure you understand the politics of the education system and what's at stake here!

Jeff was not shocked by this covert form of coercion as he had previously recognised this as one of The Head's less favourable traits. Jeff however felt compelled not to appear as a pushover.

'In a way this seems like a form of blackmail Mr Press!'

At this assertion Mr Press then slowly rose from behind his desk and walked across the office toward the concerned teacher, then placing a comforting right hand on Jeff's shoulders proclaimed:

'Hmmm, blackmail, blackmail that's rather strong language Jeffrey! How so? When Tower Hamlets benefits you do too. Alas think of it from my perspective, I could eventually to be losing you Mr Slater, one of my most valued assets. So you could say that I am the only one loser here but I'm prepared for this as long as our girls beat Monty convincingly. I'm afraid however that unlike yesterday there can be no time to sleep on it. You will consider the import of at least a verbal job application now. I've decided to bring the closing date forward to .... this morning. Indecision is a most unsavoury characteristic; you'd agree?' declared the cunning Head with confident smugness.

Jeff recognised he was clearly being put on the spot but with speedy mental deliberation could see only positives. He may have always got the best of Mr Press during the Monday morning staff meetings but on a one-to-one Jeff's light-hearted adlibs before an expectant audience were no match for the shrewd and experienced leader. Accordingly, Jeff announced that he would like to be considered for the Head of Year post and that he would have his written application on Mr Press's desk directly.

'Oh Mr Slater, before you go – gloves or bare knuckles?'

Jeff smiled wryly and thought for a moment.

'Well let's go with gloves this time and if that works perhaps mediaeval battle axes next!'

The two men shock hands firmly and parted, Jeff to elicit Ruff's assistance in preparing makeshift boxing and wrestling rings and Mr Press to the large mirror on his office wall in which to preen and congratulate himself. -

The next day by order of Mr Press a group of a dozen or more hand-picked girls were excused lessons and assembled ringside. Each was provided with a pair of boxing gloves. Some pairs were moth-eaten, some without laces but all accepted as a curiosity. Jeff had no direct experience of training boxers but he and Oliver did witness Henry Cooper floor Cassius Clay at Highbury three years earlier.

'OK Julie and Maureen you two get in the ring and see what you can do. The idea is to do as much damage to your opponent in as little time as possible ..... OK seconds out ..... Round 1,' said Jeff.

The two girls initially side stepped around each other menacingly sizing their opponent.

'How we gonna bash up Monty if you don't get stuck in,' yelled an enthusiastic watcher.

This was the cue for 60 seconds of frenzied mayhem, both girls wildly swinging their arms like crazed windmills but not making much in the way of any real contact. Their efforts and enthusiasm could not be called into question but it was clear much tactical work had to be done. Jeff consoled himself that Glenn Greaves, his counterpart at Monty would be in a similar position and that whoever could direct the girls' natural ebullience most effectively would prove the victor. There were however most definite signs that after an hour or so the girls were managing to channel their aggression and that Karon Cashman and Maureen Camilleri were Hamlets' two best bets.

That lunchtime Jeff and Oliver met up in the staff room as both were too tired to leave the confines of the school for a 15 minute break as they did more often than not. They tucked into their sandwiches whilst edging their way toward one another through the throng of equally fatigued and hungry colleagues in the staff room. Oliver, by his own quirky standards was dressed more flamboyantly than normally. Assuredly, the prospective Head of Year felt it his duty to make at least a visual impression even before the job was officially his. Wearing his favourite deep purple shirt contrasted by a rainbow kipper tie and black brush velvet slacks he looked quite the 1960s dandy. Needless to say the clothes were picked out the previous night by Louise.

'How's things Oliver? We didn't get a chance to grab a game of snooker last week did we?' enquired Jeff.

'Busy, busy, busy got lots of things going at the moment but let's make it a priority this week, yeah?' suggested Oliver.

'That's groovy, how's Wednesday? Mid-week's pretty quiet down the snooker hall.'

'Wednesday's fine ... Oh no Wednesday's unfine Jeff ... err something's come up.'

'Funny last Wednesday night I gave you a ring but I must have missed you then too. You out pulling birds up West on Wednesday's are you?' teased Jeff.

He would have been rendered wordless if he knew how close he was to the truth and that the so called 'bird' in question was none other than Louise, the focus of so much male staff attention and possibly a few female teachers too. Oliver looked a little flushed at this line of questioning and Jeff had known him long enough to appreciate that Oliver had something on his mind.

'What's up Ollie, you OK?' enquired Jeff. 'No problem if you can't make it on Wednesday then some other time eh?'

'I'm fine, just fine,' he replied loosening his tie. 'But there's one thing I can't get to grips with. I don't understand how you could possibly want our girls to batter and bruise other girls. It can give them brain-damage, it can turn them into psychopaths, can even make them infertile too!'

They looked at each other then smiled. Not such a bad thing they both agreed and laughed at how ludicrous the whole thing really was. Jeff assured that the boxing and wrestling challenge was a total one-off where no blood will be spilt and that come the day it will probably turn out to be more of a novelty event during the build-up to the end of term party than a serious contest.

'Do you know Ollie that Cockroach thinks once the media gets to know that girls and not boys from two East End schools are gonna box each other they'll be down here in droves. He's got some 'associates' as he calls 'em working for the nationals who'll give him a very rosy write-up. As for me I'm more interested in the Head of Year job he's talked me into applying for,' said Jeff innocuously. 'The interviews are soon as we get back after our summer holiday. The job's mine Cockroach assures me; it could be my passport out of here to a boys' school. All I need to do is ensure that our girls give Monty a good beating in the ring. Wish me luck mate.'

A sudden cold chill rushed through the air. Or at least it did adjacent to Oliver who sat shocked and bemused at his best friend's pronouncement. It was as if circumstances were congregating to perniciously plan on how to bring him to his knees bit by bit.

'Go for it Jeff, you deserve a break,' mumbled Oliver with pseudo magnanimity, almost choking on his cheese salad sandwich. Oliver then, in a continued effort of support listed all the other applicants and gave his friend a brief comparative assessment of their chances, effectively quoting Louise parrot-fashion. So taken by the moment, Jeff didn't question how Oliver had come by this supposed personal information of the other applicants.

'The job's in the bag Oliver. All we'll be doing in September is going through the motions. Justice and fair play has, at least to be seen to be done,' replied Jeff confidently.

'Can you really rely on Cockroach. What if he can't ….?' muttered Oliver through still gritted teeth, his words tailing off into nothingness.

'Be cool Ollie, cool! Do you honestly, honestly think that Cockroach will miss the chance of a centre spread in the London Evening Standard or a special feature on the BBC. Maybe even a Panorama Special with Richard Dimbleby?'

Oliver concurred and with an undetected sigh wished Jeff further good fortune and left for his afternoon Latin class.

En route Oliver passed the drama department wherein Louise was taking a class. To no avail through the window he waved and gesticulated in order to attract her attention. It took one of her pupils to point him out. This was something in normal circumstances he would never resort to. When she eventually turned to him, he mouthed that he would see her in her flat tonight and then held up eight fingers. Having received a comprehending nod he made his way to class dragging his feet like a forlorn infant. -

As evening approached Oliver looked from the window of his small neat 9th floor flat across what seemed a bleak, cold London skyline. He knew that his chance of promotion had likely passed. With the commensurate near doubling in salary, he had hoped that he could help Louise with her flagging acting career by suggesting she leave teaching altogether and see if she could make it on the West End stage. All seemingly a distant pipe dream now.

'Well Naked it looks like it's just you and me again boy. Just like it was in the old days,' said Oliver to his dog disconsolately. 'It seems we're destined to be stuck here up on the 9th floor for a good while yet. Unless you've got any bright ideas?' At that his companion looked up appearing to shake his head, wagged his tail and whimpered.

'I know that winners never quit or so says Lulu but only one horse can win a one horse race …. and I'm not that horse, Jeff is. Ah, what's it like being a dog Naked? You got any problems eh? Is your doggie girlfriend tough and demanding? Is your doggie best friend a job rival without him even knowing it? No, I thought not. They say it's a Dog's Life but I wouldn't mind a stint in dog world for a while. I'm sure it's better than teaching Latin and classical Greek to the Plebeians!'

Naked had never seen his master as down beat so he rolled over asking to be tickled. That seemed to do the trick, as Oliver obliged with one hand whilst pressing his eyes with the other. Having gained a little composure he left to tell Louise of the bad news.

On his way down to the third floor Oliver attempted to recall all 17 of his 'tremendous qualities' that she put to him at the Bag O'Nails just a few days before. He only got to number six before Louise opened the door. She looked pensive but smiled, kissed him warmly on the cheek and beckoned him in.

'Make me a cuppa Lulu I've got some news that might upset that beautiful face of yours,'

She remained silent and stoney-faced and proceeded to the kitchen. On her return with two cups of hot tea, she asked Oliver to cuddle up next to her on the sofa.

'I know that look Oliver so just before you say anything kiss me,' she said motioning to him beguilingly. They kissed.

'That was the best thing that's happened all day,' he admitted.

'Ollie,' said Louise longingly, 'I love you very much, you know that don't you?'

He shuddered and remained silent. Was this the build up to Louise wanting to break up?

'Although I love you Ollie I sometimes feel you let me down! That I'm doing all the work in this relationship … keeping it going, that sort of thing, whilst you're not really pulling your weight as much as you can!'

Oliver was starting to bristle 'Go on Louise, go on.'

'I know what you've heard. Cockroach told me that Jeff put in an application for the Head of Year job and that it's a done deal.'

'So you know, do you? So what's your point. I did what you said … er suggested and it's now come to this. I'm withdrawing my application tomorrow morning. Why should I just go through the motions only to become a humiliated failure!'

'My point is Oliver, I know what you're like. I know that as soon as you come up against one little hurdle you just want to throw in the towel. You never consider if there's a way around it. You just don't ever, ever consider me! I need you to help me … help us. I'm lost without you. I need my man to be strong!' Louise then erupted into a rapid surge of tears insisting that she wants a 'proper future together'. Oliver hugged her sturdily and puffed out his chest on which to rest her worried head.

'Ah, come, come Lulubell we'll get through this. We'll find a way round this we always do, don't we?' said Oliver manfully but with no plan B in mind.

'There is a way Oliver. I'm sure there is just promise me you won't withdraw your application and trust me. I'll figure out a way just leave it to me. Do you trust me Oliver, do you?'

'Of course I trust you Lou. I always do,'

Oliver and Louise gazed wistfully into each other's eyes and renewed their vow before embracing and kissing tenderly. Both were now, for the moment content.

'Let's see what's on the tele,' said Oliver.

It was a choice between Hughie Green's Double Your Money or Michael Miles' Take Your Pick. Oliver and Louise looked at the screen and exhaled mournfully. She winked at him; he nodded and turned off the TV. They then moved knowingly off to the bedroom to further cement their relationship.

For Louise, the road to success was always under construction.

A TAIL OF TWO CITIES

Chapter 6

A change is gonna come

Saturday morning saw Louise rising before 7am, about the time that she would on any ordinary school working day. Whereas she would normally struggle to the bathroom and then snuggle back into bed for a short while, this particular Saturday was different. Louise was a woman with on a mission and as many that knew her well appreciated, if Louise had an aim to realise wild horses would not stop her. Today was more than just something to do; today's task was imperative. She washed and dressed quickly. The clothes she picked out were some of her shabbier and she wore just a smattering of makeup. She then moved to her bookcase and ran her fingers along the book spines.

'A to Z, A to Z,' she muttered to herself.

On finding the said book she flicked through the pages hastily and stopped abruptly part way.

'Dellow Street? … ah there it is between The Highway and Cable Street just near Watney Market.'

A TAIL OF TWO CITIES

She toyed with the idea of wearing a hairnet but she concluded that would be going too far.

Within 45 minutes she had left her flat and reached her destination. Dellow Buildings was a near dilapidated, shabby grey and puce-coloured block of flats built just before the Great War. It was a block on an estate earmarked for refurbishment and had been so pre-Beatles. From most windows billowed full washing lines joined by some sort of pulley and spring mechanism to the block across the courtyard. It was early, not yet 8am. Although there was little stirring in the flats, the shrieks from Watney Street Market were just about audible over the deep mournful hoots emitting from the cargo ships heaving in and out of the Pool of London just a couple of hundred yards away and the dockers and stevedores going about their noisy, dirty work. In the near distance stood Tower Bridge, tall and aloof ready to swing open its ponderous arms for the first time that day.

These were not the surroundings Louise was familiar with. She was a girl from the sunny side of the street but was in no way intimidated or perturbed by some of the harsh realities of an East End in penury. She made her way up the cold worn steps to number 27 on the third floor and on knocking the door found it to be already open. She entered.

'Hello anyone there … Hello!' she said nervously.

'I'm still in bed. Didn't get in till 5 this morning,' came a nearby voice. 'What time is it now?'

'Well it's around 8,' replied Louise obligingly.

'You talking posh cos it's early are ya?' the voice said jokingly.

'No I always talk like this.'

There was a short silence then from the bedroom door struggled a dishevelled woman with long dark, dank hair who was clearly wearing last night's crumpled clothes. Both were startled at the unexpected appearance of the other.

'Hello I'm Louise I noticed the door was open … I did try to … er let you … if it's not convenient then I'll ..'

'No it's not bloody convenient Miss La De Daa. Now sling your 'ook or I'll get me big Alsatian to rip your tits off! I'll count to ten. One …' shrieked the brunette almost purple with rage. ' … two, three, four … '

Louise needed no more convincing and headed straight through the door, down the stairs and into the street. She took a few seconds to catch her breath then hurried off, taking care not to look back for fear of what she might have to encounter. It was then that the same voice could be heard from a third-floor window.

'Oh Miss La De Daa. I think I might have been bit sharp with you just then. I'm real sorry darlin'. You caught me with me knickers down so to speak. I'm always like that before I've had me first a ciggie o' the mornin. Some of these losers round 'ere call me Jezebel but I'm just as much a loser as they are really. God knows how hard I try though. Look give me a few hours and come back will ya?'

Louise couldn't decide whether to be flabbergasted at the very suggestion or relieved she'd got away unharmed. Confused, she shouted back.

'What about your dog?'

'Dog, don't make me laugh. I never had a bleedin dog, excuse my French. I can't afford to feed me bleedin self ne'er mind a dog can I? Anyway dogs round here disappear almost every night and end up down Limehouse served up with chips,' said the woman whose tone had lightened. Louise looked up and then scanned the scene noticing that the minor commotion had attracted the attention of some nearby residents. It seemed as they too wanted to know if Louise would accept the young woman's apology and return.

'OK. I'll be back at around midday,' said Louise courageously.

'Midday? ... Is that the afternoon one or the night one?' replied the woman.

'No Midday, 12 noon the afternoon one.'

'Oh I've got ya, right see you then, then.'

Louise walked home via the market bemused at the unreal scene she had just been the central player in and how the young woman invited her back without even enquiring who she was and what it was all about. 'Quite, quite bizarre!' Louise concluded.

Sure enough at precisely midday (the afternoon one that is!) Louise returned and knocked on the door, which this time was closed. She was a little more prepared and less apprehensive than earlier. Within a few seconds a hulk of a man wearing nothing but a short ill-fitting T-shirt opened the door.

'Is the …. lady of the house … available?' enquired Louise determined not to lose eye contact.

'Miss La De Da for you Janey babe,' shouted the man over his shoulder. In an instant a raven-haired whirlwind of a woman of no more than 5 feet tall pushed past the giant then turned back and gave him a big wet kiss on the lips whilst stroking his face. She then forced her way past Louise and headed down the stairs.

'You coming or what?' the woman barked.

Louise had no option but to follow.

'That's me … bruvva,' said the woman incredulously. 'We can't have a girly chin wag when there's a geezer about, can we?' she said as they reached the bottom of the stairs with Louise trailing behind.

'There's Caf's Caf down Watney near Shadwell tube that do all day breakfasts. We can get some peace and quiet there.'

As the two women entered the hectic café it was clear that they were never going to get any of the said peace and quiet in there. They decided to take a short walk to Wapping to sit by the river and watch the cargo ships being unloaded.

'Well miss La De Daa teacher. I think I better introduce myself, my name's Janey. I knew you was coming cos my Terry told me you would soon enough. I'm an unfit muvva and that ain't my bruvva back there neither. I met him last night and fuck knows how I'm gonna get rid of him. I bet you don't have man trouble like me, do ya teacher?'

Louise was a little taken aback yet again by this woman she hardly knew. She found Janey's frank honesty curious although somewhat coarse and impulsive.

'I am a teacher in fact Janey but I don't work on Saturday. My name's Louise and I've come here as a friend. Yes, it is about Terry but I haven't come to judge what sort of mother you are.'

'Louise, did you say your name was Louise. One of my fellas last month dumped me for a posh tart called Louise. It ain't you is it?'

'No I can assure you it wasn't me Janey. It's not the sort of thing I'd do.'

"It's not the sort of fing I do," mocked Janey.

'I have to say that I imagined you were going to be one of those East End dumb blondes!' replied Louise in an attempt to deflect some of Jamey's resurfacing ire.

'Well I bloody well just might be after all!'

At that Janey hauled off her bushy brunette wig revealing a shock of bright blonde hair.

'I only wear my brunette wig when I want to seem brainy but I ain't nothing more than a dumb blonde,'

The two women fell into fits of laughter at how preposterous it was all becoming.

For the next hour Louise and Janey sat by the Thames musing, exchanging anecdotes, romantic adventures and their hopes for the future. They even began to give out the odd wolf whistle to the broad-shouldered dockers that toiled up against a wall nearby. It was all good, not so clean fun the sort that women do so much better than men. It was out of character for Louise to reveal so much about herself to a stranger but she felt at ease and unthreatened by Janey who in turn revelled in the attention.

It was difficult through the frivolity for Louise to introduce the real reason for her visit. That of the boy in the tall trees, Terry. When she eventually swung the conversation around to the subject Janey's bright young freckled face descended in solemnity.

'I wondered when my Terry's name would come up. None of the other teachers at his school have ever taken as much time to get to know me as you Louise,'

'Oh no I'm his teacher but I'm from Tower Hamlets.'

'Tower Hamlets that's a girls' school, I'm sure I didn't put Terry in a girls' school … did I?' replied a perplexed and uncertain mother.

'You really are the most, dizzy girl I've ever come across Janey. No, Terry goes to Harry Gosling Primary surely you know that?'

'Of course I know what school my own bleedin son goes to. What do ya take me for, some sorta dozy cow?'

There was a brief silence whilst the protagonists reassessed their respective positions.

'Listen Louise, I have to admit I'm not really able to look after my Terry all that proper. He is my son and all that. I birthed him but his grandma is better at all that rearing stuff. She knows when to say 'no' to him. She knows all about cooking and fings like that. All I really know about is chips and beans. Sometimes he comes over but not much these last few months. He doesn't like my fella, any of 'em,' said Janey despondently. 'But what do you want with him? Has he been making a nuisance of himself with your girls there at Hamlets? Give it another ten years and I reckon he'll be a real lady-killer just like 'is dad.'

'No don't worry, he's been the perfect little gentleman,' replied Louise kindly.

It was at this point Louise came clean and told of the real reason she wanted to track Terry's mother down: She gave a detailed account of the lad being spotted in the tall trees around the school for some weeks and how he always managing to avoid getting 'Ruffed' up. She told of the disgusting shoe that remained in the undergrowth.

'Why would a boy so young want to spend so much time sitting up a tree when he could be doing other things?' ventured Louise

'You mean other things like er what, going to school? Is that what you mean? Face it Louise, if that's your real name, you're like all those other Miss Prims all you lot wanna know is why Terry hasn't been to school for a day or two, where's his school tie, ain't he got no PE kit!' scoffed Janey slowly becoming more irritated.

'That's not why I'm here. I'm here because I can tell there's something more to this than meets the eye.'

'My fist is gonna meet your eye if you don't belt up, you bossy cow!' said Janey menacingly.

Louise then jumped to her feet and with a glare strode off toward the market.

'Hold up girl. You know what I'm like, half the things I say I don't mean and the other half I don't even understand meself. Come back, there is more to all this than meets ..... whatever it is.'

Louise stopped in her tracks and turned, her mock protest although a gamble looked to have paid off.

'If I come back there's going to have to be no games.... the truth now?'

'No games, just the truth,' conceded Janey calmly. 'The whole truth and nothing but the bleedin truth, Gawd help me.'

Tentatively Louise returned and took her seat on the bench next to Janey convinced that matters were finally about to move forward.

'Terry's grandma worries me a bit,' resumed Janey cautiously 'She's a bit of a brainy bleeder really. Well ya see I was only young when I birthed Terry. I was only about 16.'

'About 16?' asked Louise.

'I was 15 … when I got caught but turned 16 when I had him. I couldn't even wait until I was 21, could I? Anyway I had him and I was real glad I did cos now I can't live without him. Can't live with either. That's why his grandmuvva over in Islington takes over alot of the time,' said Janey tearfully.

'It must have been very hard for you back then. Were you on your own? Did you get any help from Terry's dad?' enquired Louise.

'Ah bless him. He was just a kid himself not much older than me he was. What could he do, fix us up in a Knightsbridge penthouse with his dinner money! He would've if he could, he just couldn't. He came from a La De Daa family a bit like yourself. His dad worked up West and his mum ... she just drank herbal tea all day and did a bit of ballroom dancing. But she's good to Terry though, looks after him proper good, she really loves him. It's a shame Terry's dad couldn't get on with his own mum. They fell out years ago and ain't spoke to each other for donkeys. Not sure why.'

'So Terry's being cared for by his dad's mum and not yours?' asked Louise.

'My mum! You gotta be joking. My mum is what you type of people might describe as one of life's down-trodden, as thick as pig shit who don't even know what day it is since she discovered gin and vodka. She still thinks Churchill's the Prime Minister ... but I tell her he's not .... he's not is he Louise?'

'No, no it's the loveable Harold Wilson now. Churchill died in '65,'

'Yes, of course he did. As long as Terry's got his grandmuvva, his sober grandmuvva that is, he'll be OK. Once I get a bit more settled in meself he'll be coming back to live with me for good. He don't stay with me enough. I really wish he could. Every night I say a little prayer for that day to come.' Janey's eyes welled again.

'I'm sure that'll happen Janey but that doesn't explain why Terry is so interested in Tower Hamlets?' asked Louise with barely concealed impatience.

'Ain't that bleedin obvious?'

'Er … well it probably is but not quite so obvious enough to me.'

'You see Louise, Terry's grandmuvva told him that his dad is a teacher at Hamlets. I told the old bat not to, that it would confuse the poor boy but she just blanked me and sipped her bleedin tea.'

'Well who is he? What's his name? I know all the male teachers there.'

'Jeff Slater, he's a sports teacher there. He seems to be doing alright for himself. I never told Jeff that I was pregnant, his mum thought it best. She said she'd support me all she could as long as Jeff didn't know he was gonna be a dad. I really, really needed someone to turn to, I needed her help so I agreed. Now she wants to get back on speaking terms with Jeff she's gone and told Terry all about him and even where he works.'

Louise sat shocked and stoney-faced at the disclosure. She would not have believed it if the account was given to her by a third party but Janey spoke with an unambiguous direct honesty. Nevertheless, a small shadow of doubt overcame her.

'I know Jeff Slater, I know him well, we've worked together at Hamlets for the last few years. In fact, Jeff's best friend is my boyfriend Oliver. They were born on the same day. Tell me though how do I know if this thing about Jeff being Terry's dad isn't just a pack of lies?' ventured the teacher.

At this Janey slipped both arms out of her T-shirt and swivelled 180 degrees. There tattooed boldly on her back was the imposing image of Piccadilly Circus. Arching over the statue of Eros writ large the words 'Jeff and Janey 4ever 1960'.

'So Miss La De Daa do you need any more convincing?' spurted Janey.

'Well I never! No, no I'm sure it's just as you say it is. I'm sure, but don't you think it would come as a real shock if Jeff does somehow or other find out about Terry. I mean he didn't even know you were expecting. He hasn't been in contact with his mother for years. He's never even seen his son. It might be all too much for him,' said Louise.

'It might be all too much for Terry also more like, that's why I need to somehow stop him finding out more about his dad. At least for the time being but my boy's got a real strong mind of his own though,' replied Janey fretfully. -

In this, her first meeting with Janey, Louise had quickly developed a sincerity and warmth saved only for Oliver. Despite all her puff and bluster however, Janey didn't really have a bad bone in her fragile body, an aspect that Louise was quick to recognise. Both appreciated that every man has the right to know if he has fathered a child and to be part of that child's life but that in some situations there was a need for a degree of circumspection. Louise concluded that in this case Jeff's paternity should remain hidden. Within her furtive deliberations, she was not able to precisely rationalise why this newly acquired information should be kept from Jeff but she instinctively knew that the optimum time for its revelation was for some apposite occurrence hence. Oliver, she considered was her one true confidante and had to know of his best friend's teenage past. Meanwhile, Louise and Janey said their goodbyes and exchanged telephone numbers promising to meet up regularly and soon.

Louise could hardly get to Oliver's flat soon enough. Throughout her hurried walk there she mentally went through the scenarios of his possible reactions and concluded that the most likely was that he too would want the information kept from Jeff. As she approached Oliver's door however, Louise was unexpectedly enwrapped and overcome by the barely explicable sentiment that even Oliver should be excluded from the knowledge of Jeff's paternity too. Her muddled pragmatism had therefore to somehow justify this sharp U-turn. Consequently, the best she could come up with in her mind was that it would be for Oliver's good ultimately not to have to carry such an unnecessary burden when his focus should be on his job promotion, their love and her happiness.

ঔঔঔ

Chapter 7

The Good, the Bad and the Vermin

Teachers will tell you, the last week of term at any sizeable secondary modern is always rewarding, taxing and long. The prize of seven or eight weeks of ease is a major incentive in staff retention. Saying a final goodbye to the leavers, most of whom had been at the school for seven life-changing years was psychologically testing for all concerned. In most cases hatchets are buried and gratitude and encouragement exchanged. Tower Hamlets Girls School was one of thousands in England going through this annual angst. The abundance of planned school activities in the summer of 1969 was exceptional. Parents' Evening, Best Work Exhibitions, Prize Giving and of course the end of term school party, all crammed into too few days. In addition to this and by far the most eagerly awaited was however the boxing/wrestling tournament between the school and Monty. On this apparent premise Louise sought a private audience with Mr Press just before the Tuesday morning start of the day bell.

Louise slid into The Head's plush office assured that she would get what she wanted. This particular morning however Louise was emboldened in the extreme, more upbeat and dressed more glamorously than at any time during her career. Her mini skirt that was a little thicker than a thick belt went well with her tight, clinging cotton top. Louise sat back in the large leather-bound swivel chair in front of Press's messy desk. Nonchalantly she used the chair to full effect swaying hypnotically one side to the next and back again.

'I say Louise, you are on fine form today. Quite eye-popping in fact, any hot-blooded male would say that,'

'What would *you* say though, Arthur?' replied Louise pouting. 'What would *you* say?'

'Well I would have to agree. You're a very attractive ... young woman Louise,' mumbled Mr Press, like a lamb to the slaughter.

Louise folded her legs one over the other, then slowly back again. After that she unfolded completely showing almost as much thigh as there was to show.

'You like what you see don't you? Would you like to touch what you see? My body soooo needs to be pampered all over from top to bottom Arthur?' she purred as he fumbled drawing the blinds.

Press's temperature shot up and soon his toupee slid further down his forehead to almost obscure his view of her. He knew he was being manoeuvred but was too aroused to consider the consequences. Having received no real discernible reply Louise repeated her bold question but more forcefully now.

'Well yes, of course I'd like to touch what I see Louise,' whimpered and hapless seductee.

'Touch what Arthur? Touch what?'

The quivering man's fat red head took on a sweaty purple hue. Louise moved close, sat on his lap, wiggled to and fro as he loosened his tie, the cue for a rush of lustful perspiration to exude from every pore. He was happy for the moment to be helpless.

'I'd like to touch your body,' he sighed expectantly.

'From where to where?' asked Louise feigning breathlessness.

'Oh from top to bottom Louise .... The very top to the very bottom.'

'But would you like to touch my sweetest spots? Would you like to touch and caress them too?'

'I I I would if I could. Would you let me? I'd rather like to touch you everywhere Louise. Can can … I?'

'If I am to pleasure you Arthur, you will have to pleasure me too,' ventured the vamp.

'Can we discuss this later?' he said, hardly able to contain himself.

'Touching is always better after talking. Any hot-blooded male of substance like yourself would tell you that Arthur. Isn't that so?'

'Well Louise, I've never really thought about it but I suppose so.'

'Now calm down Arthur just for a teeny weeny minute and let me explain.'

Whilst continuing to writhe unhurriedly on the Headteacher's lap Louise, now insisting on being referred to as Lulubelle went on to slowly detail why Oliver was the best candidate for the Head of Year post and that although Jeff was a capable man, the school 'shouldn't settle for second best.'

Of course Mr Press quickly concurred, skilfully able to parry any brief resistance he could muster. The power deemed to Louise in this one-sided encounter was near complete and like any modern-day Mata Hari she could hardly fail to gain the malleable man's full and unequivocal consent. Having gained a further absolute assurance, Louise rechecked the office door was locked, sighed very deeply and stripped to her lingerie before her grateful and fully aroused boss ....

Within a few minutes Louise, sullied but content with her quid pro quo was dressed, out the door and off to take her first drama class of the week. -

'Let battle commence!' shouted Mr Press grandly, fresh from his exertions of earlier in the day.

At long last the day had arrived. It had been many years since Tower Hamlets girls had been part of such a keenly awaited sporting event and never, ever had they had to box and wrestle in a formal setting to enhance their already considerable tough school reputation. Twelve of the most aggressive and fearless girls Hamlets have ever produced against twelve equally uncompromising teenagers from nearby Monty. School attendance that day was at a record high. Of the 1177 girls on the school's books an unprecedented 1171 were present. The half a dozen that were not, were either too heavily pregnant, in labour or had pacifist parents. Crowd control and security was to be the staff's top priority however responsibility for this was gladly handed over to the Prefects and them in turn to some of the Monitors from the 5th year - henchgirls, the lot of them.

A TAIL OF TWO CITIES

The hockey and lacrosse fields had been divided up into six areas centred by a fully canvassed and roped ring. Ruff had done an admirable there. Alongside each ring was a set area designated for the local and national press who arrived in unexpectedly high numbers. Was this noble investigative journalism, Oliver asked, or were they just a bunch of kinky middle-aged Fleet Street hacks looking for some titillating action? The women from the St John's Ambulance Brigade were too appalled to watch but they dutifully remained at hand nearby. Those from the Womens' Institute, there plying sandwiches and hot tea demonstrated a surprising degree of liberalism with one radical even suggesting that boys should be allowed to box the girls too! Although the BBC declined the invitation a full crew from Rediffusion and London Weekend were there being guided by Mr Press, of course.

The first wrestling bout went very much as expected with Hamlets' Jacqui 'Sumo' Somers crushing her diminutive opponent pitilessly. Jeff took heart from this and immediately put Jacqui in Ring 5 to box Monty's top boxer, Linda 'The Gladiator' Greenhalgh. The gamble never paid off – 1 all. The next few bouts saw Monty take a 5 to 3 lead. Jeff and his girls regrouped and agreed to a tactical switch that simply involved an increase in violent aggression. Oliver, Louise plus several of their colleagues put aside their peaceful misgivings and converted to rabble-rousers. Indeed, all staff were amazed that the girls who would have ripped the hair from anyone that challenged them for the last scrapings of Spotted Dick at lunchtimes were able to band together so solidly. Before long the excited air was filled with chants of 'Ham-lets, Ham-lets, Ham-lets' which could be heard half way to Gardiner's Corner. Oliver suggested to some of the more vocal girls and cheerleaders that they should shout instead 'Definata et Destructium Monty' to the tune of 'Maybe it's because

I'm a Londoner'. Louise shook her head in disbelief as did all else. Even Mr Press was seen to be holding a spit bucket for one of his boxers in the blue corner. Edith, his wife of course was there too offering encouraging advice and flapping a towel to cool the combatants between rounds.

Before long the pendulum swung again as Hamlets took the next three wrestling bouts and tag match. 'Sumo' got her revenge on 'The Gladiator' and Karon 'The Crusher' Cashman was awarded a walk-over as her opponent from Monty had just started her period. Within an hour Hamlets had swept into a 7–5 lead, which was then hauled back and surpassed by a surge of Monty successes in the boxing. The excitement and frenzy was approaching a climax when some of the renegade Prefects allowed members of the public in through the school gates for half a crown a time. Most of these grown-ups however were siding with Monty and soon the away team was matching the Hamlets' chants. It took a massive renewed effort by Oliver, Louise and the rest of the staff to get their girls shouting louder and harder for their flagging heroines. Jeff was looking noticeably despondent as Glenn Greaves, his counterpart at Monty strutted between the arena confidently. There of course was more see-sawing ahead.

Another hour of perfuse perspiring, pummelling and punching resulted in a multitude of severely blackened eyes, loosened teeth and bruised egos which brought the score at the end of the tournament to an even and ultimately fair 19-19. Though, for some this was the best way to end the battle, the majority of the adults in the crowd were not as understanding, wanting a resolution and now. Half cut many of the paying fans booed and hissed, then began stamping around looking to take something out on someone! This was the cue for Ruff to push past the Prefects and jump into the main ring. An aggressive form of mass hysteria replaced the fun.

'I'll take on any of ye lanky pieces of piss.' He shouted to the crowd. 'Yous is just a bunch of southern jessie wankers. Grrrr!'

Mr Press witnessed this ugly scene and realised he had to act very quickly to at least maintain Hamlets' and of course his personal reputation. He then gathered with Jeff and Glenn and planned how they could appease the growing discontent. Together the trio concluded on nothing useful but Mr Press, being pressured by the media had to make an announcement.

'Ladies and gentlemen, boys and girls, parents and public and of course you members of Her Majesty's media.' The crowd hushed as they sensed the headteacher had a definitive announcement to expound. 'Along with my colleagues Mr Slater and Mr Greaves and after much consideration we believe that the Hamlets-Montefiore Tournament must reach a final conclusion worthy of two such magnificent educational and sporting establishments. We have decided therefore that there should be no more boxing and no more wrestling today.'

The crowd, as one jeered and derided even more threateningly nevertheless he still found time to smile at the cameras. He went on:

'But we have also decided that the most appropriate way of ending a wonderful afternoon's unarmed combat is to have one final and decisive battle … ARMWRESTLING!'

An air of disbelief swept through the throng eventually giving way to polite then eventual raucous cheers of approval. The teachers sighed and looked skyward but in the main the idea had gone down well.

Ruff, now a little more confused and some of the Prefects brought out a slim heavy table and a couple of chairs from a nearby classroom and set them up in the middle of Ring 3. Monty had chosen their biggest and heftiest girl Angela-The-Unfair, the nastiest girl from Fieldgate Mansions who was said to be related to the Kray twins. Despite this, Jeff put his faith in Christine Ingham known better as 'Chrissy the Christian' a slight and incredibly beautiful blonde girl. He had seen Chrissy's displays on the parallel bars and figured that her lean upper body strength was deceptive and would be more than enough to slam her complacent stocky opponent.

The rivals took their seats opposite each other, stiffened their backs and tensed. Angela glared at her opponent who did not respond. Chrissy had a mini version of the Bible in her shirt pocket and that's all she needed. Their hands met and gripped as the spectators calmed expectantly. They took the strain for a moment or two as instructed, then heaved. Bang! Instantly and against the odds Chrissy had flattened The Unfair's hand hard onto the table. 1-0 Hamlets. Monty supporters and the press screamed for a 'best of three', Jeff objected, Mr Press addressing the cameras appeased the hoards and agreed.

He then summoned Jeff, Glenn and Edith ringside.

'I've an idea' said the Headteacher 'How about us sprinkling a few drawing pins and broken glass on the table to give it more of a competitive edge,'

Both the teachers thought this suggestion was said in jest but Edith, knowing her husband didn't

A TAIL OF TWO CITIES

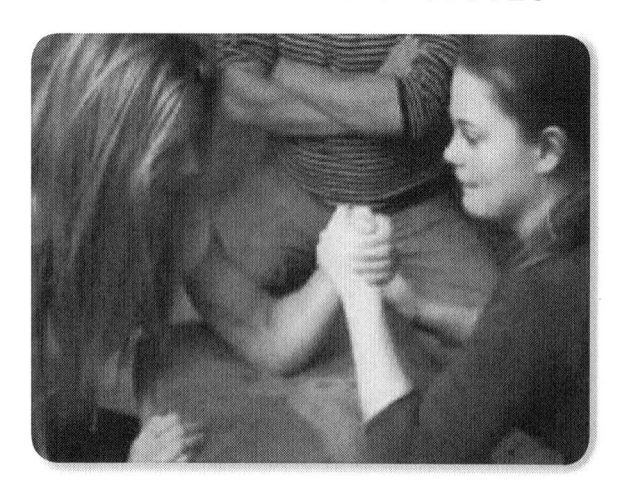

At the school gates the Prefects were counting their ill-gotten gains as the participants received final instruction. They firmly gripped their opponent's taut right hand for a second time.

'Sorry girls, this one has to be your left hand,' ordered Mr Press.

The girls duly accepted with no fuss as to do unwise would signal weakness. The Unfair, as a lefty grinned knowingly but Chrissie's assurance stayed unsaid. Bang! And in an instant it was 1-1. The championship now all hung on this final decisive battle. Monty fans were buoyed, oozing invincibility. The opponents swapped sides again readied themselves and took the strain. This time the battle was much more even, the girls yelping and wincing, puffing and gasping. Even after a full 60 seconds no quarter was given either way. It was difficult to predict.

'Come on Chrissy you can do it!' yelled Oliver.

'She doesn't smile that much for a Christian does she?' observed Louise.

'What do you expect, it must be agony and what's more she's got the responsibility of the whole school resting on her shoulders right now!'

At this point Chrissy put her left hand on her shirt pocket, looked heavenward, breathed in deeply and heaved. Crash! Angela The Unfair's huge fat fist flattened onto the shuddering table followed by the Hamlets' multitude erupting into strident cheers of thanksgiving. It had been accomplished. Chrissy the Christian had won! Within a few seconds the ominous black clouds above that had been threatening all afternoon darkened more then released their content.

'Hamlets 2, Monty 1,' announced Mr Press victoriously through the downpour and growing gloom.

This was the cue for the home support to burst into delirium - cheering, hugging and chanting.

'Hamlets, Chrissy, Hamlets, Chrissy ....'

The teachers too were taken by the moment. Even Ruff broke into some sort of celebratory Highland fling alongside a plump, blue-rinsed pensioner from the WRVS. Amidst the happy hosts, Louise quietly observed Jeff pushing his way toward Mr Press.

The job had been done. Was this to be Jeff's finest hour?

※※※※※

'Finally, the final day of the final term of the 1968/69 school year has arrived at long, long last,' announced Oliver to himself and his dog via the bathroom mirror. He was just too plain fatigued to play the Beatles Lyric Game or take on any historical persona as he did most mornings.

'Seven weeks of bliss. Seven weeks not thinking about anything but me, Louise and of course you Naked. Can't forget you. Tell you the truth dog you've turned out to be my best buddy ... the only one I could really trust,' said the teacher to his pet.

Oliver was referring to Louise and the disappointment he felt that the Head of Year promotion she had 'promised' to use her influence to fix for him was now dead in the water.

'I can do that job you know, I really can. I could make more of a success of it than Jeff. He only wants the job cos he wants out to an all-boys school. He's my best buddy and all that but I want the job for a proper upright reason. That's probably my downfall boy; I'm just too nice! Lulu's got that killer streak running through her. All I've got running through me is a backbone of jelly!'

Naked looked up sombrely and whimpered. He was always able to sense Oliver's mood and did what he could to soothe his master.

'Never mind boy. Its half day today so I'll be back early for walkies. I'll show my face briefly at the end of term party tonight, then I'm off. Well until September that is.'

Oliver groaned deeply, stroked and tickled his dog behind his ear then set off for the Tube.

That final morning at school was most uneventful and low-key. The adulation felt at the win over Monty had already diminished a little. Chrissy the Christian was her usual understated and modest self, whilst Oliver pondered on why 'a bloody arm-wrestle between a couple of teenagers' should affect his prospects so dramatically? Mr Press marshalled his troops for one final push, to prepare the hall for the end of year party that evening, and the girls obliged.

That evening the first partygoers arrived at around 7.30. The strict instruction was that no boys were allowed to the event. Mr Press had relaxed that rule a couple of years ago which resulted in a party made up of mostly boys who took to fist fighting as there were 'not enough birds to go round.' This year's concession was that ex pupils could attend as long as they had at least one current sibling in the school. For Oliver, Jeff and many of the other male staff group this was a welcome relaxation as the school hall was dotted with an array of attractive young women now in their mid-twenties who had grown into mature and poised grown-ups. The most eye-catching of these was Maggie Birkett, older sister to Jackie. She stood at 5' 6", long-legged, lean and elegantly assured in the knowledge that she would soon draw to herself inquisitive admirers and a few chancers. Oliver obliged and as the merrymaking got into full swing he approached and introduced himself. Maggie didn't remember him. Nevertheless, the two chatted, laughed and drank lemon barley water. Jeff, observing was itching to break up the duo or at least become part of them but was unable to find an opening.

'Those two seem to be getting on well,' commented Jeff to Louise.

'What two would that be?' came the nonchalant reply.

'Oliver and Miss Long Legs over there.'

Louise had been taking a very keen interest in what Oliver was up to and would have been quite prepared to cause a scene if she deemed the liaison was getting out of hand even though it might possibly have revealed one of her two big secrets. As things were however, it seemed nothing more than just Oliver being Oliver and innocently enjoying the occasion.

'He's a bit of a lad that Oliver. Always chasing any dolly bird that flutters her stuck on eyelashes,' said Jeff unknowingly.

'I thought you'd be more interested in tracking down Cockroach,' replied Louise diverting the conversation. 'You said he's been avoiding you of late, why so?' she enquired rhetorically.

'I don't really know. All I do know is that I'll be out of this school and teaching in an all-boys before not so very long!'

'Have you ever thought of settling down and perhaps ... having a son of your own Jeff ... Then you could play football and cricket all day rather than checking up on what Oliver's doing,' blurted Louise nastily before shuffling off. Of course the bitter irony was lost on Jeff who stood there bemused.

As the night progressed Louise was becoming ever more agitated at Oliver's lack of attention. He and his possible new desire were apparently clicking. Louise believed that it was time to act decisively before Oliver and 'that girl' had time to exchange telephone numbers or suchlike. She had considered a 'mishap' where she would spill her drink over Maggie's see-through top but on reflection this she deemed crass. She even thought of feigning appendicitis or falling against the fire alarm, but no. What Louise required to make her presence felt and shift her man's focus back to her was something subtler.

Once the kernel of an effective connivance had begun to form in Louise's mind then she was by nature sure to see it to an end no matter how destructive. One such seed was now about to germinate. She schemed, scanned then spotted that the cloakroom set aside for the party's adult guests was supervised by the docile Greenburg twins, Michelle and Gina.

'You two girls have been sitting there missing the fun for hours now. You've done a terrific job but even volunteers need a break. You go and have a break for 15 minutes and get yourselves on the dance floor, go on now 'Sugar Sugar' is on next I believe. I'll keep an eye on things here,' said Louise with mischief in her eyes. Michelle and Gina dutifully obliged and off to the dance-floor they skipped.

Immediately in post Louise eased down the cloakroom's shutter and hurried off to the school's biology laboratories. The large room was in darkness and eerily devoid of the hum of girls arguing over the relative merits of Otis Redding and Marvin Gaye. Louise switched on one strategic light and walked cautiously toward the frogs and mice cages there for O'Level Biology dissection. There on an upper shelf she spied a cage with two large 8-inch long portly rats. Standing precariously on a stool she reached up and placed the cage on a desk, then having spotted the chloroform spray she administered a couple or three puffs into the cage rendering the vicious, unpleasant smelling rodents temporarily semi-conscious. She then concealed the cage with a cloth and hastened back to the cloakroom with it.

There on the floor were twenty or so handbags. Rummaging through their contents Louise soon came to a large purple patent bag, that of 'Maggie Birkett' into which she delivered the slowly rousing vermin. Opening the shutters she heaved a sigh of partial satisfaction. Within minutes the dutiful twins returned. So far, so good.

'We've got a problem girls. It's getting late now. Time's moving on now and Ruff Carnegie wants the school hall cleared soon so he can clean up,' said Louise knowingly.

'But it still only early and most people haven't picked up their bags and coats yet Miss!' replied Gina.

'Maybe we could get the DJ to put out some sort of announcement then Miss?' suggested Michelle.

'No, I don't think that would be the best way to go about things Michelle. All that'll do is start a mad rush and you might not be able

A TAIL OF TWO CITIES

to cope. Then Mr Press will wonder what incompetent girls are in charge of the cloakroom!' replied Louise in an effort to redirect their thinking.

'What we gonna do Miss ... it's nearly 11?'

'Well what you two could do is go out into the hall, get their tickets and take their coats and bags to them. That's a service that they don't even do in the classy nightclubs up West,' said the teacher.

'Great thinking Miss. That'll really make Cockroach think we done good,' said Gina gleefully, seeking further approbation.

'Yes Gina, Mr Press may well make you both Prefects next term. Now come on now girls we need to work quickly'.

Seemingly at random Louise then pointed out Maggie as a 'good place to start'. Accordingly, Michelle collected Maggie's cloak ticket and delivered the bag promptly. From a distance Louise watched as Oliver and his unsuspecting 'trollop' continued their joyous and animated dialogue. She did not have to wait long before Maggie suitably unzipped her bag and reached in for her compact. - The scene of pandemonium that followed looked similar to the Keystone Cops' wackiest escapade and more than exceeded Louise's imaginings. The now fully awakened rats, one black the other white having caressed, nibbled then bitten Maggie's hand leapt from the bag and scampered menacingly around their new and heavily-peopled environment. The crowd sensing some unease jostled. Ruff, prepared as ever for violence sought and found a hockey stick. He then chased down, cornered and clubbed one of the squeaking rodents pitilessly whilst gleefully chuckling. The other rat was bigger and more agile. On witnessing this bloody cull and the tracking the movements of the other escapee, many of the now panicking partygoers lost their British reserve, hastened to the nearest exit. As for Oliver, the last thing he was to ever see of Maggie Birkett was her fleeing the fearful scene in terror aptly to the strains of Peter Sarstedt's 'Where do you go to my lovely'.

'Well Oliver, your temporary muse will be on her way to A&E now for a tetanus injection after that nasty rodent bite,' Maggie's nemesis silently concluded … Game, Set and Match Louise!

Later that night at home alone in her flat Louise felt peckish and heated up some leftovers from last night's supper.

'Hmmm ratatouille, dee-lish!'

ം‍ം‍ം

Chapter 8

'Just gimme some kinda sign yeah … '

The following Monday Oliver found himself shuffling down the Haymarket in central London on his way to buy Louise an anniversary present. His eyes barely lifted from the pavement as although he was relieved that school was out, he was melancholy at his career prospects. When in this frame of mind Oliver took to all consuming self-examination. He even considered changing his name to 'Mr Average Mediocre' and Louise would have to either accept his status or find someone with a Jeff-like charisma. Her words of encouragement the previous evening was insignificant when circumstances had conspired so perniciously against him.

The hot, breezy, cloudless day along with the effervescent colour and enthusiasm of the busy streets did nothing to lift Oliver's spirits as he tramped around with no particular destination in mind. He stopped off for a cup of tea and a bun at the Lyons Corner House on the Strand then wandered through Covent Garden before eventually stumbling into Soho. Soho was one of the city's most salubrious areas after dark but during the day functioned as a dirty, teeming fruit and veg' market echoing to the gruff and ancient cries of 'Aye, Aye Strawberries!' and 'Cherry Ripe, Cherry Ripe!' An alleyway off Wardour Street opened up into a small square, a quiet corner where fortune-tellers, tattooists and dubious mystics set up shop. Oliver had walked these streets man and boy but had never found himself there. Though in many ways a sophisticat, his basic response to 'the dark arts' was naturally negative. Previously a flaky sceptic now a firm disbeliever, he was taken by the antiquated and ram-shackled shop fronts and the unusually seductive aromas wafting from within. One of these emporia 'Mystic Dimension' particularly drew his attention,

Whilst most of the advertising hoardings promoted a soothsayer's 'free consultation' as a loss leader one particular shop sign stirred Oliver's curiosity.

'See how the PRESENT can effect the PAST'.

Oliver read it again and again and mouthed it slowly but whichever way he was not able to put any real meaning to those eight simple words. He pondered how say, if the Battle of Britain had been lost in 1940 then possibly in 1066 William the Conqueror would have fled back across the Channel as William the Conquered - How indeed could anything be so proved? It didn't add up. He could not begin to make any sense of the sign and hence felt compelled to vent his irritation.

Oliver rung the bell and entered through the dingy doorway only to be surprised at the bright vivid and classic décor of the reception area. There sat three equally bright and vivid young female employees all beseeching him to enter and relax.

'You must please sir take this cup of tea of herbs before an audience with Madam Sprigola becomes available to you,' said one.

'If she's a Madam then what does that make you?' asserted Oliver wittily.

The attempt at humour proved to be only that. The women then conversed in an Eastern European tongue. They looked Oliver up and down, chatted between themselves again before erupting into smirks, giggles, laughter followed by hysterics. Although a little disconcerting he was not to be put off. He was riled and had a bone to pick with the Madam.

'Madam Sprigola will meeting with now you. Follow sir me please,' whispered an underling mysteriously.

Oliver was led into a small well-lit adjoining room. From the ceiling down to the floor hung a hundred or more thin coloured strips of plastic about half an inch thick. It was clear that these had been the tacky plastic strips you might hang in a doorway in the summer to stop flies and other bugs entering. In the middle of the room was a poorly lit area and two well weathered deck chairs. Standing between them was the small figure of a woman clad in some sort of bright orange oversized Terylene wrap-around. Her dank bottled blonde hair was a fading tangle and was adorned by alternate red, gold and green beads. She was of course barefoot.

'Welcome. You seek an audience with Madam Sprigola, my child?' said the mystic in a deep enigmatic manner.

'I seek an audience with anyone who can tell me about that stupid sign, now can you go and get her for me? I just want a quick explanation then I'll be off,' he replied.

'Madam's spirit will not respond to turbulent karma - she takes her repose upon a bed of cosmic peace.'

'Well I'm in a bit of a hurry so can you nip round the back and wake her up?'

At this the woman took on a more serious expression rose and swept out through the velvet curtains returning seconds later.

'It is I' said the woman.

'What?'

'Tis I you seek? I am ... Madam Sprigola.'

'You! So what was all that cosmic bed palaver thingy?'

'Sit my child, sit ... you report that you have received a sign this day. *The* Sign ... You must say more but speak only in hushed tones. The Sign appears as our evolving entity and must now unhurriedly know that it has been sought and discovered before it is brought out into the full light of humanity,' replied the seer.

With that Oliver was more perplexed but took his seat in the smaller of the two deck chairs and realised where the confusion lay.

'No Madam whatever. I have not seen *the* Sign but *a* sign.'

'Speak only of this matter respectfully and to only those who have ears to hear. Continue.'

'Enough, enough! The sign I'm referring to is the one outside over the door, the one that says 'See how the PRESENT can effect the PAST'. I don't want any sort of weirdo consultation just a simple explanation will do Madam Sprigola. Is that your real name by the way?' asked Oliver impatiently.

''Of me my child I need not speak - Of me I need not tell - But when you walked along my street - I knew you'd ring my bell,' she replied.

Oliver thought the rhyme a little corny but congratulated her on coming up with something passable so quickly.

'Now look, please don't feel compelled to talk in verse. I came in because I really want to know how what happens today can have a bearing on what's already happened?' enquired Oliver.

After some deliberation the sage sighed and cleared her throat and replied.

'Take heed and address these pronouncements ....'

'Look, let me stop you there. If you're gonna explain then just do it normal-like, ok?

She thought for a moment then went on.

'Time is a strange sort of thing next weekend there's gonna be a big street carnival in Soho with floats, people on stilts and dancers that sort of thing. Now if an observer is standing on the corner watching the parade pass by he will see what's in front of him and maybe that which has passed but he won't be able to see what is coming up will he?'

Oliver wondered where this was all going but continue to listen intently

'Now just say there was someone on a helicopter above viewing that same parade. He could see the line of people in the parade from a different perspective.

'Oh I see,' said Oliver 'So you're saying it is possible to see the past, the present and the future all at the same time depending on where you're positioned. So if you're at ground level and can somehow interact with those in the parade around the corner that you've not seen as yet then the present can affect the future. So that explains the sign. How very Zen!'

Madam Sprigola seemed to surprise herself before looking relieved.

'Well I suppose I might as well confess, I wrote that sign after I'd had one over the eight so the words are correct but not necessarily in the right order. There's nothing Zen about being pissed …. my child.'

For a brief moment Oliver was stunned before laughing raucously at the woman's nonsense and his own earnestness.

'You want to get that shop sign corrected before Westminster Council gets you on Trade Description.'

'Nah don't worry 'bout them lot. The Council don't know their arse from their elbow,' she replied in a broadening Cockney accent. 'Anyway half the punters that come in here want to know what that sign's all about. Change it? No way, change it and me and the girls'll soon be out of a job. We need all the dosh we can get ... er my child.'

'You're not really Madam Sprig … whatever it is? You're a fraud. Where are you from anyway?'

A TAIL OF TWO CITIES

'I hail from a land across the water ... Peckham!'

They both chuckled again.

'Do you know I must admit that I was feeling a bit down in the mouth before I came in here to see the 'wise woman'. I was off to Bond Street to buy my girlfriend a present when I came across this place. You've cheered me up no end. Madam Sprigola, ha indeed!' said Oliver.

'It's all part of the service ain't it? I should have charged ya. Now go in peace my child. Go in peace, there's mugs out there who insist on being fleeced,' said the conwoman mockingly.

She then abruptly became more earnest and reverting into character, jumped from her deck chair and clapped her hands. Immediately one of her assistants ushered Oliver out through a now crowded reception area and back onto the hectic Soho thoroughfare. He then looked up at the sign and studied it again going back into the shop wherein he shouted to anyone there who cared to listen.

'Oh and by the way it's affect with an A and not an E. Non Est Bonum!'

✳✳✳✳✳

A few uneventful days passed, and Oliver and Louise were in their respective flats readying themselves to meet at the Bag O'Nails in their bizarre Wednesday night charade. A night out was very timely for Oliver as his mind had been taken up almost entirely by thoughts of the coming futile job interview, now just a few weeks away. A woebegone spirit pervaded. He was unable to dismiss the notion that Louise considered him a gumptionless failure and was simply patronising him so as not to puncture him further. He would rather be alone than pitied he thought. One bright spot on the horizon however was tonight, their third anniversary as lovers. A few days earlier he had pushed the boat out and bought her a gold and platinum ring costing 40 guineas from a classy jeweller in Bond Street. Oliver slapped on a dollop of Louise's favourite eau de cologne and headed West.

Six floors below Louise too was hurriedly preparing to 'bump into' Oliver. She was running a little late but knew if she really got a move on she would get to The Bag a little before Oliver was as per usual. As she was about to pull the last brush stroke through her heavy black mane the telephone rang. She toyed with the thought of just ignoring it but thinking it may be Oliver with a problem she answered. It was Janey, young Terry's mother and as so often she was frantic:

'Oy Lou, I been invited to a party. I just this minute got the invitation. My mate's mum's friend Fiona, did I tell ya 'bout Fiona, no don't think I did, we call her Fi for short, yer get it, anyway up she knows this geezer who's an actor and his friend is an actor too, so they're two actors and it's his housewarming knees-up thingy tonight, but he's not having it at home it's at the Adlib Club up West. Fancy it darlin? They'll be loads of actors there. You like all that La De Daa stuff that's why I thought of you first. Well to be honest I thought of you equal first. I was gonna ask Cath from Caf's Caf down Watney Street but I've just worked out on me calendar that she'll be on her rag about this time of the month and she can be a right dozy cow. Or maybe she's saving up for St Paddy's Day or something … So watdayasay Louise are we on or what?'

'How do you manage to say so much without taking a breath Janey? You're incredible just amazing. I'm exhausted just listening to you,' chuckled Louise.

'I know it's short notice but I can't go on me bleeding own. I'll only end up getting taken home by some posh chancer wanting a bit of East End rough. I need you Lulu to keep me outta mischief. If you don't go I'll be left sitting on the shelf in me damp lonely bedsit with all the other gooseberries!' said Janey, now resorting to exaggerated pathos.

'By the way only Oliver is allowed to call me Lulu and I've arranged to see him tonight anyway Janey.'

'You can't let me down Louise I'm nearly there.'

'Nearly where?'

'I'm in a phone box near the Adlib on Frith Street … I'm running outta bastard change. Jump in a cab Louise you could be here in less than half-hour. Don't let me down mate, I'm relying on ya darling.'

'But I've got a cab coming for me in a couple of minutes to take me to the Bag O'Nails. I don't know what ….'

At that point the phone went dead.

Louise was now in a mini dilemma which became more heart-rending as she considered further. She loved mixing with social climbers particularly those that trod the boards but she also passionately loved her one true soul mate, Oliver and would always. She got into the waiting cab, sat blankly for a few seconds then gave the driver her chosen destination!

※※※※※

Wednesday night at The Bag O'Nails had a different ambience than any of the other nights. It attracted a more cosmopolitan crowd, mostly French students who had chosen to settle in London after the bloody Paris riots the previous spring. They were content in their own small 'commune' between the Long Bar and the VIP area. Like the Huguenots before them they were mostly welcome in London and there to stay. For some of the locals the French contingent had a soured face some felt you just had to punch! Occasionally therefore a small brief fracas broke out. Door staff or patrons saw no need to separate the protagonists; it simply dissipated into nothingness and was barely noticed. Even the most liberal open city in the world had its thuggish darker element. Another smaller group of around a dozen brightly dressed men hailed from Iceland. Why they chose to make their home in London and use The Bag as its main watering hole was for open speculation.

The music played at some nightclubs toward the final months of the decade was noticeably more sombre and apocryphal. American bands influenced by the warring in South East Asia had come more to the fore. No longer the jingle-jangle of The Byrds but more the thought provoking Zager and Evans asking 'If man is gonna stay alive?' People now were listening more and dancing a little less. There remained a group of mini-skirted young women however who would dance until the lights went up. Oliver was one who would happily join them as he had often but tonight, he was less groovy and hip but more pensive and apprehensive about Louise. He scanned around once, twice and more in an effort to spot her. Then he wandered around but to no avail.

Once he convinced himself that none of the sleek women there were not Louise heavily disguised, he stood by the nightclub's entrance for a while. Louise didn't arrive. Oliver surmised she was not late or held up in traffic etc but that she had let him down because he himself had let her down.

Oliver took his place in the alcove he would normally be sitting with Louise and looked long and hard down into his glass of Guinness. An hour or passed by as did another three drinks his lips. He languished there beside himself with grief and regret and unusually quite drunk when a voice whispered in his ear.

'Good evening Oliver, how's goes it?'

Oliver turned abruptly toward the voice and spotting that it was not his beloved so sank once more.

'I don't know you, do I? How come you know my name?' he slurred.

'Perhaps you do know me …. my child!'

Immediately Oliver recognised the clue but without even looking up at Madam Sprigola began to blubber in a most embarrassing way.

'Hey there. That's just how I feel when I've watched 50 minutes of Rowan and Martin's so-called Laugh-In, but be cool man, be cool,' said the woman consolingly.

Oliver gradually composed himself and smeared his wet cheeks and nose with the back of his hand. He now looked up to put a face to the voice and was pleasantly surprised to see a plain but attractive, plumpish woman in her mid-twenties with short fair wavy hair and heavily made up radiant green eyes. She wore denim dungarees with nothing under the bib. Across her right shoulder a thin strapped bag with a black cat fashioned in beads. She had a warming smile, a protective manner and was witty too and that's what the vulnerable man needed at this time.

'Didn't think mystics came to a place like this Madam Sprigola. I thought you'd be on your flying carpet off to Transylvania or somewhere!' said Oliver trying to lift his own mood.

'No I came here on the Tube from the Rye that is Peckham!' said the woman. 'But now I'm off duty you can call me Sprig.'

'Sprig?'

'Yeah Sprig.'

'Haven't you got a real name like everyone else?'

'I prefer Sprig to Karen Sprigson. Wouldn't you?'

'Well I'm a man so I suppose I would.'

'Yeah, a man who cries too! Quite a refreshing change, a man that cries at things other than football.'

'That's the first time I've cried in ages. The first time in public probably ever. Oh yes I did cry at Wembley and couple of years ago when we beat Chelsea 2-1 in the Cup Final.'

'Who's we?'

'We are Spurs. Tottenham Hotspur, the pride of North London.'

'If I didn't know better I'd have thought you were blubbering over a woman.'

'What are you, some kind of visionary?' said Oliver unaware of the irony. They both cackled and before long he was distracted.

Oliver and Sprig talked and laughed until the early hours and soon he had mostly forgotten to check every woman that walked in. Throughout the night however various people approached Sprig and nodded or gave the thumbs-up, some even spoke in her ear momentarily before hurriedly scuttling off through the throng on the dance floor. It was all done in a friendly but efficient business-like manner.

'You must be the most popular chick in the Bag O'Nails tonight?' enquired Oliver obliquely.

'How come I've never seen you in here?' Sprig replied evasively.

'I only come here on a Wednesday with Louise my girlfriend. I bought her a ring the other day cos we've been together exactly three years.'

'And she didn't show up and that's why you were sitting alone, pissed and sobbing like a bleedin soppy baby,' said Sprig with an insensitive matter-of-fact manner.

Moments later Sprig unexpectedly became preoccupied and pensive then spotting a man standing in the near distance got up and bolted toward him. The man looked startled and then contrite as Sprig seemingly reprimanded him. She then pointed to the exit, through which the man scuttled, looking back once only to momentarily sneer at her.

Sprig was much more affable when she returned to the table. It was if a minor difficulty had been resolved.

'You seem to be a girl of some influence Sprig?' pried Oliver again.

'A girl's gotta do what a girl's gotta do. You wanna know about me don't you Oliver? Sort of nosy aren't you Oliver? I reckon you must be a teacher.'

'A teacher? Yeah, you're right. Does it seem so obvious?'

'Remember I've got mystical ooowww powers. Either that or I overheard you telling my assistants when you were waiting to come in and see me the other day,' she joked.

'You're very self-assured. Is that what they're like down in Peckham.'

'I'm from Peckham but I live over in Belgravia now.'

'Belgravia! Seems like the girl done good?'

'I'm pleased. But what about you and the vanishing lady? She a teacher too?'

'She is ... and the most beautiful one ever. No one at work knows we're a couple. They all think I'm a plank. Even the Head, Cockroach Press thinks I'm something that the cat's just dragged in.'

'Why don't you call it a day and leave and become an explorer or an astronaut. Yeah you could be the first ex-teacher on the moon.'

'I've thought about leaving this week for the first time. In September I'm being interviewed for a job that I know for a fact that my best mate Jeff is going to get. I can't believe me sometimes. I'm going for a job just to fail!' said Oliver angrily.

'Fail is not a word I ever use. If there's an answer then go out and find it. Go for it and don't give way to any suggestion you're gonna come out second best. If you think you're second best then you will be, then you're knackered!'

'Are you an American?'

'No, of course not'

'Well you sound a bit upbeat for a Brit. In-fact you sound like Louise except your language is a bit more florid.'

'I'm not florid Oliver, I've just gotta goal for myself and I'm not gonna be shifted from it.'

'So what is it?'

'What's what?'

'You're goal.'

Sprig then twisted and put her hip bag on the table. Then pointing to the image on the side asked.

'Do you know what that is?'

'A cat … a black cat,' replied Oliver cautiously.

'Yeah a black cat. A beautiful, delicious, sleek, black feline,'

'So what's your point?'

'Do you know that every year in London 233,777 cats are turned out or just left to sort themselves out. Can you believe that 232,727 homeless cats!?'

'You've just made that figure up, haven't you?'

'Well maybe, but that's not the point. From Wimbledon to Wembley. From Heathrow to Barking, stray and abandoned cats everywhere,' moaned Sprig

'So you want to rename Barking, Meoowing?'

'Very droll Oliver but if I had my way I would. No, what I'm doing is ... well I'm going to ... or planning to set up the only big cat's home in the metropolis. There's gonna be nothing like it anywhere on earth. I've got the property and soon I'll have the money to convert it.'

'Big cats, you mean like lions and tigers and stuff?

'No, domestic cats like Poppy and Tiddles ... Dimbo!'

'Oh yeah right, I've got ya. Where is this place?' asked Oliver

'Right on the river the other side in Battersea. It took me ages to find a suitable premise to buy but it had to be Battersea.'

'Why's that?'

'You sure you're a teacher? It's bleedin obvious ain't it ...' 'Battersea *Cat's* Home! Sounds good, don't it?'

Oliver picked up on the irony and laughed.

'Great idea Sprig. So you're setting up a cat's home next to the dog's home. Hmm you never know, I might be calling on you for a job. When will you be up and running?'

'Two months, three months max. Just need to find another £2000 for the last bit of the conversion.'

'Where will you get £2000 in just two months? It won't be from palm reading or whatever Madam Watevaernameiz gets up to that's for sure!' asked Oliver disparagingly.

'I'll sort things out, don't you worry.'

'My beautiful dog is amazing. You'll get more sponsors if you helped stray dogs. They're man's best friend you know.'

'Well Oliver, if your dog has got you as his best friend then the poor thing has got real problems!'

As the evening wore on it was clear to Oliver that whilst Sprig could be determined and sometimes entertaining, she was only happy to talk vaguely about herself and her plans up to a point. Anything beyond that he soon discovered was taboo. He found his new acquaintance puzzling, funny and a little awe-inspiring. What lay therein, he convinced himself was best not known but anyway he remained curious.

Soon enough the lights came up and the DJ announced that it was 'chucking out time.' Oliver said his goodnights to Sprig and commented how much he had enjoyed meeting her again. She reciprocated with the encouraging conclusion that if he set himself a target he should not be put off, 'Jeff or no Jeff'. Oliver sighed then wrote his telephone number on a beer mat – not reciprocated and handed it to her with a peck on the cheek before slipping away into the sultry night … and to Louise!

Chapter 9

The Cowboy and the Angel

A black cab pulled into Wardour Street then slowed to an easy halt outside The Ad- Lib Club. The door gently swung open and out stepped Louise looking pale and perturbed, culpability clearly written across her concerned face. She had never let Oliver down in such a mean and deliberate way.

'How can I ever look Ollie in the face again after this?' she mumbled to herself.

Needless to say Janey was delighted that Louise had chosen to disappoint Oliver but made no mention of it for fear of antagonising her. They gave each other a sisterly hug before checking their lippy and hair in their compacts. The narrow, busy pavement was not the place to converse so the two girls joined the short single-filed queue.

'How you feeling darlin?' asked Janey

'How'd you bloody think! Oliver's waiting at The Bag only a mile away. I can see him sitting there all alone and worrying his little head over me. This'll need some explaining. Doesn't even know about you and Jeff and Terry and all that. He'll go up the wall.'

'Don't tell him. Men are all the same. Just flutter your eyes, sit on his lap and wiggle your bum. Works for me every time and my bum's half the size yours!' advised Janey in her usual coarse manner.

'Must you! … Oh well. We're here now. Might as well make the most of it.'

'That's the spirit Louise. I always come to these knees-ups. They're even better than the Happenings. Just think, you might just get chatted up by 'Dangerman' or Terence Stamp or David Bailey. Now he's a real babe. I'll probably end up going home with one of The Kinks …. again! You know why they're called the Kinks don't you?!"

Louise had never been to The Ad-Lib before but it was well known throughout the city as a magnet for the glitterati from stage, television and film. Janey was clearly excited as she witnessed well known faces brush past on their way to double peck the cheeks of another of their illustrious contemporaries.

'Blimey, Louise don't look now but there's that bloke off the tele, he's in … he's one of the teachers in 'Please Sir'. You fancy teachers don't ya?' exuded Janey thoughtlessly.

'Does Captain Scarlett come to many of these dos Janey?' asked Louise sarcastically.

'Oh yeah. He never misses. You get a lot of the army types 'ere when they ain't out shooting foreign wrong 'uns.' came the unexpected but sincere reply.

As the evening progressed both Louise and Janey had numerous drinks bought for them, cocktails of course by both men and women and as often, asked to dance. Janey, without exception accepted whilst Louise declined graciously, still inwardly fretting about Oliver. On returning from the dance floor and leaving one of her suitors behind, Janey flopped on her seat took off a shoe and started massaging her toes. Louise noticed that Janey's full blonde wig had slipped and twisted so she hinted that they go to the 'ladies'. Janey, by now slightly tipsy, hotly refused adding that all men should accept her as she is because she's 'Janey, and not the Duchess of bleeding Duke Street!' This was the first clue that Louise had of a possibly memorable night.

Louise set off to the restroom leaving Janey manipulating her throbbing bunion. As she passed the VIP bar she barely caught some words directed at her.

'Good evening Louise. It's been quite some time, hasn't it?' came the deep mellifluous tone.

Louise turned and stared quizzically at the man responsible. He was an elegant bear of a chap, greying and in his mid-50s. She recognised the voice more than the face.

'Think hard Louise, think hard,' he continued.

'It's coming, it's coming,' said Louise clicking her fingers. 'No it's gone.'

At this the man took a long yawning breath and then into song.

'Consider yourself at home. Consider yourself, one of our family.'

'Arnie Slater. Of course how could I ever forget, Mr Arnold Slater? How are you old-timer?' said Louise excitedly.

'Come on let's sit and reminisce. You can tell me how life's treating you and all about the modern day teacher,' he said.

Arnie Slater was Louise's drama and dance teacher and greatly encouraged her as a teenager with a dream to work on a career as an actress. He himself had progressed tremendously in his vocation and was now directing on the West End stage. He was quite simply Louise's mentor and inspiration and second only to Oliver as an influence. Arnie was also Jeff's father.

'You've still got that mischievous choirboy look Arnie. Or should I say Sir,' joked Louise.

'No, Sir will do,' he joked back.

'Well from what I've heard and read you're well on the way to a real knighthood.'

'It's good of you to say so Louise but that's a long, long way off. That doesn't mean I'm not pleased how things are going though.'

'Jeff tells me you're putting on 'Hello Dolly' at the Lyric soon. That's got to be my all-time favourite musical, Arnie,' hinted Louise, fluttering her big eyes appealingly.

'It might be later than sooner at this rate. Can't get the staff these days sweetie. I'm having a lot of trouble casting. But enough of me, how's things at Tower Hamlets Louise? Have you cast your spell on any of your colleagues yet? Have you got the Head teacher eating out of your hand?' Arnie was inadvertently nearer the truth than he would have ever imagined.

'Well you know me Arnie … you know me.'

'Jeff's going for some sort of very important promotion pretty soon he tells me. It's a very important jump in his career if he's successful but mum's the word, you know. He's still ambitious but I wish he'd just bloody settle down and make me a granddad. Jeff'll be joining us pretty soon … said he'll be here in about half an hour.'

On hearing this shock news, Louise choked and gasped before making her excuses and hurrying to the Ladies. Could she allow Jeff to meet his estranged teenage sweetheart and mother of his son Terry?!

The Ladies toilets in The Ad-Lib were sizeable but nevertheless cramped with self-aware egotists. It is customary for women never to pay a visit on their own but with at least one of their friends or colleagues. This ritual was no doubt used as a point of congress where women can reassess how their evening is progressing and come to some consensus as to their next collective or individual move. Of course, men are the main topic of their deliberations. Louise stood in front of the mirror attempting to appear busy on her face but all the time thinking that her dilemma was of far greater import than any of the trifles she heard talked around her. When Jeff arrives in less than 30 minutes how would he react when he sees Janey? More importantly how will Janey to him? Janey was a firebrand even when sober! Louise concluded that she should just let the situation unfold naturally without any intervention.

'What will be, will be,' she mumbled to herself.

In an instant however she reconsidered and panicked: Jeff will know that she and Janey are friends! How could the origins of that be explained? Just as pressing was Janey's knowledge of Louise's love for Oliver and that couldn't be allowed to slip. That this should remain under wraps was imperative. Louise now had to become proactive; there was 'no reasonable alternative'. She couldn't stop Jeff from arriving, nor could she just go home and miss the opportunity of setting up a possible 'Hello Dolly' audition with Arnie. The only option left was to somehow and in some way get rid of Janey!

'Ohhh I could have been with Ollie in The Bag O'Nails now, instead of all this!' mumbled Louise to herself in the mirror.

'I've just come from The Bag and if you ask me it's just full of men on their own, picking up tarts and taking them home for, you know what! That's what always happens there on a Wednesday,' said a stranger from the next mirror.

'Thanks that's all I need to hear,' replied Louise despondently.

One of Louise's great fortes is conceiving a workable plan and seeing it through. It had stood her in good stead and got her out of many tight corners before as at the end of term party. This ruse, whatever it would be, would have to be different though and more considered given it depended on several variables of which she had no control. She'd give it a go anyway.

Louise edged her way past Arnie through the crowd without being detected and moved toward Janey. It was clear that Janey was well inebriated and hence looking to cause a scene.

'I thought you'd pissed off to The Bag so you can check up on that tosser Oliver. What sort of name is Oliver for a man anyway? Wos wrong with Steve or Ronnie or Dave a real proper man's name … but Oliver? Anyway, I think all the men in here tonight are a bit La De Daa like you Louise. None of 'em have got much about 'em. All too bleedin busy posing and accidentally on purpose rubbing up against ya on the dance floor. Next one that does that I'll bloody castrate 'em,' slurred Janey her anger gathering.

Louise had no time to get uppity and anyway she was too busy looking around for a likely victim!

'Excuse me Janey. I won't be a mo,'

Louise got up and moved swiftly across the dance floor where she approached a dapperly dressed young man who was clearly there on his own.

'Hi there my name's Samantha. How ya doing?' said Louise.

'I'm just swell lady, just swell,' replied the man.

'My friend guessed you were a Yank. Whereabouts?'

'Texas ma'am. The Lone Star State.'

'Oh yes, the state that alone wanted to keep slavery but nevertheless Texas sounds terribly romantic. My friend guessed you were from Texas. She's very astute you know. Rich London girls normally are especially when they've had a drink. She always drinks a bit too much when she's feeling very vulnerable! Us girls can be so easily taken advantage of you know,' said Louise pointing to Janey.

'She's cute. Your friend got a name?'

'They call the little lady Janey in these parts buster,' replied Louise in a mock American accent.

'The lady will be leaving with a cowboy tonight ma'am,' drooled the Texan confidently adjusting his Stetson and sipping his bourbon.

Louise was not particularly confident that Janey would take the American bait, also he seemed in no real hurry to act. Louise then searched around for a replacement/reserve and fixed on another lone man. This one was tall, unshaven and leather-clad. How he was ever allowed into The Ad-Lib was anybody's guess Louise pondered. She knew that Janey had a thing about Hell's Angels so he may be quite the ideal. She approached:

'What Chapter you from mate?' asked Louise, attempting to sound as much like Janey as she could.

'The Stepney Sabre-Tooths. Why.... You interested in joining up ha ha?' replied the grinning biker.

'I wouldn't think of joining you lotta poofs. But I know a girl who would. She's been asking about ya all night. Can't take her eye off ya. It's a shame really cos she ain't gotta leather jacket but she's got thigh-length black leather boots,' said Louise knowingly.

All that was left now for Louise was to sit back and watch as the leather Lothario went recruiting.

Janey was sitting as demurely as the alcohol in her blood stream would allow her when the biker skulked over. Quite unexpectedly and simultaneously so did the Cowboy. Through the crowd Louise was not able to see precisely what occurred but as the scene unfolded it seemed as if both men saw the other as an interloper and started gesticulating, then disputing loudly and then jostling. Before long a full-scale, table upsetting punch-up ensued with neither the Biker nor Cowboy prepared to give up on Janey - testosterone, alcohol and the male ego making a heady and dangerous mix. Unsurprisingly Janey, who had been sporting for a fight since she had finished her fourth Bacardi got involved. It wasn't clear if she was trying to separate her paramours or had sided with one of them against the other. What was clear however was that several forceful and uncompromising club security men ejected all three. When the dust from the fracas had settled all that remained was Janey's limp blonde wig under a table, which Louise surreptitiously collected and stuffed in her handbag. In triumph she sighed, swished her palms together thrice and said 'Job done!'

Seeing that Louise was a close observer of the debacle, Arnie gallantly pushed his way over to her side to offer protection.

'Two men fighting over a thing like that. I don't know what's happening to London,' complained Arnie to Louise, 'in my day, in the '40s women would never be seen making a spectacle of themselves in public. That one looked like a typical fishwife anyway.'

'Well Arnie, that so-called fishwife is the mother of your grandson.' she whispered inaudibly.

A TAIL OF TWO CITIES

'It's just as well she's gone Arnie. She was only in the way. Now where's that son of yours?' replied Louise with a calculating poignancy only known to her.

As the temperature cooled and the Ad Lib reverted to normality Arnie and Louise found a relatively quiet corner, drank some more and talked of previous times. Throughout, Louise found it difficult to manoeuvre the conversation over to Arnie's current production at the Lyric. For his part he knew that Louise in her younger days had talent and a certain stage presence, but he was experienced and wily enough not to put himself in a position where he would be actually compelled to ask her to audition. His world now was not one of keen amateurs, but top international singers, dancers, musicians and choreographers of which Louise could certainly not be included. She was an East End teacher.

Arnie ordered another bottle of Champers when Jeff arrived and spotted his dad entertaining Louise.

'Louise, fancy you being here. I didn't realise that The Ad-Lib would be your cup of tea,' pronounced Jeff.

'There's a lot of things about me that might surprise you Jeff!' replied Louise.

'Hey I've just seen a Rocker outside being taken away in an ambulance. There been any trouble in here?'

'John Wayne 1, Peter Fonda 0,' said Louise under her breath. 'No not really,' she continued, 'Just two stupid men fighting over some sad, mad girl.'

'Wouldn't you just know it, there's always some girl involved,' replied Jeff.

'Yeah, but this was no ordinary girl Jeffrey.'

'What do you mean?'

'Oh nothing … nothing really.'

'Come on son have a drink and take the weight off. Now what's this, I saw you and your pupils on the TV last week boxing or some such ludicrous thing,' asked Arnie.

As the night wore on the three of them exhausted most subjects ranging from 'the ridiculous ease Great Britain was giving up her Empire' to the size of Prince Charles' ears. It then became apparent that Arnie was not even considering offering Louise an audition. She wasn't going to be put off though. There was one last throw of the dice - She took the opportunity, when Arnie was chatting nearby with a couple of thespian friends to seductively ask Jeff if he wanted her telephone number. As a long-standing admirer, the Classroom Casanova gladly accepted. Louise sighed jotted it down on a beer mat and handed it to him, giving him a peck on the cheek before slipping away into the sultry night …. and to Oliver.

Chapter 10

'A Bleedin' Great Decision'

At precisely 4.37 am Louise's cab pulled up outside her block of flats. She paid and alighted. The starry early morning sky was clear, ordered and peaceful. Only the rattle and clink of a nearby milk float and some pigeon cooing broke the tranquillity as the Hackney Carriage dissolved into the imminent dawn and headed back to the capital's centre. The calmness outside did nothing to balance the turmoil Louise felt inside but only added to her sense of apprehension at having to explain her non- appearance the previous night to her man. She stepped gradually and very deliberately across the pavement somehow feeling she had to tiptoe. After a momentary delay she stopped, took a few paces backward and craned her neck looking upward to see if there was a light coming from Oliver's flat on the ninth floor. It was, like her mood, dark. Louise could not somehow persuade herself to press the lift button and go up to her third floor flat so she turned and spotting a nearby red phone box took refuge therein and, overcome by remorse sobbed and cried aloud into the night's stillness. 'How could you do this Louise, you selfish, selfish cow!'

Arriving back from The Bag O'Nails at this precise moment came Oliver. His disposition was one of worry more than disappointment. Had Louise happened upon an accident tonight? Was this her way of saying 'It's over Oliver, you ambitionless wimp?' More than anything he was just simply exhausted and decided that, to clear his head and reassess he would walk the 7 miles or so from the West End to the East End.

As Oliver neared his block, through the brightening twilight he spied a silhouette in the telephone box. As he neared still more he discerned the figure it to be that of Louise who popped another mint into her mouth. His heart raced as he quickened his pace, approached and flung open the kiosk door almost separating it from its hinges.

'Where the hell were you tonight?' he yelled 'and I want the whole truth Louise and nothing but....'

'Ohhh Oliver... Ollie it's a long story. I couldn't get hold of you before you left to tell you,' she balled wide-eyed and startled.

She reached over to hold him but he backed away and spurned her, becoming even more incandescent.

'Don't touch me, don't even think of touching me. I can't even bare to look at you!'

Louise recoiled and squeezed herself further into the corner of the red kiosk, shocked at Oliver's forceful assertion and steaming rage. He then shoved the kiosk door closed and leant on it, effectively barring her exit.

'What's the number?' shouted Oliver over his shoulder.

'What's ... what's ... what number?' she replied.

'The number of the phone there?'

'What do you mean? …. What for?'

'Just give me the number!' screeched Oliver louder than ever.

'OK! Alright! It's 790 2704,' replied a confused and tearful Louise.

At this, Oliver took three or four short paces around to his left and went into the adjoining kiosk where he hauled up the receiver and dialled the seven given numbers. It rang just once.

'Louise its Oliver,' he said angrily seemingly unaware of how ludicrous those three words sounded.

'I guessed it would be you,' she sobbed 'Why you doing this Oliver, why don't we just talk to each other face to face rather than playing this stupid game on the phone?'

'It's not a game and it's not stupid. I just can't … can't bear to set eyes on you. So get explaining quick. I haven't got much change!'

Throughout much of the night Louise had thought of several plausible untruths to present to Oliver when this inevitable moment arrived but such was her panic at the unreal situation, she just came up with the first concoction that entered her head embellishing as it progressed.

'My mum has had a fall. She fell and hit her head when she was … err shopping. No one came to help her. They just left her there until a kind woman and her daughter … or daughter-in-law stopped and helped her to her feet and then she went all dizzy and couldn't see straight and then she blacked out and then after the ambulance came …' she was starting to ramble when the money ran out and the phone was disconnected.

'I've only got a 10 bob note, ring me back now on 790 0055,' shouted Oliver loud enough to be heard. Louise rummaged through her handbag and purse and finding a shilling returned Oliver's call.

'Hello, who's calling at this unearthly hour?' yawned Oliver jokingly, his fiery temper now having almost totally subsided on hearing the sad account of her mother's fall.

'Hook, line and sinker!' Louise callously thought to herself, as she quickly regained her composure.

Oliver immediately hung up the phone and rushed around to the adjacent kiosk. She too was on her way to meet him. They hugged each other tightly as the last of their tears dried. Both were greatly relieved but for very different reasons.

'I can't tell you how worried I was Lulu. You'd never believe what was going through my head. How's your mother, I know you don't see much of each other but how is she now?'

'Oh she'll live. The doctor's given her something for her headache.'

Over Oliver's shoulder Louise then noticed a clump of Janey's blonde wig sprouting from her handbag that she held against Oliver's back as they embraced. He was so taken by the reconciliation that he failed to notice that the extended embrace was designed to give Louise time to fiddle with her bag. Like everything that Louise had cooked up that night, it was all done behind Oliver's back and as always, totally successful.

✺✺✺✺✺

A TAIL OF TWO CITIES

The following Sunday Oliver sat at home listening to the radio. He'd always make a point of tuning into 'Round the Horne' on the Light Service. So important was this 30-minute comedy respite that he would never allow himself to be disturbed. This afternoon however the telephone rang frequently. Oliver eventually relented thinking it perhaps Louise who had gone to visit her 'recovering' mother. The repeated programme would be aired again on Wednesday night anyway he consoled. Oliver quietened the volume and answered.

'Hello, Oliver speaking?'

'We can reach an agreement that suits us both if we just put our heads together,' said the cryptic caller.

'I know that voice,' replied Oliver 'It's the so-called Madam Sprigola!'

'I think you know me well enough now to call me Sprig especially when I'm not on duty,' she joked.

Oliver thanked her for a memorable night at The Bag O'Nails a few days prior and explained how Louise's mother had fainted while shopping.

'Anyway, what's all this about an agreement that could suit us both?' enquired the teacher.

'That's why we've got to meet soon. It's very important Oliver, very, very important. This is too important to chat about on the phone!' said Sprig mysteriously.

Her persistence and earnestness intrigued and slightly concerned Oliver. He took no more persuading and agreed to meet her at the Reno-Nile Café, Petticote Lane in an hour. -

The last summer of the most memorable decade in peacetime England was a true swelterer. Temperatures often reached the mid-70s even touching 90 degrees once or twice. So much of the British disposition is dependent on whether the weather chooses to be kind. Second guessing the vagaries of the English climate would always make a suitable opening gambit. As Oliver walked day dreamily along a blistering hot, busy Whitechapel Road he wondered if, 'what do you think of this weather?' would be asked more often today in England than, 'Do you fancy a cuppa tea dear?' Probably a dead heat he concluded.

Whitechapel Road was not only a beating heart of the East End; it was ingrained on Oliver's heart too. He loved everything about it. Indeed, he was born just over there in The London Hospital and always lived and worked within a few miles. He enjoyed the squalor, squabbling, variation and vibrancy of the street market and the general organised clutter of the place. He felt proud to have hailed from an area steeped in such a gory and glorious history that shaped the East End, London, England, Europe, and indeed the world. Oliver took the opportunity to tag onto a guided tour for history seeking enthusiasts and tourists as they moved along the wide, dusty thoroughfare. -

The Blind Beggar Pub was noted as the venue where Ronnie Kray shot dead Jack 'The Hat' McVitie a few months before. The portly tour guide dressed as a pearly king took pains to emphasise the word 'Allegedly' as the case was soon up at The Old Bailey. Next they came to the huge Charrington Brewery where its Victorian founder, John Charrington sold his successful business when he saw the destructive results of his brew and gave the vast proceeds to the London Temperance Movement. Goldrink's, the Jewish Deli nearby was once the place where, for a farthing you could see the horrific freak show that was John Merrick, The Elephant Man.

A TAIL OF TWO CITIES

'His skeleton remains in the hospital opposite. 100 years later it's still used for medical purposes.' Next stop was an ordinary looking camera shop which 60 years prior held the 3rd Communist Congress attended by, amongst others Trotsky, Bulgarin and Lenin himself. Adjoining, was once the home of a disillusioned Jewish tailor, Abe Sapperstein. 'As many did at the turn of the century, the poverty-stricken disaffected young man set sail for the New World to eventually found New York City's Harlem Globetrotters. Tiring of basketball Sapperstein was also said to gone further west, to California to help set up one of the first Hollywood film studios.'

The tour guide then moved on to the subject of The Salvation Army founder William Booth, The Sidney Street Siege, Winston Churchill, Peter The Painter and of course Jack The Ripper and his infamous Whitechapel Murders of 1888. - Soon enough Oliver noticed the time and broke away from his free tour to hurry along Brick Lane to his rendezvous with Sprig.

By the time he reached the Reno-Nile cafe, Petticote Lane's Sunday market was at its height. It was probably the worst meeting place at the worse time. Sprig was pacing outside as Oliver jostled through the crowd toward her.

 'Whose bloody idea was it to meet here? We can't talk here. Let's walk,' said Sprig.

Before long they had forced their way through the tumult and found an oasis, a quite teashop off Bishopsgate.

'Let's sit here and talk and I'll get straight to the point', said Sprig seriously. 'I think you could use my assistance Oliver.'

He looked apprehensive, 'Go on.'

'The capitalist world Oliver, is built on commerce but long before Pounds, Shillings and Pence, bartering was the only currency we had,' pronounced Sprig.

'Is that what you call getting straight to the point. Let's skip the macro economics lecture before we both die of old age,' he said impatiently.

'As I was about to say Mr know-it-all teacher, I can for sure make you and your lady friend Louise a very happy couple indeed. In return you will help me set up my cat's home.'

'Your cat's home? That place over in Battersea you've been going on about.'

'Precisely, but cat sanctuary is a better description. I know that you really want that promotion at work more than just about anything. Even though Louise is certain that you'll get it, you're even more certain that the job is Jeff's.'

'And now you're going to tell me that Louise and me are both wrong?'

'No Oliver, I'm gonna tell you that Jeff won't even be interviewed for the job because, you and me will make sure that he's elsewhere!'

'Elsewhere, where elsewhere?'

'Listen Mr teacher weren't you bloody wondering why so many people were coming up to me in The Bag the other night?'

'Well it did cross my mind,' said Oliver getting increasingly exasperated.

'You see the people there need me or they need what I can give them ... What I can supply for them ... do ya get my drift Oliver ... SUPPLY FOR THEM!'

A TAIL OF TWO CITIES

'So you're telling me you supply drugs.'

'My oh my. I'm shocked Oliver. I thought you were a little more wet behind the ears,' said the surprised dealer.

'Well I knew it wasn't Scotch Mist they were after. I suspected all along but thought it unwise to mention it.'

'There was I thinking you were so naïve.'

'Maybe I am sometimes Sprig but I still don't get all this about bartering, the job and Jeff.'

'OK, I'll explain. I deal in drugs, narcotics like pills, uppers and downers and sleepers. I also handle Pot. Some of the best stuff in all London. What I do Oliver the Labour and Tory stiffs see as uncool. Now just imagine if the pigs, who are so very uncool themselves were to spread their uncoolicity towards say … Jeff things could become difficult for him!'

Oliver almost choked on his own cream tea and thought a while before speculating.

'Well Sprig I can tell you that Jeff stays well away from that sort of thing. He's Mr Fitness personified ….. but can you imagine the heat on the street if the cats from Scotland Yard find Jeff has been dealing in … substances … narcotics …. drugs. Tut, tut Jeffrey and you a respected teacher too.' mused Oliver.

'Oh, it seems like the penny's dropped Mr teacher and so surprisingly quickly too but drop the pretend American gangster lingo, that's my job. There's quite a dark side to you isn't there Oliver.' she replied.

Oliver sat dumbfounded at himself and that he was even prepared to listen to a relative stranger discussing such treachery. After all Jeff's his 'best mate'.

'Jeff's my best mate, we grew up together!' said Oliver more rationally.

'That maybe true but equally true is that Louise thinks you're a wimp who's going nowhere fast. Isn't that true Oliver? In fact, you said those very words to me! Would *you* stay with someone like you? Would you?' asked Sprig.

Buried deep in his guts, Oliver could feel ambition and ego furiously battling against friendship and British fair play. Nearly doubling his teacher's salary seemed appealing too. His head spun with possibilities, probabilities and scenario.

'You've obviously thought this through Sprig so go on, say what you planned to say.'

With no further hesitation Sprig described in detail how they would break into Jeff's mews in Chelsea and plant a substantial stash of pills and Pot where Jeff would not find. A short time after this Oliver would anonymously contact the police with full information of the callous 'school teacher dealer'. They will then dutifully raid, find the stash, arrest and even remand in custody 'the felon' and this all before his job interview.

'Brilliant in its simplicity, I'm sure you'd agree Mr Oliver Cherry, future Head of Year,' proclaimed Sprig with a fair degree of satisfaction.

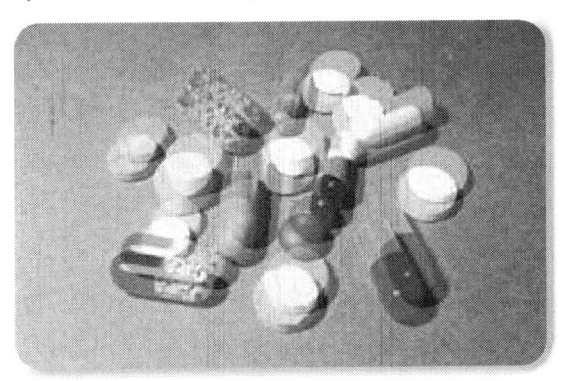

A TAIL OF TWO CITIES

Hardly had Oliver been as totally overwhelmed as at that moment. He remained quiet for a minute or two as Sprig observed the contortions on his clammy but thoughtful forehead.

'So what's in it for you then Lady Macbeth?' he enquired.

Sprig then placed her sequinned shoulder bag on the table and pointed to the beaded black cat on the side.

'In a sense this is what I mean by a sort of bartering. I will provide this unspeakable service for you. You will in turn be required to roll your sleeves up and do some grafting and building work at my cat sanctuary. Of course you will be required also to hand over a nominal fee for the …. err necessary,' responded Sprig coldly.

'Go on, how much?'

Sprig brought out a pen from her bag, wrote a £ sign and then three figures on a napkin and handed it to Oliver who stared at it and smiled.

'That's not quite as nominal as I'd hoped Sprig. I'll have to raid my piggy bank or even take out a loan!'

'You could even get Jeff to lend you the money. You can save up and pay him back when he's done his stretch!'

Sprig cruelly suggested.

'So Oliver, am I to understand that it's full steam ahead?'

Oliver looked long and hard at the ceiling and then at Sprig before holding his breath and exhaling fully. He then suddenly jumped to his feet and quickly moved toward the door.

'Let me sleep on it Sprig. I need time. Time!'

As quickly as Oliver went through the door he spun on his heels and came back to retake his place sitting opposite Sprig.

'Let's do it Sprig. Let's just do it! I need this job really badly. Of course it's not right but it just has to be done if me and Lou are gonna make it!'

Sprig looked delighted. 'You've made the right decision Oliver. A bleedin' great decision. Other than myself I can think of one particular woman who'll be so very proud of you when you announce you've finally got that promotion you so deserve. Who know where it'll lead!'

Chapter 11

Where do you go to my lovely?

The hot days and warm nights in London during the summer of 1969 was taking its toll. People sensed that others sensed people were generally becoming more tetchy and irritable so too Oliver, Sprig, Janey, Jeff and Louise who were all individually and insidiously being consumed by self-interest each having their own narrow agenda: Oliver, yearning to gain promotion and his lover's approval - Sprig desiring to save a London cat and start going straight - Janey longing for a man to simply love and have her son Terry back with her - Jeff craving to teach in an all-boys school and continue his philandering. As for Louise, she was simply Louise, on the surface beautifully transparent but below unable to defeat the darker side of a conniving nature. Throughout the next few days things would move on at a rapid rate of knots – The unfolding had begun as three almost simultaneous telephone conversations would direct how things would eventually turn out for the hapless quintet:

CALL 1 - Louise to Janey

LOUISE: Hi Janey it's me Lou.

JANEY: Yeah, my bloody fair-weather friend. You know what they say Louise 'A friend in need is a friend that pisses off and leaves you in the lurch!'

LOUISE: You left *me* in the lurch. I went to the bar or the ladies or somewhere and by the time I got back you'd gone. I was left on my own in The Ad-Lib, a strange place that I've never been to before. It was your idea to go. You were the one that thought it would be a good idea. You Janey invited me! I put my friendship with you Janey before Oliver and you just abandoned me there. I feel you've really bloody let me down Janey and I thought you could be trusted but obviously…...

JANEY: Alright OK I'm sorry about that Louise, sorry. I didn't think that it was me who wasn't there for you.

LOUISE: You should try thinking of others a bit more next time you just leave unannounced. Anyway, what happened to you?

JANEY: You wouldn't believe it. When you was in the loo Lou, two hunky geezers came over and started chatting me up. Two big bleeders both at the same time!

LOUISE: No, get away!

JANEY: It's true. Yeah, on my Terry's life! One was a Hell's Angel from Stepney and the other some sort of American, from New York City in Texas he said.

LOUISE: They must have been attracted to your bunions!

JANEY: I don't know what got into 'em it was if both the bleeders thought I was Miss World or something.

LOUISE: You're a very desirable woman Janey it's as simple as that. So what happened next?

JANEY: Well before you could say 'Carnaby Street' there was a ruck.

LOUISE: A what?

JANEY: A ruck. Aggravation. What is it you La De Daas call it ... Fisticuffs ... an alter-bloody-cation. Two men fighting over me, how bleedin romantic is that!

LOUISE: Wow, and then what?

JANEY: Well as I was trying to get out of the way some bloke in a dicky bow picked me up and suggested I leave. Well I'm not 'aving no suited-up gorilla telling me what's what, so I had to ......

LOUISE: You had to what Janey?

JANEY: Well things got out of control so I pulled his hair, kicked him in the bollocks and called him a twat ... that's when things got really outta control?!

LOUISE: So they threw you out?

JANEY: Not just me but my men too.

LOUISE: Your men?

JANEY: Yeah my two men. We all got booted out. My men carried on fighting on the pavement outside.

LOUISE: I bet the fella in the Stetson won.

JANEY: What's a stepson?

LOUISE: No, a Stetson, a cowboy hat.

JANEY: Yeah, dead right he did. How do you know he had one of them on?

LOUISE: Er, well don't all Americans wear Stetsons? So, who did you end up with?

JANEY: The Yank of course. The biker went home on .... er public transport. We're all friends now though. Me and Hank are out again tonight. I bully him but he says I'm adorable. I says, too bleedin right I am. He's lucky to get his hands on some classy London crumpet! So what happened to you after I left?

LOUISE: Well after I got over the shock of being on my own I bumped into an old teacher friend of mine, Arnie Slat .... whatever his name is. He's a big wig up West and he's about to offer me a part in 'Hello Dolly' can you believe.

JANEY: About to?

LOUISE: The old duffer was probably too busy with all the comings and goings but his son came later and no doubt if I flutter my eyes at him he'll be able to sort things out with his dad. The young man is taking me to dinner soon, although he doesn't know that yet!

JANEY: Wow Lou. I don't know how you do it. A part in a West End show! A hunky new man! Give him one for me sweetheart!

LOUISE: I think you've beaten me to it.

JANEY: To what? What do ya mean?

LOUISE: I don't know I … er I talk … rubbish when I'm excited.

JANEY: What about Oliver?

LOUISE: Oliver hmm. Let's just say Oliver is a very understanding man. Anyway, must go. Like they say, People to see, places to go.

JANEY: OK Lou, good luck, go break a bleedin leg!

CALL 2 - Jeff to Oliver

JEFF: How's it going Oliver old bean?

OLIVER: Oh Jeff it's you. I was just thinking about you, amazing.

JEFF: Something good I hope?

OLIVER: Well er …sort of. You OK, what's up? How's things going? I haven't seen you since we broke up from school.

JEFF: Yeah, terrific mate. Things have never been better. I've got a copper-plated guaranteed promotion come September and I've got a new lady on my arm.

OLIVER: You and your birds Jeff. Another floozy?

JEFF: No this one's different. It's a bit too close to home so won't say anything yet. I'll be asking her out to dinner soon but don't wanna appear too keen. We'll probably end up in the sack. It's best not to say too much about her until I know if we've got a future, don't wanna count my chickens. Until then, Mums the Word, if you know what I mean.

OLIVER: London's number one lover-man!?

JEFF: Yeah, me and Mick Jagger. Anyway, Ollie mate – snooker, Thursday, how about it?

OLIVER: I'm not sure Jeff. I'm not sure I'm up to it.

JEFF: Up to what? It's snooker, not the bloody marathon. Come on now, Thursday! I need a chance to get my own back on you.'

OLIVER: What, what do you …. er… mean 'your own back'?

JEFF: You beat me last time remember?

OLIVER: Oh yeah, I see, so I did.

JEFF: Thursday then Ollie, same time as usual?

OLIVER: OK. Alright. Thursday it is.

JEFF: Great. See you there.

CALL 3 - Sprig to Oliver

SPRIG: Sprig!

OLIVER: Alright Sprig you OK?

SPRIG: Time marches on Oliver. Time to step up a gear and get the job done. There's cats all over London depending on me.

OLIVER: They don't just depend on you, you know. You're not the only drug dealer in London are you?

SPRIG: Cats Oliver, cats the furry type that go meeoow.

OLIVER: Oh right cats, I see what you mean. Anyway, guess what?'

SPRIG: A bottle of snot.'

OLIVER: Will you be serious woman! I've just spoken to Jeff and agreed to play snooker with him on Thursday.

SPRIG: Brilliant Oliver, brilliant.

OLIVER: What do you mean, brilliant? We're just about to condemn the man to prison. He's my best mate, Jeff is.

SPRIG: It's brilliant because it just makes your case stronger. If you're playing snooker with your *best mate* just before he gets busted then that's brilliant. Who's gonna suspect *you* if..... Best mates don't do things like that to each other, do ya see?

OLIVER: Is that supposed to make me feel better about myself? Sometimes you'd be better off just keeping your big bloody mouth shut.

SPRIG: Oliver, Oliver I've never heard you resort to that sort of working-class industrial language. One is shocked, one is!

OLIVER: Puto te oportet ad insanium.

SPRIG: Stop with your Roman lingo nonsense will ya!

OLIVER: I'm sorry but I've not been sleeping too well lately.

SPRIG: Why's that?

OLIVER: Why's that? Why's that? I don't do this sort of thing often. You might be part of the criminal fraternity but I'm a bloody teacher. People look up to me.

SPRIG: Precisely, and people will look up to you even more when you're Head of Year. You could be Deputy Head in six months. You getting cold feet?

OLIVER: No, No, a bit nervous perhaps. It's just that I've always been part of the non-criminal overworld.

SPRIG: Oliver, you have to understand: Jeff equals enemy, promotion equals friend. You need to focus and stay focussed. Let me help you. Now just imagine this completely made up scenario - Louise is the most precious thing to you, right?

OLIVER: Right

SPRIG: Picture this, Jeff takes her out one night, romances her then they go back to his place for a bit of how's ya farva! Wouldn't you want some sort of retribution then, wouldn't you?

OLIVER: You're starting to turn my stomach now. Of course I'd want revenge.

SPRIG: Well there you go then. Keep such an image in your imagination and that might help you keep your eyes on the prize.

OLIVER: OK, OK let's stay calm now.... calm.

SPRIG: That's good Oliver. Calm and focussed, calm and focussed and before long you'll be half way up the slippery education pole and running a giant school all of your very own. So what we need now is a time when Jeff is not at home for at least a couple of hours. That'll give us more than enough time to break into his place, plant the wotsits, make our escape and voila, Robert's your dad's bruvver! Ha Ha …..

OLIVER: Try not to reduce everything to a Carry On film plot.

SPRIG: Don't be so uncool Ollie, just find out Jeff's movements in the next few days so we know when the coast is clear.

OLIVER: Well come to think of it, he did say he was going out with some new tart he's just picked up.

SPRIG: Good, well find out the details when you play snooker and let me know. There's a city full of neglected felines out there depending on you and your financial contribution.

OLIVER: Hmmm.... Anyway gotta go now, Thunderbirds has just started.

SPRIG: Righto, and make sure ya get ya skates on.

ಉಉಉ

Chapter 12

Monopoly, Daffodils and Chelsea

That evening Louise came up to Oliver's flat on the ninth floor. Although it was her birthday, they decided to celebrate by enjoying each other's company exclusively and having a quiet night in with some booze. Besides that, Naked was feeling a little off colour, so Oliver deemed it best that he stay home and keep an eye. Near tangible tension tinged with an aura of foreboding pervaded that stormy night. Cracks of thunder and flashes of lightning didn't help. Both independently believed that their relationship could be stumbling toward oblivion, but neither was quite able to pinpoint why.

They opened an expensive bottle of red wine symbolic, Oliver thought of a last supper and sprawled on the floor with the Monopoly board between them. Louise was a renown board game Maestro. Before long she had most of the hotels, all the houses and £650 cash against her opponent's £25. Oliver threw the dice and ended up in jail. An omen perhaps? He shuddered. A while later he took a short break to feed Naked. On his return his £25 had been reduced to just £15. He was too distracted to realise that he had been cheated and not for the first time.

Louise took a long-dissatisfied sigh followed by a deep, deep breath as if preparing to make an announcement. She stared hard and mournfully at Oliver; her eyes full of regret. Then she cleared her throat:

'Ollie … Oliver. Let's just finish it put an end to it … finish it now!'

There followed a long, long chilling interlude. Oliver gazed up at the ceiling hoping this moment would pass. His eyes welled. He took a gulp of his wine and then another and another. It was at this point that it quickly dawned that perhaps Louise wanted to 'finish' playing Monopoly and nothing more but nevertheless one lonely tear had already rolled and forced its way from the corner of an eye. It was noticed. Oliver inwardly composed himself concluding that he'd take advantage of this unusual circumstance to somehow gauge how Louise ticked.

'Finish … Finish it? … I knew that this day was coming Lulu. I just knew it. I thought you would perhaps leave it until after the interview. It's your birthday, a good time to move on I suppose. I've failed you I know so, it's all that I really deserve ….' he feigned.

'Monopoly Oliver, Monopoly. Let's finish playing Monopoly!' said Louise. –

'Monopoly. Monopoly of course we should finish playing Monopoly. It's a boring game anyway. Fancy a cuppa Lulu and biscuits …. Chocolate ones? Do you know, I think I've got something in my eye, must be hayfever? I know, I'll go and get some fish and chips. Come on Naked let's go. Yes, two birthday fish suppers coming up and a gherkin ……..'

Not discerning her lover's tactic, Louise could endure his writhing no longer.

'Oliver … Ollie, enough now stop! Just listen!' Louise then gave him a reassuring hug, pecked him on the cheek and sang

'Me and you. You and me. That's the way it will always be.'

True, Oliver was reassured but his coming crime and current discomfiture resulted in a strange irrational indulgence.

'No Louise. I know you think I'm not pulling my weight in this relationship but it's clear that you're just biding your time seeing if I get the job, then *you* will decide our future ….'

Louise interrupted the distressed man before he swung fully into another pathetic rant.

'I LOVE YOU!' she shouted and repeated over and over.

Oliver went still then after a moment's thought said.

'Louise, promise me that you will never ever say those three words again. Not in that order, anyway and not for a while yet. I don't deserve your love right now. Promise me. Say you promise you won't say those three words!' he insisted.

'What's got into you?' she replied.

'I know this might sound irrational, but you must promise me! Say it! Promise me now!'

'OK Oliver OK if it makes you happy then I won't say the words 'I love you'. Are you happy now?'

Oliver immediately calmed and due to his unspoken guilt resolved in his mind that after he and Sprig had completed the foul deed and he eventually got his promotion, he would only then be somehow worthy of Louise's love - but not before. He understood this was wrong and irrational but he was doing it for love, he was doing it for Louise and Jeff would have to suffer the consequences.

※※※※※

Jeff too was a man of much complexity and variation with a bountiful reputation as a womaniser with accompanying kudos. More often than not, his vast experience of women resulted in him adopting the overused adage 'treat 'em mean, to keep 'em keen'. Partly at the cajoling of his father, he had now reached the point in his life where he would be required to throw off the Classroom Casanova tag and replace it with something more establishment-based, having say, Ted Heath rather than Jim Morrison as his mentor. Of course, as Head of Year a certain degree of refinement would be expected. This image make-over could be enhanced by a long-term relationship. Louise perhaps, and it would certainly get his dad's approval?

As Louise predicted, Jeff dutifully phoned to arrange to meet. They agreed to dine at an exclusive eatery near the Victoria Embankment. Jeff offered to pick her up in his E-Type but Louise explained that this would not be necessary as she was 'a strong independent woman' but perhaps more to the point, their liaison had, at all cost to be kept from her lover and his best friend.

The Bijoux Plage French Restaurant during the middle of the week had a quiet and genteel vibe. Standing in the shadow of Big Ben and overlooking the serene gently flowing Thames, it was the ideal sophisticated venue Jeff needed to impress and romance his date. To Louise, where they met was immaterial, she just wanted a part, a big part in 'Hello Dolly' and Arnie Slater via his son Jeff would unwittingly or otherwise be her passport. If Louise was anything, she was ambitiously adaptable. She was also astute enough to appreciate that when a man talks about himself excessively then it's a clear sign of some form of insecurity, which must therefore be indulged and even humoured but rarely challenged if ambition is to be sated. Simultaneously Jeff wasn't sure if Louise was genuinely interested in him or maybe she had an agenda!

The night was moving on and Jeff made no mention of his father or the West End show. Indeed, for an hour or more Jeff continued to monopolise almost all the words spoken and centre it on his favourite subject, himself. As the evening wore on it was becoming a tedious monologue. Louise was becoming frustrated and impatient at her inability to change course. Finally, she could take no more and, in an attempt, to redirect his thinking, impetuously revealed the secret Janey imparted to her when they first met by blurting out:

A TAIL OF TWO CITIES

'Jeff, bloody well shut up and listen to me for a change. Did you know that as a teenager you fathered a son, a boy called Terry who is being brought up by your estranged mother? You must remember Janey; she's a good friend of mine now. She's the gymslip mother of your son. Your dad Arnie desperately wants to be a grandfather and, would you believe it, he bloody well is!..... Ha Ha Ha Ha Ha....'
–

Well a dramatic outburst like that, Louise thought would certainly stop Jeff dead in his tracks and take the wind out of his egotistical sails but in reality, it was to be left merely to her imaginings. She therefore prudently continued to bite her lip and fake adoration!

Eventually however Jeff was to show his hand:

'Louise I wasn't going to reveal this to you but it's difficult to keep strong feelings in check when they insist on being set free. Tonight, as I was preparing to come and meet you something inside compelled me to write this poem. Do you mind if I air it?' Jeff reached into an inside pocket and unravelled some paper.

'WORDSWORTH HAD HIS DAFFODILS

SHAKESPEARE, LADY ANNE

LIFE WITHOUT TRUE LOVE MY DEAR

IS NO GOOD FOR ANY MAN –

AS THE SUMMER DAYS RECEDE

LEAVES WILL TUMBLE FROM THE TREES

BUT WHO WILL KEEP ME WARM AT NIGHT?

IT'S YOU MY LOVE, LOUISE –

There was a short silence whilst his stunned subject measured an appropriate response.

'That was touching. Very, very touching. I'm choked, completely overwhelmed! You're quite the wordsmith and very sexy too may I say,' said a woman eavesdropping from an adjacent table.

'That's good of you to say so Madam,' said Jeff, with not a hint of abashment.

'Perhaps you should see about getting it published. I think your young man has got an awful lot of talent don't you think so sweetie?' enthused the mystery diner to Louise.

'I think Jeff's got a lot to offer but I'm sure he doesn't appreciate it himself!' replied

Louise using her well-practiced and cloaked ambiguity.

The evening was drawing to a finale, so Jeff suggested they take a stroll along the Embankment. Louise agreed recognising that she may well be forced to play her trump card. They sauntered along the wide boulevard past Boadicea's grand statue and Cleopatra's Needle and up as far as London Bridge before returning the way they came.

'I've got a Mews House in Chelsea, Louise,' speculated Jeff.

'Yes, you mentioned it earlier, several times in fact,' came the semi-caustic reply. 'Oh, your dad lives just off the Kings Road, doesn't he Jeff? Even though you live so close he's probably so busy at work that you hardly get a chance to meet up I bet?' conjectured Louise as well.

A TAIL OF TWO CITIES

The two tiring, but highly perceptive teachers then took to an odd unstated form of pseudo-Victorian surrealism to reveal their respective agendas and save their reticence. -

'My motorised vehicle is stationed yonder, Miss Elsmore,' mused Jeff.

'And it's pointing in the direction of your romantic Mews residence in Chelsea Master Slater darling?' she replied.

''Tis but a few miles away. We could away presently and be there in a matter of minutes. 'Tis important, I'm sure you'd agree, to the modern man of the late 1960s that his say er physical ambitions and aspirations are satisfied despite it being an initial liaison. Our education establishment in the East End can be so dreadfully restricting.'

Louise looked up and sighed calculatingly.

'Tis of equal import to the modern gentlewoman of the late 1960s that her umm career ambitions are satisfied too!'

'Ha Ha. You refer of course to a role in papa's production of Hello Dolly coming soon to the capital's famous West End?' he replied intuitively.

'Precisely Master Slater, precisely!'

'Take it as read Miss Elsmore. I shall converse with father on the morrow and utilise my considerable influence. Once he is convinced and he will be, I will inform you of the happy news immediately thereafter.'

'You will be sure to succeed now. You will be absolutely certain to win him over Master Slater!'

'Without question! You have my total assurance as a gentleman of my word. Rehearsals commence anon. Now let's retire to my abode wherein I will test your resolve and virtue!'

Louise looked skyward again, drew up another deep breath and silently mouthed.

'Come on then. Let's go. Let's bloody well get it over with!'

Chapter 13

'Dastardly Deed Day'

At the precise moment Jeff and Louise were ordering their main course at the Bijoux Plage Restaurant, Sprig pulled up outside Whitechapel tube station in her battered bright orange 1956 American Jeep. Oliver was waiting and got into the passenger seat. He forced a nervous smile and the Jeep set off for Jeff's pad in West London. The time had finally come. 'Dastardly Deed Day' as Sprig light-heartedly referred to it. Oliver was more candid.

'No we'll best call it, 'planting-drugs-in-your-best-friend's-house-then-call-the-police-anonymously-hence-committing-him-to-jail-all-for-the-sake-of-a-job-and-Louise Day.' That's more to the point don't you think Sprig?'

Sprig agreed that although his was more accurate it was a little long-winded and didn't sound quite as sinister. Sprig really loved sinister.

Crowbars, jemmies and other fiendish tools rattled in the back seat as the Jeep moved stealthily through the City, along The Embankment, past The Bijoux Plage where, unknown to the felons Jeff and Louise were enjoying their dessert. They parked about 50 yards away from Jeff's house down a narrow poorly lit side street.

'Do you think we ought to synchronise our watches?' asked Oliver.

'Why, where are you going?' replied Sprig.

'I'm coming with you, aren't I?'

'Umm, you're a bit nervous aren't you 007? You've never been dastardly before have you?'

'No, I bloody well have not and I can assure you that tonight marks the end of all my dastardlyness!'

Sprig ordered that they both get into the back seat to prepare. She was wearing a black velvet flared catsuit, her usual unusual dark green and red suede gloves revealing her sweaty palms and navy-blue tennis shoes. He thought she looked more like Emma Peel than a burglar/drug dealer. Oliver wore what he thought was more fitting; something like Patrick McGoohan would don in 'Dangerman'. Black slacks, black polo neck, black woolly hat and black leather gloves.

'And all because the lady loves Milk Tray,' Sprig joked.

She opened a plastic container which held within dozens prellies, purple hearts, black bombers, maybe as many as a hundred in total. As well as these, at least three hefty blocks of cannabis resin.

'Uppers, Downers, Stay-As-You-Arers, sedatives, stupefiers, stimulants plus some of the best high-quality Pot to come to Western Europe from Morocco for years. There's enough here to send a small hippy commune skyward for a fortnight. I thought about adding some Lucy in the Skys but it seemed a bloody shame to waste it all on your so called best mate Jeff!'

said Sprig heartlessly.

It was only in seeing this that the complete enormity of the situation and its inevitable consequences really hit home to Oliver.

At the precise moment, Jeff was inadvertently impressing a fellow diner with his ode to Louise, Sprig and Oliver loaded up a small tatty holdall with the required accoutrements that also included a bottle of milk which Oliver needed to settle his stomach when he was nervous. Having checked the internet using Google Earth, Sprig was familiar with the layout of the mews around Jeff's. They checked that the coast was clear and covertly slipped out of the Jeep walking promptly and perhaps suspiciously in single file to Jeff's house! Having successfully negotiated a small wall and a higher fence the two made their way to the back of the Mews. There was hardly any moonlight; the night was almost pitch black and strangely tranquil although they could hear the thudding of each other's heart.

'Right Oliver, I'm gonna mooch about a bit and see what I can see, you keep me covered,' whispered Sprig.

'Sprig, how exactly do I do that. How do I keep you covered?' replied Oliver anxiously reaching for his milk.

'Will you behave Oliver and just bloody keep your eyes and ears open, that's all. You can do that can you?!'

'OK, OK don't get too tetchy. I'm a teacher remember. I teach Latin not larceny. I've never done anything like this before.'

'And neither have I!'

'What .... what did you say? You've never done a burglary before? How come, I thought you're from Peckham?!' said Oliver.

'No, I mean I've never done a burglary with a blithering idiot before! Now shine the torch on the kitchen door,'

'Right, I'll shine the torch on the kitchen door and I'll hold the bag, this heavy, heavy bag and I'll keep you covered and I'll do this and I'll do that ...' muttered Oliver to himself mockingly.

Sprig pushed the door hard with both hands, top, middle and bottom checking where the locks could be.

'Shit, shit, shit and shit. It looks as if we'll have to force the kitchen window' said a disappointed Sprig.

Meanwhile, at The Bijoux Plage Jeff was paying the bill.

By torchlight, the hapless couple then surreptitiously made their way around to a high kitchen window. Oliver needed some more milk. Sprig reached up on tiptoes straining to touch even the bottom of the frame. She then started to feverishly and inexplicably scratch at the top of her back.

'You got an itch?' said Oliver

A TAIL OF TWO CITIES

'No, no just a little problem. I can't seem to get...' said Sprig with a degree of irritation in her voice. 'Oliver, I'm gonna ask you to do something I've never asked a man to do before and never will again. I need you to help me take my bra off. Don't get the wrong idea but I can't stretch up and sort the window out, bleedin bra's too tight.'

Oliver looked suitably shocked, but not for the expected reason.

'You're a lezzy ..... a lesbian aren't you?' asked Oliver.

'Aren't you too?' Sprig replied.

Sprig's puzzling response was designed to throw Oliver into some confusion. It worked.

'Why I put this catsuit on for a job like this I'll never know,' complained Sprig.

'I think it looks cool,' said Oliver in an undertone.

'Look Oliver all you have to do unzip the back then unfasten the bra clip. And get on with it, this is a burglary not some sort of kinky back garden, after dark seduction.'

Oliver thought a while and carried out the instructions efficiently. Sprig took each arm out of the catsuit and slipped her bra off exposing two very hefty firm size 36E breasts each with an erecting raspberry sized nipple that responded naturally to the night chill. Oliver was stunned and clearly mesmerised.

'Oliver ... Oh Oliver. Wake up Oliver! When I said keep me covered, I didn't mean keep shining the bloody torch on my tits!'

At precisely the second Oliver was putting his accomplice's bra in the holdall, his lover was walking along The Embankment hand in hand with his best friend.

Oliver kept a watchful eye whilst his crime partner sought a point of entry.

'Sprig look, there's something coming, it's a cat....'

'Well, is it a talking cat Oliver?'

'No!'

'Is it a talking cat carrying a night vision camera off to the nearest phone box to ring the pigs?'

'Well ...no.'

'Well then I think we need not worry, Oliver, don't you?'

'No... you don't understand. I know that you like cats alot don't you?'

'Oliver, you're starting to do my head it, you are!'

'Sprig, Sprig. Look over here Jeff's left a window open. Can you believe it? Thanks mate.'

A TAIL OF TWO CITIES

Sprig hurried over and confirmed the discovery.

'Brilliant Oliver! You're a natural. Right take your shoes off. We're going in.' Sprig first then Oliver. They hauled themselves up and in through the high kitchen window. Oliver managed to get a furtive squeeze of Sprig's bottom in the process. Although she realised, now was not the time for her famed right upper cut.

Meanwhile Jeff and Louise had just set off for Chelsea in his E-Type.

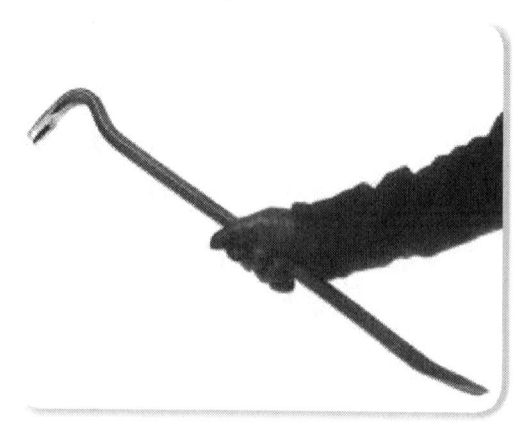

Sprig's torch was failing so she commandeered Oliver's and the two moved quietly through the kitchen and into the living room.

'You got the bag Oliver?' asked Sprig

'Oh no, I've left it in the garden! ... Just kidding. I thought I might as well enjoy the experience while I'm here,' announced Oliver vainly trying to break the tension.

In almost complete darkness they discussed where best to hide the stash of narcotics so Jeff would not discover them. They crept furtively back into the kitchen.

'Behind the cooker. Whoever goes behind the cooker?' said Sprig in a less than hushed tone.

Oliver agreed. They edged the cooker side to side making just enough room for the stash. Oliver rummaged around in the holdall and pulled out the small container of pills and pot. He held it against his chest, exhaled slowly and mumbled a prayer of forgiveness to an entity he had given up on in recent years.

'Come on Oliver. Stuff the stash behind there. We've not come this far to bottle it now,' insisted Sprig.

With an increasing sense of foreboding he obeyed and they at once sidled the cooker back into its original position.

Jeff and Louise meanwhile, were travelling down The King's Road as Sprig and Oliver painstakingly covered their tracks, exited the way they entered and hurriedly put their shoes back on in the garden. Calmly and quietly the two criminals scaled what needed scaling and made their way undetected back to the Jeep. Before getting into their getaway vehicle they gave each other a knowing smile and chuckled with nervous relief. They then embraced warmly and congratulated themselves on a successful mission accomplished without a hitch. Oliver almost embarrassed himself as he held his braless accomplice too close for too long.

'Get down now!' yelled Sprig.

Oliver thought of course this was Sprig's reference to his burgeoning manhood.

'Get down, there's a car coming up!' she repeated. Oliver quickly turned.

'Bloody hell it looks like Jeff's,' said Oliver.

Sprig had no intention of doing any such thing herself and watched as the car passed slowly by and turned into the cobbled Mews.

'Don't worry Oliver. Jeff doesn't know me from Eve and neither does the woman he's with,' proclaimed Sprig to fellow felon who by now was lain near prostrate on the pavement.

'The woman he was with wasn't the sort of tart you said Jeff usually goes for. In fact, I think she looked quite fanciable, I must say,' remarked Sprig longingly.

'I can't believe it. I just can't bloody believe it. That was close, another couple of minutes and we'd have been caught red handed,' said Oliver to his unconcerned associate.

'You're a weirdo you are. You've never really said much about yourself, have you Sprig?' enquired Oliver as he got to his feet and dusted himself down.

'All I know is that you deal drugs, have got a sizeable bust and like cats. What else is there about ya?'

'I'm about to give you a bunch of fives. Now I'd like you to drop the interrogation and get in,' came the evasive reply.

Oliver got the hint and did again as bid. The Jeep moved off into the night at precisely the moment Jeff gently closed his bedroom door!

᎗᎗᎗

Chapter 14

Lulu in a stew

There was no way on earth that Oliver was going to sleep that night. Having just completed the most dangerous, thoughtless and cruel act he would ever commit. Pacing to and fro and looking for yet another distraction only partially held at bay the insidious self-loathing that would engulf him.

'I know you told me not to Naked but what could I do?' he pleaded to his dog.

'I wasn't brought up this way. I'm essentially a good man brought up to be a gentleman but now I've gone and done a terrible thing to Jeff, your Jeff!'

This was a reference to Jeff who bought Naked for Oliver as a 21st birthday present some years before.

'Well dog. We're both wide awake so we might as well go for a stroll. It'll do us both good. Well it will me.'

As the sun was about to come up Oliver and his dog trudged dismally through Victoria Park nearby. Nothing stirred at that time of the morning just the dawn chorus and a few grey squirrels preparing for the coming autumn. He eventually sat on a dewy bench. Naked looked up at Oliver with sombre expression sensing that his master wanted to get something off his chest.

'Jeff used to be my best friend you know boy. As kids we used to play football over there, cricket there and knock-down-ginger in those flats. I kissed my very first girl Lyn Snow sitting on this very bench and then Jeff kissed her too right after me. Then she kissed me again, then Jeff, then me. By the time we let the poor girl home she had chapped lips and a stiff neck. We made a promise to each other then, to get our own girlfriend and not share the same one. Oh well at least I've got Louise and he's still happily single.' They both sat silently for a while.

'What's it like being a dog Naked? You happy? It's all taken care for you. Winalot, Water and Walkies. You don't ask for much do you? Us men have got it all to do. Normally we do manage to somehow do them all but it's just that … err we're not that much good at any of 'em. Look at me. I was a pretty good footballer at school but I was no Jimmy Greaves. I was never gonna play for Spurs. But I was good at languages. I bet I can speak better Latin than Greavsie though. Then before you know it dog you're teaching Latin to girls who think it's a complete waste of time. Do you know I told 'em that they still speak Latin in Latin America and they believed me hah hah! Tu credis hoc! Ohh but then when I met Louise, when I set eyes on my Lulu I knew my life would never be the same again.' Naked stared up at Oliver and whimpered, as he would do every time Louise's name was mentioned.

'That woman has turned my life upside down Naked. I never thought a man could love a woman as much as I do her. It's a wonderful, wonderful ache. I wouldn't have done such a terrible thing as I did tonight to Jeff unless I really, really had to. He's my best friend you know, my very best friend. God forgive me, wherever you are!'

In a short while Oliver took back his composure, wiped his cheeks, patted his dog and set off for home. It was now about 6am. Oliver looked up at Louise's flat and considered joining her for breakfast as he would on many occasions however weariness and remorse had now got the better of him as he pressed the lift button for the ninth floor. Placing his head on the pillow he reflected on what was unquestionably the most eventful and significant day of his life. At that very moment Louise placed herself on the bidet in Jeff's bathroom attempting to flush away her guilt.

✳✳✳✳✳

Louise arrived home from Chelsea mid-morning. She was surprisingly perky given the exertions of the previous night. Although much of her wanted to relax a while and perhaps have a short nap she was running on adrenalin, unable to contain herself. She telephoned Janey to inform her of the role she had likely landed and how excited she was at the prospect of finally appearing on the West End stage.

'A lifelong ambition was soon to come to fruition,' she yelped.

Louise discreetly chose not to explain to Janey what had to be sacrificed, fearing some sort of 'casting couch' jibe. Furthermore, Jeff and Janey's brief history as teenagers was always in the back of Louise's vigilant mind.

At lunchtime Louise called up to see Oliver who was still in bed. He eventually came to the door dishevelled and still bleary-eyed. Louise blustered through the door and went straight into the kitchen. Oliver fed the dog and shuffled off back to bed.

'I can't stay long Ollie darling. I'm expecting a call from an old agent friend of mine. I might just have a surprise for you later sexy,' she boasted.

By then he had drifted back asleep and had heard none of it. He was never one to sleep late but she was too future-focussed to notice or query this.

Around an hour or so later Oliver was woken by a relentless tap, tap, tapping noise quite unlike what he had ever heard before. He ignored it for a time then, when he could stand it no more stumbled out of bed to trace the sound's source. The answer came from the kitchen. Therein stood Louise wearing a skin-tight leotard, orange bandanna, black tights and bright silver and red tap shoes. She was whirling around the kitchen floor like a clockwork dervish.

'Is it April the first Lulu or are you off to the Notting Hill Carnival?' joked Oliver sleepily.

'No Oliver sweetie, it's August 24th and I'm off to The Shaftesbury Theatre soon!'

'Louise darlin, it's early. Can you just explain, I haven't got the energy to interrogate you?'

Louise continued to prance up and down Oliver's polished kitchen floor and embellished her 'agent friend' yarn. As always, Oliver had no reason to disbelieve her. Naked's eyes followed her every move and growled in an inaudible undertone. He never warmed to Louise anyway and furthermore, to extend her 'stage' she had shifted his bowl!

Oliver ate his Co-Co Pops and watched as Louise went through some of her dance steps and old routines.

'Will you count and help me keep time Oliver sweetie …1 and 2 and 3 and a 4 and 1 and 2 …'

'That's the second time you've called me 'sweetie' this morning err this afternoon. You're turning into a lovey' said Oliver.

'I've always been a lovey sweetie, always. It's just that as a teacher one's true vocation tends to be submerged. Tower Hamlets tends to do that to one. Now I feel lucky. In the next few weeks I'll have a part in a massive production and you my prince will be Head of Year!'

'Well I feel pretty confident now that I'll get the job but when will you know for sure about yours?' asked Oliver.

'That's the attitude I've always wanted you to have Ollie but how come you're so upbeat about your promotion all of a sudden?'

'Things change don't they?' he replied with hidden regret in his voice.

'Things are changing for me too. Things are changing for us Oliver, me and you …. us Oliver, us! Anyway toodle-pip must fly, expecting a call,'

Louise then pecked him on the both cheeks and flounced out of the door. Oliver thought it rather risqué for Louise to go down six floors dressed like a Tiller Girl but there was no stopping her, she'd gone out the door like a whirlwind, much to Naked's relief who then nosed his bowl back where it belonged.

Throughout that afternoon Louise paced and complained to her silent telephone. 'Bloody well ring will you, ring!'

Jeff had promised her he would clear the role with his dad and definitely call her around 3.30pm to confirm. Louise's mother and several friends had called but she made these quick 'hello/goodbye' calls. The line had to remain free. She was becoming all the time more agitated and angry.

'If only I had a cat to kick, if only!' she would mumble to herself but the phone sat there undisturbed and silent. Oliver phoned and asked if she wanted to come up and watch the BBC's new comedy, 'Monty Python's Flying Circus' that evening but she made her excuses and declined.

Louise had almost run out of all hope when at last the telephone rang. She did not want to appear too anxious and pick it up immediately so decided to let it ring a while. After a few long seconds she answered.

'Hello, Louise speaking.'

'Bonsoir Mademoiselle. I am wanting to speak with Mademoiselle Ellesmere, Mademoiselle Louise Ellesmere,' said the caller in a clearly discernible French accent.

'Elsmore, Yes that's me,'

'My name is Jacques, the owner of The Bijoux Plage Restaurant, I do believe you and a gentleman friend dined wiz us last night. Is zat so?'

'Yes, yes I was with a Mr Jeff Slater the son of Arnie Slater,' replied Louise expectantly.

'Yes, I'm sure. Did you realise Mademoiselle that you left your purse under the table? I took the liberty of looking inside and got your number. The contents are all intact. Perhaps you'd like to come and collect it sometime soon.'

Louise sat there deflated and still. In her blind anxiety she felt that Jacques and Arnie (the eternal practical joker) were somehow connected and that the Frenchman was the purveyor of her much-anticipated good news but she soon discovered that the caller was genuine.

'Yes, yes thank you, thanks. I need it so I'll er come and pick it up this evening.'

The time was now just after 9pm. Oliver was alone in his flat still reflecting on the previous night and morbidly considering his next move and the consequences thereof. Louise meanwhile still had received no word from Jeff. She found it almost impossible to reason that Jeff may have hoodwinked her so flagrantly and therefore concluded that there was some sort of unexpected hitch. Something like, Arnie having to unexpectedly have to pop over to Paris to sort out some of the dancers' costumes and hence Jeff not able to contact him easily. 'Yeah, that's it,' she said. 'Jeff'll phone tomorrow,' she murmured to herself ruefully.

Louise then decided to collect her purse from the restaurant and set off for the Tube. She came up at Charing Cross and walked down The Embankment alongside the Thames, again past Cleopatra's Needle and Boadicea. She paused for a moment or two and looked down at the ebbing water and reflected that only 24 hours previously she had sauntered this way arm in arm with Jeff. She then continued walking up to Westminster undaunted.

What now confronted Louise was to shock her to the core and change her attitude toward everything and everybody indefinitely! As she was about to enter the restaurant, she saw Jeff of all people sitting at the very same table as the previous night. Well at least she thought it looked like him. She quickly withdrew out of sight and reassessed. She put her head around to check. Although he had his back to her it certainly looked like Jeff. She looked again assuming the necessary angle whilst remaining in the shadows. It definitely was Jeff, without any doubt it was he but who was his companion? Louise peeped around again trying to do so inconspicuously. Horror of horrors, it was a woman! She was easily identified - Maggie Birkett the Tower Hamlets ex-pupil that Louise was forced to separate from her Oliver using vermin as a spoiler at the school's end of term party.

Louise was in a quandary as to what her next move should be. Should she casually approach him, should she confront him or should she tip up a few tables like her hero Nina Simone would when similarly affronted? Whilst there remained a slim chance that Jeff would come up trumps with Arnie, the Simone approach was dismissed. Louise now recognised however that she had probably given herself to a man that had no real interest in her stage ambitions and that rankled in the extreme!

Spotting a phone box Louise decided that she needed to discuss it with a friend before she did anything too hastily.

'Janey, it's me Lou. I'm outside the restaurant that me and Je ... er the man I was with last night went to,' Louise flustered.

'You're gonna end up a fat old cow you will. He's spending a lot of money on you. You sure you're not having to have to lie on your back. Nosh for dosh they call it you bleedin you old slapper, you!' replied Janey innocently with her usual amount of tact.

'Will you listen fa bloody once. He's with another woman and he never phoned me today about the stage job like he said. I've even told Oliver the job's mine and that I won't be teaching for much longer but dancing for a living. What the hell is happening here Janey!?'

'Excuse your French Miss La De Da. I've never heard you use such language,' said Janey.

'Can't you ever take anything seriously. Can't you?!' yelled Louise who was now about at boiling point.

'I am Lou. Ever thought of hiring a hitman? Better still, I know some people who could arrange a teeny-weeny accident! If that's too much then just fleece 'em and you-know-what 'em. If they're lookers then do what you need to do and then fleece 'em. It works for me!'

It was then that Louise became engulfed by a momentary calm, one of her clear thinking lucid moments. All her anger had suddenly dissipated and she began to smile inwardly to herself.

'Janey, I have business to attend to,' proclaimed Louise mischievously.

A TAIL OF TWO CITIES

'Go to it girl. Let me know how you get on. Gotta go now meself, my Sabre Tooth Angel from Stepney needs taming!'

Louise gently replaced the receiver and slowly began a transformation in which the telephone box was ideal cover. As she watched Jeff and Maggie eating and making chit-chat nearby, she took out from her bag Janey's dank blonde wig, which she had since the Ad-Lib debacle, tidied it and put it on. Then she made her face up differently, aided by the small mirror on the phone box side. Now with a pair of semi-tinted glasses the metamorphosis was complete. She emerged from the phone box like a super hero then strode across the pavement to the restaurant. An unsuspecting Jacques opened the door and greeted her warmly. The new 'Louise' confidently breezed in taking up position on a table adjacent to the enwrapped Jeff and Maggie, neither of whom cast even a cursory glance her way.

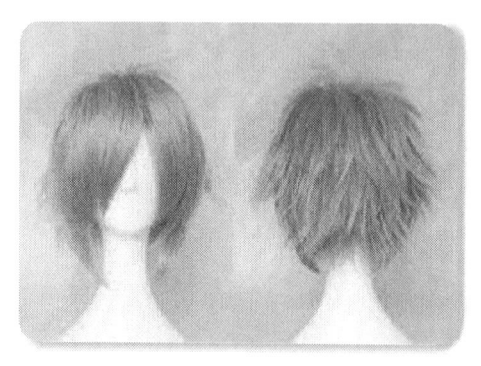

Whispering to Jacques that her 'companion' would be joining her soon, she ordered a Babycham and tuned into her neighbours' conversation. They were discussing mundane things such as their respective backgrounds, school days and alike. Maggie confessed she had always dreamed of becoming a model. Louise sighed! Then after a while Maggie described how finding two rats in her bag still gave her sleepless nights. Louise smiled! As their conversation became slightly stilted Jeff looked earnestly across the table.

'I wasn't going to reveal this to you Maggie but it's difficult to keep strong feelings in check when they insist on being set free. Tonight as I was preparing to come and meet you something inside compelled me to write this verse. Do you mind if I air it?'

'WORDSWORTH HAD HIS DAFFODILS

SHAKESPEARE, LADY ANN

LIFE WITHOUT TRUE LOVE MY DEAR

'TIS NO GOOD FOR ANY MAN –

AS THE SUMMER DAYS RECEDE

SOON LEAVES WILL TUMBLE FROM THE TREE

BUT WHO WILL KEEP ME WARM AT NIGHT?

IT'S YOU MY LOVE, MAGG-IE

Louise sat mortified and could hardly believe her ears. Her first reaction was to jump up and expose the deceiving cad but held back. Then Maggie took Jeff's hand and said.

'Jeffrey, no one's ever written anything like that for me before. I don't know what to say. It's really good how you poets get things to rhyme. You really are the most romantic man I've ever met. Does this mean that we're a couple now?'

'In my heart we were a couple the moment I set eyes on you that very first time er Maggie,' said Jeff, oh so sincerely.

Louise felt like vomiting on hearing such corny superficial scripted nonsense. It took an inordinate amount of effort on her part not to jump up and warn the poor misguided young woman what fate was about to befall her.

'Shall we take a stroll down the Embankment Maggie? I've got a Mews in Chelsea that I'd like to show you.' repeated Jeff.

Within minutes Jeff had paid the bill. Wooing complete, he and Maggie walked straight over to his car, there seemingly now no need this time for a starry-eyed promenade. -

Fundamentally Louise held some degree of admiration for Jeff. She could see they had much in common and appreciated that in affairs of the heart most people deserve each other! What she wasn't able to accept was that she was his victim and that she had slept with a man who had no intention of keeping his side of the bargain. Hello Dolly seemed more distant than ever. She'd cheated on Oliver, the man she loved and for what? She felt disgusted with herself. Something had to be done, someone had to pay, someone had to get their 'come-uppance'. From that day on Jeff Slater, the Classroom Casanova was a 'marked man'!

Louise then made her excuses and paid for her drink. She had to take off her wig and glasses before convincing Jacques that she and 'Mademoiselle Ellsiemore' were one of the same. Only then did he reluctantly hand over her purse. –

She needed to get things off her chest so rang Janey and told her she was on her way over!

※ ※ ※

Chapter 15

True love's a many splendid thing

That Louise needed a sounding board, a listening ear to vent her ire was in no doubt. That she should have chosen Janey to satisfy this function successfully may not have been the best choice. Normally Oliver would suffice but there could be no one on earth less appropriate than he in the circumstance Louise now found herself immersed in.

There was a calmness that settled over Louise on her journey. This quickly flip-flopped to rage then outrage, to serenity followed by more acute rage. She was however more measured when she finally arrived at Janey's dingy flat. As was so often the case the door was not answered by Janey herself but a man usually referred to as her 'brother'. This time was no exception however the man looked familiar. He wore a smart leather jacket, pristine white tea-shirt, neat stonewashed jeans and had his long light brown hair tied back in a ponytail.

'You're that posh chick from The Ad-Lib?' he enquired.

Louise immediately recognised him as the decoy biker she indirectly introduced to Janey as a distraction some weeks before.

'Does Janey know you know me?' whispered Louise menacingly in the hallway.

'I don't even know I know you so how am I going to tell her!' he replied.

'I'd like you to keep it that way. We don't want to confuse things. Do you understand?!'

'Gotcha gorgeous,' obliged the biker and led her into the living room.

Janey was sitting cross-legged on the sofa next to a huge teddy bear almost equal to her diminutive stature. The biker sat opposite. On the table stood an empty Party Seven beer can and two full to overflowing ashtrays. All around were strewn articles of clothing, shoes, crockery and various paraphernalia. The whole place seemed to be in some disarray even by Janey's shambolic standards.

'Janey what's gone wrong, the flat is a state. You OK?'

'The place is fine and so am I!' she replied.

It was clear that she had drunk at least five of the Party Seven!

Louise then heard the toilet flush and moments later out from the bathroom came a tall man, made taller by his large cream coloured Stetson. Being now partly prepared, Louise recognised him immediately as the cowboy from The Ad-Lib. It was obvious and much to Louise's relief that he did not remember her either.

'These are my two friends Louise. The ones I met that night up West. After a rocky start we're now all the best o' mates. Here we have Strange John my Hell's Angel mate from Stepney and Mr Clint, the cowboy DJ from New York City in Texas.'

Both voiced a few warm words of welcome. It was clear they were on their best behaviour trying to outdo the other in politeness.

'I was hoping we could have a little chat Janey. I've had quite a night,' said Louise.

'Go on then, chat away sweetheart. I'm 'ere just for you Lou,' Janey replied.

'In private Janey. Just you and me.'

Janey suggested they go into the bedroom. She then ordered the two enraptured men to 'get this bleedin place tidied up and quick whilst us girls put the world to rights.'

They unhesitatingly obliged.

Janey's bedroom was no more organised than the room they had just left. Louise further digested the scene but saw no point in commenting again rather she simply made a small space on the bed and plonked herself thereupon. Janey decided that this was pointless and sat on a pile of clothes that acted as a pillow. She then rested backward on the headboard and asked Louise what had caused her to be so unusually flustered. In no time at all, before she could even begin to summon up even the merest account of recent happenings Louise descended into a torrent of tears. This was a most serious matter, Janey concluded and immediately went into enforced sobriety.

'Do you want me to start crying too? It'll show we're really good buddies, like we're in a sisterhood.' Janey enquired thoughtfully.

Louise gave her a quizzical look and didn't answer but proceeded to give a full account of how last night she was wined, dined and duped. The story amazed her comforter who in some way took solace at not being the only woman to have been deceived so. Louise was, for obvious reasons, careful to refer to Jeff as simply 'this man' and then 'the lying bastard'. Janey too was becoming increasingly outraged as Louise's calamity further unfolded, more particularly regarding the rehashed and recited 'poem'.

'I can't tell you how sick I was that this man, the lying bastard read the same shitty verse to her as he did me not 24 hours before,' moaned Louise.

'Well Louise, of all the bastards in all the bastard world you met up with King Bastard, the bastard daddy of them all. Not only that, 'Louise' rhymes with 'trees', but it don't really with 'Maggie'. I wonder if he'll take me out for some French nosh tomorrow cos my middle name's Denise!' joked Janey.

'I don't think you'd appreciate that Janey,' said Louise knowingly.

'I'm sure you're right darlin,'

'I won't be taking this lying down though Janey,' shouted Louise determinedly.

'Too late for that sweetie,' came the obvious reply.

'The lying bastard will bloody well pay for treating me like some stupid cow. I really wanted that part in that show. I'm not cut out to be a teacher for ever more, I need to dance, I need or act, be creative!' bawled Louise working herself back up to a crescendo. 'I've been working on some of my old routines for no reason, no bloody reason. He'll pay he will. He'll pay!'

Janey made several attempts to reason with her friend, advising her once more to leave things be and move on, citing examples when she herself had done the same after being humiliated by men who similarly promised her the earth so they could get 'a leg-over.'

Louise vowed not to be so accepting stating that only some form of settling of scores would enable her to move on.

Soon after Louise had exhausted her tears and anger, the bedroom door knocked. It was the cowboy wearing a pinafore. He was enquiring if he should now wash the dishes?

'Please your bleedin self,' came Janey's disdainful reply.

'I'll take that as a 'yes' Janey,' replied the Texan and scuttled off to the kitchen.

Louise was suitably amazed at what she had just witnessed commenting that Oliver had to be forced or even threatened before he takes up any form of domesticity.

'Oh my hunky cowboy really likes being told what to do. In fact, he gets off on it. Moans and groans if I'm not ordering him about would ya believe. I always keep the flat shitty to give him something to do.

He'll be doing the bedroom next. The biker's the bleedin same. You might look at him and think he's Mr Tough Guy but he's really more like Mrs Mop than Steed. What's more they don't expect anything physical from me. They're mostly more interested in …. each other than me, so that's real groovy. The only rule I've got is they don't do anything to each other while I'm about. Turns me bleedin stomach all that palaver does!'

Louise tried to encourage Janey to think more openly about such things.

'Perhaps we should all be a bit more liberal and understanding. I reckon the 1960s will go down as the decade of enlightenment, you'll see,' proclaimed Louise.

Such hypothesising was really too much for Janey preferring to focus more on the here and now.

'I understands what I understands that's all! Do you know Lou if you and me hadn't gone to The Ad-Lib that night I would never have bumped into my two little poofy char ladies. It turned out to be a real good night for me that did. Funny how things work out, ain't it!"

※※※※※

It was a couple of hours later that Louise returned home. She was cheered and encouraged by Janey's superficial approach to even the most important matters but it wasn't in Louise's nature to simply 'forgive and forget'. It wasn't normally in Janey's either, such was her contrary character. Louise was still mostly dejected and deflated by the whole experience with Jeff and what might have been if he was as sincere as he led her to believe. The more she pondered and tossed it around in her head the more she felt the uncontrolled resentment welling once again. Standing in the lobby she got into the lift and started to consider where to next? Her right index finger shifting between the 9th and 3rd floor buttons. Eventually it fell on the 9th.

Oliver was in bed and drifting when she rang his buzzer. He soon awoke and answered the door. Like most people that get a call at a time they least expect Oliver thought this could be only bad news.

'No one calls at 2 in the morning to tell me I've won the pools,' he mumbled to himself as he shuffled to the door. He was correct, it was bad news. Instantly Oliver got the sense of the occasion from Louise's grim expression and without a word being traded opened his arms into which she gladly enveloped. Louise wept. Oliver held her closer for a few seconds, led her into the living room and asked her what had happened. Even in her high emotional state she was careful not to let anything too inflammatory slip, therefore took effortlessly into invention.

'I just needed some company,' she said. 'Was sitting in my flat feeling a bit down for no good reason. Then I popped over to see my mum in Soho for a while and that just made me feel worse. She always thinks I'm up to no good. Now I simply want to be with you Ollie!'

Spouting spontaneous untruths effortlessly and with great conviction came easy.

It's rare that Oliver had to take the role of Louise's emotional prop so he gladly and willingly accepted his part of comforter and support. He had read, perhaps in Vogue or Cosmo that in a

situation like this, the man must never ever ask if it's her 'time of the month' even if his experience of her 'moods' demonstrated that there is likely to be no other cogent explanation. He also recalled that the woman simply wants a shoulder to cry on and not someone to rationalise and problem-solve, something that he and most men find difficult to resist. Consequently, Oliver reverted to banal platitudes as well as vague and unchallenging questioning like 'so how did that make you feel?' and 'what will you do next?'

'Life can be tough sometimes for a woman Oliver. Just keeping going day in, day out can be a real struggle. I'm constantly swimming against the tide. It makes you wonder what it's all about?' she bemoaned.

'The Hokey Cokey, Louise,' he replied cryptically.

'The Hokey Cokey?'

'Yeah. That's what it's all about,' said Oliver trying hard to remain straight-faced.

The gag seemed to do the trick and when the penny dropped Louise gave way to a brief chuckle.

'Stay tonight Lulu? Stay here close to me, will you? You don't have to go to your flat. I need you too don't forget,' sighed Oliver wistfully.

Within a minute, Oliver drew the thick orange curtains, stripped off and beckoned Louise into his warm welcoming bed.

A TAIL OF TWO CITIES

Mostly at Oliver's instigation, he and Louise had agreed earlier on in their relationship that they would not sleep together often.

'This would keep their love fresh,' Oliver would assert. Surprisingly, given recent events, this suited Louise too as she came from a moralistic background where marriage and stability were of greater import than the permissiveness that was the pervading wind of the laissez faire '60s. Enjoying their tingling bodies therefore was a rare treat. They both resolved that on these infrequent occasions they were going to indulge themselves and each other fully and not discuss mundane matters such as the weather or cricket as many staid couples who behold no further mystery of one another tend. They would speak only of themselves as a couple held together by 'an invisible bond of loveliness.'

That night their bodies lay primed only for the pleasing of the other. They needed the closeness. They needed most of all to let go. Oliver kissed Louise's lips affectionately then more forcefully as he ran his fingers through her copious black tresses. She was wanton and prepared to be submissive. He slowly then teasingly nuzzled and kissed her again, lingering when he felt he must. He became more inflamed and driven by her stirring! She too was consumed by the feel of his compact torso, firm limbs and solid manliness.

Slowly, slowly they were beset by a warmth and tranquillity which gradually ebbed and radiated over and through them. Louise's angst and tensions had instantaneously softened. The lovers had never enjoyed the experience to the extent they did that night. They were bound together, one with the other physically and intimately. Both held their secrets tight to themselves as they did their lover and as they tried to sleep a menacing sense of foreboding prevailed.

ಞಞಞ

Chapter 16

Peace in our times?

Over the next 48 hours Oliver considered the most apposite time to contact the police and enact the last part of his 'dastardly deed'. The drugs were in place behind Jeff's cooker, so the hard bit was complete, now it just needed the finishing touches. He had arranged to meet Sprig on Thursday near her cat sanctuary in Battersea to finalise matters. She was keen to show him around and demonstrate that her ill-gotten gains of which he was to contribute was altruistically put to good use.

Sprig arrived for their appointment first and was happily rocking to and fro on a swing in the children's section of Battersea Park when Oliver approached. They welcomed each other affectionately and Oliver sat on the swing next to her. The weather was bright and sunny for the moment but with rain threatening. As they exchanged more pleasantries and discussed mundane things, Sprig sensed Oliver was uneasy. They then walked past the boating lake and funfair and onto her building project. She unlocked the heavy steel doors and commenced a detailed guided tour. She was clearly proud of what she had achieved to date.

'Well Oliver, this is what all my endeavours over the last two years or more were for. Soon, London cats will have their answer to Battersea Dog's Home. A sanctuary for every abandoned moggy. A comforting refuge for all forgotten felines. In a couple of months they'll be a grand opening. Through a cat loving celeb agent friend of mine I've managed to get a few big stars to come to the opening party. They've also donated wads of cash too. I've sent invitations out to Diana Rigg, Sid James, Mick MacManus, Keith Richards, Gerry Anderson and maybe even Roger Moore, 'The Saint' himself and guest of honour, the simply gorgeous Mary O'Brien.

Of course you'll be coming too won't you? You can even bring your lady Louise, we've not had the pleasure have we?'

announced Sprig joyously and perhaps somewhat optimistically.

'Thanks Sprig, I'll be here but I somehow think Louise won't be able to make it. She's so taken up by her tap dancing and all that at the moment I can't drag her away from my kitchen floor. I've just left her there this morning working herself up into a sweat frenzy. Even thought the job she wanted seems to have fallen through she's still hopeful something'll turn up somewhere else. Don't worry though I'll be here. I wouldn't miss it. I know how much this all means to you. I have to ask though; who's Mary O'Brien?'

'You'll just have to turn up and see!' she replied with a glint in her eye.

With that he then reached into his jacket pocket, pulled out an envelope and smiled ruefully as he handed it to Sprig. The envelope was stuffed with £10 and £20 notes.

'There you go Sprig my 30 pieces of silver as agreed!'

'Ah yes I see, a Biblical reference. Remember Ollie blood money is as good as any according to the gospel of the bank.'

Sprig gleefully counted and recounted the cash.

'This is a bit more than we agreed Oliver.'

'Yes, the rest is for your efforts the other night. You were risking an awful lot for me with not that much in return. Burglary is a very serious crime and you could have got some very serious time if we'd been caught. We very nearly were, remember? You did it mostly for me, my school promotion and Louise. Anyway, I quite like cats so what's an extra twenty quid.'

'I'm shocked Oliver but you can't call it a burglary if we took nothing, in fact we put something there that wasn't. Made a sort of contribution,' joked Sprig ironically. 'But I'm really bleedin bowled over. This money will make up for the shortfall. What this means is that I'm now on the straight and narrow. No more dealing in pills. No more mixing with London low-lives. The new Sprig is born! This place is where I'll be spending my time from now on. No bleedin where else,' she announced flamboyantly.

Sprig was becoming emotional. The harshness of character and the tough bravado that Oliver had known was dissipating. He warmed to his born-again friend and congratulated her on her revision.

'It's now time for me to make a significant announcement,' said Oliver.

Sprig listened attentively.

'First I need to tell you that I'm not, repeat not going ahead with it. I've thought long and hard and I am not, definitely not going to frame Jeff. I also think you need an explanation as to why I've changed my mind.'

Sprig listened even more intently.

'A couple of nights ago Louise stayed the whole night at my place, something that doesn't happen often. The feelings we had that night were more special and passionate than I can ever remember.

If I was to go ahead with it, I could never live with myself. I'd have to keep the biggest secret I have away from the woman I love. It would destroy me. Slowly but surely it would totally destroy us too. More important than that Sprig, Jeff is my best friend in the whole world. We've always stood by each other. As kids we rode on the back of milk floats together, we've fought for each other and fought against each other but we've always stayed friends. Framing him and effectively ruining his life was way, way, way out of proportion. No Head of Year job is worth that. He'll get the promotion and get the move to the all-boys' school that I know he's always wanted. They'll be other jobs for me. Lulu will understand, I know she will.'

After Oliver had finished explaining his change of tact there was a short lull in which neither spoke but continued to walk through the near empty echoing building. Oliver was trying to gauge Sprig's response. It eventually came:

'You're a good man at heart aren't you? To go through all you've done recently, to put so much at risk and then to give me, what must be all your savings shows the sort of man you are. I don't know Jeff but he's got a good best mate in you and Louise could never find a man with the courage you have. It's much harder to be a good decent man than a complete tosser. That's why there's so few Olivers around. You've made the right choice.'

'To be honest with you Sprig I couldn't get a bank loan so I had to lend the money I've just given you from….. a colleague'

'Don't tell me….

'Uh ha.'

✶✶✶✶✶

The following week Louise too found that she had choices to make.

A TAIL OF TWO CITIES

'One and two and kick and four and. One and two and kick-kick four and … What do you think Naked? Do you think I've got what it takes to be a star, do you?' panted Louise to the dog.

Oliver's kitchen floor was more sizeable and echoey, a better choice than her own. After an intense 30-minute work-out she fell to the floor breathless and sweaty. She was working on a routine that she was choreographing herself, something she could perform if called to any audition. She was now determined somehow to turn Jeff making a fool of her into a positive and use it act as a springboard and incentive for her to 'reach for the stars'.

It was a Saturday and Oliver had decided to go for his usual weekend swim at Vicky Park Lido. Louise was keen to impress him when he came home and worked all the more feverishly as his return became more imminent. Whilst recovering on the kitchen floor her eyes fixed upon a book tucked under Oliver's fridge. It was a small volume the like of which she had not seen before. She was curious and carefully slid it out. The book looked important, leather bound with a small strap with lock and key. The key remained enticingly in situ. On the cover in large gold embossed lettering read 'Diary 1969'. For Louise there was no dilemma as to whether it was ethical to read her man's private recordings so she opened it immediately and thumbed through the pages as Naked sat and observed.

Louise was pleased by much of what she read initially as it confirmed the deep-felt affection Oliver had for her. Eventually, as she flicked through to the more contemporary entries her expression altered radically - She then read how Oliver had met a woman, a 'Madam Sprigola, some sort of pseudo mystic weirdo in Soho' and even how they were to meet again at the Bag O'Nails some days later. She also discovered that he was with this woman whilst apparently worrying that Louise had not arrived at the Bag! Louise still seething by recent memories of how she had been deceived by Jeff had now discovered it was happening again. This time the deceiver was her Oliver! – She was then immeasurably staggered as she read how Oliver planned to frame Jeff and the trouble that he and his accomplice had gone to in planting the drugs in Jeff's home and the plan to contact the police thereafter.

'Bloody hell……. I never thought you had it in you Ollie, you dark horse you, and all for the Head of Year promotion and little old me,' said Louise to herself.

In the next entry Louise discovered that Oliver had met Sprig in Battersea only two days before, gave her a wad of money and decided that 'Jeff was too good a friend to hurt so irreparably,' and that the plan to set him up had now been 'totally abandoned.'

Louise was by now utterly bewildered by these revelations and read them repeatedly until she truly made sense of it and appreciated the gravity of it all. She was further amazed at how Oliver managed to carry the huge burden of his actions without her ever having the slightest suspicion that there was anything at all amiss.

'I thought that I could read Oliver like a book, but it took his diary to find what really makes your master tick,' said Louise to Naked, shaking her head in disbelief.

She then placed the diary just where she found it and tried to continue with her dancing. Within a few short minutes however she had given up, such was the impact of what she had just inadvertently learnt. Oliver arrived soon after refreshed and ravenous as he always was after a bracing outdoor swim.

'Fancy some fish and chips Lou?' he asked.

She barely gave him a reply but made her excuses and took her leave. Now was not the time for her to show him the new steps that she had worked so hard to put together. Louise gazed out the window of her flat perplexed. Was it Oliver's secret liaison with another woman, his loyalty to Jeff, the burglary or that he simply chose to exclude her from his scheming? That evening Louise was as unsettled as she had been for a while and there had been many restless times more recently than at any other time she could ever recall. She felt confused, uncertain and more insecure than usual not able to rationalise how and why the diary's revelations affected her so but sitting around and doing nothing simply exacerbated matters. The more she sat alone and mulled over events the more she became incensed, first with Oliver and then Jeff who still remained the focus of her ire.

As was becoming more the norm these fretful days, Louise telephoned Janey to sound off and vent her fury and disbelief. The call lasted a full hour. Therein Louise explained to her friend in substantial detail, (with the necessary subterfuge) the conniving she had discovered in Oliver's diary. Janey was taken aback too by the account despite apparently not knowing the main players.

'Well if you ask me Louise these people who deal in drugs need to be swung from the highest tree no matter how La De Daa they are. I like the odd cocktail or two but I know where to draw the line.

What's the world coming to, where will it all end? It's all coming over here from America I reckon. Following the Yanks we are. We're all like them little hamsters that fling themselves off a cliff. You can't go into a nightclub these days without one of these bleeders giving you grief. Offer you all sorts of stuff they do.'

And so the litany went on, with both the women condemning and high-mindedly debating the drugs menace and how evil men can be.

From nowhere and within a second Louise had one of her now regular moments of focussed lucidity!

※※※※※

The following day - 9.04 am Monday 29 August 1969 -

Caller : Is that the police at Leman Street.

Police : Yes madam, how can I help you?

Caller : I need to talk to you about something of great importance.

Police : Of course, your name please.

Caller: My name is Mrs Anonymous.

Police: Oh, I see. Anyway, go ahead.

Caller : It has come to my notice that Tower Hamlets Girls School on the Commercial Road in the East End is awash with all forms of evil drugs, pills and Pot. You'll know that too of course.

Police: Yes Madam alas it's happening everywhere in the capital. Sign of the times I'm afraid.

Caller : What are the police doing to stop this poison getting out of hand?

Police : As much as is possible but we need as much help from the public as we can get ......

Caller : ..... Precisely. I do hope that I can therefore be of assistance to you. I have proper good information that the drugs are coming into the school by way of one of the teachers can you believe!

Police : This is a very serious allegation. You are aware of that madam?

Caller : Oh yes officer, I'm very aware of the consequences for the teacher in question but what if we all sat back and did nothing. Where would we be then?

Police : Exactly.

Caller : You'll appreciate that I have to remain anonymous but I can assure you that the information I have is kosher. The teacher's name is Mr Jeffrey Slater of 1 Alexandra Drive, Chelsea. Although I can't be sure of his actual supplier I know he keeps a substantial amount of narcotics in his kitchen, possibly behind his cooker. Have you taken note of that? Can I trust you will act appropriately and get your bloody finger out officer?

Police : Of course Madam. That goes without saying. That's just the sort of information we need to keep this evil trade away from our kiddies. Hmm Jeffrey Slater, 1 Alexandra Drive, Chelsea.

Caller: That's correct officer. Well I shan't delay you any further. Get it sorted young man!

Police: Of-course madam. Thank you for the info. London needs more of your type. I will inform the bobbies from the Drug Squad at Paddington Green right away. Thank you once again.

Caller: 'tis simply my civic duty officer. Some people are just not what they appear to be and he may be a teacher but he still needs to be taught a good hard lesson exploiting people, taking advantage of them all for his own gratification. Justice needs to be done!

Chapter 17

31st August 1969

The last day of August was a real scorcher. Typically, Londoners went about their business bemoaning their circumstance with unconscious masochistic longing for a return to familiar damp and foggy days. Oliver was more practical, using the greater part of the sultry afternoons for a siesta. The school year was to start next week and he had energy to conserve. As he lay dosing on the sofa, Louise was in the kitchen kicking, twisting and stretching, honing herself for another tap-dancing marathon. There was the usual telephone standoff when it rang as neither was prepared to stop what they were doing and attend to it. Eventually Oliver conceded.

'Hello Oliver speaking.' - It was Jeff.

'Ollie listen to me I can't talk too long but I'm in big, big bloody trouble. I need your help man like never before. You wouldn't believe what's happened. It's like a bad nightmare. I've been well and truly dropped in it!'

Oliver sat and listened as Jeff told him that seven police officers had forced their way into his house in the early hours, searched everywhere and eventually found a haul of drugs behind his cooker. He was then arrested and was about to be thrown into a cell at Paddington Green.

'Ollie, you gotta bloody believe me I don't know anything about drugs. You know how I feel about that sort of thing, don't you? I keep telling them the drugs have got nothing to do with me but they won't have it. They say I'm responsible for the drugs getting to our girls at Hamlets. They're gonna throw the bloody book at me!'

Oliver remained rooted and speechless unable to console or advise his bereft friend. Louise knew from his reaction that, whatever it was, the call was of a most serious nature. Just when Oliver believed that he could be stunned no further, Jeff continued:

'Ollie, I hope you're listening to me. The police have just asked me if I know someone called Karen bloody Sprigson, they call her Sprig or something. They found a torch or something tucked away next to the cooker and when they examined it they had the palm print of this woman. They reckon she's my bloody accomplice cos she's got drug convictions as long as your bloody arm. They won't believe anything I say. I keep telling them I've never heard of this Sprigson woman. You've gotta do something and help me mate. You've gotta!'

Jeff then broke down. Oliver somehow summoned up a little composure.

'Jeff, Jeff tell me. Tell me how can I help you? I can ... just let me know,' he stuttered.

'I couldn't get hold of my dad, he's over in Paris casting for the show so you're gonna have to get hold of him there asap. What I want you to do first is get the best solicitor you can find and get him here today. Did you hear me Ollie, today! Come and see me mate. They're taking me to The Scrubs tomorrow. Look, they're telling me I gotta go now Ollie. Please help me mate!'

The phone brrred then went dead .....

Oliver dropped the receiver on his lap and sat open-mouthed and motionless. Then he slumped back on the sofa and clasped his head. He was so numb as to not be able to demonstrate any form of emotion; the news was simply too ghastly to process. Gradually the reality of what he had done or, more aptly what he hadn't done, began to sink in until it soon overwhelmed him. He curled up into a ball and wished the world away.

'Oliver, Oliver what's happened tell me what's happened? Who was on the phone?' insisted Louise as she wrestled the silent receiver from him. 'Is it Jeff? Has something happened to Jeff? What's it all about and please don't say the Hokey Cokey!'

In an instant Oliver then jumped to his feet, collected his thoughts and hurriedly put his shoes on.

'Well yes there's a problem. A big bloody problem. Think of the biggest problem you could ever imagine then times it by a million, even then it still wouldn't be big enough. I need to get my head together I'll tell you all about it when I get back ... Come on Naked ... Walkies,'

With that, Oliver and his faithful dog shot through the door.

Naked found it difficult to keep pace with Oliver who was so intent on reaching ground level in the shortest possible time that he bypassed the lift and rushed down dozens of flights of stairs. Out of breath, the man and his dog pelted across a busy street to a nearby phone box. Oliver spun out the numbers on the dial quickly and impatiently jumped up and down on the spot as the phone rang ... and rang.

'Come on Sprig, pick up the phone Sprig. Pick it up will ya!' She didn't. He realised that Sprig was in as much trouble as Jeff. In his mind he ran through events the night of the break-in searching for clues that never came. He did however recall that her fancy red and green suede gloves covered the fingers but exposed the palms. His 'best mate' Jeff and his 'accomplice' Sprig were facing a long stretch. The nightmare for Oliver and his two friends had begun but some obvious questions needed to be answered!

Louise was waiting with a hot sweet cup of tea when Oliver and Naked returned. She guided him to the sofa, tugged his shoes off and cuddled him.

'It's bad news isn't it Ollie? Tell me what's going on,' she asked stroking his hair comfortingly.

Without giving away his role in recent happenings Oliver explained that Jeff had been arrested, having been caught in possession of a large hoard of narcotics and that he was on his way to Wormwood Scrubs. Louise sat poker-faced.

'Well is there any truth in it do you think? Could he possibly be a dealer?' she asked cautiously.

'Oh what do you mean woman! What do you think? You know Jeff, he's not like that. Stuff can get into school any way. It doesn't have to be a teacher!'

'My mother often says that there are many people these days leading double lives and that when the truth comes out everyone's flabbergasted,'

Louise could see that this was the last thing Oliver wanted to hear and backtracked a little. 'You know him better than anyone else so I can understand how shocked you must be. What can we do to help poor Jeff?'

Louise and Oliver between them discussed and agreed a strategy of action: Today he was to find the best solicitor around to represent Jeff and tomorrow visit him in The Scrubs. Meanwhile she was to track down Jeff's dad Arnie in Paris and give him the distressing news. Oliver then flicked through the Yellow Pages and after numerous telephone calls arranged to meet a Miss Felicity Challinor that day's duty solicitor. Within an hour Oliver was pacing up and down in the legal firm's plush Holborn offices. By the time she'd finally called him in he had past frantic and was now sweaty and nervous. He painstakingly went through with her Jeff's sad plight again mentally divorcing himself entirely from his significant part in Jeff's arrest.

'Mr Cherry, Oliver it's imperative that we work promptly. We need to pull things together immediately. I don't need to tell you how serious this matter is for your friend and colleague Mr Slater,' said the legal expert. 'If you are as certain as you are of his innocence, is there anything, absolutely anything, even of the smallest detail that you can tell me now that will assist him. In narcotics cases like this, quite often it's the evidence gathered in the first couple of days after the arrest that decide how many years' imprisonment the Crown Court will deal out, if the Defendant is found guilty of course.'

This would prove to be a pivotal moment in Oliver's life. In the few fleeting seconds before a response was required he had to decide whether to come clean and be totally self-sacrificing for the sake of his friend or continue to be massively selective.

'Er well I can't think of anything', he replied quickly deciding on the latter. 'All I know is that Jeff is totally innocent. I know him better than anyone and drugs are something he would always avoid,'

Oliver's courage had clearly failed him.

'Is there anyone who you can think of who might hold a grudge against him, someone looking for some sort of reprisal, someone wanting to get him out of the way? Anyone jealous or resentful of him - a friend, a disgruntled lover, a colleague?' enquired the solicitor persistently.

Oliver was here given another opportunity to divest himself of the vital evidence he held but declined to take it having now betrayed his friend thrice!

Miss Challinor ended the short interview abruptly and prepared to journey to Paddington Green police station to meet her new client.

'With the quantity of narcotics involved we could be talking about a number of years if convicted. I'll need you to give evidence when this eventually gets to Court. He will need you and as many of his workmates at Tower Hamlets School you can muster to act as character witnesses. These drug cases seem to get to a final hearing within weeks. See what you can do there Mr Cherry when you return to school next week. I'll be in touch presently.'

Oliver heard little of what she had said after the word 'years' but

Miss Challinor's demeanour, prompt response, precision and experience reassured him. He had done all he could to secure Jeff competent representation. That out of the way, he needed to somehow do something positive for Sprig whilst at the same time trying to find the answer as to how the police got information known only to himself and Sprig. The following day he went to the Madam Sprigola's Soho palm reading place to delve around a little. This proved fruitless as it was now converted to an upmarket delicatessen. With that same objective Oliver went to the venue he first met Sprig. -

The Bag O'Nails had its usual busy cosmopolitan buzz about it. A rock band was playing live and there was clear evidence that some of the patrons were too 'spaced-out' for it to be natural. Cautiously Oliver approached a group of such characters and listened into their conversations in the slight hope that Sprig's name might be mentioned. Although much of what he could pick up on was mere chitchat and banter one individual did mention Sprig by name. This thin, dark haired woman was well spoken, confident and in her late 30's. She was dressed in a similar casual way to Sprig and smoked a cigarette from a long red and green holder. It was her towering height, at least 6' 2" however that turned heads. When the opportunity arose Oliver approached and asked if he could have a private word. She agreed but firmly refused his offer of a drink!

Oliver found it difficult to find the correct form of words so stumbled around hoping that she herself would present him with a practical opening.

'Now let's not beat about the bush,' said the woman. 'You want some sort of private word with me do you? Now get to the point little man!'

'I'm Oliver and you are ….?' he ventured, carefully sidestepping the slur and warmly extending his right hand.

'Oliver, Oliver. So, you're Oliver are you!' she sneered.

At that she gave him a troubled glance and disappeared into the crowd.

Oliver found this response as alarming as it was unexpected. A stranger knew him by name! Clearly there was a need to be extra cautious as a new pensive vibe about the place made him uncomfortable and hesitant. He did make a few more cursory enquiries about Sprig but he sensed being stonewalled. Futile to continue he finished his beer and left for the Tube. He was oblivious as to what now was about to befall him!

Just before reaching the subway leading down to the ticket office Oliver was hit from the rear by what felt to him like a hefty gust of wind which, within a second became a hurricane. Such was its force and surprise that it unsteadied him before knocking him off his feet. He then found himself on the cold pavement ringed by several hooded figures one of whom was responsible for putting him there by expertly kicking him swiftly in his calves. Oliver naturally made himself small. He was being attacked and he knew it. Kicks landed from every possible angle crashing into his chest, arms, back and legs. One shuddering blow after another. The assailants stepped

A TAIL OF TWO CITIES

up their brutality and began to trample on his weakening wincing frame. Maybe as many as a dozen feet were near simultaneously coming down and into him with constant viciousness. It was more than he could take. Momentarily, as the pain became too awful he felt like giving up but as quickly as his assailants came, they went, silently melting away into the dark Soho alleys. Oliver groaned. He lay there bloodied and alone. He was hurt, quiet badly hurt!

'I saw everything from my bedroom window. I saw the lot from start to finish young man,' came a voice.

He remained curled into a ball and was in no fit state or minded to look up and put a face to the voice. He lay there for a short while as the Samaritan stroked his head tenderly.

'An ambulance will be here soon. It's best to stay as you are. You might have broken something.'

Eventually Oliver felt safe enough to slowly unravel his bruised body. His helper was a small greying woman in her 60s. She had a calm reassuring manner.

'Thanks lady,' Oliver groaned. 'Are you sure that they're not coming back for more?'

'You can call me Mrs Spencer but thanks for addressing me as a lady. Yes, I'm quite sure they won't be back. Try not to move too much. With such a commotion its almost certain the authorities have been notified. When they get information from an onlooker they usually arrive soon after,' she reassured. 'I've never seen five such nasty women before.'

By this time Oliver was beginning to spit blood. She handed him some tissues and cradled his head.

'Women? Five women?' he spluttered on a caught breath.

'Yes, at least and none of them touched your head did you notice? Anyway I can see there's an officer on foot approaching and I can hear the sirens so the police are heading this way.' she replied.

'Look, I don't want to see anyone. I've gotta go. Help me to my feet lady will you please!'

The pensioner gave Oliver a long look. 'You're quite shaken but you will certainly recover well from this dear,' replied the woman with surety. 'If able you must get up and go right away. Here, I'll help you but you must assure me you will see a doctor at the earliest opportunity. That must be your first promise!'

Oliver agreed and the kindly lady assisted as required and bade him well. He then stumbled along a side street and out of sight.

'Where did he go to madam?' a breathless policeman asked the lady.

'That's your job not mine! I'm a simple member of the public,' the benefactor knowingly replied. -

Oliver somehow found his way home. He took off his shirt and inspected the damage. His strong but battered torso was now the colour of fallen leaves and a mass of emerging deep bruises. The cuts and small lacerations were particularly painful. His legs had taken a pounding too but it was his breathing that caused him most concern. Thankfully his face was untouched. In keeping with the pledge given to the helpful Mrs Spencer he phoned for the night doctor who arrived soon thereafter and patched him up, recommending he attend Casualty when able. Despite the pain as soon as his head hit the pillow he was gone.

The last day of August 1969 was a real scorcher in so many ways. For Oliver Cherry his sweet trouble free past existence had slipped away into the night as he sensed that as autumn approached more troubled times lay ahead.

ঌঌঌ

Chapter 18

'I need to speak to Mrs Spencer'

Naked's morning routine told him that Oliver was sleeping in far too late so pounding around on his owner's bed and generally making a nuisance of himself was required. Quite the wrong thing to do to a man so battered and tender following last night's exertions. It was the first day of September, the beginning of the month, the chance to meet and defeat new challenges Oliver would often imagine. The pseudo-persona of a Greek god or an Egyptian Pharaoh wasn't going to lift his mood even the Beatles' Lyric Game failed to enthuse. These times were different and resolutely embedded in reality.

'Ahhh … get down Naked. Yeah it's a bit late for walkies. I'm gonna have to rest up for a while. Louise will see to you. Battered within an inch of my life last night boy.'

Oliver tentatively eased himself out of bed and stumbled to the bathroom then to the kitchen where a small bowl of Sugar Puffs was just about all he could manage.

Back in the bedroom he inspected the damage in the wardrobe mirror. His trunk remained a pulsing mess of swellings, small cuts and an oozing slit on his side seemed like he'd been speared. His legs and upper arms were equally distressed as if he'd been the plaything of some fiendish medieval tormenter and felt so too.

'Had seven bells knocked out of me by half a dozen loony bloody women. Can you believe that Naked! They didn't take my money though. Ooooch, they must have done it just for kicks, if you'd excuse the pun. Gotta go and see Jeff later so be good for Lou, she's going through a lot too.'

Naked was Oliver's other great companion and an invaluable ray of sunshine. His dog would also provide a pair of sympathetic canine listening ears, albeit twitching.

'How did it ever come to this? Only me and Sprig knew of the stash we planted and then the next thing you know Jeff's been busted and it seems they've got Sprig too. It just doesn't add up boy!'

Louise dutifully arrived later that morning. Given his shocking news yesterday she tentatively gauged Oliver's mood. Never one to miss an opportunity she brought down her tap shoes so she could give it a blast in the kitchen when he was away on his prison visit. He, in turn did what he could to cover up and disguise the pain he was enduring and blamed his unusual gait on an old football injury that had flared. -

The visiting area at Wormwood Scrubs was very much as expected with the grey and black colour scheme suitably reflecting the disposition of angry inmates and despotic officers alike. It had the same effect too on Oliver and no doubt all visitors to this gruesome Hammersmith institution. Oliver knew he had to be strong for Jeff and carry on the pretence whilst at the same time holding back from grimacing as lightening speed shocks of agony zipped through his body reminding him of the night before.

Oliver's heart sunk as Jeff was lead in and sat opposite on the screwed down canvas tube chair. Jeff's healthy honey brown skin was sallow. His bouncy jovial character was now submerged under a confused pessimism. Was this really the Classroom Casanova, the man with a quip for every occasion, Cockroach's scourge? Oliver had never seen him less vital.

'This place is like hell on earth. At least the Birdman of Alcatraz had something to occupy himself with. All I do here is read the bloody walls. One-minute life's bobbing along as ever with a signed and sealed job promotion and all the birds a guy could desire then next I'm in clink for God knows how long. The only person that seems to believe in me is Miss Challinor,' bemoaned Jeff somewhat justifiably.

'I believe you too Jeff. Believe me I know you're completely blameless I'm certain you are!'

'Well let's hope I'm up before Judge Oliver Cherry when we get to The Crown Court ay!'

'Who could this Karen Sprigson be Jeff? You said the police reckon she's somehow mixed up in all of this. Might she have some answers? Where is she now?' Oliver enquired surreptitiously.

'I don't know. I've never heard of her. For all I know the police might not even have caught up with her. She might be guilty and free and I'm stuck here. I can't see how Her Majesty gets pleasure out of presiding over this sort of injustice!'

'I'll see what I can do Jeff. If I can somehow get hold of Sprig .... er Sprigson or whatever her name is then maybe we can get some proper answers. Believe me this is as much a mystery to me as you!'

About half an hour later a bell rang and Jeff was escorted back to his cell. Despite being saddened by the whole scene Oliver was now inspired to assist his friend, without implicating himself of course! On the journey back home Oliver went over last night's attack on Wardour Street in Soho and wondered if the lady who saw the whole incident from her window might just be able to throw up an unlikely clue or two. He knew the woman's name and the street where she lived but not much more.

Late that afternoon Oliver got the information he needed via Directory of Enquiries and dialled the number he had been given.

'Hello, I hope you can help me but I need to speak to Mrs Spencer,' Oliver speculated.

'I'm glad you've phoned. Was sure you would. You're the young gentleman involved in the altercation last evening, aren't you?'

'Hello Mrs Spencer, yes that's right. I must thank you for your help.'

'I take it that you did as promised and got some medical attention.'

'I did, sort of but it's going to take a while before I'll be up and running again. I start work again next week.'

'You're a Latin teacher aren't you?' she asked.

'Yeh but how did you know that?'

'Well er ... doesn't the new school term start next week?

'It would have been better if I'd been a judo expert and not a teacher. Then I might have been able to fight back,' he joked.

'I don't think any one person could have stopped that lot Oliver. It all seemed so unnecessary. This was no random thing. You were their specific target that's for sure.'

Oliver and Mrs Spencer chatted for neigh on a couple of hours during which time he slowly warmed to her open approachable nature and welcomed her serenity and erudition. She cracked jokes too. Soon enough he sensed that he had nothing to lose by telling her all that had happened in recent weeks including his role in planting the stash with none of the gloss or omissions. This was quite a risk for someone usually so cautious. He also spoke of his tremendous love for Louise. That Mrs Spencer was a stranger, Oliver reasoned, meant she did not have an agenda of their own hence likely more objective and trustworthy. As well as that he needed a sure-footed adviser, a role Louise would have always filled prior. Mrs Spencer listened long and hard without forwarding an opinion then asked.

'If you were a target picked out by that gang then they are likely to be connected with your friend Sprig. Perhaps you might attend the opening of the Cat's Sanctuary you mentioned and see what might transpire and more importantly who might arrive. Make me a second promise Oliver will you? If you do go you will keep the lowest of profiles. There may be great danger there. I can certainly help you but you must phone me first thing in the morning.'

Despite her reluctance to elaborate Oliver committed and thanked his new sagacious friend for listening free from reprimand. He felt somehow unburdened and inspired by the kindly older woman.

❋❋❋❋❋

There was now less than a week before the 1969/70 school term, a chance for most teachers to prepare themselves, mentally and in any other way for the expected onslaught. Louise had some unfinished business to attend to. At this point Arnie was still out of town but his PA informed her that he was expected back later in the day. Every 30 minutes Louise telephoned Arnie's office until she eventually caught up with him and arranged that they meet urgently! Arnie agreed.

Louise arrived as scheduled but was kept waiting over an hour before the impresario came out of his 'meeting'. Arnie apologised extravagantly, as those in the theatre world tended to. He explained that his trip to Paris was to put the finishing touches to the casting of the 'Hello Dolly' musical and that unless things started to move much more rapidly the debut curtain-up would have to be postponed. Given his frustration Louise for a moment considered that now was not the best time to inform him of Jeff's predicament but having reconsidered she felt that she had no real alternative.

The news rocked Arnie most literally and he fell back in his large leather chair. He held his head in his hands and swivelled side to side.

'He can be a bit of a rogue, a bit of a ladies' man, I'm surprised he hasn't made a pass at you but drugs, no way. There's got to be some kind of mistake, either that or he's been set up. You read about these things don't you. How's he coping, do you know?' lamented Arnie.

'I know that one of our colleagues has seen him at the Scrubs and he's baring up well enough.'

On hearing these words Arnie broke down and bitterly complained about the system, the police and how London was turning into some sort of debauched cesspit. Louise was acutely aware that Arnie was now at his lowest and hence his most vulnerable! Skilfully and without appearing in the least mercenary, she coaxed Arnie into giving her a role in his upcoming stage production promising him her total devotion to duty. Preliminary rehearsals start in a fortnight and although it would not be a major part it would nevertheless require her full time commitment. He agreed to having his people draw up a favourable contract that in effect would result in her nearly doubling her teachers' salary.

It would have been crass in the extreme for Louise to act out the exuberance she felt within on hearing this spectacular news. Although floating up to cloud nine it was hard for her to keep her feet on the ground, but both feet were firmly kept planted until she offered Arnie her final commiserations, departed and stepped out into the busy Mayfair thoroughfare. There she yelped and punched the air clicking her heels all the way to the bus stop.

'I'm gonna dance ... I'm gonna sing ... I'm gonna do most everything,' shouted Louise to any passer-by who cared to listen 'I've got what I want! Oliver's sure to get the promotion now and as for Jeff ...... Well I didn't even need him to influence his dad in the end anyway. So I'll see ya later, Jeffrey Slater.'

As events transpired the first day of the new month had turned out exceedingly well for Louise.

※※※※※

Heel! **Toe!**

Step! **Stomp!**

Shuffle! **Flap!**

Hop!

No one deserves it as much as you do Lulu. You're going to light up the West End with that beautiful smile of yours not to mention those long, long legs,' enthused Oliver on hearing the news.

They then hugged tightly and joyously spun one another around and around. Oliver's body would have been a little too delicate to have done such a thing a day prior.

'I can't tell you what this means to me Ollie. It's what I've wanted since forever and ever and ever. I'm actually in 'Hello Dolly'!

'*Hello Lulu, well hello Lulu. It's so nice you've got the job in the West End....*' sang Oliver as Louise tap-danced around the kitchen.

'We could do with some good news Ollie darling, don't you think? Things are gonna really turn around for us now sweetie. When you get the promotion and I start at the Lyric people won't recognise us. They'll think we're two beautiful angelic lovebirds cast down to earth to brighten the place up. Before you know it I'll have a starring role and you'll be the head teacher of the most massive school on the planet. The sky's the limit for Louise and Oliver. Oh darling I really love y…'

Oliver quickly placed his hand over Louise's mouth before she could finish the sentence and said,

'I was going to say let's not get carried away Lou but why not let's just go with it sweetie. Oops, I think I called you 'sweetie' sweetie. Help! Help! I'm turning into a Lovey, all's lost and before you know it I'll be quoting from the Bard's Scottish play. Come Dame Louise tonight we away to a local hostelry!'

Which is exactly what they did. Although a tremendous struggle, Oliver put to one side his heavy guilt. It was the first time in a while that he felt able to ignore his secret wrongdoings and truly enjoy himself as he would so often in sunnier times. The night was a celebration of their great love for each other and a chance to repeat their vows.

They were more than merry and amorous when they came back to Oliver's. So they ended the night with a treat reserved only for special occasions, a mutual foot massage!

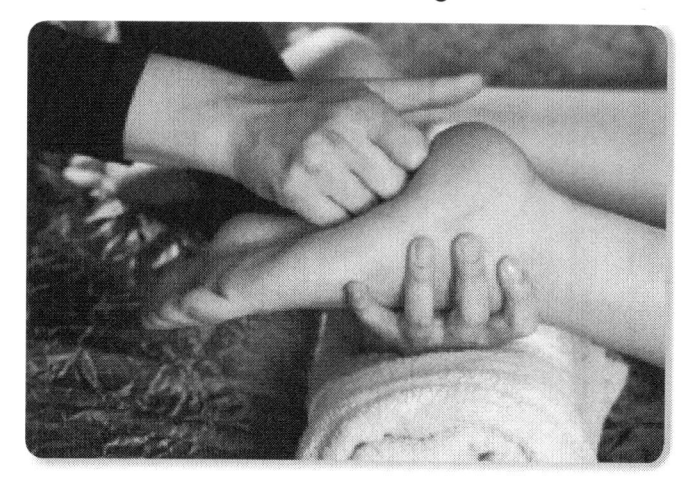

Chapter 19

Hey look, it's Mary O'Brien!

This day was a day that Oliver had tried to dismiss from his mental record without success. The grand opening (or otherwise) of Sprig's Cat Sanctuary had arrived and he was driven not to miss it. In the proceeding few days he had not managed to move matters forward in any way. Sprig's whereabouts was still unknown and quite why Jeff's home was raided remained a mystery too. Oliver believed that even if Sprig herself wasn't around she would have somehow appointed an 'associate' to see things through and open as planned. All in all he concluded that by recent measures this was a relatively uneventful short period marked only by Louise signing her 'big break' contract with Arnie.

What Oliver was to face in Battersea was one of the great imponderables but one conclusion readily reached was that his assailants were somehow connected with Sprig, so they'd be no red carpet rolled out for him today, despite being an unknown major benefactor. Nevertheless, he felt capable and duty-bound to try and help Sprig (as well as Jeff) and to do so he would need to at least to track her down. He could perhaps glean some information and then if at all possible, start reparation.

Oliver recalled the promise made to Mrs Spencer to contact her on that morning and dutifully complied. He did so only to find her even more of an enigma than before. She instructed him to arrive at her apartment on Wardour Street on the dot of midday where, in the lobby he would find an envelope containing a letter and some keys. He was to read the letter and then stand on the pavement just below her window. Oliver recognised that there would be no point asking his mentor to fill in with some more detail so did exactly as urged.

Arriving on Wardour Street with ten minutes to spare Oliver retraced his steps from The Bag O'Nails to where he was bashed up, again attempting to illicit some clues. He felt nervous, as if being observed. Indeed, he was but by Mrs Spencer specifically and no one else. Having got no further in his investigation, Oliver timely entered the lobby. There on the table between The Times and The Telegraph was the aforementioned envelope. He eagerly gathered it up and read its contents:

Dear Oliver you must go to Battersea now but it is imperative that you remain incognito. Under the table you will find a crash helmet. The keys are for the motor scooter outside. Remain on the scooter at all times and do not remove the helmet until you arrive back here where you will leave the scooter, helmet and keys where you found them. Take care - Mrs Gloria Spencer.

A TAIL OF TWO CITIES

This was the strangest of letters from a woman he had never really seen. Oliver was unperturbed; he figured that if his new helper was going to go to all this trouble then it was likely that she would have his interests at heart. Furthermore, Oliver was a Mod some years back and a chance to take to the road and cross 'The Water' on a scooter again more than appealed.

On the journey to Battersea Oliver pictured what he would be confronted with. What he actually saw when he arrived on his scooter should not have really surprised him. The windows of the entire building were boarded up. The large metal sign above the main entrance had been blacked out and swung at a frighteningly hazardous angle squeaking in the light breeze as in a spaghetti western. The guttering on one side of the pathetic building was barely held together. Work had clearly been abandoned. In short, the building was much nearer to being condemned than functioning, with no memory of Sprig or a distressed cat in sight. Despite the sorry scene there nevertheless was plenty of activity. Oliver stayed on the scooter and observed the comings and goings: Perhaps as many as ten women of varying ages walked the pavements nearby. They seemed reasonably kindly, often acknowledging passers-by with a courteous 'good afternoon' but it was their apparel that gave them a semi-sinister aura - Black polo neck sweaters, black denim jeans and deep red Dr Marten boots. They all had short bristly mostly untreated hair, which to Oliver looked incompatible on one or two of the women who were clearly pushing 50.

From an unobtrusive distance Oliver witnessed a number of expensive cars roll up. At one stage there were so many almost bumper to bumper it looked like an Imperial State Visit easing down The Mall on its way to Buck House. The leader of the group, a tall, stiff, statuesque woman would then approach its driver explain to the passengers that 'Battersea Cat's Home' would definitely be opening but alas at some date, hopefully in the near future.

There was then a profuse apology that this information came so late. The cars then coasted off back over the river. It seemed that all the 'faces' that Sprig invited were not told of this beforehand. Oliver sat on his scooter and watched Diana Rigg, Gerry and Sylvia Anderson and several other cat-loving luminaries arrive and soon went. When things seemed to be slowing the leader shouted excitedly to her underlings that 'Mary's coming.' This caused a minor hubbub as they all gathered into a sort of guard of honour formation. The car pulled up and the back door was opened. From it came the instantly recognisable and slight frame of Mary O'Brien, known better as Dusty Springfield. Her admirers didn't have to say outright that they adored her very presence but they were close at hand and fawning to the extent that she would have easily elicited the sentiment. The star was given the news and graciously posed for a few photographs surrounded by the deferential women in black. She then signed some autographs for the awestruck before being quickly spirited away. It was all over within five minutes.

There was no sign of Sprig and even if he had hung around until midnight Oliver was now certain she would not be making an appearance. He was further sure that if Sprig had been around the first few dozen London cats would have already taken up safe residence. Dispirited and unsatisfied he then turned the key in the scooter's ignition but before he could take off he felt a slight tapping on the back of his helmet. He instinctively felt it unwise to turn and investigate however simultaneously a hand then stretched from his rear and abruptly turned the scooter's key, cutting off the engine. A tall woman in black who seemed eager to drag him from his bike confronted Oliver. The brief melee lasted a matter of seconds before Oliver managed to shove away his attacker, turn the key again and shoot off down the road into the oncoming traffic and then back on the correct side off the road. Through his rear view mirror he could see that this had alerted several of 'the troops' of which the more youthful vainly attempted to catch the speeding bike.

This time Oliver got away by a whisker, a cat's whisker! Paradoxically he was emboldened rather than shaken by the experience. It was now abundantly clear that these women were somehow connected to Sprig and probably held him responsible for her almost certain arrest and hence the likely collapse of the Cat's Sanctuary project.

He reasoned however that Sprig herself would know he wouldn't have gone to the police with information about the stash at Jeff's. Why would he? Therefore, this mob was exacting their own irrational revenge and Sprig herself he believed was the only one able to rein them in.

Morbidity began to insidiously creep over Oliver back in his flat that evening. It was a foreboding brought on by menace and uncertainty.

'That's one good thing us being so high up, we're not likely to get a brick through the window up here on the 9th floor,' said Oliver to his dog. The fear of a knock on the door was always present nonetheless.

It was time to report in to Mrs Spencer. She answered the telephone quickly and seemed to be concerned about Oliver's well-being. He told her of his narrow escape that afternoon and lamented that he had not seen Sprig.

'She's been locked up. There's no other answer. Sprig and Jeff, both of them in prison for something that shouldn't be. What can be done to help 'em? Prison days' last a week I reckon specially when you're innocent!' said Oliver.

Mrs Spencer seemed more and more bothered how events were unfolding.

'The tall woman, the one you describe as the leader. She was tall, very tall well over 6 foot you say?' asked the lady.

'Yes, I'd guess she would be nearer 6 foot 4.'

'She's not the only tall woman you've met recently, is she Oliver?'

'Yes, I know what you're getting at, she was the one in the Bag O'Nails the other night. It's the same one. She got real uptight when I asked about Sprig!'

'Perhaps your asking antagonised her?'

'What do you mean?'

'Well it seems that on the two occasions you've clashed it was you that approached them Oliver.'

'So you're saying that if I keep away they won't bother me?'

'I'm sure you're correct there. This doesn't seem to be Sprig's doing does it? Keep away from them and I'm certain they will stay away from you. Is that what you want?'

'More than ever. I'm back at school soon and I don't need any more headaches.'

He was now much less fearful. Like all contacts Oliver had with his new adviser and guide he felt so much better after. Her knack of confirming his suspicions and relaxing him eased his mind sometimes adding another dimension to his thinking.

'Old Mrs Gloria Spencer, the provider of peace of mind,' he would say to himself. Now he had head-space to focus on the Head of Year promotion interview next week. –

The contrast in attitude between Oliver and Louise as they readied themselves for the return to school was marked. In her handbag Louise had a typed letter of notice for Mr Press. Her future was now the West End and not the East End. Her lover meanwhile was unable to summon up the wherewithal to play the Beatles Lyric Game (BLG) as he often did whilst preparing for work on Monday mornings. His mind was set on his interview later in the week and not the Fab Four who the newspapers reported were in nearby Twickenham working on their last album 'Let It Be'. A minor part of him out of guilt and respect for Jeff thought it best to withdraw his job application. This idea soon passed as now more than ever he felt duty bound to keep up with Louise, as regards professional progress at least. He'd gone this far and could now not turn back. The only way to stay focussed he maintained was to put to one side all unanswered questions, stay away from the women in black and to give attention to his work and his love for Louise. It was comforting to know that Mrs Spencer was always there in the background to be called upon if required.

Mr Press and some of the more enthusiastic teachers had made the effort to come into school a few days before the new term. As well as ingratiating themselves on him they were used to generally tart up the place and literally paper over the cracks. The school hall was festooned with blown-up media photographs of last term's memorable 'Sporting Victory Against Monty'. Pride of place went to pretty Chrissy Ingham whose sheer power and commitment won the deciding arm-wrestle. Again, Ruff had somehow managed to commandeer various much needed tables and chairs from a nearby school that had an excess, the floor of the main school hall was now highly polished hence highly dangerous and the toilet cisterns on the first-floor girls' bathroom each had a chain and not before time.

Given Oliver's bid to become Head of Year it would have been to his advantage if he had made his presence felt during this period but he had other priorities. In his pigeon-hole he found a letter from the London Education Authority informing him that his interview was definitely set for Wednesday morning, a relief for Oliver as he knew that Mr Press got some sort of sadistic joy from springing the odd surprise on all his staff.

Jeff loved the banter of the Monday morning staff meetings and that he was not there this day only added to Oliver's guilt. Mr Press then stood up to address his teachers and after welcoming the three new rookie staff members to their number asked for all present to take note of this sad news:

'Many of you will know our sports' teacher Mr Jeffrey Slater. Indeed, many here today would regard Mr Slater as a close personal friend.' Was this a reference to Jeff's fraternising with several women teachers, Oliver pondered. 'I have to announce today that Mr Slater has handed in his notice and will no longer be joining us here at Tower Hamlets this term or indeed again.'

Oliver had no emotion left in him to fake surprise at the announcement. Louise looked to the floor eager to avoid any interaction with her colleagues. There was an audible joint gasp from the room and even more so when Mr Press instructed that all staff would have to 'chip in' on sports lessons until a permanent replacement was found. He then went on to tell of his holiday in Scotland with Edith 'my wife of course' and numerous grandchildren. He wished his staff well for the new school year and dismissed them.

'Nothing seems to change. A teacher's lot is just the same old, same old,' Oliver thought, as he stood in front of his first group of unappreciative schoolgirls. It was his first Greek classics class of the new school year. That day he went through the motions and wished he had a 'Magic Boomerang' like that Australian boy in the TV programme of the same name: The boy would sling the boomerang in the air and time would stand still during which he could correct errors that he had made and put all things right again. Oliver yearned for such power. But what's done, he consoled was done.

At the end of that first day Mr Press was waiting outside the classroom for Oliver. They then went to the head-office. The Head knew that

Oliver and Jeff were good friends and asked Oliver if he knew that Jeff was supplying drugs to the school? Oliver was visibly indignant at that and the Head's subsequent questions seemingly presented as fact. Oliver forcefully pointed out, in Jeff's defence, that nothing had been proven in a Court of Law and that no decisions as to guilt should be made by anyone at school until then. Oliver was more at ease when the more comfortable subject of the Head of Year position and Wednesday's interview was broached. It was then that Mr Press dropped his bombshell.

'Mr Cherry, my colleagues from the Education Authority and on the interview panel are hoping that given your close and long-standing friendship with the accused that you would consider withdrawing your application until after the matter has been resolved in Court. Drugs have been coming into the school and tongues have been wagging and fingers pointed.'

'But the case is months off and my interview is in a couple of days!' protested Oliver, pointing out the obvious.

'Precisely, Mr Cherry. In the circumstances, should you fail to reconsider it would seem as if you're flouting common sense. This wouldn't look too favourable on your personnel file and might really have a serious baring on any future promotions prospects that may interest you. As one of East London's brightest young Classics teachers it would be an awful waste of talent if you were to…err languish in your present post for another 10 years, wouldn't it Mr Cherry? Surely you've got more ambition than to lead a stagnant career?!'

'…so let me see Mr Press, you and the bigwigs think that Jeff and me are running a drugs racket at Hamlets so you're not giving me much of an option are you? If I withdraw I obviously don't get the

A TAIL OF TWO CITIES

job and if I don't and attend the interview it would be a total waste of time!'

'Your words not mine Mr Cherry,' said Mr Press knowing that the battle had been won. 'Do I take it that I will have a gap in Wednesday's interview schedule to fill now Mr Cherry?'

The question was to remain unanswered. Oliver stood bolt upright and, for a long moment glared ferociously at his callous tormentor. Marching quickly out of the door, he made a point of slamming it hard behind him.

The realisation it had all been for nothing was a fact that Oliver found difficult to accept. As a man of principle he would never normally resort to grossly underhand tactics to further his career in the manner he had done. 'After all it was just a job anyway' he pointlessly said to himself in consolation but he wasn't really consoled.

That night Oliver came to view it all as some kind of mild unseen retribution. Mild, in that he, unlike others at least still had his liberty.

His blinkered and greedy Louise-inspired ambition had been rightly thwarted. 'Just desserts, indeed,' he concluded. When discussed that evening Louise's summation was, as expected vicious, raging at the injustice of it all. 'So we're living in a land where guilt by association prevails, are we?' she asked plausibly. She had sacrificed an awful lot of herself with the lecherous Cockroach, allowing him to violate her body and for nothing. For her the disappointment was slightly more tolerable however, owing to her new vocation. As regards the head of year job, it was all one big unnecessary mess and an ill conceived disaster from its very conception. Later that evening, alone in his flat Oliver whined to his dog at the futility of it all. - Quite independently both Oliver and Louise had given so much of themselves to gain less than very little.

☙☙☙

Chapter 20
Nylon

'PAUL IS QUITTING THE BEATLES' shouted the headline in the London Evening News.

'That's all I need,' lamented Oliver to Louise.

'...so what's gonna happen to the submarine?' she replied.

'The submarine?'

'Yeah, the yellow submarine they all live in. Who'll get that in the divorce settlement?'

'Not sure if they can work it out but they'll probably get by with a little help from their friends Lou.'

He mourned the passing of his favourite band a fact that added to his woes. He had the weekend to lick his wounds. She however had no time to think of what might be, given that she was no longer a drama teacher but a professional actress and dancer. Things were going well and the first main dress rehearsal was tomorrow afternoon.

'Lulu I've got an awful lot of marking to do. Could you take Naked for his evening walk?'

Louise never really warmed to Oliver's pet. She was always envious of the attention and affection he afforded him. Naked had a keen and innate sense of smell and whenever in Louise's presence he smelt treachery.

'Hmm, well ok just this once mind. Get me his lead and I'll let him have a romp in the park,' she agreed grudgingly. -

It was a clear evening in Victoria Park just before sundown. This was the time of day when younger kids and kite-flyers were making their way home and dog owners walked their pets. Naked was particularly lively this evening as Oliver had been so involved with his work that he had not taken him out that morning as he would normally. Louise spent a few minutes throwing a ball for the dog, which he returned ready for more. A short while later she slipped the lead back on the dog and headed for home. With no warning

Naked had spotted another dog and made a bolt for it. This took Louise very much by surprise and with a thud, the sharp yank on the lead pulled her forcefully to the ground.

'Aghh my ankle,' cried Louise. 'My ankle, you stupid, stupid bloody dog.'

She struggled to her feet and winced in agony as she put her right foot to ground.

'Ahh it's twisted. I can't walk. I can't even stand. Ahhh, I can't do anything. How can I dance like this you mad bloody dog? This is all down to you....YOU!' yelled Louise waving her fist at the bemused hound.

Louise became even more incandescent when she realised that her ankle had not just swollen but was likely sprained. Naked wondered what all the fuss was about and continued to sniff around nonchalantly as Louise tried to find some movement in her stiffening joint.

'You dog are responsible for this. You're gonna pay you rabid thing!'

It took Louise 30 agonising minutes to limp back to Oliver's. She returned there alone.

'Oliver, I've lost him, Naked's run off. I took his lead off to give him a bit of a run and before you know it he was gone,' confessed Louise convincingly.

'Gone what do you mean gone, gone where?'

'Gone, he just ran off across the park and into the distance, completely out of sight.'

'Where to, did he run across a road? Did anyone catch up with him? You must know more woman!' Oliver was now advancing toward a full-on panic.

'I tried to catch him but he was determined to get away. In the chase I fell and did some damage to my ankle. Look Ollie it's really bad!'

'Just ... just soak it or something. I'll go find him.'

With that he pelted out the door. Louise took his advice and cursed her misfortune at such a crucial time.

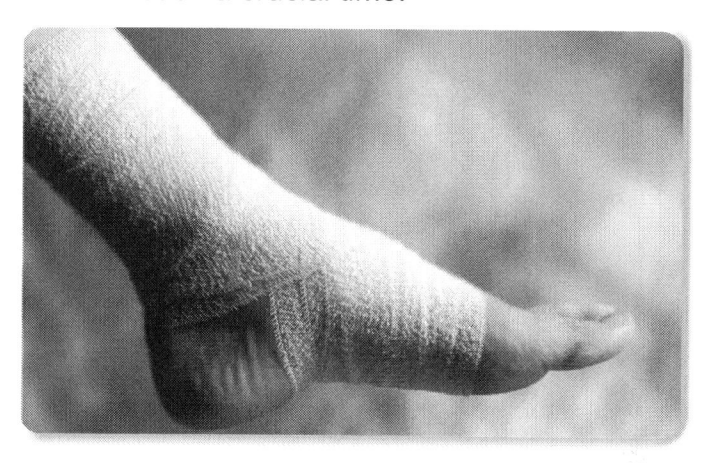

Around an hour later Oliver was back home. He too returned alone. Louise had fallen deeply asleep on the sofa with a bowl of now tepid water next to her. His was a brief visit as he had come back for a quick cuppa and to telephone some friends and acquaintances that lived close to elicit their help. A short while after, Oliver and his hastily assembled posse had gathered in the park to conduct a swoop of the area and surrounds in search of his missing dog. Forces marshalled, they each went their separate ways with the instruction of returning in an hour which, in turn they all did. The dragnet was unsuccessful. Oliver sighed deeply his distress obvious. He thanked the assembly as they disbursed. He then flopped dejectedly on a park bench. It was the same bench that he had sat with Naked at sun-up just a few weeks before. Then in his life Oliver had Louise, Jeff, Sprig and Naked – now all but Louise had left him.

※※※※※

The next few weeks saw mixed fortunes for Louise and Oliver. Louise, now with mended ankle made her 'Hello Dolly' debut at The Lyric and then onto The Shaftesbury. A plethora of London, Manchester and Paris luminaries attended a lavish party marking the opening. Sadly, there was a black cloud, Louise's mother who inexplicably missed her daughter's debut having pulled out at the last minute. The all-important theatre reviews ranged from vindictive to ecstasy – one well known newspaper critic claimed to need 'smelling salts during the second half' and another wrote that the show 'the sizzling show simply smelt of success.' The majority opinion however was positive and the resultant houses were full to overflowing. Along with Lionel Bart's 'Oliver!' the production soon came to be the West End's biggest musical hit of the season, beating even the 'West Side Story' and 'South Pacific' revivals. Louise was now in an environment, in which she thrived, surrounded by like-minded, creative and ambitious go-getters. Arnie enjoyed having her around and she reciprocated in every way that she thought necessary to move up the slippery theatrical pole. Her lively presence with the cast was increasingly being felt and appreciated.

Prospects for Oliver looked less rosy: Cockroach had appointed Sarah 'Stupid' Stringer as Head of Year, an ignominy Oliver found hard to swallow. Keeping his enthusiasm for teaching was also increasingly arduous. There was no sign of Naked who Louise reminded was now 'gone for good'. To Oliver, life without his trusted companion was bleak in the extreme. Other things were resting heavily on Oliver's mind too, none more so than when Miss Challinor informed him that Jeff and Sprig's drugs case was to be heard at The Old Bailey on 1st December. She confirmed that a certain Karen Sprigson had been remanded in custody and would be Jeff's co-defendant! Things were making more sense now but only slightly.

Remarkably the love that Oliver and Louise shared during this period of divergence seemed quite unaffected. He was able for the most part to keep his grieving and confusion under wraps so as not to take the shine off Louise's glow. He did however have the need to refer and defer to Mrs Spencer when things became intolerable. She would kindly decline every time when he requested to meet with her directly but as long as she was there for him at the end of the phone he was not too bothered.

1 Dec 69 – The day had arrived. Miss Challinor had informed Oliver that he would not be called as a witness, something he was ambivalent about anyway. Jeff, she said 'was going to fight tooth and nail' to prove his innocence. Oliver having taken time off work planned to support Jeff and Sprig in his own way by attending every moment of the trial. Louise, in support of Oliver would offer verbal reassurance. The outcome of course was, for differing reasons of great interest to them both –

The public gallery at Grand Court 6 at The Old Bailey had a reputation that proceeded it. It was the scene of Dr Crippen and the Great Train Robbers' convictions. Recently it held the Kray twins preliminary murder trials. It was an austere, windowless and wood panelled arena marked out for battle, with its wigged combatants pacing back and forth with a confidence that only familiarity with the surroundings brings. Oliver's heart sank when Jeff ascended from the cells.

His appearance was every bit as melancholy and aggrieved as at Oliver's regular prison visits. Sprig cut a different figure entirely. She sat a few yards from Jeff, upright but without any sign of tension. Her demeanour was one of quiet determination, in many ways similar to a group of woman clad in black sporting regulation red Doc Martens crammed into the public gallery a few seats from Oliver. One of them he recognised as 'The Leader'. Recalling Mrs Spencer's advice that if he kept away from them they would him. But for a few sneers and intimidating glares, it turned out to be just so.

Oliver had not set eyes on Sprig since she showed him around her cat's sanctuary in Battersea some months prior. She was clearly taken aback when she noticed him in the gallery above. He in turn was puzzled. Did her expression say 'How-could-you-be-so-cruel-Oliver?' or more worryingly 'Beware-of-me-and-my-troops-when-I'm-outta-here Cherry!' He wanted to shout out the truth but he did not have a clue what that was himself. He was also concerned that should Sprig resort to a verbal outburst in court implicating Oliver then his 'innocent' role would be dangerously questioned by some present.

Miss Challinor was on the defensive from the first minute of day one to the end of the five-day marathon. The forensic evidence against Sprig was the undeniable palm print found at the scene. The evidence against Jeff was compelling too with the Crown continually hammering home the fact that the stash was found hidden at Jeff's home and Tower Hamlets School had a recent influx of narcotics and that this 'was likely an inside operation'. Although Jeff's prosperous lifestyle was mostly at the behest of his successful and wealthy father this seemed not to register with any of the stern-faced jurors. The Judge spoke very infrequently but on those few occasions The Court hung on his every word. The inference that lay behind the Judge's enquiries seemed very much weighted in the Prosecution's favour particularly when suggesting that Jeff's lifestyle exceeded that of a man on solely a teacher's salary. Again, Oliver picked up that the jurors concurred. Any hope that the two defendants might just slip through an incredible legal loophole had all but evaporated by the end of day three. If justice was to be done a miracle was needed, and soon.

Alas, there was no such miracle, no dramatic last-minute undisclosed piece of evidence a la Perry Mason, no sudden seizure struck the Judge, not even a bomb scare or faulty fire alarm.

Miss Challinor valiantly strained out a truth of a sort but Oliver, Arnie, The Leader and her troops looked decidedly pessimistic.

It was now late on a Friday afternoon and time for the foreman of the jury to conclude. He took to his feet whilst the other jurors looked on knowingly. His expression gave no clue. The Court Clerk ordered there to be silence.

The verdict: Jeffrey Jack Slater - 'Guilty' ...... Karen Hannah Sprigson - 'Guilty' both of obtaining and the supply of Class B narcotics. The word 'Guilty' resonated momentarily before all in the grief-stricken gallery bowed their heads. Soon the court echoed to moans below and shouts of derision above as the disbelief exhibited across the faces of the convicted two progressed to shocked and anguished wails. The Judge eventually got the silence sought and after a brief outline of how drugs were changing London into a 'modern day Sodom and Gomorrah' adjourned for an hour to consider sentence. The steely eyed Judge returned merely 30 minutes later, which all supporters of the convicted two viewed as ominous. They were right to think so - Both Jeff and Sprig would be serving 18-months imprisonment!

Jeff and Sprig were then handcuffed and slowly led away, their dejection patently clear. Oliver held his head, too bewildered to look either of the prisoners in the face. Arnie unashamedly bellowed aloud long and hard. The 'troops' all of whom were there to support Sprig silently filed out, solemn defiance marked across their faces. One of their number had been taken from them. Meanwhile, Louise's reaction to the harshness of the sentences was quite imperceptible.

Initially Louise was at her most reassuring and endearing that evening working out the earliest date that Jeff and Sprig would be released for 'good behaviour.' She helped distract Oliver by flicking through one of their old photo albums. This raised a temporary smile or two. They then played a few hands of Rummy topping things off again with a most relaxing and mutual soothing foot-massage. However, in attempting to underhandedly disparage Jeff she produced such a furious outburst in Oliver, she was forced to make her excuses and leave for her third-floor refuge as quickly as her dancing feet would carry her. This day was yet another low point for Oliver and he wondered if things could ever be the same again. A short telephone conversation with Mrs Spencer the next day did improve his dire outlook but again this was only temporary.

✶✶✶✶✶

What was needed now, for Oliver particularly was a change of scene, failing that a chance to really let his hair down. A massive blow out would be 'just what the doctor ordered.' Such an opening eventually presented itself with the huge celebrations being planned all over London marking the end of the 1960s and ringing in the 1970s. Mr Press, Sarah 'Stupid' Stringer, Ruff and others were organising 'An End of The Decade Rave Up' in the school hall just before they broke up for Christmas with the quirky themed idea of playing music from the 40s and 50s only. This paradoxical notion had to be reversed when less than 50 of the 700 tickets were sold. Either way Louise would not be persuaded to attend despite having a night off from Hello Dolly. There was also the possibility of Oliver and Maggie Birkett reacquainting. As Rave Ups go, the school did themselves proud and it was regarded as a success. Indeed, any event that turns out to be uneventful at Hamlets could be regarded as a success.

A couple of weeks later, with Christmas over Louise had the winning idea of going to the usual Trafalgar Square revelries followed by a party that Arnie was hosting on the stage of The Shaftsbury starting just after the midnight chimes. She set about persuading Oliver that more fun was to be had there than almost anywhere else in

London. She put a convincing argument and Oliver as ever bent the knee. -

Well over 800,000 people from all over the planet crammed into Trafalgar Square and its environs with eyes and ears focussed on Big Ben at the far end of Whitehall. The night was crisp and blowy but the heat of the masses was tantamount to being oppressive. Oliver and Louise held each other closer than ever before in public as Big Ben the huge distant bell forged in Whitechapel chimed. As always the turning of a page is for some a form of reflection and planning. Oliver who greatly missed his friends and his dog felt it best not to look back at 1969. Louise's outlook was more progressive.

'Say that we'll always stay together Ollie. Promise me that here and now will you?' pleaded Louise.

'You don't have to ask it Lulu. We'll be together after time has run out! Goodbye and good riddance 1969. 1970 is our year!' he replied ruefully.

As Big Ben rang in the changes and with fireworks and the refrains of Auld Lang Syne surrounded them they pushed their way through the heaving joyous tumult and made their way to The Shaftsbury that was dark that night.

Given that the main frontage was closed off, the side stage door entrance was the only point of access into the theatre. The party was beginning to swing so Louise hustled Oliver in past security and into a quite dimly lit long anti-room containing endless racks of extravagant stage garments.

'OK Ollie take your pick,' said Louise excitedly running her extended arm along the clothes. 'Didn't want to worry you before mister but this party is strictly fancy dress. Arnie does stuff in style so go on, any one you want is yours.'

Oliver thought for a short moment and smiled his approval. Like most Englishmen having the chance to dress up was an opportunity he would not want to miss.

'Chief Sitting Bull, Marie Antoinette, Pharaoh, Shakespeare how can a guy decide,' proffered Oliver taking no time at all getting into the spirit of the occasion.

'You were put on this earth for one reason only Oliver. That to be a latter day Elizabeth the first,' said Louise.

'Brilliant. She's my heroin,' shouted Oliver.

'Given Jeff's fate perhaps we better refer to her as your hero,' said Louise insensitively.

Ten minutes later Oliver was transformed. He had singled out a long green and gold billowing gown with puffed arms and peppered with fake jewels, a matted ginger wig, a six-inch ruff accessorised a glittery royal tiara and orb. Louise meanwhile was somewhere nearby preparing.

'I'm done, now let's have a look at you Lou,' said Oliver proudly.

A couple of minutes later Louise emerged from out of the darkness dressed as a decidedly provocative French Can-Can girl. Oliver was immediately animated and even more so when she lifted her frilly dress and did the customary twirls followed by an eye-popping final bow. That she chose to wear no bloomers, indeed nothing at all under her dress encouraged Oliver to grab her by the wrist and lead her to 'who knows where'. They found themselves in the dark dusty orchestra pit. There, good Queen Bess pinned his mademoiselle against the wall and ran his strong hands up and down and over her tempting body. As the party swung noisily on the stage above the Queen lifted his dress and then hers. Within a few fumbling seconds both were sufficiently aroused and at their most giving. She yelled out passionately and ordered 'Elizabeth' to make her 'happy' knowing that they could not be heard.

With no notice they heard a sharp metallic-sounding clunk and from the back of the theatre shot a harsh beam of light. The Queen and the Can-Can dancer had been rumbled and were illuminated by the strident white light of a powerful Super Trouper. Unknown voices from the surrounding darkness shouted unrefined comments such as 'Go on Queeny off with head, pousser fort!' and 'Je t'amie madam, Ooh La La!'

Oliver was now too stirred and in no mood to pay them any heed. Louise liked the idea of performing semi-incognito. As the two 'entertainers' moved toward their finale their audience of lusty voyeurs, no doubt almost equally stimulated bellowed out their kinky orders all the more vehemently. The crowd hushed as the Queen's last few authoritative lunges rendered mademoiselle helpless. Both their cries of delight echoed throughout the cavernous auditorium and slowly subsided into content whimpers. There then followed a brief almost tangible silence. After that a familiar metallic sound followed by near total solid darkness. This was drama at its most realistic the like of which the Shaftsbury Theatre could never dare stage to a paying audience. Even 'Hair' the most permissive show of the 1960s didn't take things this far.

As the satisfied couple could hear the spectators moving away in the distance, Oliver and Louise caught their collective breaths and tidied themselves up. 'Well Lizzie I thought you were the Virgin Queen,' joked Louise.

'And I thought you would be wearing les pantaloons mademoiselle!' he said straitening his wig and searching around in the dimness for his sceptre.

'It's always best to start the New Year with a bang don't you think? Perhaps we'll sell tickets next time ma cheri!' claimed Oliver.

This was the most fun they had had together for many months and although it was completely out of character for Oliver to be so flagrant he suggested they repeat the experience later, 'perhaps in Piccadilly Circus!'

Strangely when Oliver and Louise joined the party no one mentioned what they had witnessed just minutes earlier. 'Unseemliness was not the thing the Brits get involved in' thought Oliver. All in attendance were too intent on making the best of the occasion rather than possibly embarrassing fellow partygoers in regaling what they had witnessed.

Soon the whole up-stage was crammed with the most extravagant costumes, at least half a dozen Caesars, a few Canadian Mounties, geisha girls, strippers, Eskimos, policemen, flamenco dancers, a couple of Rudolph Valentinos, more than enough Charlie Chaplins, Mick Jagger, and a passable Winston Churchill or was it W C Fields? Arnie came as Henry VIII, which meant that Oliver, somewhat ironically referred to him as 'dad' throughout the night. Taking Jeff's place just for an evening seemed not to concern Oliver as it likely would have done some months before.

Given Arnie's recent heartbreak over Jeff, the entire Hello Dolly cast was intent on making it a night he would remember all decade. He however had a surprise up his sleeve for them. On calling for everyone's attention he perched himself atop a 1920s pseudo Cadillac there as a production prop:

'This has been quite easily the most tremendous production I have had the good fortune to produce and direct,' said Arnie emotionally. 'But like all good things it must eventually come to an end and we must bring the curtain down on Dolly for the final time in September. So we've got nine months to keep those box-office tills ringing before we say farewell to one another,'

The drunken crowd jostled and cheered then jeered at the news.

'You are such a talented troupe I'm sure you'll all go on to great success on the West End stage but that will have to be after we have returned from..... Broadway where I hope you'll all be joining me!'

This was not quite understood by most there.

'So what are you saying then Arnie,' shouted a Viking.

'I'm saying that this production and its entire cast are transferring to New York in the Autumn, or should I say The Fall! Goodbye London, hello New York, Hello Dolly!'

The stage went into complete jubilant uproar with all sorts of hugging, backslapping and chanting of Arnie's name. Louise too was as ecstatic as anyone and for a while Oliver lost her in the festivities. Arnie was clearly taken by the wholehearted support of them all. Oliver glanced at him and caught a hint of melancholy in his eyes that Jeff was not there to enjoy the good news as well.

The celebrations had yet to reach a high point so Oliver took the opportunity to find an empty office to clear his head and contemplate his future with Louise when the show transfers to America. He was pacing around the office when he heard footsteps slowly approach. Oliver felt vulnerable and gripped his sceptre and orb at the ready to defend himself if called for. The steps stopped outside the door. There was a brief hush. The handle of the door turned hesitantly as Oliver held his breath. When the handle could turn no more the door gradually creaked opened inch by inch.

'I wasn't sure if you'd be in here,' came a disembodied voice, before its owner's arrival.

In through the door stood a tall portly figure clad in regal ermine and gold. It was Arnie. Oliver was mightily relieved.

'You can put your weapon down now Bess,' joked Arnie.

'I didn't know who to expect. I nearly wet myself!'

Arnie asked Oliver to sit down as he had something important to ask him. Oliver did as bid and through his tight-laced dress could feel his heart pounding heavily.

'Louise is an important member of my cast and I don't want to lose her when we transfer. It's obvious that you've got strong feelings for one another and I don't want that to change just because of the show. I've also known you all your life Oliver remember and you've been a great support to Jeff.'

The passage of time had eroded Oliver's guilt but he was curious as to where this was all leading and politely and somewhat nervously asked him to get to the point.

'Come to New York. Louise will want you there too I'm sure. She's been a breath of fresh air for us all and has gained alot respect. You're not in the cast but the company will pay all expenses. A year away from London will be good for all of us. Don't give me an answer now but don't keep me waiting too long Oliver. New York, New York it's a wonderful town!'

Oliver was struck by an instant sense of relief in that Arnie's generous offer had put another very palatable option into his 1970 equation.

'Oh Elizabeth, I'm sorry about your mother but she had to go but I don't know what I'm gonna do with that Bloody Mary!' said Arnie confident that Oliver would appreciate the historical.

With that 'Henry' smiled and headed back to the celebrations.

The 70s had started most unpredictably for Oliver and Louise alike. The prospect of getting away from London and Tower Hamlets for at least a year or so appealed to Oliver immensely. Just as immense was Oliver's natural caution. Even though it was quite late he decided there and then to telephone Mrs Spencer, his mentor and protector. Perhaps she could guide him?

Mrs Spencer was awake and not in the least put out at Oliver calling at such a time, indeed she was pleased to hear from him.

'It's likely that there's a problem Oliver. Well I'm listening,' said she compassionately.

'Well err …it. Oh a happy new year to you. Well it's more of a dilemma Mrs Spencer.'

Oliver appraised her of Arnie's generous offer and elicited her advice. She thought for a moment or two.

'Tell me Oliver. Do you and Louise believe that you both have a long-term future together, after all it's nine months before the show transfers? Indeed, are you sure about her as a partner, as a person?'

'Oh yes, now even more than ever. We've vowed always to stay together and I really do trust her and love her as much as any man can love anyone or even Naked. Louise is everything to me.'

'Well if that's how you sincerely feel then it's off to New York with you and don't forget to send me a postcard of The Statue of Liberty. Take care Oliver, think wisely about things. For you it's a new dawn, new decade, New York!'

~~~

Chapter 21 (A New Chapter)
Noah, Jeremiah and the Jews

BOAC flight 4359 left London Heathrow at precisely 0930 hours on Friday 23rd September 1970 having been delayed more than an hour. That small inconvenience did nothing to dull the excitement that Oliver, Louise and the rest of the 'Hello Dolly' cast emitted. They were embarking on a new adventure in the New World. They had seen so much of New York in films and on television. They had read that fortunes were there to be had for those bold enough to go for it. They were going to take full advantage of their talent, youth and opportunity and they figured if they couldn't make it there, they couldn't make it anywhere!

For Oliver there would be no more Tower Hamlets, no more girls who failed to see the beauty of 'the dead languages', no more Cockroach and no more awful Jeff and Sprig regrets. Were it possible to look differently at his place in the world then he'd certainly take the opportunity. Through much of the seven-hour flight he resolved to become more forthright, less flaky, more focussed and less, much less reactive but more proactive. It was a time to fulfil his unknown potential and goal set and in doing so make more of a success of things. Louise? Well Louise was different. She was leaving behind events that she dare not bring to mind but once across the Atlantic she would be working from a clean slate. Her American ambition meant she was going for a leading and not a supporting role on stage and in life. It was now onward and upward, quite literally.

There was a certain sadness at leaving wonderful London felt deeply by many of their number with one or two even resolving silently to themselves never to return home again, like the Pilgrim Fathers before them. Some of the cast had never been abroad and several had never even been on a Green Line bus. As the plane taxied and sped off along the runway the whole party spontaneously burst into refrains of 'America' from West Side Story. In fact, such was the general exuberance that throughout much of the flight almost every song with 'New York' or 'New York City' in the title or lyrics was sung and sung again much to the disquiet of a few jaded passengers not of their company. Normally an utterance from Arnie was akin to a Papal Bull, so all held their breaths when a senior member of the cabin crew asked him to get the troupe to quieten things down. Arnie simply shrugged dramatically, threw his head backward and in his best Gielgud-esk voice said grandly 'weren't you ever young and in love?' That seemed to have the desired effect and the singing started up again.

The seven-hour flight flew. Before long the Manhattan skyline could be picked out in the far distance and minutes after the dot of the famed and aloof Lady Liberty. All busied themselves as they touched down at JFK.

'How you feeling Oliver?' asked Louise.

'Just swell ma'am!'

'Ollie, is there anything that you really want to do more than anything whilst in America apart from the obvious that is?'

'All I want is for you to fulfil your dream Louise. Seeing you happy will make me even happier.'

Unknown to anyone, Oliver had in his breast pocket his most precious family heirloom, his beloved late mother's diamond and emerald engagement ring as well as her still gleaming wedding band. His ever-constant rabbit's tail was in his bag tucked under his seat. These were entrusted to him the week she died some five years before. He, at that time could never have realised that they had any value other than emotional but now they did, as he planned to ask Louise if she would be his wife. He was certain that the time was approaching when she should become Mrs Oliver Cherry and was able to easily dismiss the inferred misgivings that Mrs Spencer would often make known. He had it all mapped out in his mind's eye. Having read about the idyllic views of Manhattan at night as seen from Brooklyn Bridge he resolved, when the time was right that this would be the ideal venue for his romantic proposal: Louise would melt into his arms, they would hold each other close and tenderly kiss. Through teary eyes Louise would emotionally accept and thank her new fiancé for making her the happiest woman in the whole wide world. Well something like that!

Back in the real-world Arnie had arranged things faultlessly so that as soon as they had passed through US Customs they would be directed onto a bus. It worked perfectly as they quickly left the airport grounds and onto the streets of the largest of the city's five boroughs, Queens. In this city they noted the cars drive on the other side of the road and tend not to obey traffic lights as rigidly. Indeed, the lights seem to have no need for amber. The police cars' sirens make an ear-shattering racket and the Fire Brigade is known as the Fire Department, a much funkier epithet. Most striking was the sheer life and movement on the streets particularly as they crossed over to Manhattan. The city was completely laid bare for the world to observe and they cared not who did the observing. Good, bad or indifferent New Yorkers performed brashly without the flamboyant mincing so common to Londoners. The air the place exuded suggested that if a job needed doing expeditiously then asking a New Yorker would see it done well and done quickly.

The streets heaved together with a sense of peril. Here was a world of many races flimsily dressed and ambitious. All around children playing bent on exploiting the enjoyment to be had in the gaps between the cars, 'trash cans' and fire hydrants. Then, but a few blocks further on a contrasting neighbourhood, a patch of near pristine sobriety, a residential oasis for the more genteel and a respite where life simply happens to its moneyed citizens who now have few serious issues to resolve or deals to seal. Their years of hustling had long passed to be replaced by a slow and easy smugness. 'It could be Holland Park or Mayfair in the 1950s,' Oliver thought.

Even in the suburbs the main thoroughfares were wider, the apartments were taller and the people a good deal sweatier and heftier, a sizeable proportion even obese. Also with New York being on the same latitude as Rome a September temperature of 90 degrees surprised none of its populace. New York City, as much as they had seen so far was a truly fascinating place with more vitality and vagaries than any film or book could depict or fashion.

The bus stopped and started through much of Queens and part of Brooklyn but it wasn't until it met with Manhattan Bridge that traversed the East River did its passengers truly catch sight of the New York City of renown. Huge clumps of exceptionally tall skyscrapers surrounding the UN headquarters then an equally vast clump of brownstone tenements, all laying in an orderly tight mesh. The bridge was high off the flowing river below, which appeared to be almost as busy with small bobbing vessels as the streets with cars and yellow taxicabs. Running almost parallel sat Brooklyn Bridge, Oliver's 'Proposal Bridge.'

Arnie announced that they would all be staying in various parts of the Lower East Side of Manhattan just a few miles south from the theatres of Broadway in Midtown. This meant little to most aboard who by this time just wanted to alight and start pounding the streets of their new temporary home. The Lower East Side was, as the name suggests on the bottom right of the island. It could roughly be defined as an area with Houston Street to the north, the East River to the east and south and by the Manhattan Bridge and the Bowery on the west. It was well known in song and the written word as the bustling and teeming magnate for immigrants stretching back nearly a century. Two hundred years prior the area was prime farmland and attracted crew from famed ship captains such as Rutger and Delancey whose names could be seen on local street signs even today. Oliver and Louise would be stationed in a small apartment above some shops and a community hall on Hester Street.

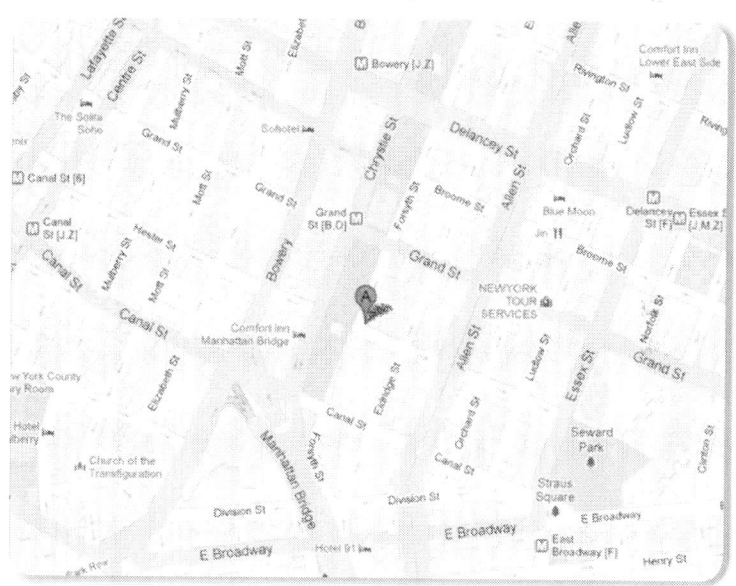

'I suppose this place could be described as compact!' joked Louise as she ran a rule over the four small rooms.

'More compact a flat I have never seen. Do you know Louise this will be the first time we have ever lived together? What do you think?' enquired Oliver hopefully.

'Well why not. It's what I want, don't you?'

'Oh well. Let's give it a go,' he replied feigning nonchalance.

There was a knock on the door and before it could be answered Arnie put his head around.

'Louise, Oliver let me introduce you to Irving. He's one of our stage lighting people that we've brought over from Philadelphia. He will be sharing with you two for a few days until we've got something more sorted.'

In no time at all Arnie had breezed out leaving behind Irving holding a small case. The three of them looked at each other momentarily trying to gauge a reaction. Oliver broke first and into a smile, Irving using his huge hand wiped away some perspiration from his brow and nose then extended it in welcome toward Oliver. Louise frowned and sighed very apparently.

Irving was an overweight, tall and slightly unkempt man in his early 30s he had obviously made an effort with his appearance, but this was undone by the rigors of the sweaty journey from Pennsylvania. He must have weighed in at around 250 pounds and this together with the hot oppressive weather presented Oliver and Louise with none too pleasant a sight and odour.

'Welcome to our humble home Irving. I guess this will be your room for a few days,' said Oliver doing his best to alleviate the apprehension.

'I can't see you settling in New York?' came Irving's first words. 'Not with a name like Oliver. I reckon Chuck or Jack, a man's name, a name that will give you some status without having to work for it. So what's it gonna be Chuck or Jack or maybe Hank. Yeah that'll be your New York name, Hank. It's got certain manliness to it!' said Irving demonstrating not a shred of initial English reticence.

'Yes Oliver, I believe Irving is correct, Hank is much more appropriate, don't you?' said Louise sarcastically.

'OK then Hank tell me what did you do in London, England?'

'I taught Classics,' replied Oliver grandly.

'Classics, you mean like Mozart, Beethoven and Bark them guys?'

'And Rembrandt too,' said Oliver picking up where Louise had left off.

'Those guys were cool. Now I suppose I'll be sleeping in *this* room,' said the American placing his bag on Oliver and Louise's king-size.

Louise picked up the bag and summoned Irving to the second bedroom. She plonked his bag on the small bed and left without a word, closing the door behind the portly Pennsylvanian.

Nevertheless, within half an hour Louise and Oliver had got their new apartment just so. Both were anxious to get out and find their way around. Looking out of the window the broad streets were remarkably quiet with few people on the sidewalks. Only the odd car and yellow taxi moved down along Hester Street. There were however some curious goings-on underneath their apartment as they could hear a lot of thumping and shouting. From what they could pick out it sounded like an army officer ordering his men in some sort of fitness work-out regime.

※※※※※

A small Chinese owned grocery store was Oliver and Louise's first port of call. The owner, Mrs Choy was welcoming and informative. She had a sister and cousins in Islington and Brixton and was planning to visit the UK next year she informed. Mrs Choy pulled out a small tourist map of the Lower East Side she had kept for occasions like this and handed it to Oliver.

'I must tell some warning here in your first day. You stay must away please from the men in the community hall below your apartment. Community Hall ha! That's what they call it now but really this place is a synagogue temple. Men there are Jews who try always to be great in this part of New York,' said Mrs Choy.

'What do you mean exactly?' asked Oliver.

'Today, Friday yes? This area has had most Jewish people for many, many years so no one drives car or buys in my shop on a Friday you see. They don't care, always they buy and drive.'

'It's their Sabbath yeah,' said Louise.

'The men in the hall are Jewish and do thing in a way very different you know from us Orientals. The Jew drive car every day, they turn on lights, they eat anything but on Friday they change. They are kind gentlemen but everyone thinks they up to no good. Mr Choy, my husband think they are not really fully Jews but more like Jewish,' she quipped unknowingly.

We ask but they don't tell us what they really do. Jews who say yes to Jesus, Jesus, Jesus are very, very confusing to us. Just be carefully English people.'

This all seemed too ominous for Oliver who had known Jews all his life and was born and raised amongst Jews in the East End of London. The newcomers decided that there would be no problem in seeing what all the commotion was in the hall below.

Indeed, when Oliver and Louise pushed open the door of the community hall they were welcomed in and asked by several breathless men wearing track suits if they would like to join them in coffee and matzos. The men had just completed one of their regular strenuous work-outs. When Oliver jokingly mentioned that they only drink tea in the afternoon one of them rushed out to Mrs Choy's to make the necessary purchase.

Along with their tracksuits they wore the traditional Jewish broad brimmed hats with their customary long black curls of hair protruding through. The walls had several posters announcing that they were 'Jews Supporting Jesus.' They seemed comfortable with this apparent contradiction.

'My name is Jerry but some call me Jeremiah, take your pick. As a rule we don't have females in this hall for our keep-fit sessions,' said one of them addressing Oliver.

'Oh, why is that?' replied Louise careful to keep fixed her eyes on the man.

'Well it's the women themselves you see. They can get a little embarrassed exercising with us. They have their sessions on Monday, Wednesday and Friday. All's welcome,' said Jerry.

'Hi there. My name is Noah' said another, introducing himself with a wide, warm smile. 'If you are from England it is not likely you would have come across JSJ but we're hoping soon you people will all know too. He poured himself another cup of coffee in quiet contemplation then continued:

'The Gospel of Jesus is simple. It says we're all wrongdoers, every one of us, to some extent or another. We were born that way. To be acceptable to Almighty God we must acknowledge this, that we're wrongdoers and ask for forgiveness via the blood of Jesus who died in the place of our sins. Its Jesus and only Jesus that can do this and not by us trying to live a godly life. From then on, we can ask God to be with us and live the life we were made for. Romans 10 verses 9 and 10 sums it up. It's so important cos we all have to give an account you know.'

'What sort of account?' asked Louise.

Noah gave no reply.

'What sort of account and to who, to whom?' insisted Oliver.

'And what about me and Louise? How will we get on in all this?'

'That's for you both to decide individually. It's our aim to tell others about the Gospel of Jesus and then leave them to think,' said Noah kindly.

'So what's the membership fee? How much to get on board your Ark brother Noah,' asked Louise finally revealing her incredulity.

'It's all free Louise, anything Jesus does for us is free. That's so different from the world we live in.'

At that, the couple decided to take their leave, Oliver thoughtful and Louise disgruntled.

'Oh, and do keep the noise down boys. I need my sleep!' said Louise as a parting shot.

Oliver pondered whether this first meeting with such an unworldly group would have a bearing on their stay. Louise was, as expected much more immediate in her assessment.

'They're cranks Ollie. All of them are a load of cranks so wrapped up in themselves that they can't see that the whole world outside their little coven have got it right and their little group are the misguided ones. I bet there are as many crackpots over here as there are in London. We'll probably meet some more later today.

Jews Supporting Jesus, huh I ask ya! Anyway who's ever heard of Jews who are into keeping fit, that'll be a first! Have you ever heard Woody Allen's sketch on the first Jewish world heavyweight boxing champion? Check it out then you'll know what I mean.' -

It was now time to get a feel of the place, so the two valiant and curious East Enders went on their first Manhattan jaunt. - In Midtown they visited the Empire State Building, Macy's and wandered down Fifth Avenue, along Broadway and then 42nd Street. Through Times Square and past Madison Square Garden they strode, eventually ending up wearily downtown in Washington Square, hours later. The smell, swift movement and raciness of their enormous surroundings dizzied them. They knew beforehand of the city's fast pace but the sheer extent of it all had them feeling quite unimportant as well as stimulated and awe-struck like never before. New York City had little of the splendour of London or the beauty of Paris neither was it graceful. What it did have was a modern day trashiness and effervescence seen rarely elsewhere on the planet. Oliver and Louise were left well and truly agog by its unapologetic brazenness, single-minded purpose and burgeoning majesty. The city promoted itself by simply being itself and you could take it or leave it. Oliver and Louise were clearly planning to 'take it.' They were in love with each other and New York City.

҈҈҈

Chapter 22

We want to be alone

It was their first Monday. Arnie had given the company and stage crew the weekend to acclimatise but now rehearsals for the Broadway production of 'Hello Dolly' had to start in earnest. The bus was due to pick Louise up at '8 am sharp' but she had overslept, was running late and had to make sure that Oliver and Irving knew it. She did make it to the bus on time but was ill-prepared and was forced to skip breakfast which, for Louise was almost sacrilege and totally against the 'dancer's code'.

Louise was in no better mood when she returned exhausted that evening. The apartment was cramped and hence required order and everything putting in its proper place. She had independently decided where that place should be. It was clear that although Oliver had made an effort, Irving was intent on not

living by Louise's rules. Oliver thought it best to, whilst their new flat-mate had his own set of domestic standards reflecting his ad hoc appearance. The inevitable clash ensued with Irving referring to her as a 'Prima Donna at the centre of your own universe.' Louise retaliated calling him 'A grease monkey hic with a chip on his shoulder!'

'What do you think Hank? How do you want the apartment to function? You want rules or are you cool?' asked Irving as he piled some sort of yellow and puce coloured Chinese food into his already full mouth.

'I think you should understand you are our guest and act accordingly. Fair's fair and we want this to be a happy ship with a crew of happy sailors,' replied Oliver firmly yet diplomatically.

Despite this the inevitable final straw came when Louise took out a bottle of fizzy lemonade from the fridge and poured herself a glass. When she had finished she commented that American lemonade was suitably cloudy and superior to anything she had tasted before. Was it because of the bits of real lemon floating in it? Irving corrected her.

'Sorry to disappoint you little lady but just after I'd eaten a hot hot dog I needed a drink. There were no clean glasses so I had to drink out of the bottle!'

'Yuk', Louise's face rapidly reddened. She then rushed out of the apartment and down into the street. Through the window Oliver could see her run across the road to the payphone opposite. She returned minutes later saying that she had just spoken to Arnie and that he would arrange another apartment for Irving to move into 'in the next few days'. To this Irving seemed totally unconcerned, a stance that annoyed Louise all the more. They spoke not again that evening but immense tension remained. As if to wilfully goad, Irving went out and returned with several cans of beer. For the next few hours he burped forcefully and broke wind both with as little decorum as he could muster. That night Louise cried tears of rage into her pillow, not prepared to be comforted, such was her frustration. That particular evening proved to be the low point. -

The subsequent days moved into a week and a week then into a fortnight throughout which Arnie was unable to find an apartment for Irving. To the American's credit however he, at first vaguely then, little by little complied with Louise's wishes until it was practically total. Indeed, domestically Irving transformed into quite the ideal flat-mate contributing over and above what could equitably be expected. Unreasonably Louise was not in any way appeased or pleased with Irving's new commitment. Far from it! What she resented was the firm friendship that was developing between Oliver and Irving. In some ways it was comparable to that which Oliver and Jeff had enjoyed back in London. Irving was somewhat in awe of his English buddy's Noel Coward-type wit whilst the American's dry humour and strange idiosyncrasies would constantly amuse Oliver. Further and much to Louise's chagrin, Oliver was comfortable with being referred to as 'Hank'!

Soon enough, Louise as well as being exhausted by her ever-tightening work schedule was feeling slighted and even excluded. She had vowed that the next time Irving said 'sock it to me baby' she certainly wouldn't let the opportunity pass. This whole situation had to stop. An opening soon presented itself when Louise accused Irving of using her toothbrush. Oliver was not in the least bit moved and Irving just looked confused. Oliver was equally unimpressed when Louise suggested their intimate times would increase 'if there was one less person living in the flat'. Oliver did not exactly dismiss this notion but he did not rise to it either!

One Friday evening all three were at home relaxing after a gruelling week. Louise was particularly content given

that she had Saturday and Sunday off, her first two blank days for a while. Oliver would always make a point of watching 'American Bandstand' on TV every Friday but on this occasion Louise disturbed him and asked him to come into the bedroom leaving Irving snoozing noisily on the couch.

'Ollie, listen I can't find my best earrings and necklace you know the ones you bought me in Brighton a couple of years ago. I need them for Sunday,'

Both then set about a cursory search, albeit Oliver half-heartedly before he eased back in front of the TV.

Over the next few days several other valuables that Louise had brought with her from London went missing. Oliver was becoming more concerned but put forward nothing as a possible explanation. She however was careful not to lay the blame at the door of anyone, preferring to bide her time. In this she did not have to wait too long.

A TAIL OF TWO CITIES

'Irving I know you don't go in our bedroom but I had a couple of gold rings in my jacket pocket. In a sort of secret pocket in my best jacket. You seen them knocking around?' asked Oliver.

Louise was at this point out at work.

'Not much of a secret pocket then was it?' replied the American. 'I can't say I have but I'll keep an eye out Hank,'

That evening Oliver began to panic.

'These mean a lot to me Lulu. Both rings have been in my family for generations. I've searched high and low then back again!'

Louise, who could empathise then went to extraordinary lengths to track down Oliver's missing heirlooms. Indeed, she went as far as pulling up the bedroom carpet as perhaps 'they had slipped out when we unpacked.'

It was a further 48 hours before Oliver concluded that the rings were not misplaced but that something unsavoury had occurred.

'Do you think Irving's behind this?' Oliver nervously asked Louise.

'What do you mean?'

'Can he be trusted Lou? He's here on his own a lot of the time.'

'Well if the rings aren't here, I don't see how else they could have disappeared. Shall I ask him when he comes in later?' she proposed.

'No, no. I'll handle this. If he's short of a few bob then he's more likely to tell me and not you.' he said scratching his head.

As expected Irving knew nothing of the rings' whereabouts or indeed Louise's jewellery however the awkward situation was made all the more fraught by Irving's indifference.

'Hank, a guy like you should get his act together. Anyway what sort of real man wears rings like that unless he's looking for another guy?' said Irving totally unaware of the situation's gravity or Oliver's pending marriage proposal to Louise.

Oliver became instantly incandescent and kicked over the small table with Irving's beer. Irving jumped to his feet immediately and they stood eyeball to eyeball for a few seconds before they simultaneously grabbed one another. They grappled and struggled to maintain a foothold before crashing into the wall and then onto the floor. The two men were not prepared to hold back and struck each other with hardened fist violently about the body, head and face. Both combatants managed to momentarily haul themselves apart to regroup when they set about one another again with increased ferocity, punching, kicking, elbowing and making a huge commotion. Louise stood and observed, arms folded, silent and unconcerned with the battlers or the damage occurring!

The factions battled on for the best part of five minutes as it became more of a sweary wrestling bout than a rugged boxing match. Both blooded men were intent on giving no quarter, not at least until the whirr of a police car siren and the reflection of a blue light flashing brought the warring parties to attention. Irving broke loose from Oliver's head-lock, moved to the window and saw two officers talking to a local man who was pointing up at their apartment.

'I'll come for my things later,' groaned Irving who inexplicably appeared more troubled by the law enforcers than the altercation itself. Irving then grabbed a small towel from the bathroom and dabbed it around his bloodied eyes and lips before wrapping it around his injured hand. He then pushed open the back window to the fire escape, wedged himself out and descended as fast as his bulky frame would allow him.

'Don't bother dropping by I'll throw your bags out at midnight. Me and Ollie can do without a bleeding thief back in our flat. We never wanted you here in the first place. We want to be alone. Sling your hook ya robbing git and leave the keys!' screamed Louise in a Janey-like fashion to the fleeing assailant.

Later that evening, when calm had subsided into relief, the dust quickly settled. Louise was remarkably impressed by her man who she had never seen taking a firm stand on anything really. His 'backbone' was developing she thought. For the first time ever

Louise and Oliver were now a couple living together and alone. With little effort she had got what she originally had wanted. When didn't Louise get what she had wanted?! What's more Hank was now back to being Oliver and Oliver was now stronger, more perceptive and driven than ever before. The night's events changed him in ways he even was unaware of.

Change was in its early stages: Although she was far from top-billing on Broadway, Louise was most definitely lapping up all the excitement the city had to offer. Locals accordingly were taken by her English charm, quick wit and tremendous poise which in turn gave her more confidence and assurance. In addition, her natural beauty was more on display than ever before. Perhaps for the first time in her adult life she enjoyed an inner clarity similar to that of the hero in a final scene of a Bogart/Cagney gangster film or an Agatha Christie stage play. This resulted in a new Louise Elsmore, one that had to fulfil her still ill-defined ambitions, one that strove to progress to the next, still to be conceived level. She wouldn't rest until she had identified her new goal and then attained it. -

The Hello Dolly Wednesday matinee was paradoxically the cast's busiest and most exhausting day but to Louise something to look forward to as it gave her the opportunity to saunter around Manhattan in daylight hours, perhaps to indulge in some window-shopping or day dreaming. It was on one of these midweek, midtown strolls that Louise happened upon a wall decked with a poster – THE GREAT SHOE DEBATE –, TELL US YOUR PREFERENCE, HIGH HEELS OR FLATS?

The billboard went on to say that although this may seem a curious question, your answer says much about 'You, the 1970s woman'. Louise was suitably intrigued, given that for many years she had gathered herself a footwear collection of around 40 pairs but sadly had to leave most of them with a teacher friend in Hackney before setting off for the States. In fact so many pairs had she that Oliver held the notion she had some sort of 'freaky foot fetish'. The 'Great Shoe Debate' was to be held in a small anti-theatre at Carnegie Hall on Seventh Avenue later that month. -

Later on that afternoon Oliver stared restlessly out of the apartment window into Hester Street. At that moment he became taken by the idea of becoming a part of the city's action rather than observing it longingly. What he needed now was something to fill in the long days. He toyed with the idea of buying a dog, something like his long lost Naked. Though never a scrapper, he also considered the virtues of taking up some sort of martial art just in case his path crossed that of Irving's who by now had disappeared completely from the scene. Neither suited him quite as much as finding worthwhile employment. Not having a Green Card to present to a potential employer could prove tricky however but word on the street was that many staff seekers saw this as merely DC trying to stifle business as Green Card = red tape. If you could do the job, looked reasonably decent and had at least a smattering of English then in New York you were employable whatever your status. Oliver set out forthwith.

At the corner of The Bowery and Division Street stood a small smart bookstore ornately decorated in racing green and gold, a tidy sophisticated oasis amongst the hurly-burly. As so many retail outlets did, the store's window contained a card advertising vacancies. Oliver could easily envisage himself working in this semi-cultural setting hence enquired within. A small sharply dressed Italian woman was immediately impressed by the applicant and asked if he'd like to be interviewed there and then? Somewhat surprised, Oliver agreed. The woman then promptly grabbed him by his wrist and led him behind the scenes to the stockroom where she introduced Izzy, her husband. They chatted for a few seconds.

'So you're a Limey? You got a Limey accent that's how come I know you'res a Limey!' proclaimed the man, satisfied with his accurate deduction.

'Got it in one! My name's Oliver and I've come about the job advertised.' he replied jauntily.

Izzy, a portly red-faced man in his sixties put down his overflowing sandwich and smeared the back of his right hand across his mouth. He then looked Oliver up and down intensely before slowly circling, his arms clasped behind his back sergeant major-like. As he started his second circuit he uttered:

'Umm ..... so I guess you're going back to England soon so you'll want a job that's flexible, well paid and in keeping with an educated guy from Europe? Now hear this, my wife Claudia's from Italy, I'm a Jew and you're a Limey but we're all in the States now so we gotta get it together and make some money. We give a service for the people, they give us money. With that money we buy nice things someplace else and so it goes on. That's capitalism! It's as simple as that. I think the idea was invented in England as a matter of fact. OK here endeth the lesson. I'll see you here tomorrow at 9 sharp.'

'Is that an interview?' asked Oliver incredulously.

'That's as good as it gets, unless you wanna interview yourself and show me how it's done Mr Olivier!'

'No that's fine and it's Oliver and not Olivier. I'm a teacher not an actor. So I'll see you tomorrow then,' he replied resolutely.

A TAIL OF TWO CITIES

'Yes, as I said 9 sharp,' repeated Izzy.

Of course there was no thought given to terms and conditions. That was for another day.

It wasn't the most comfortable of first meetings or the most conventional interview but at least Oliver had a job and a job in keeping with his pseudo-status, he thought to himself back at his apartment. Somehow Oliver enjoyed the laissez-faire let's-get-the-show-on-the-road approach many New Yorkers had. To him it was refreshing and 'cool' just like James Dean or a slim leather-clad young Elvis in his early days. Back home he slumped on the chair and smiled contentedly at himself in the mirror across the room. All things considered it was a successful afternoon's work of which he looked forward to relating to Louise that evening. Mrs Spencer too would be pleased that he had found something to occupy himself. He had had told her he'd planned to go job hunting when they spoke on the telephone the day before. Oliver, now gainfully employed was now beginning to feel part of things again and becoming a 'librarian' would do nicely at least for starters.

Chapter 23

Books Smooks!

The traffic roar, the movements and bustle on the street below, together with Oliver's excitement roused him naturally from his deep slumber just after 7 o'clock the following morning. Beside him lay Louise exquisitely restful with her long lush dark hair filling the space around her radiant haloed face. Her perfectly proportioned and even features were loveliness personified. This picture of natural allure was however somewhat tarnished by the hardened greeny-brown mucus that flapped quickly up and down at the entrance of her left nostril. As she breathed out it rattled to the left and to the right as she inhaled. Oliver loved her just the same but thought it best to divest her of the offending intruder that had semi solidified overnight. This he had to do without stirring her and anyway, the endeavour could prove to be a bit of fun before breakfast!

The most obvious implement to get the job done quickly and with little kafuffle had to be a cotton bud. Oliver took out a bud from the packet on the bedside table and slowly edged it toward the vibrating booger quietly humming the Mission Impossible theme music as he set to task. 'Dum Dum Dum Der, Dum Dum Dum Dah ….' It was easy and with one or two tiny upward motions the offending sticky secretion was taken. Louise barely noticed that the obstruction had been removed. Oliver looked at it hanging from the end of the cotton bud and winced. There was however flailing from the other nostril yet another more sizeable emission. This too had to be disconnected. Imperceptibly he wiped the first booger on Louise's right cheek then set about the second. He held his breath and moved in. This proved to be a more testing operation. It was more deeply imbedded and fastened to the nostril wall. Louise was becoming twitchier and rolled over onto her side forcing Oliver to leave the cotton bud in her nose. When she'd settled he moved to the other side of the bed and like a highly trained dental technician completed the extraction causing his 'patient' no discernible discomfort. This hefty hardened snot was so similar in appearance to the other, Oliver believed he had no other choice but to place it on Louise's left cheek. This would enhance the natural symmetry of her face, he concluded.

Emboldened by the whole experience and still with over an hour to get to work, Oliver continued working on both nostrils but now the excavation required considerably more depth. He, at this point could barely hold his laughter. By the time he had finished Louise had five blobs of mucus neatly placed around her face, one on each cheek, her chin, forehead with the wettest and most unpleasant on the tip of her nose. A job well done Oliver decided. Mission Impossible made possible deserved an extra big bowl of Corn Flakes! Some half an hour later Louise woke and stumbled off to the bathroom.

'Aghh my bloody face!' she screeched.

'Yes I noticed that you're getting a few spots lately. Perhaps you're a bit run down Lulu?' said Oliver giving away nothing.

'Ahhkk spots! These are not bloody spots,' came the anguished retort.

'Well what else could they be? They look like spots or zits of some sort or other to me Lou!'

There was a short intense silence before Louise opened the bathroom door and stared fresh-faced momentarily at Oliver who made every effort to appear unconcerned and entirely innocent. Shaking her head in puzzlement (and possibly embarrassment) she trooped back to the bedroom saying nothing more before briefly falling back into bed. -

Needless to say Oliver chuckled to himself throughout the short debut walk to the bookshop. He now refocused fully on the job in hand. Never before had he done what many would consider a menial job although he recalled having been a milk monitor at primary school and stacked shelves at The Co-Op in his mid teens. Nevertheless, working in a bookstore in a foreign land was a small challenge Oliver relished.

A TAIL OF TWO CITIES

On arrival Izzy was pushing up the metal shutters and greeted Oliver with a firm appreciative handshake. The day was bright and glaring so Oliver boldly suggested pulling down the opaque internal window blinds. Before Izzy had a chance to consider, his wife Claudia rushed out and spoke quietly in her husband's ear. Immediately then Izzy pulled down the metal shutters.

'No need to come in Mr Olivier. Just wait there, we'll join you soon,' said Izzy somewhat uneasily.

On the face of it this mini drama seemed ominous, but Oliver had conditioned himself not to be surprised with anything Manhattanites got up to as these were some of the more bizarre people on the planet.

Izzy and Claudia emerged a few minutes later and locked the door of the store.

'We won't be needing you here today Olivier,' said Izzy.

Before Oliver could protest or correct him on the name again, Izzy declared.

'What I've got for you though is even better. Follow me.'

'I don't need all this aggro!' Oliver said to himself but out of curiosity he duly obeyed and trailed behind what must be New York's other Odd Couple.

They had only walked some 200 yards or so from where they had set off when the couple turned into a shop doorway and rang the bell. A small, chic, elegant African-American woman opened the door. She was perhaps in her late 20s with determined, confident eyes set in a kindly face. The air was heavy with the allure of expensive perfumes. She fixed her eyes on Oliver and beckoned them in.

'This is my good wife's beauty Vintage Emporium,' said Izzy triumphantly to Oliver. 'Manicures and makeup and lady-type things. You'll fit in nicely I know it. The ladies will think we got a bit of panache and kapow with an English guy called Olivier seeing to them. Now Belindy here will show you the ropes,' said Izzy.

'But I don't have a clue about nails and things. I thought I'd be working in the bookstore!' pleaded Oliver.

'Books Smooks! Who's ever made money out of paper? I keep telling Maury that books are for losers. Beauty and things like that. That's where the big bucks are,' barked Izzy defiantly.

'Leave him to me Izzy,' said Belindy in a clear, certain tone. 'I'll settle him in.'

Oliver thought for a moment, scanned the surroundings and approved of what he saw.

'Ah! Books Smooks. You're so right Izzy. Whoever made money out of books!' said Oliver having had an apparent near instant rethink.

'I knew you'd see it my way Olivier but I may want you to give me and Claudia a hand out the back if we have a big job on. Take good care of Olivier, Belindy.'

With that Izzy and Claudia hurried through to the back of the Emporium.

Vintage Emporium

A TAIL OF TWO CITIES

Being thrust into a strange situation via a set of odd circumstances could have unsteadied most men. Not Oliver though. He always relished new challenges. The tingle such events provided would naturally outweigh any apprehension. Oliver did however find his beautiful work colleague's warm and unabashed direct gaze somewhat confusing but after a couple of minutes she broke the ice.

'Belindy's my real name but those who I really take to call me Linda. I would like you to call me Linda,' said the woman part seductively.

Oliver knew a come-on when faced with one and responded accordingly.

'Most people call me Oliver but those I take to call me Lord Olivier. What would you rather Linda?'

'You're a Lord a real English Lord?' she replied aghast.

'I am, my dear one of only four. Lord John, Lord Paul, Lord George and myself Lord Olivier.'

'So what happened to Lord Ringo?' Linda enquired catching on.

'I'm afraid he's a drummer and drummers can only become Dukes. Surely you know that!? Duke Ringo of Starr does it ring any bells Linda?'

'Well maybe! Oh you English are so cool. I always wanted to be a royal princess when I growed.'

'When I grew you mean, you should say when I grew not growed. Oh and its autumn and not fall and maths and not math and anti-clockwise and not counter-clockwise…'

'OK Olivier I guess you know best,' she said submissively. 'You English guys are so uptight and awesome at the same time.'

'And you're a tasty bit of crumpet too Linda!'

They both laughed. The ice had been broken.

Linda did all she could to make Oliver feel at home in the hour before the Emporium opened. She attempted to excuse Izzy's unorthodox style and explained that the bookstore was owned by Maury, Izzy's younger brother and that Claudia ran the Beauty Emporium. Izzy though was one of New York's most skilled taxidermists and Oliver was told he would become Izzy's part time assistant when things were slack in the Emporium which was convenient as the 'workshop' was in the back. Izzy specialised in stuffing the recently deceased and well-loved pets 'of Manhattan's rich and stupid.' It was clear however that Oliver was more taken by Linda who he initially thought to be some sort of feeble minded, vampish seductress but throughout the morning her sweet sincerity together coupled with her quite obvious allure fascinated him. She had a kindly inner strength of character and was also as bright as a button. As it turned out Linda was in no way taken in by Oliver's 'Lord and Duke' nonsense as he had at first believed. Most importantly Linda would laugh at his jokes. All in all, Oliver was charmed!

Over the next few weeks Oliver became the Emporium's star attraction fascinating and entertaining all its well-heeled patrons as soon as they crossed the threshold. He had a humorous nick name for each customer and would make full use of his naturally engaging wit, swarthy looks and exaggerated stories of the highlife in Swinging London which of course including 'taking tea with the Queen' and teaching Jagger to move! The clientele lapped it up and cared little for veracity.

Although Linda confined him to solely menial nail filings and polishings Oliver was content enough. His role was to keep the

A TAIL OF TWO CITIES

ladies satisfied and this he achieved magnificently. On the odd occasion when the atmosphere was flagging Oliver would stand in the middle of the floor and recite some Latin prose from Homer's 'The Iliad'. The ladies were wowed and engrossed again and again. Before long word had spread and they were coming in from as far away as Yonkers and The Hamptons. Izzy and Claudia soon saw Oliver and Linda as a great double act and their prime assets and compensated the couple generously with both money and praise. Ultimately Oliver was used less and less helping Izzy stuff cats, dogs, rabbits, parrots and hamsters.

'OK Olivier that'll do in here now,' Izzy would often say from his taxidermy. 'Now go out there and give them sweet ladies some culture!'

Oliver was only too content to oblige, as he wanted to spend, as much time in the Emporium as was feasible.

More pointedly, he somehow missed Linda when they were separated.

Chapter 24

'Persons of the Opposite Gender'

POG

'Springtime, springtime, springtime! Give me April in New York than in Paris any day. I never thought things were gonna work out so well for us in America Lulu,' enthused Oliver.

'Me too. The show's going well, we're still packing 'em in, you love your job and we've got the apartment to ourselves for as long as we like. Who knows maybe soon we'll move over to Greenwich Village. Do you miss London ever?' asked Louise.

'Well …. I miss Naked that's all. I really miss my dog.'

Louise hurriedly prepared for the gruelling matinee ahead. Oliver had the day off so the two decided that they should seize the moment and stroll into midtown. They'd eat and Oliver would drop her off at the theatre before making his way past the tall and glorious towers thereafter heading the few miles downtown and home.

A TAIL OF TWO CITIES

The crisp bright morning was beginning to warm. Oliver and Louise walked slowly for an hour or more along the fast-moving streets and avenues hand in hand still adoring the hectic and demanding city.

'Hey Oliver,' said Louise excitedly. 'Let's go in here and check this out. It's some sort of discussion about shoes of all things,' Louise loved footwear of all description and had bought umpteen pairs since arriving in the US.

The couple had stopped outside Carnegie Hall where another inspiring but quirky 'High Heels versus Flat Shoe Debate' was soon to begin.

Oliver stared at the advertising board and scratched his head as memories of the first time he had met 'Madam Sprigola' in Soho sped back into his mind.

'What's there to discuss? You've always liked high shoes. It's part of what makes you, beautiful you,' said Oliver dismissively.

A small stocky woman who was about to enter overheard their dialogue.

'The shoe debate is for woman only. That's the rule. It's not for them but for us!' she said directing her advice to Louise.

'Well there you go then, the Women's Institute, American style. You enjoy and I'll see you tonight. Have a nice day!' said Oliver somewhat pleased that the decision had been made for him. He gave her a peck on the lips and strode off somewhat gleefully.

'Yuk. Why do you let him do that to you … and in public too?' said the woman to Louise.

'What?!.... What's it to you Miss Dumpty! Have you ever had a pen stuffed up your hooter, you nosy cow?' replied Louise brandishing a biro and reminding herself very much of Janey again.

'You gotta lot to learn missy. A lot to learn,' said the stranger. -

The Carnegie Hall was packed wall-to-wall with an odd mix of chattering, gesticulating women. Women from around the world dazzled Louise with their colourful array of flowing national dress and their equally colourful language. In contrast, dotted around in pairs were women dressed darkly, wearing black polo neck jumpers, black jeans even some with purple shiny boots. This 'Praetorian Guard' was on hand to guide people to their seats and other such innocuous duties. Were they there too to quell any unrest if needed Louise posed?

'Sit here, sit here alongside me,' said a young professionally dressed woman to Louise.

'I can tell you're new here, stands out a mile, I'm not really dressed for the occasion but what the hell,' the woman continued.

Louise could sense the descending hush and sat beside her new acquaintance.

'Hi my name's Louise,' she said warmly.

'Hi I'm Scott but that's my last name, the name I was born with. So tell me now, what's your real name?'

'Elsmore, my real name's Louise Elsmore,' she replied obligingly.

'What's with the shoes and the names and the no-go zone for men. I don't get it?' asked Louise.

'Well Elsmore you gotta lot to learn,' said Scott.

'Hmmm. I've been told that already,' she replied.

A TAIL OF TWO CITIES

There then came a distant and approaching hum of engines. The crowd quietened and from the right side of the stage descended a huge red high heel shoe about the size of a small car. Lowering simultaneously at the other side an equally gigantic boot, the type worn by middle aged, well-educated English ramblers. The caption in the centre read:

'FOOTWEAR TELLS THE WORLD THE WOMAN YOU ARE'

The lights dimmed and onto the stage strode a tall, barefooted woman in her 30s carrying a plastic bag. She took up her position behind the microphone and said simply

'You decide!'

From her bag she took out a red high-heeled shoe and put it onto her right foot. There was a notable air of discomfiture amongst the audience as she did this. Then from her bag she took out a Wellington Boot slipping it onto her other foot. When complete she repeatedly kicked her right foot into the air like some deranged court jester. The audience duly hissed and booed. Quite the reverse when she flailed her booted foot as the crowd took to their feet and cheered and applauded voraciously. Louise somehow felt taken by the rapturous moment and joined the enthusiastic appreciation. She seemed however to be the only one who saw the distinct humour as the woman on stage completed her mime and limped off back into the wings.

'I thought you Americans had no sense of irony,' joked Louise to Scott.

'That's not irony that's for real,' Scott replied.

It was obvious that the two women had missed each other's point.

Following a brief fan-fare the main speaker came to the microphone. She was a young statuesque woman, very much in the mould of Angela Davis. When the clamour had not entirely quietened she held aloft her arms and on slowly bringing them down to her side began:

'There is honour, grandeur and an indefinable strength amongst our gender pool. We learn from a young age about how many ribs we have. We learn from an early age about the X and Y chromosome and we learn from an early age that we can't read maps! Our fathers, brothers, uncles, grandfathers teach us this and dare I say it, our menfolk too. Let me ask you all, raise your hands those here today weighed down by the childish demands of their spouses?'

To much amusement an estimated 80% put their hands up.

'We have always had to do it on our own and the modern world suggests that the other gender have manipulated situations cunningly. We, yes us are freeing up their time so they can play football, fart and philander. Even our own offspring, our boy children could well follow their father's manipulative example if we women allow our repression to perpetuate. Now let me ask you this, who amongst us truly loves the POG they live with and their lifestyle?'

There followed an uncomfortable fidgeting of bottoms on seats.

'POG what's that?' Louise whispered to Scott.

'POG..... PERSONS OF THE OPPOSITE GENDER!' came the stern reply.

'Persons of the opposite gender! Why don't you just say men?'

'Listen Elsmore I don't know your circumstances, but you are required here to act thoughtfully!' said Scott tersely.

Louise looked around expecting most of the positive responders to do so again to this. Only a handful in the auditorium raised their hand. These woman, Louise noted looked to be sitting on their own and had no similar guidance.

Louise, normally courageous and unabashed at displaying her love for Oliver at any opportunity, declined to join the brave, honest or naïve small group.

'Some of the audience here have come from as far away as the Polynesian islands in the Pacific,' the speaker continued. There was a brief ripple of acclaim from a few large women in resplendent garb.

'Pacific island cultures glory in womanhood. They marvel at a woman's ability to cut the crap and get the job done. This irrefutable fact is understood and appreciated by the POG in their land. We in the western world need to look to these women. We need to start from the bottom and emulate that which we yet have and we do this by starting from the bottom by that I mean our feet, our shoes. Tongan women are leaders in their communities and all wear shoes that are flat to the ground. Flat to Mother Earth. No high heels to impede their long march to progress, no stilettos to stumble them as they stride toward equality or to foolishly impress their POG. We must learn from this.' And so the able orator went on for another hour.

There was something comically English about the Monty Python type juxtapositions the speaker used to emphasise her radically feminist stance, but it was put with such genuine heart-felt zeal that Louise soon became compelled to gradual self-examination. Though far from a repressed woman, Louise accepted 'that too much power was in the hands of too few and that these were almost all POG'. Reflecting, she asked herself if these could take in Mr Press and Arnie. Surely Jeff and many other young men who had damaged a naive and immature Janey could be included? Louise left Carnegie Hall intrigued and thoughtful but now even Oliver would be under suspicion.

✳✳✳✳✳✳

The brightening springtime days of April and May 1970 blossomed into the regular hot sultry summer months. Air conditioners whirred, Manhattan's traffic continued to battle with its pedestrians, the war in Vietnam expanded into a South East Asian conflagration and the Nigeria/Biafra war ground to a halt. The popular culture struggled too: A Purple Haze eventually enveloped Jimi Hendrix in London and the Doors were slowly closing on Jim Morrison in Paris. In between Janice Joplin's Holding Company finally lost its grip. All failed to handle their own adulation and gave way to self-indulgence. Meanwhile John Lennon had sent back his MBE to Buckingham Palace in disgust before soon after announcing to the world that he and Yoko were jumping off the hectic London merry-go-round and were on their way to New York City to settle 'happily and anonymously'. Beating them to it were Oliver and Louise who now were as established as they would ever be. In the Spring air they blossomed. Oliver was sometimes prone to the occasional dark day with thoughts of Jeff and Sprig suffering innocently 'amongst society's detritus in a dank prison cell' thousands of miles away but these moods were becoming less bleak and frequent. Mostly though he felt emancipated by his work at Izzy and Claudia's Vintage Beauty Emporium where spending time with Linda was a real treat. Linda reciprocated effortlessly, and Oliver often felt mesmerised by her. Louise's life was evolving too but down a quite unexpected path.

Over the last few months the fledgling New York City Women's Movement had won a place in Louise's affections, which was enhanced by what she referred to as the 'rational rightness' of the cause. This re-evaluation seemed inevitable and although she was not fully in tune with the more flagrant inconsistencies presented in some of their harsher doctrine, she fathomed many of The Movement's principles would, in her lifetime be accepted as the norm. She avidly read the feminist pronouncements of Dr Tracey Frankish, Margarita Quinn and Professor Ann Hall and was now helping with 'The Movement' in organising events and fund raising. She even went as far as pawning Oliver's two most precious gold rings she had 'found' prior to Irving's 'escape' and donated the proceeds to the crusade! Louise was keen to explain to her fellow radicals that rings and their like were symbolic of the controls POG utilised in 'maintaining the status quo in their favour'. She felt it judicious nevertheless not to discuss any of her underhand dealings not only because of her non-Green Card status but because she sensed the workings of a sinister element within the faction that was at least as dishonourable as herself and she did not want to appear to be part of that pernicious sub group.

There was no doubt that Oliver treasured the few spare non-working hours he and Louise had amongst their frantic work schedule but Hello Dolly and the Emporium's continuing success mitigated against this. Friday nights though turned out to be Oliver's night to switch off when Louise was still at the theatre. He would start the evening by bringing home a take away and a cheap bottle of plonk and, kicking off his shoes he'd settle down to watch 'The Beverley

Hillbillies', 'Bonanza' and 'I Love Lucy' on TV. It was however a chance glance out of the window that was to unsettle him. Down below Oliver noticed as many as half a dozen people sitting on a wall opposite his apartment. They were seemingly going nowhere and quite definitely encamped. All were uniformed in black clothing and on their feet solid well-polished boots. Oliver's reaction was dismissive initially but decided to monitor the group's activities. Throughout the next hour the assembly remained on the wall staring toward the apartment. It was then that Oliver set upon a closer investigation and put his shoes on with the idea of innocently walking around the block to see if his increasing paranoia was justified. As he walked through the lobby about to enter the street it struck him that the dark gang were all women. He was immediately zapped by a bolt of real consternation and relived the night in Soho when he was badly beaten by such a mob of booted female thugs and the near miss when on his scooter in Battersea. He hot-footed it back to the apartment to gather his thoughts. At times like this Oliver could call upon the advice of Mrs Spencer. After all, if he had not been the victim of a hefty thumping on Wardour Street he would have never met her.

As so often Mrs Spencer was just the comfort and reassurance Oliver needed. On the telephone, later that evening she told him that although this group would likely have a similar ethos to various groups of female heavies springing up all over England they were essentially aiming to increase their numbers amongst like-minded woman rather than cause injury.

'Women must have their way Oliver,' she'd profoundly say.

'But women do have their way. Take Louise, she always gets what she wants and does it fairly but with dogged determination.'

'Is that her only tactic though Oliver?' she replied.

'I really want to know your take on these mad Storm Troopers outside the apartment and not your view on my Louise!'

'Go and take a look out of the window now Oliver' she countered.

Careful not to be seen, he edged to the window and peered out.

'All's quiet, it seems that they've gone home for the night to polish their steel toecaps. Now maybe I can get some peace before Louise gets back.' said Oliver calmly slipping out of his shoes again.

Oliver was thankful to Mrs Spencer for her soothing words and thorough advice. She would emphasise that few things in life were truly important and that most of the fears and worries he had rarely come to fruition. He spoke of how at times he was missing London and even the girls at Tower Hamlets School. She advised him to remain in New York and work hard at The Emporium.

'I see only good things for you at The Emporium. I think you've landed on your feet there Oliver, stick with it,' she said confidently. -

That night Oliver slept soundly and at peace with Louise in his arms. He had determined that it would be better not to worry her about the dark women he supposed were watching him from the wall opposite until at least the following morning. Over breakfast Oliver spoke casually of his experiences the night before knowing that she had no knowledge of his Soho debacle the previous year. Louise listened attentively as Oliver explained all. She made no comment other than to remind him that 'New York has as many cranks and loonies as London.' Equally she more than suspected that these women were from The Movement and was fully aware of just how intimidating a small radical component could be and how dim a view they took of her cohabiting with a POG. Quietly she resolved to sort them out head-on, Janey-style.

The next day Louise attended her regular early evening meeting at The Movement's new midtown headquarters opposite Bloomingdale's on East 59th Street. She was of course less interested in hearing the new radical thoughts of the guest speaker fresh in from Australia than the others attending that evening. Louise had a pressing matter to discuss with Scott and her partner Hubble.

'Some of the girls have been hanging around outside my apartment on Hester Street. Now I know you're gonna tell me that they're nothing to do with The Movement but I know different. Who are these trollops, what do they think they can achieve by intimidating me like that? I've already told you that when the time is right I'm planning to ditch my POG but you're just making things worse. Now back off all of you,' yelled Louise belligerently.

Temple, who many regarded to be politically left of The Movement picked up Louise's bellicose warning. She put a reassuring arm around Louise but such was the Londoner's indignation it failed.

'Elsmore there is much you have to learn about us here in New York,' Temple said softly.

'Why the hell do people keep telling me this. I'm a woman in my own bloody right and do not need to be patronised by you or anyone here,' screeched Louise for all to hear.

'The apartment you share with that POG of yours….er it's on Hester Street on the Lower East Side, correct?' asked Temple.

'You bloody know it is. You're probably one of those who's been skulking around there last night,' claimed Louise.

'You better come with me. I've got something that might alter your perception of things completely' said Temple with confident insight.

Temple, Scott and Hubble led Louise up a couple of flights of stairs and to the back of the building.

'Take a look out that window Elsmore,' said Temple.

Louise complied. Looking up at her as she looked down were as many as a dozen young men. Some were sitting on trashcans nonchalantly eating popcorn whilst others were immersed in reading. What seemed to be the oldest in the gathering was avidly scrawling on a clipboard.

'Recognise 'em?' asked Hubble.

Louise looked hard.

'No, should I?' said Louise remaining indignant.

'Jews Supporting Jesus,' replied Scott.

'Hmmm ….. Jews Supporting Jesus, Jews Supporting Jesus? We got a load of them just below our apartment. They're into keeping fit and suck like I believe,' said Louise.

'If they were only interested in fitness then they wouldn't spend half their day staking out The Movement,' said Temple.

'What, a stake out?!' asked Louise incredulously.

'Well let me explain Elsmore. You'll have noticed that the JSJ are all exclusively POG. That's fine by us but what isn't is their view on the world's women. They see us as degenerates who are seeking to subjugate if not destroy womankind. They set the rules and we should abide by them! So long as we're carrying their offspring or seeing to their needs, we're good little girls. If we dare challenge their set order they want to crush us!' replied Temple decidedly.

'They would crush you too Elsmore,' added Scott.

'And your mother and your sister and all womankind if given the chance,' Hubble confirmed.

'These are not JSJ. The JSJ wear a sort of uniform. Hats, curled tussled hair and all that. These men are just men. Anyway, why are that lot out our apartment?' asked Louise.

'They believe that we'll all melt away if they intimidate us,' replied Temple.

'They want to scare us back to the kitchen and bedroom,' said Hubble.

'POG want fall the perks whilst giving nothing in return,' pronounced Scott.

Louise took a deep gulp and winced.

'They think they can bind our wrists and ankles to the bed, abuse us and that we get some sort of pleasure from that! Would you?!' snarled Hubble. 'Would you?'

'They want but they are not going to get. So their response is predictable. Like all spoilt POG they stamp their little feet if things are not to their liking. But strong women believe in like for like. So that's one of the reasons why we were on Hester Street last night and again tonight and so on. We are not taken in by the JSJ in civilian clothing. We can be equally menacing if called to be so Elsmore. We expect you to back us and not back off!' said Scott bluntly.

'People who follow Jesus are cool and peace-loving, aren't they? Now look, I think I know what's happening here. It's a simple misunderstanding it seems. We live above a community hall. Any group can hire it out and meet there,' argued Louise looking down at the men on the street outside.

'Who knows, perhaps they just use the same hall as the JSJ or are some JSJ breakaway group acting as a decoy. Anyway, we don't trust them, any of them!' said Hubble.

'So, what are you saying? Are you saying these POG are simply into plain harassment? If they're harassing the Movement why don't you report them to the police?' said Louise stabbing her finger angrily at the window.

'The cops! The cops are all POG and those that aren't are just sad women who deny their gender calling. Now are you with us or not Elsmore? You must decide now! Are you prepared to stand and fight against these authoritarian despots or will you continue to wallow in the filth of the downtrodden and have them smear their soft excrement in your face?' implored Hubble explicitly.

Louise saw the need for a measured response and thought for a moment.

'I'm a woman first,' she replied quietly. 'Freedom, equality, power that's not too much to ask.'

'That's just what we need to hear Elsmore. The Movement must be built on a foundation of ambitious strong women like yourself. Strong women work well together. What you need to get into your head is that we live together or we live on our own. To play a leading role in The Movement Elsmore you have to ….. rearrange your domestic situation,' said Hubble ominously. 'And you have to do so quickly!'

Chapter 25

The Good, the Bad and the Shaven Headed Witches!

'Louise, Lulu come and take a look at this quick!' shouted Oliver in an increasing state of alarm. He got no response.

'Louise quick …. what you doing?' he repeated impatiently.

'A number two!' she replied. Louise was in the bathroom and in one of her frivolous moods.

'You need to see this now! How long you gonna be?'

'Oliver weren't you ever told that it's quite ungentlemanly to ask a lady of my standing and status how long it takes for her to evacuate?' Louise could be as coarse as any man when the mood took her. 'Can you imagine Prince Philip being so impudent when Her Maj is sitting on her other throne?'

'Pro rectium anus ass regardum andrex!' replied Oliver obscurely.

'Well this must be serious. It always is when you prattle on in Greek,' said replied.

'It's Latin actually as you well know and it means 'wipe your arse and take a look at this. Now!"

'OK Ollie I'm seeing to my pert botty now….. I'm pulling up my silken bloomers now or shall I go commando today? Have I got time to wash my hands Ollie dear?'

'No time for merriment sweetheart. If you don't get your skates on you'll miss it.'

Their New York adventure was now to move on apace and things between them would be shifting. –

Eventually Louise came smiling from the bathroom.

'There, look they're there!' said Oliver anxiously.

'Where?'

'They're there,' said Oliver pointing at the window.

Louise's demeanour altered instantaneously, she knew just what to expect. She peered into the street below at a handful of The Movement's fervent fundamentalists who had come to make their presence felt with the JSJ group that could he heard thumping around as they exercised furiously below. From the window Louise was immediately recognised and the women waved at her knowingly. She responded with a barely perceived wriggling of the fingers on her concealed right hand which was held tight against her chest, she turned.

'What's the big deal Ollie?' she said.

'The big deal is that these girls have been hanging around outside night and day. It can only mean trouble,' he said.

'Girls, Girls! They're not girls. I see only women. Women Oliver not girls…. all of them over 21 years old don't you think?'

'Why can't they do something useful? Even the Gestapo didn't just hang around,' he replied with equal scorn.

'Do you think that because we're mere women we should be at home doing the washing up, making the beds or popping down the shops. If women want to sit out and enjoy the sun then let them be. Wise up Mr!'

'And they'll be sitting out there tonight enjoying the moonlight will they? They've been there ages now so you need to wise up Missy!'

Louise was now in no mood to placate Oliver by explaining that the women were only interested in the bizarre POG flexing below and not him. In fact she became so indignant that she only fuelled his misplaced paranoia.

'Perhaps they're waiting for you Oliver. Maybe they want to give you a real good hiding because you're such an outdated Victorian tosser!'

'Don't be so …. Stupid,' he said.

'I'd watch your back if I were you Oliver dear. There's only one murder a week in London but I heard there's a dozen murders ever day in New York you know!'

With that Louise gave him a sardonic wink and left for the theatre content that Oliver had been rattled. Indeed so shaken was he that when he left the apartment for the Emporium he slid out through the back exit. He wouldn't be trailed. -

Linda could see that Oliver had something on his mind the moment he walked in. Without enquiring directly she suggested he put his feet up read the paper for a short time before the first appointment arrived.

'I've got you under my skin. I've got you deep in the heart of me - So deep at the start you're really a part of me. I've got you under my skin - I've tried so not to give in………..'

Linda's mellifluous tunefulness emanating from the next room cheered him. She sang so sweetly that it proved the ideal distraction and antidote for his troubled mood. Louise had never ever spoke to him with such vehemence as she had done that morning so he welcomed anything that would take him out of himself.

'You've a beautiful voice Linda,' remarked Oliver.

'I only sing when there's a need to,' she replied.

'So why are you now?'

'I can tell that you might need a little uplifting. Your British stiff upper lip was quivering when you arrived. Things not going too well?'

'Things are fine Linda. Never better but thanks for asking and thanks for singing.'

He felt it somehow disloyal to Louise to complain about her in any way hence the cover up. Up until then he believed that it was only Louise and more recently Mrs Spencer who related to him well enough to appreciate his feelings.

'You'll make someone a very happy man one day Linda,' he said.

At that moment a small smiling, round woman entered the Emporium: the first customer of the day. –

Throughout the remainder of the week Oliver and Louise's disagreement fell from mild irritations to, on one occasion, a raucous slanging match. He would storm out of the apartment in a huff and she would sulk for hours on his return. The next day they would half-heartedly attempt to patch things up but it never lasted.

It would be her turn then to storm out and he would sulk and so the cycle continued. There is never one sole reason for the bitterness and so never one simple solution. One conclusion that they were able to reach separately however was that Louise was changing and Oliver didn't like what he saw. Although he did pull his weight on household matters it was not a strict even split. Louise sensed that he was becoming more like Irving than even Irving himself and sought to redress this by stipulating who should do what particular chore. He accepted this but when she then decided that household duties should somehow be tied to their respective incomes Oliver remonstrated.

'I work longer hours at the Emporium than you do at the theatre.'

'Maybe, but I earn a lot more than you do Mr!' retorted Louise.

There was a momentary silence whilst she considered a more cutting addition. It didn't take long.

'So, little Oliver you either get another job to keep up with me or …… ship out! What's it to be?' –

During the short walk to work Oliver was now more miserable and dejected than at any time since arriving in America. Unaware of The Movement's influence on Louise he was unable to rationalise why the woman he loved so had converted into a 'Screaming Banshee.'

'That's because you never put your foot down at the beginning,' suggested Izzy. 'Take my Claudia, now there's a woman who knows how it works. We're from the old school Olivier, which is a damn sight better than the school you kids got now. I work, Claudia works and we split it down the middle 50/50. She's a crazy Italian and I'm a clever Jew. Both second generation and both still really loving life, America and each other. So you see Olivier just because the

Italians fought for Hitler it don't mean that us Jews can't eat pasta on the Sabbath. You gotta reach an agreement or you gonna have to accept a Dictator. Ain't that right Claudie honey?'

This was one of Izzy's regular nonsensical pearls of wisdom that more confused Oliver and even Claudia than answered any question. What Oliver did ascertain was that domestic peace could only be reached at a price.

'Hey Olivier!' said Izzy. 'This kid Louise, she screwing around cos all I know is when a woman changes her feelings there's always something else going on in the background and my bet is it's some other guy she's keeping in the background!'

The possibility of Louise having 'an affair' had never crossed his mind. Indeed, the thought of such an occurrence so disconcerted him that he immediately dismissed it from his thoughts.

Claudia gave a female prospective:

'She likes alots of men, she works in the show business and be's with alots of men. She likes alots of sexy loving eh? She pretty too eh?'

Linda was within earshot in the adjoining room as the discussion on Oliver's fraught home situation proceeded. She thought it expedient not to get directly caught up but knew that Oliver would welcome a diversion.

'Who's for coffee?' she asked.

'I'll have one if you're making!' Oliver replied.

'Coming up,'

Linda soon came in with the hot beverage. She approached Oliver wearing her usual warm smile and handed him the cup. From her pocket she took out a small folded piece of red paper and handed it to him without explanation. Oliver opened it.

It read: *When I look at you I like what I see. Call me anytime 021-716 4747. Love Belindy xxx*

By the time he looked up Linda had gone but he could hear her singing.

'Something in the way he moves, attracts me like no other lover could - Something in the way he woos me…. Your'e asking me will his love grow. I don't know, I don't know'

Oliver sighed deeply and read the note over and over as her tender voice filled the air and aroused him. He was passionately stirred by the idyllic combination of her resonance and words but his heart was inclined toward his Lulu and to Lulu exclusively.

✻✻✻✻✻

Friday night: a full week had passed since Oliver first spied the women in black who were still encamped across Hester Street. He had almost gotten used to them, even recognising some of their faces. They were clearly working on some sort of rota but Oliver still couldn't figure out why they were content to simply monitor his movements and not approach him. He had spoken to Mrs Spencer in London on the telephone earlier in the evening but she failed to convince him that the black-clad stalkers had nothing to do with Sprig, his incarcerated former partner in crime. Mrs Spencer however was much more concerned about the state of his relationship with Louise.

'Perhaps it's time to move on Oliver? Have you considered a future with that charming young lady at the Emporium? I just have a nasty feeling about Louise. I'm not sure that she has anything but her own interests at heart,' she ventured.

'Louise and me have vowed to stay together. This is the first really big test we've ever had. These sort of things always happen to couples who are really in love. I've managed to get a $75 advance from Izzy my boss because Lou thinks she's having to subsidise me. She's a big Broadway earner, whilst I file and polish finger nails and tell made up stories from the land of yore!'

'Be careful Oliver, very careful. There's things about Louise that make me uneasy. Be aware of how love can string you along,' she counselled compassionately trying to wean him away from any pending danger.

'I know Lulu better than anyone on earth. 'Tis simply a rocky blip and nothing more.'

Later that same night Louise left the theatre exhausted. Hello Dolly was still spoken of highly on Broadway and the box office had never been busier. Although she was pleased with the success, the relentless pressure of show after show was becoming more an ordeal than pleasure. As the traffic thundered down The Great White Way, and before she could hold out a tired arm to hail a taxi one of the same pulled up revealing its two surprise passengers - Scott and Hubble. The two shaven-headed radicals now nursed an acute dislike of Louise which was keenly reciprocated. All three basically shared the same outlook on the new role for Womanhood but there the consensus was to end.

'Elsmore, well there's a coincidence. We're heading downtown to relieve some of our partners outside the freaky JSJ on Hester so do ya wanna ride?' said Hubble grinning widely.

Louise would never have chosen these two as her late-night travel companions but she was too weary to object.

'I'm totally, totally shattered and completely bleedin' knackered,' said Louise.

'Knackered?' said Scott.

'Yeah, knackered. It means washed up or wiped out, whatever it is you say,' replied Louise.

'Short cropped hair.... that's what women in The Movement expect. So you think you're different do you?' complained Scott.

'I can't be bothered with all that stuff about my hair right now,' she replied.

'You're never bothered about anything but little Miss Louise. I bet ya gotta go home now and cook and clean for your controller I suppose or is he out with his floozy,' Scott calculated.

'You seem to know alot about things. In fact, I've already warned you two to keep out of my affairs. When the time is right I'll fix Oliver and I don't need any of your bloody help. How the hell can The Movement get anywhere with you two stirring weirdo idiots spilling poison everywhere,' spewed Louise who was by now more agitated than exhausted.

'Remember Elsmore we got our people outside your place each and every day. We know who's coming and going!' said Hubble with fake concern.

That was it! Without a moment's hesitation Louise swung her hardened fist fully into the side of Hubble's face whose head in turn sprung sideways crashing into Scott's unsuspecting nose. This sparked a massive and brutal free for all in the back seat of the yellow taxi that swerved in surprise. Although outnumbered Louise, overrun by indignation battled with a force that can only emanate from unbridled rage. Given their limited space, the three combatants managed well enough in their kicking, gouging, scratching and hair pulling to inflict considerable harm to one another. The distress that the backseat battlers were accountable for would have sent most cab drivers into apoplexy but this New Yorker was hardier, and rather than remonstrate he steadied and continued the journey monitoring the catfight through his rear-view mirror. His only direct involvement was to quietly plea to the hanging St Christopher emblem hanging from said mirror for safe passage. He weighed that the last thing he needed was three angry bloodied women spilling out of his vehicle onto the city streets only to be crushed by a Wal-Mart truck. Were that to have transpired and this being New York, he'd probably be off the road for a week whilst reapplying for his licence and this wouldn't do at all! -

The melee ended with the journey. Scott and Hubble's numerous radical associates, who on seeing the fracas came to their aid. Louise didn't have a chance and having broken away hurriedly left the scene exchanging insults.

A TAIL OF TWO CITIES

'That's just the start Elsmore. Now go and do your womanly duty. Your supervisor is up there waiting with a list of chores for you before he goes on his next date,' screeched Hubble derisively.

'Go fuck yourselves the lotta ya,' she responded with equal rancour.

'Go get your hair cut, you disgrace to womankind,' yelled Scott.

'I'd rather have a red-hot poker shoved up me Jacksy than look like you shower of bleedin' baldy wankers!'

Louise was becoming an East End fish wife believing that not even Janey would have come up with such a retort.

To date Louise had never involved herself in a slanging match in the street. Such a flagrant and public demonstration of wrath was previously thought to be uncalled for and decidedly uncool. Louise was changing however. Imperceptibly she felt that life was spinning unmanageably into oblivion and beyond. Further, she now had the seed of a notion that Oliver; her Mr Reliable was being unfaithful. This conception was to ferment over the weekend until she determined to take back some control or at least endeavour to do so. She hadn't concluded quite how this could be done but she was determined not to have Scott and Hubble at some point smugly say

'Well we told ya so!'

☙☙☙

Chapter 26

The Naked Truth

The prospect of the rigours of another trying week was beginning to weigh heavily on Oliver and Louise. Their mutual suspicion remained closeted adding to the strain that they now imposed upon their relationship. For days now they barely spoke and in bed they distanced themselves as much as the king size bed would permit.

'You got alot on this week?' asked Louise fishing.

'Nothing more than usual. I'm working just half a day today but Izzy wants me to do one or two sessions in his brother's bookshop,' Oliver replied.

'I thought you were employed in the Emporium only?'

'Well yeah, but I'm just going to have to cover for a bloke who's on a week's holiday,'

'You gonna be working there on your own?'

'No there's someone else there who'll be running the place.'

'Oh yeah, this person got a name?'

'Pedro, Juan, Carlos or something Spanish I think. What you got on this week?' enquired Oliver.

'Just like every bloody week. Arnie's holding a meeting. He's thinking of a Thursday matinee as well as Wednesday. The man's a bastard slave driver!'

'You don't usually use language like that Louise.'

'Well that's how you and the rest of the world make me feel right now,' she said crashing her full cup hard down onto the table and showering the area with hot tea.

Oliver was again shaken by her unprovoked mini-tantrum. Although he had seen it several times before they were now regular occurrences and were attached to a sneering disdain.

'Perhaps you need to clear your head and get out for a walk before you work,' said Oliver thoughtfully.

'Perhaps you need to get out for a walk and keep walking!' she replied her face reddening with anger.

'I'm going nowhere Louise, nowhere!'

They parted that morning equally miserable both unable to identify the origins of the en-passe or figure out a likely remedy. Their respective aspirations were different however, Oliver to just have fun whilst hoping to reawaken their love and Louise intent on living her own life as a single woman accountable to no one but herself. She was now convinced her POG would hold her back and needed an excuse, a pretext to sever the lacklustre connection with her 'flatmate.' She now set her mind to secretly follow Oliver that afternoon to see if he actually was cheating on her. -

A TAIL OF TWO CITIES

Oliver's disposition and outlook bucked up as soon as he entered the bookstore where he was greeted by a most delightful yapping Dalmatian puppy that came bounding up to him.

'I thought you'd like him. Everyone does you just can't help yourself,' said Linda.

'Oh, it's you. I thought that you were at the Emporium today,' asked a surprised Oliver.

'Izzy thought I deserved a change of scene as well. Claudia's working the Emporium and we're doing the books for half a day. You OK about working here alone with me?' she ventured nervously.

'A change of scene, a beautiful woman and a little puppy, what more could a man want!' replied Oliver wistfully.

This was the sort of answer Linda was hoping for. She recognised that Oliver thought her attractive but he had as yet never acknowledged such or indeed her brief note to him.

'Yeah I got the puppy from my friend last night. It's mine if I want him. What do you think?'

'Of course go for it. He's beautiful, aren't you boy!' said Oliver tickling the dog under its chin as it yelped and nuzzled pleasingly.

'You thought of a name for him yet Linda?'

'No not really. You got any ideas?'

'Hmmm. I can choose, can I?'

'Go ahead.'

Oliver looked deeply at the dog and then to Linda. He gradually became watery-eyed clearly moved.

'Well we could call him …. Naked.'

'Naked! As in no clothes naked. Why Naked?'

'Back in London I had a puppy dog given to me as a 21st birthday present by my best mate Jeff. He was truly loyal and devoted to me and me alone. I mean the dog and not Jeff. He never saw the faults in me, never thought I wasn't pulling my weight in the apartment, never had dark moods and never thought that I should go for a long walk and not come back,' said Oliver remotely.

'What happened to him?'

'Well Louise took him for a walk and somehow, don't ask me how, he got lost or ran off or something,'

'Was this walk a …… long walk?'

'Yeah'

'He just ran off! Did he normally do things like that?'

'No never,'

'So what do you think really happened?'

'I told you, Louise said she called him back but he just …'

Oliver was stopped dead in his tracks and for the second time ever doubted that Louise, his Louise may have been less than honourable.

'I don't know what to think anymore. Just don't know who she is or what she wants or why she's so miserable. But anyway my dog was called Naked and I think it would suit this little fella here,' he said perking up a little.

Linda took the dog from Oliver and silently paced around the bookshop. She wore a thoughtful expression and would momentarily glance in Oliver's direction before declaring.

A TAIL OF TWO CITIES

'OK Naked it is!'

Oliver sighed, then smiled, then pecked Linda on the cheek and thanked her graciously. Naked seemed pleased too. The rest of the working day Oliver spent entertaining the puppy and studying Linda's curves and beauty taking care not to be noticed.

That afternoon Louise attended one of The Movement's fortnightly discourses given by yet another 'internationally renowned feminist guest speaker'. It also gave her the opportunity to test the water with Scott, Hubble and others following the taxi bust up. They and most of the usual radicals where there to lap up the new thinking on 'Repression, Realisation and Resourcefulness'. Though the words spoken were much of the same there was a new emphasis on how the modern free woman should present herself to the world. Heels were still of course outmoded, but they all knew that anyway. Now however it was long hair that was equally derided and with this in mind many of the women there were sporting short, even cropped hair. Louise was feeling considerable discomfort being the proud possessor of a long, thick substantial dark mane which she had no intention of relinquishing despite this and Scott and Hubble's promptings. She asked herself why she was out of step with so many of The Movement's adherents when she ultimately shared their belief that woman need commensurate representation in all areas of life. Louise drew the line at wearing a 'hair uniform'.

When the meeting disbanded several women, all on the radical wing, though not Scott or Hubble approached Louise. They bluntly harangued her about the length of her hair and the need to present a standardised front to Persons of the Other Gender. Louise was in no mood to fight her corner. What was foremost in her thinking was keeping tabs on Oliver's whereabouts that day and to do this she needed to get to the bookstore before it closed.

※※※※※

Arriving at the bookstore at lunchtime was quite a sacrifice for Louise such was her anxiety. It meant that she had to miss an important meeting at the theatre wherein Arnie was going to extend the contracts of most of the performers given the proposed Thursday matinee. Those in the cast that didn't get to the gathering could be putting their future with the Hello Dolly production at some risk. Despite this Louise encamped in a busy antiques shop opposite Oliver's bookstore and waited for the shutters to come down.

Sure enough Oliver emerged and waited momentarily on the sidewalk. Following this from her vantage point she noted -

A young, attractive woman close behind holding a small black and white dog. Oliver and the woman spoke for a minute or two and began to laugh somewhat raucously. They obviously knew each other well. The passing busses and trucks made it difficult for Louise to see and interpret all that occurred from the other side of the road but it appeared that the woman handed the small dappled dog over to Oliver. She then took out a small black and white leather strap from her bag and attached it to the dog's collar. The woman then pecked Oliver on the cheek and before much longer they parted, the woman jauntily heading downtown and Oliver and the dog the other way. -

Louise was livid. Could this be the woman Scott and Hubble had seen with Oliver? Did The Movement actually have Louise's best intentions to heart? Was her Ollie a philanderer despite their vows to one another? YES! YES!! and YES!!! to all three questions she concluded. She left the antiques store, crossed the road and followed Oliver unobtrusively at a safe distance, stopping and staring into the nearest shop window each time Oliver crouched to attend to the puppy. After a while she decided that to follow them any further was futile. She had seen with her very own eyes the kiss and the warmth Oliver shared with this 'other woman'. She could almost feel the heady heat Oliver and 'that trollop' generated. No more proof was needed. Oliver had to go!

It was now 2.15pm. Louise had put aside the whole afternoon to trail Oliver but she managed to gather the required evidence in barely no time at all. There was still time to get to the theatre for Arnie's meeting. After all, why should she put her career at risk for a 'no-good, double-dealing, perfidious POG!?' She hailed a cab and headed uptown. On arriving at the theatre Louise paid the man hurriedly and rushed in. Minutes later another cab pulled up some 50 yards away from the theatre's stage door. From it leapt a small Dalmatian puppy on a black and white lead at the other end of which was Oliver!

Louise was met inside the theatre by a couple of her stage colleagues, one of whom announced that Arnie wasn't well and the meeting was postponed until the same time tomorrow. In point of fact Louise was quite relieved by the news as her mind was so scrambled she wouldn't have been able to play any active part. Not wishing to go back to the apartment where she knew Oliver would likely be, she resolved to indulge in a spot of retail therapy and Macy's was just a few blocks away.

Along the crowded sidewalks no more than a hundred paces behind strode Oliver and the new Naked in hot pursuit of Louise. It was the puppy's first experience of negotiating himself safely around the legs of speeding humanity and although managing well, was unable to easily keep up with his new master.

'Come on boy, let's be having ya,' said Oliver to the pup cheerily. 'If we don't keep up we'll end up losing her and we'll never know if she really is seeing someone behind my back, will we?' Oliver then picked up the puppy, held him close to his chest and hastened through the city throng past Madison Square Garden and onward.

In the shadow of The Empire State Building Louise stood forlornly looking up at the Macy's monolith before finally summoning up the wherewithal to enter through the heaving host of thoughtless, harried shoppers. Oliver, picking up on the intention panicked knowing that he couldn't take Naked into the busy department store. He was convinced that Louise was but minutes away from a prearranged liaison with her secret lover in one of the store's many restaurants and that there never really was a meeting with Arnie. Oliver then secured the dog's lead around a signpost, stroked him reassuringly and hotfooted in after her. Sure enough Louise went to the nearest eatery and ordered. Oliver took up a nearby position in Women's' Casuals and waited for the inevitable tryst. His target was content to simply read her magazine and sip her tea whilst occasionally glancing around to observe her surroundings. Her scanning startled Oliver, which prompted him to take further precautions. He purchased a small chequered peaked hat with earflaps and straps from a nearby display counter, never losing sight of the woman who had inflamed him so. He pulled the peak as far over his eyes as reasonable and tied the straps under his chin. Together with his dark glasses Oliver's disguise was complete, surely no one, not even Louise would recognise him now. It was predictable however that the bizarre man wearing a 10-year-old girl's peaked cap and dark glasses would attract the staff and consequently store security's attention. So Oliver, the spy who was following the spy was himself being spied upon.

It was a full half an hour before anything of note happened. Louise slowly rose from her table and collected another cup of tea from the self-service counter before returning to her read. Patiently Oliver remained indiscreetly close convinced that some concrete evidence of Louise's disloyalty was soon to show itself and it was this that prevented him from going to the bathroom. He stood for some time swaying on the spot and grimacing but just before embarrassingly giving way to nature on the floor of the Sportswear Department he charged to the nearest men's bathroom which, he was informed was on the floor above.

Sure enough the inevitable had occurred. Yes, by the time Oliver had resumed position his quarry had disappeared! He cursed his bad luck resolving to continue the trail tomorrow and the day after and the day after that, in fact as long as it took to verify Izzy and latterly his own contention that Louise's treachery lay behind her recent callousness. Oliver then divested himself of his disguise and morosely returned home on the subway with Izzy's words ringing in his ears: 'when a woman changes how she feels there's always something else going on and my bet is it's some other guy!' –

During this period all too often for Oliver's liking, a handful of shaven-headed women in their intimidating garb were on 'patrol' on Hester Street making their presence felt with the JSJ brethren. 'Street furniture' Oliver referred to them as. This day however the women were there in greater number and seemingly more agitated too. Down in Mr and Mrs Choy's grocery store Oliver overheard some customers expressing their outrage that the police had failed to follow up the residents' complaints and have the women moved on. Mr Choy, ever the capitalist took a more pragmatic line appreciating the business that the loiterers had brought him.

'You know anything about these lady with bald head Mr Oliver?' asked Mrs Choy.

'We've got them in London too. They've got nothing better to do than sit and stare up at my apartment. I'm not hiding myself away anymore. Anyway don't give two hoots,' replied Oliver.

'They stay outside now because you no longer give them your hoots? You must start again with your hoots then maybe they leave.

Your lady Louise talks to them very friendly but they always stay here,' said Mrs Choy innocently.

'What! Louise knows these women?' he screeched.

'Well she talks with them many mornings Mr Oliver and will sit with them on the wall there for long, long time too. They like to talk! Them ladies from England too?'

Such was Oliver's distrust of anything he hadn't actually seen himself that he semi-convinced himself that Mrs Choy was somehow mistaken but nevertheless yet another seed of doubt and confusion was planted. By the time he reached his apartment he was deflated, angry and confused.

That evening Oliver and Louise avoided even eye contact speaking only in a cursory manner. Of course neither of them appreciated the comic irony of being followed incognito by one and then the other. Nevertheless, Louise made it apparent that their future lay apart. Like a fisherman without a hook Oliver was feeling decidedly helpless and hapless. Louise's stony heart was dark and getting blacker and more vengeful. She wanted only to extricate herself from Oliver but knew he would not leave willingly. Having given it some thought she resolved to enlist Uncle Sam to assist in the sundering!

※※※※※

That night Oliver and Louise again lay as far apart as the bed would allow, quickly withdrawing any part of their body should it accidentally touch upon another's. It was idiocy and they both knew it. Not long after they had both eventually relaxed into some form of sleep Oliver abruptly sat bolt upright with the cry of.

'Naked, Naked …. Naked!'

Louise was equally startled.

'You've been dreaming …. What about Naked? He's long gone, probably picked up by the dog wardens,' said Louise.

Oliver jumped out of bed and walked around fretfully gesticulating and pleading to the unknown for help. How was he to explain his forgetful neglect to Linda? And where was the poor puppy now?

'Oh God I am such a stupid air-head …. Err yeah the dog wardens or maybe someone would have taken him,' he feigned.

'He's likely living the life of Riley with some posh family in Hampstead,'

'What? Hampstead ….. Oh no not …. My Naked…. Some other dog …' Oliver's voice trailed off and he continued to chide himself.

'Naked the Dalmatian?' enquired Louise attempting to cease the moment.

Oliver was too embroiled in his moment of anxiety for Louise's telling comment to register with him. It was her attempt to surreptitiously inform him of what she had witnessed outside the bookstore that afternoon. He in turn was in no mood to explain who the new Naked was lest he be forced to spell out how, where and more worryingly, in what circumstance he had lost the puppy. Neither of them slept soundly that night. -

"I'll come clean. I'll just come out and say to her 'Linda I'm terribly sorry but I took your puppy to Macy's yesterday. I was following Louise who was about to meet her new lover so I left him tied up outside there. Sorry but I simply forgot I had him with me'"

So went Oliver's imaginary rehearsal that morning as he prepared to face his trusting workmate. He remembered how devastated he was when Louise told him that she had somehow let his Naked get away from her at Victoria Park some twelve months prior.

'Would Linda take it so bad?' he asked himself.

For the moment anyway it did take his mind off the problems he and Louise were having.

His heart pounded like at no other time since he had arrived in America. He remembered how distraught he felt on hearing Jeff and Sprig's prison sentence and when he had 'lost' his mother's rings. This feeling now was up there with the worst of them. As he approached The Emporium his pace quickened. He instantly became emboldened and felt the need to tell Linda of the bad news immediately and at once to get it out of the way. But as soon as it came his courage fled from him. He could feel his feet dragging as if shod by leaded diving boots. The last few yards were tortuous.

When he finally made it through the front door rather than being confronted by an angry face he was met by a small yelp. Seconds later a small black and white Dalmatian puppy bounded up to him scratching at his feet imploring to be gathered up. Linda appeared and asked.

'What happened to you Oliver? I was worried all night about you!'

'You were worried about me!? I'm fine but how come Naked's here? How did you get him back?'

Linda explained that the puppy was spotted by a kindly passer-by and taken to the cops of the 14th Precinct. Using his nametag, they contacted me early yesterday evening and soon after puppy and owner were reunited.

'I was up all night worried about you,' said a greatly relieved Oliver tickling the dog fondly.

'I was up all night worried about you Oliver but somehow Naked worries about nothing' replied Linda curiously.

He apologised and then told her of his escapade in Macy's tracking Louise and how he was so consumed by it all that he simply forgot about the dog.

'Maybe it's time for a change!' was Linda's advice.

Oliver simply sighed. -

Things remained much the same over the next few days. Louise was as vexatious, unfeeling and distant as of late, the Movement's Hester Street vigil continued but at the same time however Oliver's flagging male ego was replenished by the now more welcome attention given to him by Linda. Even though he was able to softly spurn these advances she accepted it all with a good heart.

Friday evening: Oliver's time to chill out, relax and enjoy his own company came slowly. Although unusually Izzy wanted him to work the following day Oliver was determined that he would make the most of having the apartment to himself rather than feeling like an unwanted discarded toy. Tonight though his peace would be disturbed by a long distance call from London.

A TAIL OF TWO CITIES

'Oliver!'

'Hey there Mrs Spencer. Oh dear, am I in trouble? Good to hear from you anyway. How's life back in the old country. Coronation Street, crumpets and four seasons in one day as usual?!'

Oliver's surprise was genuine as they had a rule that he would be the one that instigated contact.

'Thing's are fine in London but what about America?'

Oliver sensed from her tone that this was more than just friendly chitchat.

'Come on old girl what's it all about? Let's be having ya.'

She spoke at first ponderously, alluding that she was concerned about Oliver's well-being.

'No need to worry yourself about me little lady. I'm enjoying my work and things. Life's bobbing along mighty swell!'

Mrs Spencer was becoming exasperated having previously always been able to lead Oliver imperceptibly down the path she wanted the conversation to go but tonight he was full of bluster. She then became more direct.

'Oliver, how's things with Louise, are you getting on well, are there any problems? It's important that you be honest.'

Oliver had never heard her so blatantly earnest before. His manner then immediately changed accordingly dropping the bravado.

'Well seeing that you asked me, Louise and I are on the verge of breaking up. She's changed. I don't know if it's another man she might have met at the theatre or somewhere. All I do know is that things have gone past the point of no return,' he replied, no longer choosing to conceal his misery.

'Oliver there is something you need to listen to very carefully. Something that might come as a bit of a shock,'

Oliver sat down, turned off the TV and tuned in intently.

'Go on,' he said.

'My name is Gloria, isn't it?'

'Yes, Mrs Gloria Spencer, that's right,'

'Well yes, Mrs Gloria Spencer. Spencer is in fact my middle name. My full name is Mrs Gloria Spencer .... Elsmore.'

'Elsmore ... as in Louise Elsmore?!' bleated Oliver.

'Precisely,'

'So who are you? How come? What are you trying to say?'

'I'm saying Oliver that Louise is actually my daughter. It's something I've kept from you but now is the time you must know. Things are changing rapidly for you and you need to know this.'

Oliver sat silently and still. Could this be some sort of conspiracy? Has the old lady got some axe to grind? Was it in fact perfectly true? All the imponderables ebbed backward and forward through Oliver's distorted thoughts.

'It's true Oliver. Louise has never introduced us, she wouldn't but when you were beaten up on Wardour Street that night I recognised you immediately from a Tower Hamlets staff photograph Louise left with me,'

'Are you…. are you really being honest with me, this isn't some sort of perverted joke at my expense is it?'

'Well let me try and convince you. Your friends Jeff and Karen Sprigson the one that's called Sprig. They're in prison and both there because of your stupidity and ambition, put into you by, no doubt by my daughter.'

'I know I've been stupid, evil even but I didn't inform the police. I planned to but in the end I couldn't go through with it. Honestly! They were arrested though as if I had done …'

'No you didn't inform the police Oliver, I know you didn't …… but Louise did. As you know we speak occasionally on the phone so I know that …. she read your diary and there it was in black and white, your plan to get your best friend off the scene for the sake of a job!' she replied unsympathetically sighing.

'My diary, my diary she read it in my bloody diary. I hid it under the fridge … I can't believe it. Noooooooo….!' he bellowed repeatedly.

Oliver was totally immersed in his anguish. He hid his eyes at the patent realisation that Louise, his 'little Lulu' the woman he trusted and loved beyond anyone had duped him so easily and so convincingly. Vows and pledges meant nothing to her. He then wept bitterly for himself as much as anybody else. Presently Oliver composed himself.

Mrs Spencer continued:

'Your troubles started the day you met my daughter. She was always an ambitious and even scheming little girl and even moreso as she got older but she was beautiful and that helped her get by. She seems to have had a grudge against your friend Jeff and had to get her own back.'

'Why didn't you tell me earlier that you were her mother?' he blurted abruptly.

'Oliver I know from bitter experience of my own how being young and in love can cause you to ignore all the warning signs. Let me tell you how it was with me: During the war I was engaged to the most wonderful dashing sailor. War changes so much and separates couples to opposite ends of the world often. He was stationed in Burma for well over a year but that didn't worry either of us. We wrote to each other at least twice a week and planned to marry as soon as he got back to England after the war. But it was a long war Oliver, a war in which when you're apart from the one you love they gradually became a sort of distant cousin or a pen-friend even. Time went on and I got lonelier so sure enough I was swept off my feet by an equally dashing GI. He not only promised me the earth but in a way he delivered. I got nylons, chocolates, perfumes and all the Spam I could eat even though I couldn't stand the stuff ha ha! My friends and family warned me over and over again that he'd be gone soon and that I'd better get used to life without him. Of course I took no notice.'

'So what happened?' asked Oliver. 'No don't tell me, I know where this is going. Your American soldier gave you the GI Blues and went off?'

'Precisely Oliver,'

'So if you'd have warned me about Louise I would have dug my heels and....'

'Buried your head in the sand. That's what would have happened wouldn't it? You needed to find out for yourself.'

'So why are you telling me now? How come?'

'I'm telling you now because enough is enough! Louise called me earlier today. She was angry, furious even. She's now a closet radical feminist whatever that is and wants to live on her own she says and you won't leave so she's going to make sure that you do. She's planning something Oliver and soon,'

'But what? Did she say any more?'

'Only that .... Uncle Sam would sort things out!'

'You got a brother over in New York Mrs Spencer cos Uncle Sam is the packet rice you can buy over here?!'

'That's Ben not Sam! No, Uncle Sam, in other words somebody or something in authority! Whatever it is Louise means business. I'm telling you this Oliver because despite you indirectly causing trouble for Jeff and the Sprigson woman you're basically a kind and trusting man. Sometimes a little misguided but essentially, you're a decent young man. My daughter could learn much from you.'

The initial shock of Mrs Spencer's revelation had passed its high point. Oliver needed some answers to events that he had deliberately placed unresolved in the far recesses of his memory.

'What about the jewellery, my mother's rings?

'Would it help if you knew?' Mrs Spencer replied.

'What about them?' roared Oliver down the phone.

'She stole them then sold them Oliver and pointed the finger at Irving!'

'I'm scared to ask but, but …… what about Naked?'

'Well, she took Naked for a long, long walk and bus ride and somewhere near the Millwall Docks simply abandoned him.'

This last piece of shattering news failed to crush him as might be expected, rather Oliver was steeled by it. He quickly focussed on his next move, not revenge but some form of final poignant 'divorce' from Louise. He needed the opportunity to reveal his new-found knowledge and after going over the incidents with his informant for another half an hour thanked Mrs Spencer for all her guidance and support.

Oliver sat down with furrowed brow evaluating his options and tossing around in his troubled mind a life without the woman he had adored for much of his adult life. His considerations and their consequences frightened him but this time papering over the massive cracks would never be an alternative. -

It was well after midnight, just about the time Louise was to arrive home from the theatre. Oliver had, in his head put together a mental script designed to imperceptibly guide Louise to confessing all and that without revealing his source: Holmes-like Oliver would pace the room thoughtfully then present his impeccable watertight case. He'd be stern with the hints of the compassion all juries expect however each piece of evidence would see the reprobate slowly fold then crumble acknowledging all through bitter, regretful tears. Over and over again broken wrongdoer would tell the court what an amazingly wonderful man Oliver really is and of her folly in not appreciating his brilliance. Such would be her shame that she would feel compelled to pack up and leave the apartment immediately. Magnanimously Oliver will allow his now chastened ex-partner to stay one more night, sleeping on the Lazy Boy of course, before finally handing Louise her toothbrush at the door the following morning. Quite brilliant in its simplicity Oliver imagined!

1.30am: Louise had still not returned. Oliver was concerned. Even the longest Hello Dolly overruns saw her home well before 1am. Soon after the telephone rang. It was Louise.

'Oh Oliver it's you!' she said in a surprised tone.

'No this is a burglar there is no one here at present how can I help you?' he said derisively.

'Listen you need to know that…. Senga one of the Manchester girls … I mean one of the women in the cast is leaving for home …. going back up north she is. So we're having a bit of a farewell knees-up then I'll be staying over at her place in Tribeca or Flatbush, can't remember exactly. I'll say goodbye then. Don't wait up!'

That was the full extent of the conversation. Louise had hung up quickly, giving him no opportunity to take the matter further. It was all becoming more curious. Such a thing had never happened before. Why now?! Oliver was furious that he'd somehow been thwarted and unable to implement his imagined interrogation. It had been a long, emotional and exhausting night. But it was a mere postponement of the inevitable. He would live to fight another day.

✳✳✳✳✳

The following morning at the Emporium was pretty run of the mill. As ever it was Linda's role to have the customers look better than when they first came in whilst Oliver enhanced their mood by generally making them feel better about themselves. So as always customers paid up and left altogether enriched. It also served as a welcome distraction from the planned showdown. He felt a foreboding since Louise's brief call last night. Who would strike first? Throughout the morning he was primed for the possible unfolding of Louise's final move against him. He did not have to wait long:

Just before lunchtime Oliver caught sight of a flash of light coming from the street. It came not from directly outside but a little further down the busy road. Oliver went to the window to investigate but by now the blue light had stopped. Two police cars had pulled up and its officers fell out onto the sidewalk and involved themselves in conversation. In New York this was a routine sight. Oliver continued unconcerned and went into the back to collect some stock. Moments later, coming from the salon Oliver heard a man's voice.

'Morning ma'am. You gotta Oliver Cherry working here?'

Oliver peaked around the curtain and saw three New York cops towering over Linda. She looked scared.

'Well I think he knows my boss Izzy,' replied Linda vaguely playing for time.

'We got a report recently that Cherry is from Europe and is working as an illegal alien. We've checked with US Immigration and he's no Green Card. We need to take him in and check him out. I'm telling you this from the start so you'll know we expect the truth from you,' said the officer sternly.

'Well thank you for your consideration officer. You say you gotta a report from who?! Cops can't harass people just cos they gotta report. Where's the proof. You can't just deport someone just like that.' Linda was now becoming obviously obstructive.

'We need to run this past your boss. Now let me take down some details,' replied the cop officiously.

Oliver quickly descended into a state of silent and controlled frenzy. He had though, heard enough. At any time now the cops could start to search the entire place and discover the English 'alien' cowering. He then quietly turned the key to the weighty security door that lead to the back alley. Inch by inch he dragged open the thick heavy portal just enough to surreptitiously edge himself out into the litter-strewn alley there to make good his getaway.

This freedom of sorts was short-lived as at the end of the passageway stood another police car with two of New York's finest casually standing guard. Oliver stood close to the wall. The two burly officers hadn't spotted him. He then took refuge amongst the refuse hiding between an overflowing dustcart and a dumpster, by piling some old boxes on top of him. Corny, but this sort of thing worked in the movies so why not now Oliver supposed. The hide was complete.

'No sign of him anywhere Clive. You guys down there seen anything?' yelled an officer.

The three cops had finished searching inside and were now out in the alleyway no more than ten feet from where the pursued was concealed. Oliver crouched perfectly frozen. He could breathe no shallower.

'I told you he wasn't here. Does the Mayor know how much time you cops waste. The city's full of murderers, rapist and street crime and all you wanna do is waste tax-payers dollars looking for no one,' said Linda clearly trying to engage them in some form of fatuous controversy as a distraction.

Sure enough the three cops had had enough mooching. Now they were to leave empty handed and joined their two colleagues at the end of the alley.

It was a further twenty minutes before Oliver was sufficiently confident to make himself known. As he tentatively threw off the trash and emerged from amongst the garbage he felt like a renegade, a wronged man who by stealth had evaded capture much like David Jansen in 'The Fugitive'. Reality was to hit home soon after as it was he, Oliver who was 'the one-armed man.'

When he was sure that the coast was clear he cautiously made his way back into the Emporium.

'You're here Oliver, you gave 'em the slip. So where did ya go, how did you do it?' asked Linda excitedly.

He explained, in full gallant detail how he'd overheard the cops and hidden in the alley just yards from them. She was suitably impressed and lead him into the stockroom, peeled off a couple of chicken bones that had embedded themselves at the back of his shirt, dusted him down and then planted a huge alluring kiss on his lips. Oliver was suitably taken too, quite the hero!

'Looks like this was Louise's final throw of the dice. So it's Oliver 1, Uncle Sam 0,' said he grandly.

This grandeur however belied his acute nervousness and uncertainty. What was to be his next move and where to now?

The only thing was to lay low for a while at the apartment and regroup. He asked Linda to tell Izzy of all that happened and said he would call tomorrow.

He had no idea as to what tomorrow would bring.

Chapter 27

Visitors

Hardly ever did Oliver find himself at home during a weekday afternoon but these were exceptional times. He estimated that the NYPD had commenced their search for him there prior to calling at the Emporium. Now more resolute than at any other time, he resolved to confront Louise with all the newly gained evidence of her devious schemes including her latest bid to have him deported and out the way. His tormentor had to be beaten and well beaten.

Outside on Hester Street numerous prominent members of the New York Women's Movement were vigorously discussing their differences with officials from the Jews Supporting Jesus group – all this in front of a mixed bag of curious vocal locals. This neighbourhood skirmish was now becoming the talk of the Lower East Side. The Chois were happy to give a Chinese perspective to the women regarding the complimentary roles of both genders with Mrs Choi occasionally scuttling back over the road to their small store when a customer entered. Italians, Irish, Eastern Europeans and a former Black Panther added to the mix of women with conviction. This was one of the few moments when the JSJ leadership ventured out to take on The Movement as they were always decidedly outnumbered and outshouted. – On close examination New York City was far from the 'melting pot' she claimed to be but more a crucible containing a multitude of ingredients that refuse to stir into a single cohesive broth. From his window Oliver could hear a full spectrum of views on 'Women's Liberation in today's society' followed by the JSJ rebuttal. His mind however was fixed on one particular woman.

Throughout the afternoon the telephone rang and rang. No one of Oliver or Louise's friends or colleagues would call so persistently knowing that both would be at work. He knew this and also appreciated that the caller could be just one person, in the business of checking up. Of course Oliver chose not to answer.

As the time neared for Louise to return Oliver put the first phase of his new well thought out plan into action: He changed into a white tea shirt and in the kitchen doused the front of it with tomato ketchup. He then smeared the sauce convincingly enough before arming himself with the largest pointed kitchen knife he could find. This was to be Oliver's ultimate vengeance. Intermittently Oliver checked the comings and goings on the street below. Except for a handful of the regular uniformed Movementarians the street was now relatively quiet. From the window just around midnight he spotted Louise heading home some 100 yards away. Then turning all lights off he lay spread-eagled on the sofa with the vicious knife placed strategically on his 'blooded' chest which in turn he covered with an open newspaper.

Through the open window Oliver could hear Louise's footsteps on the sidewalk approaching.

'So you still here Elsmore, still living above those Jesus freaks, still running around looking after your POG?' came a woman's voice.

'I'm still here Hubble and I'm going nowhere,' said Louise with a touch of irritation.

'Like I said you can't be part of us until you've sorted out your domestic arrangements and you've done something about that damn long hair,'

'As far as my home life is concerned The Movement can rest assured that I've taken care of that once and for all! Free at last, free at last, go back and tell them all I am free at last!' replied Louise in a triumphant Dr King-like mocking tone.

'That's groovy but what about the damn hair Elsmore. Time for a shave don't you think?' said Scott with a determined glint in the eye.

'Thought I told you fatso my hair's got nothing to do with our freedom. We'll get our freedom no matter what I've got on my head. So now why don't you just piss off home? The Jesus Jews will probably all do the same too,' said Louise harshly.

She felt it best to leave the conversation there as any talk with Scott and Hubble about her precious flowing tresses would only incite further venom.

To Oliver ear-wigging as he lay there in the darkness this was the first time he had an inkling of Louise' connection with 'those crazy bald layabouts' as he often referred to them. Reference was made to a fracas in a taxi that she had with Scott and Hubble and this perplexed him all the more. Moments after, Oliver could hear Louise outside the door. Turning the key she inched the door open and could be heard heaving a sigh on discovering the apartment was dark and seemingly empty. A couple of days prior she was told by US Immigration that all 'illegal aliens' would be detained immediately before their eventual and inevitable deportation. With this in mind Louise reflected then confidently entered, turned on the light, locked the door, kicked off her shoes and went in to the bathroom humming contentedly as she showered. Her nemesis meanwhile lay undiscovered and motionless on the sofa trying not to rustle the newspaper as he breathed. Presently Louise came from the bathroom dressed in a bathrobe and a towel wrapped around her head.

'Ahhhggg' shrieked Louise. 'Waaah!'

She had discovered 'the body'.

Louise panicked and rushed over and looked for any signs of life. Oliver's arm then flopped onto the floor as did the newspaper revealing the sharp blade as well as the apparently bloody and fatal stab wound. She then reeled and staggered backward crashing into the table then onto a chair.

'No, no, no, no. Oh God…No!' she yelled hysterically. 'You stupid, stupid bastard Oliver. I just wanted you out of my life… out of the country. I didn't want you bloody well dead,' she wailed bitterly.

That was enough! Oliver now had heard all he needed to know and resurrecting himself sprang to his feet causing the horrified woman to let out an ear-piercing screech before curling into a ball on the floor.

'My little ruse had worked even better than I'd guessed with an admission too. So you wanted me out of your life … out of the country did ya? Couldn't bloody face me last night. You want blood, well here's some blood for ya!'

Oliver now in total anguish then smeared some of the ketchup from his shirt across Louise's fretful contorted face and top.

'I'd have done anything for you, anything! You were my entire world but you wanna shit on anything good just so you can…..'

At that moment there was a heavy knock on the door. Oliver and Louise stood statuesque and silent as the wrapping continued.

'Oliver Cherry…… Oliver Cherry we know you're in there,' came a firm deep voice. Oliver then crept to the door and peered through the spy-hole.

'It's a man…… Two of them' said Oliver under his breath.

'They look like they've got guns under their shirts, both of them. They know my name. Immigration people!' Oliver whispered more loudly.

Louise's gnarled face blossomed into a full but hardly discreet smug smile.

'It looks like you and Uncle Sam have won,' admitted Oliver, now totally downtrodden and deflated. He leaned against the rattling door and stared at the ground a weary, washed up and beaten man. There was a brief moment of stillness.

'Well Oliver don't be rude aren't you going to let the officers in?' replied Louise self-satisfied.

'Oliver Cherry, Mr Oliver Cherry open the door or we'll be forced to break it down!'

'You wouldn't want that would you Ollie? I think you better do as they say, don't you Mr Cherry?'

He hesitated still further then slouched away from the door beckoning Louise to do her worst.

'Let 'em in!' he conceded.

She needed no persuading. In an instant two huge plain clothed men strode into the room. Between them they set an imposing and totally overwhelming figure. The first around six and a half feet tall and almost as wide, the second slightly taller and just as broad. Both giants were tanned with bleached gingery blonde hair. As if they had just returned from vacation they sported eye-catching bright yellow and blue Hawaiian shirts and yes, under their shirts they were clearly packing a firearm each.

The two men stood motionless and silent with eyes burning down heavily on a calm but resigned Oliver.

'Well aren't you going to say something?' asked Oliver.

On cue the two heavies parted and from between them strode a familiar form. It was Sprig! Oliver gasped and soon Louise sensed that Sprig and Oliver somehow recognised one another. Sprig then moved to one side revealing another figure. It was Jeff! Louise grimaced in sheer horror. Her demeanour altered radically as she now realised that the whole scenario she had envisaged was now not to be.

'Sprig…er Jeff. You're not … in London. You're in America,' stuttered Oliver.

This was the first time all four had been in the company of one another. Jeff and Sprig were momentarily as stunned as Oliver and Louise because of the apparent bloody carnage they had interrupted. Jeff and Sprig were there, in New York of all places and not behind bars at the Scrubs or Holloway!

'That's right Cherry and we're here on business and not as tourists,' growled Jeff.

'Although there will be a good deal of pleasure to be had eventually Jeffrey,' said Sprig menacingly.

Then like some nasty vengeful Gestapo commandant Sprig wondered around the room arms clasped behind her back and glancing down at the knife and 'blood' said.

'Looks like if we had arrived a bit later we'd have witnessed a

murder. That would have saved us a job hah haa.'

'Let me introduce you to our accomplices. On my left we have Hansel and on my right Gretel. I'd ask that you be gentle with them, they've cost us half a year's salary. Now tis a warm sultry night so let's say we embark on a spot of late-night sightseeing. It's our first time in the Big Apple and freedom smells good!' announced Jeff theatrically.

'Me as well as him?' asked Louise pointing to Oliver.

'But of course Louise you need to witness the sad demise of your little Cherry,' said Jeff sarcastically.

A TAIL OF TWO CITIES

Louise smirked again.

'Touchey Oliver you're fucked,' said Louise under her breath.

'Where to, where we going?' asked Oliver.

'Let's just say you won't need your swimming trunks where you're going,' said Sprig who seemed anxious to get on with proceedings.

'What about me afterwards?' asked Louise fretfully.

'Well all you'll need is your taxi fare home. Of course what you see tonight will be kept schtuum. 'Ansel and Gretel here will be only too pleased to pay you another visit Louise and finish you off if you blabber. Is that clear, is it?' scowled Sprig aggressively.

Of course, Louise agreed.

Rather than Jeff and Sprig adopting the typical 'good cop, bad cop' routine it was now more a case of 'bad cop, wicked cop' with Sprig exuding the greater malevolence.

It was then that Jeff and Sprig went into a huddle in the kitchen leaving Hansel and Gretel to mind their charges. On returning Jeff announced that Louise was to be 'disposed of as well' as the risk of doing otherwise was just too great. Louise smirked no longer and winced pleading with Jeff to trust her silence. Her exhortations were dismissed and he ordered his two burly goons to tie their hands behind their backs.

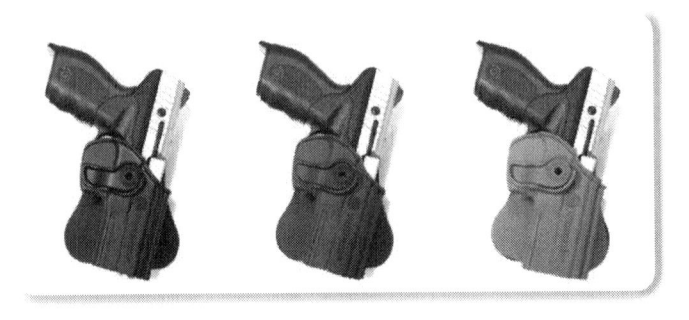

This was all now very serious. Louise was approaching hysteria but calmed when Sprig ordered Hansel to 'shut that stupid cow up'. Louise was still in her bathrobe so Sprig went into the bedroom and pulled out some clothes for Louise to put on.

'At least let me get dressed in the bathroom,' pleaded Louise. Sprig glanced at Jeff who sighed, nodded and untied her. At Jeff's command Gretel went into the bathroom, checked the window etc and on his return whispered Sooty-like in Jeff's ear.

'Get in there and dressed sharpish unless you both wanna meet your Maker right here! You'll not need any make-up,' barked Jeff.

This threat startled Louise all the more who marched promptly with her clothes into the bathroom.

Louise chose the bathroom ahead of the bedroom to change for a reason. There ensconced and realising that she had no more than a few short seconds she immediately reached up to the top of the bathroom cabinet and patted around until her trembling hand fell upon a small key, a key to the bathroom's window lock. With a feverish struggle she unfastened the catch and leaned out waving frantically across the road until ultimately attracting the attention of Scott, Hubble and several other adherents to the sisterhood who were continuing their threatening vigil. At last the women approached to investigate.

'Listen good. I can't go into detail but there's some people in the apartment from London. They've got guns and they're gonna take us somewhere and do us both in. This is no joke. It's really bloody real,' said Louise in a stifled whisper to the incredulous audience below. They laughed of course.

'Yet another fantasy,' they replied but she was asked to clarify why the Londoners wanted her and her POG dead.

'I don't fucking have time to make a bloody statement just get the police or the bloody FBI or someone now,' said Louise again in hushed tone hauling up her panties.

'Well if this isn't your usual load of English bullshit Elsmore then you'll do something for us, for our collective, won't you,' replied Scott with casual disdain.

'What the bloody hell can I do for The Movement at this moment in time?' said Louise even more frantically.

'Cut your hair! If it's true about these so-called visitors of yours, you'll prove it, you'll cut your hair and you'll do it now, yes right now this minute won't you!' sniggered Hubble.

Louise could hear movement on the other side of the bathroom door. Sprig was restive. Having no alternative Louise reached for some scissors and quickly sheared away at her hair whilst simultaneously putting on the rest of her clothing. She then threw the great clumps of thick auburn hair down to the joyous but somewhat perplexed women below. The tresses cascaded down and separated in the warm Manhattan breeze.

'Now will this do? You gonna help? You have to help me Hubble, I'm about to be shot dead,' hissed Louise in desperate terror.

The women stood there stony-faced looking up as their protagonist's hair continued to fall to the ground before them.

'Shame you never did that that night in the taxi Elsmore,' said Scott who, even now remained wholly unconvinced of Louise's tale of woe.

'You fucking, fucking fuckers!' seethed Louise knowing that she had been duped.

'Time to take a ride,' shouted Jeff banging on the bathroom door.

'Ok Ok alright. I've just, just, just err started my monthly,'

'Well get it sorted sharpish,' said Jeff conscious that Hansel and Gretel were being paid by the hour.

'And they'll be a damn sight more blood before the night's out won't there Mr Cherry!' said Sprig.

Aware that Oliver was visibly intimidated, Sprig sought to exact a slow and torturous revenge on the man responsible for her lengthy Holloway incarceration. Then taking out some thin nylon cord from her pocket she bound Oliver's hands firmly behind his back a second time and chuckled exuberantly as the cord tightened deeply into his flesh. She then pushed Oliver over toward Gretal who held him tight allowing Sprig to rain down heavy slaps into Oliver's face.

'I did a lot of porridge cos of you Cherry. You fucked up my Cat's Home; you fucked up my life and now you're gonna pay for that with yours,' spat Sprig mercilessly.

Oliver winced but remained silent. This time the blood ran for real. He glanced over to Jeff in the pessimistic hope of respite. He got none.

A TAIL OF TWO CITIES

Moments later Louise emerged from the bathroom fully dressed but still with ketchup spread about her face. On her head was a blue baseball cap that she had found in the bathroom. Having observed Oliver's bloodied face she assumed that in the mayhem he had received a face full of ketchup from his sauce-soaked tea shirt. She showed no concern on being corrected. Gretel then bound Louise as Oliver and then the party made their way out onto the rickety metal fire escape. Given Hansel and Gretel's combined hefty weight Jeff wisely ordered each of the heavies down the steps with their chosen allotted captive singly. Once all down on street level Hansel reversed a car down the narrow darkened alley. Jeff then opened the trunk and ordered the prisoners in. Of course to decline was futile nevertheless Louise attempted to whereupon she and Oliver were firmly guided therein by the two hulks at the instruction of their paymaster.

'Where you taking us?' quaked Louise, who from being a young girl was afraid of, not just of confined places but confined darken spaces particularly.

'Where the sun don't shine, where the sun don't shine!' came the fearfully doom-laden reply.

Chapter 28

… And in the end, the love you take, is equal to the love you make!

To Oliver the closing of the trunk seemed as to the sealing of his fate. 'How did it ever come to this?' he fretted as he yearned for the simpler, easier life as a rookie classics teacher in inner city London. If only he could return to the years when he and Jeff kicked a ball down Henriques Street, played kiss-chase, knock-down-ginger and fought over who'd be the first to take Denise Sternshine to Saturday morning pictures at the Mile End Odeon. That was an effortless time, a more innocent time, 'a time before Louise!' Now he found himself trussed up in a dismal foreign dungeon alongside his tormentor en-route to some sort of execution.

'Many, many innocent people have had their lives taken from them' he silently consoled, but that was usually for a loved one, a point of principle or an unshakeable belief. Oliver's demise would be for nothing more than the love of a vengeful, self-consumed woman. That she was to die alongside too meant nothing.

Louise was less resigned - heaving, kicking, screaming, recriminating and threatening throughout the bumpy journey.

'I'm gonna have to die because I'm a bloody witness to them bloody killing you for, what I don't know!' bawled Louise in the darkness, her face pushed up against Oliver's buttocks.

'You'd be fucking banged up now in some festering American cell waiting to be sent back home if I had my bloody way. Try and wriggle out of that with your fancy fucking Latin shit talk you bleeding bastard loser you. Jeff won't kill me I got information, big information that he wants and I'm the only one who can give it to him. You'll be dying on your own you bloody will, you mad git. Jeff won't want to even lay a finger on me. I'll have him on his knees in front of me begging before the night's out. Jeff won't lay a finger on me!'

'What information, what you talking about you stupid cow? Nothing's gonna save your skin now. No amount of scheming …. and lying….. and conniving … and cheating or anything's gonna get you out of this one Lulu darling,' shouted Oliver dismissively.

'You're the one that's fucked Oliver, I'll be on the first plane back to London before your body's even cold. I'm telling ya, Jeff won't even lay a finger on me. I got stuff he wants to know!'

And so it went on until the car gradually eased to a stop then, after a few seconds into reverse.

From outside the now motionless vehicle the captives could pick up a dialogue:

'This'll do nicely, or maybe just a bit further along?'

'Come on let's just get it over with and stick to the plans we made. We've already had to change things around to kill the woman as well. Two murders wasn't part of the deal'

'OK lads get 'em out the boot.'

At this the trunk opened slowly. Oliver and Louise had arrived at their place of execution. –

'Right you two, on your feet,' ordered Sprig.

With some difficulty, they did as bid.

'Where are we, where is this place?' asked Louise.

'Brooklyn Bridge with the East River I believe it's called below. Isn't that correct Hansel?' asked Jeff rhetorically.

The large man confirmed with a nonchalant nod.

With no warning the two tethered and terrified detainees were then roughly manhandled along the bridge's timber sidewalk. As cars and trucks rushed past Jeff ordered the group to stop then directed them all back toward the Manhattan side of the bridge when eventually a voice cut through the darkness.

'Hey guys, you guys up there, I'm just below you down here!

A TAIL OF TWO CITIES

Jeff ordered them to a halt and leaned over the barrier acknowledging the voice that came from the bridge's maintenance walkway that ran some 150 feet below and was situated just 15 feet above the unfriendly, black East River.

'You got him?' asked the same voice.

Despite the distance and the whirling wind the voice's timbre and inflection was familiar to both the abductees who were however unable accurately to identify.

'We got the girl too, you'd be pleased to know. Now we're all happy!' replied Jeff to the still unknown enquirer.

Jeff then commanded that they all make their way over the high barrier down the metal steps leading to the maintenance walkway, a lengthy, precarious exercise at any time but all the more so for the tethered two. Thoughtfully however Jeff conceded to Louise's request and agreed to have Hansel untie her. He gave no such charity to Oliver. –

The walkway beneath the road was strewn with all sorts of paraphernalia, metal support bars, rusting drainage piping and discarded fast food rubbish, old newspapers and their like. Making it all the more inhospitable was the baleful howling wind that rattled through the harsh, cold steel bridge supports. Was this the secluded setting in which Oliver and Louise were to spend their last waking moments?

In times past Oliver would creatively ponder his end. For him he envisaged a sudden heart attack brought upon by the gratuitous sexual demands of Diana Dors and Hattie Jacques together! Or maybe as a gallant and heroic 3rd World War Harrier pilot defending England from the invading Communist hordes of Chairman Mao and Kruchevcev. Murdered in some foreign field by an angry childhood friend and a vengeful, cat loving lesbian spiv never figured. -

Oliver and Louise remained silent awaiting Jeff and Sprig's next move when from the gloom strode the large figure of a man. That man was immediately recognised as Irving.

'Bleedin hell!' gasped Louise.

Oliver was equally bowled over as the last he'd seen of him after their brief but memorable cohabitation was him scuttling down their fire escape. Oliver did however recall this scuttling was accompanied by cries of future revenge!

'So ve meet again!' said Irving mocking any number of baddies from a Bond film.

'What you gonna do with us? How do you know Jeff?' asked Louise noticeably shaken by Irving's role in all of this.

Before any answer was forthcoming Jeff intervened. Taking out a small hand gun from his pocket he ordered Oliver and Louise to sit on the barrier with their backs toward the water. Not much more than a dozen or 15 feet below ran the unforgiving, murky waters that separated Manhattan and Brooklyn. On either side of the death-row prisoners standing very close by were Hansel and Gretel silent and uninvolved but nonetheless an unavoidable watchful presence.

A TAIL OF TWO CITIES

There then followed a hush as Jeff paced to and fro thoughtfully considering the right words. For the first time since the last day of the Old Bailey drugs trial Oliver and Jeff looked at each other full in the face. There was an immediate and emotional connection. The Brits present knew of the long history the two men had together which added to the moment's poignancy. Teary-eyed Jeff softly ordered Gretel to pull Oliver from off the barrier and untie him. Jeff then approached his old friend slowly. The two men embraced tightly and sobbed. Sprig and Louise looked to the ground not wishing to be part of the men's private grief, even the two heavies were moved but whyso they never knew. When the two old friends eventually separated Jeff wind milled his arm far back and forcefully swinging it round landed a vicious right hook full in Oliver's face. Oliver recoiled at the unexpected jolt before falling semi-conscious into the gantry's cold steel floor.

'Get up, get on your feet!' bellowed Jeff belligerently.

Oliver was unable to respond but was hauled to his feet by the two paid henchmen.

'Nearly two years I did. Two years in the Scrubs. That's friendship for you. Every day locked up with piss heads, weirdos and dope fiends while you and your trollop are living it up in the West End. You break into my place, you then plant all sorts of drugs and then you grass to the police without saying who the hell you are and tell them I'm dealing out drugs to the girls at school. What was you hoping to get out of it?' hissed Jeff whilst further man-handling his dazed ex-friend.

Oliver eventually struggled to his feet again clinging on to the barrier but was too stunned to give a coherent answer.

'How did you find out where we were?' spluttered Oliver.

'Didn't you think I'd catch up with you?' bawled Jeff. 'Did you think I'd let you just shit on me and get away with it. As soon as I got out of The Scrubs my dad told me that slag of yours was here in New York. Just after that Cockroach was good enough to invite me to his retirement do and offer me some sort of forgiveness for all my bleedin misdemeanours. He told me that you and Louise had a hush-hush thing going on together. So when I couldn't track you down at home it figured that you, you bastard were over in America too with that bloody floosy. When I met up with Sprig my so-called co-defendant we decided that it would be in our common interest to make a trip across the pond. Then we met up with Irving here through my dad's theatre and he lead us right to you. So now we're gonna mess with your life like you did ours. The only difference is that for you Mr Oliver Cherry, this-is-the-end!'

Jeff then wrenched Oliver's head backward by his hair and threw him back on to the barrier.

In amongst the brutality Sprig, whose role in all of this was still not fully appreciated by Jeff, needed to exact some retribution of her own. She did so in no uncertain terms slapping Oliver repeatedly about the face. Sprig's onslaught only came to an end when a quick gust of wind swept in blowing Louise's cap clear off her head and down into the gloom thus revealing her hastily scalped hair. There was a bewildered silence as all tried to figure quite what met their eyes? Louise remained motionless sitting on the barrier. Her obvious discomfiture and pending fate left her too pathetic to even offer up a sham explanation! None present questioned the shorn as more pressing matters were at hand.

A TAIL OF TWO CITIES

Brief was this bizarre interlude and all too soon attention refocused on Oliver, the accused, who used this short time to draw upon a deep reserve of composure.

'I'm the baddy in all of this aren't I?' whispered Oliver at the commencement of his mitigation.

'Well Cherry I wondered when you'd have something to say,' snarled Sprig caustically.

'What if I told you that it honestly wasn't me that grassed on you Sprig or you Jeff?' mumbled Oliver.

'I'd reply, 'you're a delusional cretin trying to save his skin," came Jeff's derisive and expected reply.

'Well I won't say it but I'll show you, then you decide for yourselves,' said Oliver whose plea to be untied was granted by Jeff expectantly.

Oliver then stumbled around in his pockets causing both Hansel and Gretel to close in on him guardedly.

'Leave me be,' invoked Oliver harshly before hauling out a small book which he handed to Jeff.

'So!' said Jeff. 'This is your way of getting out of this is it? Saving your skin are we Cherry?'

'It's a diary from 1969. My diary!'

Oliver had put the diary in his pocket whilst waiting for Louise to return home at which time he planned to dramatically confront her with the evidence as told him by her mother now known more accurately as Mrs Gloria Spencer Elsmore.

'Right; I've marked the page with a bit of paper. Go on read it, read it aloud now!' pleaded Oliver pensively.

'It says 'Dear Ollie - When I look at you I like what I see. Call me anytime 979-0201. Love Belindy kiss, kiss, kiss'... Can't see how this floosy is gonna keep you alive Cherry.'

'I knew it, I bloody knew it you cheating bastard,' said Louise having had her doubts confirmed.

Oliver seemed mildly flustered at this most inopportune of gaffs and though, given the dire circumstance it hardly mattered, however he felt unable to turn his head to face her.

'Not that, not that. Read August 29th,' Oliver insisted.

At this Sprig immediately jumped into a near frenzy.

'Let's not mess about Jeff. We ain't come three thousand miles to read his bloody memoirs. Let's just get it over and done with and do him good and proper right here, right now like we planned. Now! Now! Now!' she protested anxiously trying to thwart the discourse's unfavourable new direction.

Sprig, again screaming for blood forcibly commandeered Gretel's gun waving it around her head like some whirling dervish. It needed Jeff to physically disarm Sprig, something only the British or those that have little appreciation of the dangers of a loaded gun would have ever attempted. The two heavies simply shook their heads and sighed rolling their eyes skyward in disbelief at this near comic spectacle.

'Listen Sprig I want revenge as much as you do, now shut the fuck up,' barked Jeff.

'You gotta read it Jeff. It's proof that on August 29th I planted the drugs in your house cos I wanted the job, the head-of-year job remember. I must have been mad. I admit it I planned to get you out of the way before the interview. It seems stupid now but that's the truth. I did it for me and Louise's future, I wanted to earn enough so she could give up teaching and get into acting. It was her dream,' confessed Oliver confusingly.

Jeff read on and on then gasped not just at Oliver's ridiculous intent to sign his own death warrant but Sprig's involvement in both supplying and planting the stash.

'So that's why you didn't want me to read it,' Jeff screamed at Sprig. 'You wanted me hung, drawn and quartered too!'

It was now Sprig's time to defend herself but it wasn't needed.

'No Jeff leave her out of it, it was my idea. Sprig didn't know you then remember? It was her palm print that gave her away. She was just there to help me get rid of you,' implored Oliver.

'Get rid of me! How this gonna save you now?' yelled Jeff brandishing his firearm precariously.

'That's not meant to, but you gotta read on - Read August 31st and the next day,' shouted Oliver hastily. 'Read it out loud Jeff - August 31st 1969, read it out,' yelled Oliver.

Jeff's head was now spinning but, suspicious at first calmed and narrated as bid:

"August 31st: Didn't sleep too well last night. In fact didn't sleep at all. I love my Lulu and I always will, but Jeff's my best mate. Took Naked for a dawn walk in the park again. Been doing that a lot lately. Recalled that Naked was Jeff's 21st birthday present to me. Decided there and then that my friendship with Jeff meant more to me than anything. How can I do this to him? Friends are friends; Jeff I'm sure would never ever wilfully hurt me. I'm going to arrange to meet Sprig and tell her that there's no need to grass up Jeff. I'll meet her tomorrow and tell her it's off and that I can't go through with it. Next time I'm at Jeff's I'll try to somehow get the stash and flush them. Still going for the interview though and may the best man (or woman) win. Looks as if I'll have to do some private tuition if I don't get the promotion or Louise will never get out of Tower Hamlets."

Once more Jeff's eyes welled as he read the next few days' entries. Now his tears were those of regret tinged with even more puzzlement. The whole atmosphere was transforming into one of palpable apprehension. No one spoke but waited intently on Jeff's response.

'It doesn't make sense I don't get it, I don't see how the Old Bill knew. When they raided they went straight to the drugs behind the cooker,' said Jeff.

Clearly implicated and embarrassed Sprig realised now and no later was the right time to offer Oliver her support.

'He's right Jeff, a few days after our break in and plant, me and Ollie met up and called the whole thing off. I didn't say much at the time but I was pretty relieved too, even though I didn't have a bleedin clue who you were at that time. He even dipped into his savings and borrowed some money off you Jeff to help finance my Cat's Sanctuary in Battersea. What I do know is that Oliver cares about all the people close to him, sometimes too much. He gets himself into a fuss at times but means no real harm.'

'Bloody amazing, so I lent him my hard-earned money to give to you so you could get me done. Bloody hell but that doesn't explain why we got bloody picked up. How'd the police know?' yelled Jeff.

'Well it wasn't me, it wasn't Oliver, it wasn't Naked - God rest his soul and the diary can't talk,' said Sprig querying.

It was then that the key moment of perspicacity that Oliver had skilfully directed Jeff and Sprig toward suddenly and simultaneously dawned.

All eyes instantly shifted toward …… Louise!

'You nosy, malicious cow. You read his bloody diary and grassed us up to the police. I should have guessed it, should have bleedin' known, it'd be a woman,' roared Sprig grievously.

Unlike the spotlighted Oliver of minutes before, Louise's countenance and demeanour clearly betrayed her guilt. She however wasted no time in jumping to her own defence denying the authenticity of the diary whilst unwisely referring to Sprig's overweight problem!

Choosing to suspend his usual veneer of buffoonery Irving, who had observed the drama unfold from the side-lines saw that this was now his moment to step forward:

'Well I don't mean to sound like some kinda smart Alec but I could have guessed that little miss innocent there would have had something to do with it. That girl's got 'danger stay well away' written all over her pretty face,' he continued 'Those rings Oliver, the jewellery that meant so much to ya that went missing from the apartment, she stole 'em not me! She wanted me out of the apartment and used you to do her dirty work. I took the wrap. It's obvious now, she's poison!'

There was then another short thoughtful hiatus.

'You got it in one. That Elsmore woman told us she stole the rings and sold 'em for big, big bucks. We never trusted her as well.'

This surprising and revealing new entrant came from Scott who along with Hubble watched the happenings from another works gantry suspended below the bridge's sidewalk nearby. In an effort to validate Louise's bathroom window account they had followed the car from the Hester Street alley to the bridge.

'Elsmore'd steal from her deaf, dumb and blind grandma if she had a chance,' accused Scott acrimoniously. 'Whatever you chose to do with her Jeff, your secret's definitely safe with us,' Scott added.

Louise hung her head shamefully lost, partly defeated but never remorseful. Even at this most grim occasion 'The Movement' was there not to assist but to strip her bare and pile on the agony. Her sisterhood in which she had invested so much faith proved as supportive as any similar brotherhood when men turn against one another. 'People' she thought, unable to see her own role in her current plight, 'not just men, are complete shits!'

Jeff and Sprig were unnerved by how their well thought out plan was now veering out of their control and now hastily undertook to get the matter dealt with before Scott and Hubble were joined by a whole precinct of Manhattan's NYPD. Notwithstanding her emotional and unconvincing denials and parries, Louise's chickens had all come home to roost, well almost all. It was now time for Oliver to make known his true feelings known and ask Louise what genuinely motivated her:

'Naked …. What happened to my dog? For once in your life tell the truth Louise!' said Oliver in quiet anticipation.

She wouldn't answer. Oliver calmly repeated the question again and once more.

'He had to go, the dog had to go alright! I couldn't bare the bloody thing near me, looking at me, wagging his bloody tail and jumping up the minute you walked in the room, so he had to go. I just took the dog over to Millwall Docks and simply… left him there. Well you wanted to know so now you bloody well do!'

For Oliver this was now the proof he needed. Louise had evolved into all the things that disgusted him.

'Why Louise, why? How have you turned out to be such a spiteful cow? You weren't always like this were you?'

'You don't know what I had to do with Cockroach to get you that bloody promotion Oliver!' cried Louise.

'Whatever it was I'm sure it was with you in mind more than me. It always is with you isn't it?'

Oliver heaved a deep sigh again then continued:

'You know it's hard to believe this now but here on Brooklyn Bridge was where I'd planned to propose to you when the time was right. I even had my speech worked out in my head. I would have done it all for you, given up anything for you, walked to the other end of the world if you wanted me to. I loved you more than any man could love a woman and what hurts the most is I always thought you loved me just the same back.' Oliver was now choked and overcome but gathered himself to resume. 'I never, ever doubted that what you said, you sincerely meant and that I was as important to you, as you were me. You deceived me not once but over and over. Ha, stupid, deluded me would never ever have known any different but it was plain to see that you thought that the whole bloody world revolved around you and what you wanted. Think about it Louise, you got rid of my dog, stole my mum's rings, forced Irving out onto the streets, tried to get me deported and to top the lot got Jeff and Sprig locked up and all without a care. There's gotta be alot more evil than that you've done but it's all too late now you gotta take what's coming to you. What's more you are prepared to see me, an innocent man die tonight and say absolutely nothing ... nothing! The world needs rid of you once and for all.'

Oliver's lengthy regretful lament was felt by all. Jeff, Sprig, Irving, Scott and Hubble even the crime hardened hirelings could not fail to be moved by Oliver's sombre chronicle of recurring treachery at the hands of the woman he cherished and put foremost in his affections. It was the fact that she stayed silent when the focus was on Oliver and was prepared to remain tight-lipped right up to what would have been his sorry demise that spawned the pervading feeling that she, and she alone had to pay the ultimate price. So embittered was Oliver that he was to be the only one of her numerous victims who could rightfully pull the trigger. Jeff of course agreed with the sentiment.

Oliver ordered that Louise be forced to sit on the safety barrier. Gretel hoisted Louise up onto the rail where she remained with a still brazen and accusatory attitude. Occasionally she would gingerly turn her head glancing down to the freezing and inhospitable waters that coursed just a short drop below. An innumerable number of American suiciders or victims of some unsavoury act had been swallowed in its depths but such thoughts were far from Louise's mind as she again began to screech her supposed innocence whilst at the same time throwing out more poisonous vitriol.

'You've only brought this upon yourself Lulu belle,' derided Irving.

'You're done for woman!' added Sprig characteristically.

'You were never much good to The Movement anyway Elsmore but the hair looks pretty cute!' mocked Hubble above.

'You've been weighed and measured and been found wanting,' cited Jeff poetically.

Louise found this last condemnation quite the most sanctimonious and irksome.

'You, you bloody hypocrite, ya didn't say that the night we spent together at your place in Chelsea did you Jeffrey?!'

Jeff and Oliver's eyes met but the former was unable to hold the contact, preferring to shift his gaze downward.

'Well ok it's true Ollie, but remember I didn't know you were a couple then did I,' declared Jeff uncomfortably.

Oliver then swung his furious attention around.

'But *you* did, didn't you Louise? What more have you done! What else?' roared Oliver.

Louise for the first time that fateful night quaked inside realising that things were now truly closing in on her. She'd played her trump card and lost.

Oliver then approached Sprig with outstretched palm.

'A gun. Give me a gun!' said Oliver.

Sprig yanked a weapon from Gretel's holster and gleefully handed it to him. Oliver took the weapon and violently shoved it in Louise's chest. His eyes and whole countenance told her that this was finally the finish.

'Don't Oliver, you can't do this to your Lulu…. Remember our vow Ollie….. Jeff do something, do something!' Louise spluttered.

Her pleas went unheard as Oliver's finger tensed on the trigger but Louise was not done yet:

'Jeff, Jeff before I go. You need to know something real important. It's good news, really good news for you. You've got a son; you're a father. Remember Janey … Janey the girl you knew from when you were a teenager. You didn't realise it but the last time you saw her she was pregnant with your baby. You've got a son, a beautiful son, the son you always wanted. He's called Terry and looks just like you. I can take you to him. I can't remember the address but I can definitely take you to them. Janey would love to see you again. She needs you too. I can take you to 'em both but how can I if I'm six foot under. You can play football with him, be a proper dad to him. Terry's never had a dad. He's your flesh and blood. Do something Jeff. I'm no good to you dead how will you ever know your son? He needs you. I …. need …. you!' begged Louise.

Though not borne out of contrition this truly was Louise's very final throw of the dice and the information alluded to in the trunk of the car. She held it back for such an unlikely emergency. Could she ever have conceived that the boy perched in the tree in the grounds

A TAIL OF TWO CITIES

of Tower Hamlets School, Ruff's vexation and Janey's 'little darling' might someday become her potential salvation?

'Kill her Oliver, she's lying a bloody gain!' barked Sprig.

Jeff was now bewildered and in part swayed, barely able to forward a coherent sentence. To be a father to a son was his most enduring and earnest desire. Louise knew it too.

'No, no leave her…. leave her be. I need to know more. If she's right and I've got a son then…..' conceded Jeff his voice dissolving into the drone of the thoroughfare above.

Oliver interrupted, groaned and met Louise's pleading cow eyes with a look of undiminishing abhorrence.

'What's she playing at now Oliver?' asked Jeff.

Oliver sighed deeply and responded.

'Yeah, yeah she's right Jeff, for once she's telling the truth,'

'You knew about this!?' spat Jeff.

'Yes, I knew about Terry before he was born,' admitted Oliver. 'Your mum made me swear never to tell you because as a teenage father you'd never be able to finish your education. It might have wrecked your life she thought. She always had high hopes for you mate. To make amends somehow, your mum decided that she was gonna do as much as she could to help Janey bring up Terry and when the time was right she was gonna take him to you and try and patch things up. Don't worry Jeff, I can take you to your son. I know where he is in London. You don't need her. But first things first!'

Louise's wretched callousness was there for all but the blind to behold. The game was now up. Her game was now up! Oliver continued to hold the gun at her chest again outlining in summary all her contemptible acts. After each point was made the prod of the gun he held close to her chest became all the more forceful so much so that Louise could barely keep a grip of the rail she sat on.

'This is a far, far better thing that I do now than I have ever done,' cried Oliver in his anguish and tightened his index finger on the trigger to the point of no return. At that moment he jabbed her in the chest with the gun one last time so forcefully that she fell backward and almost simultaneously Oliver finally fired the gun with the bullet hitting the water.

Baaang ….!

The single gunshot seemingly echoed clear across to Brooklyn. Louise was forced backward and disappeared down and down into the dark waters beneath, her falling body emitting a deathly fading wail of woe.

'Agggghhh!'

Then came the splash and the eeriest of silences.

The sound of the 'body' hitting the water and then resurfacing was the sign for all witnesses to instantly escape the crime scene and with little regard for the other all clambered hastily up the steel bridge supports to the street level's wooden sidewalk. Oliver watched as first Hubble and Scott headed east toward Brooklyn soon to be followed by Jeff and Sprig and eventually Irving who in a form of controlled alarm made their way swiftly over to the Manhattan side. The two massive mercenaries remained unperturbed and emotionless.

'I ain't seen nothing like this ever!' said a bemused Hansel to his partner. 'Seems we gave the Brits Peyton Place but these guys have given us the real damn thing!'

A TAIL OF TWO CITIES

With that the two enlisted thugs climbed up and disappeared into the New York City night. Now only Oliver, still holding a warm gun remained.

Oliver took a sombre look downward. Then amongst the din of the traffic over 100 feet above he could faintly pick out:

'Oliver…. Oliver I love you!'

These words shocked him to the core. He was minded of that evening in Whitechapel when he utterly forbade Louise to use those three words. Meanwhile her thrashing about continued. It was difficult to look down.

'Oliver, I really love you!' she continued.

The words rang out again but now more faintly than before. Oliver then stopped dead in his tracks. He pondered momentarily as his heart pounded and his confusion settled. Spotting a red and white roped life ring he tossed it in the water 15 feet below. He then tied the attached rope at the other end loosely, very deliberately loosely to a metal side bar at his feet before making his way up to the bridge and the passing traffic. He watched as she swam hard to reach the buoy. Oliver's job had been accomplished. With the help of the Gulf Stream, his one timer lover's rotten body was to be washed up on a Cornish beach in a few months he imagined. His emotions were spent and his body exhausted. Now was not the time to play the Beatles Lyric Game nevertheless that was just what he did. The song that came up was 'She Loves You' and Oliver imagined Jeff singing it to him. From his pocket, he took out the fluffy brown rabbit's tail that so often accompanied him providing some form of comfort over the years. He hurled it down into the gloom saying 'Well, I won't be needing you anymore.'

He gave Louise one last fleeting look as the tied knot loosened still further. A few minutes passed. Then spying an emergency telephone box he picked up the receiver:

'New York City Emergency River Patrol, how can I help you? Hello New York City Emergency River Patrol, can I help you in any way?'

'I've just seen a nasty, evil, malicious, conniving, bald English woman fall from Brooklyn Bridge into the East River. If you fancy you might wanna help her out, but no rush!'

'I need some details quickly sir. Do you know her? Is she injured in any way sir?'

'No madam. Hic liber esset a magna scaena musicis….. '

'What language is that sir?'

'Latin.'

'Hold the line sir, my colleague here is from Latin America. He maybe able to help….' -

So, in this age of wisdom and foolishness, darkness and light, hope and despair, Oliver's spring of hope and winter of despair with Louise had given him some of the best and worst of times.

A TAIL OF TWO CITIES

It was the best of times, it was the worst of times,
it was the age of wisdom, it was the age of foolishness,
it was the epoch of belief, it was the epoch of incredulity,
it was the season of Light, it was the season of Darkness,
it was the spring of hope, it was the winter of despair,
we had everything before us, we had nothing before us,
we were all going direct to heaven,
we were all going direct the other way -
in short, the period was so far like the present period,
that some of its noisiest authorities insisted on its being received,
for good or for evil, in the superlative degree of comparison only.

Charles Dickens, A Tale of Two Cities

THE END

Clive Van Cooten

A TAIL OF TWO CITIES

86683 words, 354 pages, 1262 paragraphs and 6307 sentences with full stops, too many to count!

BY

Clive Van Cooten

A TAIL OF TWO CITIES

Book Cover and art work by the amazing, talented and patient Ryan Griggs (Ryan Griggs Graphic Design) from the great city of Manchester, England, United Kingdom

Contact: RYAN@SOCIALBEINGZ.COM

*Time and Place: Chapter 13 contains a glaring yet deliberate error!

JOHN 3 v 16

JOHN 3 v 16

JOHN 3 v 16

JOHN 3 v 16

A TAIL OF TWO CITIES

'A TALE OF 3 CITIES' BY CLIVE VAN COOTEN PUBLISHED VIA AMAZON IN JANUARY 2021 WITH THE ACCOMPANYING STAGE MUSICAL TO FOLLOW

Printed in Great Britain
by Amazon